WICKED CITY

Also by Alaya Johnson

Moonshine
Racing the Dark
The Burning City

WICKED CITY

A ZEPHYR HOLLIS NOVEL

ALAYA JOHNSON

St. Martin's Press
Thomas Dunne Books
New York

This is a work of fiction. All of the characters, organizations, and events portrayed in this novel are either products of the author's imagination or are used fictitiously.

THOMAS DUNNE BOOKS.
An imprint of St. Martin's Press.

Map by Kristine Dikeman

www.stmartins.com

Library of Congress Cataloging-in-Publication Data

Johnson, Alaya Dawn.
    Wicked City : a Zephyr Hollis novel / Alaya Johnson. — 1st ed.
        p. cm.
    ISBN 978-0-312-56548-0 (hardcover)
    ISBN 978-1-4299-4141-9 (e-book)
1. Vampires—Fiction.   2. Lower East Side (New York, N.Y.)—Fiction.   I. Title.
    PS3610.O315 W53 2012
    813'.6—dc23

                                                                    2011032867

First Edition: April 2012

10 9 8 7 6 5 4 3 2 1

For my family

ACKNOWLEDGMENTS

Sequels are notoriously tricky, and this one would not have been possible if not for the support of my friends, colleagues, and family, for whose help I am incalculably grateful. I would like to thank Lauren and Alexis, for helping me navigate a thicket of story problems; Amanda, for being so excited to read more; Justine, Abby, and Rachel, for helping me sort out the messes of early drafts; Eddie, for regular care and feeding when I was on deadline; my fellow members of Altered Fluid, for early-morning title brainstorming and general writing advice; Kris, for the beautiful map; Jill and Cheryl, for drinks by the Piazza Nettuno; Karyn, for continuing to be the most awesome editor Zephyr or I could have asked for; and, finally, my readers, whose enthusiasm has encouraged me throughout this process.

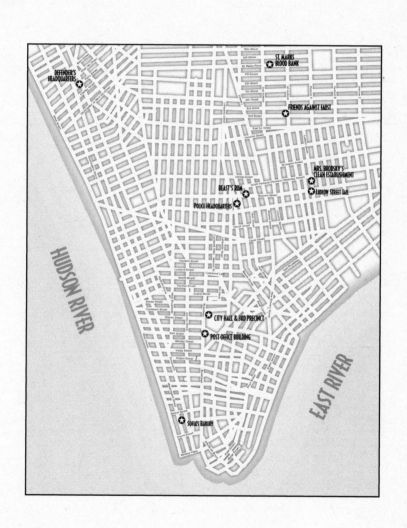

WICKED CITY

CHAPTER ONE

In the depths of late summer, when airless nights meet dog-eared days, the cream of New York City society flees east to the beaches of Long Island, where dinner parties last the weekend and hangovers last the week.

But instead of sipping champagne by a fountain at Scott and Zelda's, I was standing on East Twenty-eighth Street in an evening dress far too hot for the weather and T-strap heels far too small for my feet. The latter had just recently been splattered with that most unsavory of New York excreta: the blood and fatty remains of an exsanguinated vampire—or, in common slang, a popper.

"I did always hate these shoes," I said, attempting philosophical resignation.

"Aren't they your only ones?" Aileen said. My roommate was staring at the remains of the unfortunate vampire with equal parts fascination and disgust.

"I already have three blisters."

"I don't suppose you can afford a new pair?"

I sighed. "Not really." I hadn't been paid in nearly two weeks, as my night school classes were on temporary hiatus until August. Money and I never had much to say to each other, in any case. Too many people needed it more—the vampire charities, the immigrant charities, the socialists and the communists and any number of women's rights organizations. I owned a sensible pair of leather boots that served me adequately. Evening shoes were a luxury I had never bothered to afford.

And yet now their loss made me unaccountably melancholy— bloodstains have yet to debut in the Parisian fashion houses. Having already made a mess of myself by walking unwarily near the popper, I gingerly stepped closer. The remains of baggy skin could tell me nothing of the poor man's appearance, but the absence of any stake or scorch mark from a blessed blade made me conclude that he had expired from natural causes. Common enough, particularly in the heat of summer. My friend Ysabel, who ran the Bank on St. Marks Place, always complained of the low donation rates in July and August. The poorest vampires used the Banks, and every summer a few dozen of them died of blood starvation. And when a vampire died, he popped.

"I wonder who he was," I said softly. Worn gray trousers and a patched shirt were drenched in exsanguination. Familiar as I was with popped vampires, I had no desire to explore further. Vampire blood burned.

"You could ask Amir, you know," Aileen said.

"About the popper?"

She rolled her eyes. "Heavens, no. The shoes. What good is having some filthy rich djinni prince at your beck and call if you can't ask him for a favor now and then?"

I stood and stepped carefully away from the mess. Nothing I could do for him now—the cleanup crew would take him to the medical examiner's, and from there the potter's field. For a moment I contemplated asking Amir to conjure his identity, so perhaps I could inform his family, but I shook my head. That sort of request would mean a wish, and a wish entailed precisely the emotional entanglement I was determined to avoid. When you have a past like mine with a djinni like Amir, extreme caution is warranted.

"I'm not some gold-digger, Aileen," I said. "I earn what I have."

"Lorelei Lee would ask for a lot more than a new pair of shoes," Aileen said, sighing. "But have it your way. Maybe we'll get lucky and find a speakeasy with dim lights."

"Horace's has dim lights," I said glumly. But as we had discovered, our favorite speakeasy was closed for a private party. Horace and I have a working relationship (I have been known to open for the house band), but he hustled us out the door and said to come back next week.

Which left us here, staring at a popped vampire on a quiet stretch of the East Twenties, wondering what happened to our special night out.

"I don't suppose you know of another one nearby?" Aileen asked.

"The Puncheon?"

"Very funny," she said, sighing. New York's most exclusive speakeasy wouldn't give two girls from the Lower East Side the time of day. "Should we go home?"

I was inclined to agree, but my attention was caught by a strange commotion at the other end of the street, near Lexington. A crowd had gathered around the entrance of some establishment—a gentleman's club or a restaurant, judging by the awning. A reporter's camera flashed.

Aileen and I glanced at each other. "That looks interesting," she said.

She started to hurry toward the crowd, but I hesitated. I hated to leave the poor vampire's remains just lying there, trickling into the gutter with all the other refuse of the city. On the other hand, I couldn't do anything to help him. A clean-up crew had finally arrived in an ambulance wagon parked across the street.

"Zephyr!" Aileen called.

I swallowed, took one last look at the popper, and hurried to catch up. I would speak with Ysabel about getting blood out more efficiently to the most desperate vampires. Perhaps that way I could save someone from a similar fate.

From the back of the crowd, it was difficult to see the object of their focus, but it wasn't hard to hear about it.

"Mr. Lindbergh, a picture for the papers?" called out a reporter. From over the shoulder of a short gentleman, I caught sight of the famous aviator's suit jacket and gray hat as he hurried to the car parked on the curb. They said the man who had crossed the Atlantic in an airplane had a boyishly handsome air, but I couldn't see his face well enough to tell. The city had thrown him a ticker tape parade a month ago, and I wondered if a man could grow tired of adulation.

The gathered crowd lingered for a few minutes after Charles Lindbergh drove off, chatting animatedly about their brush with fame.

"He *was* handsome, don't you think?" Aileen was saying.

"I have no idea," I said, a little snappish. My feet hurt and the prospects for making it up with alcohol had grown quite slim. "I can vouch for his fine taste in millinery, at least."

Aileen clucked her tongue. "You're no fun," she said. "We just saw the most famous man in the city."

"I saw his hat," I said.

"No fun *at all.*"

Aileen was my best friend, but sometimes she was insufferable. "Then why are you out with me?"

"Because my regular partner has defected to the Hamptons. Traitor."

The traitor in question was Lily Harding, a peculiar mix of debutante and hard-nosed lady reporter. She had formed an unlikely friendship with Aileen, mostly founded on their shared love of late nights, nice gentlemen, and fine spirits. Never mind that Aileen and I shared a small room in a boardinghouse on Ludlow Street, that Aileen was an Irish immigrant, or that she told fortunes for a living. Lily could be a snob about a lot of things, but it wouldn't be smart to bet on what.

"Sorry to be such a disappointment," I said. "You two are out all the time—don't you know of any other speakeasies?"

She took a look at my shoes and winced. "We wouldn't get in," she said.

Well, then.

"Pardon me?" A gentleman slightly taller than my collarbone had turned to face Aileen and me. "If you don't mind my intruding, I take it you ladies are looking for a gin joint?"

Aileen nodded. "Absolutely!"

"I'm going to a nice place not two blocks up. I'd be happy to take you there."

Getting a lead on a gin joint from a stranger struck me as a dubious idea, but I did not argue very strenuously. I wanted a night out nearly as much as Aileen, after all.

The short gentleman chatted with Aileen about Mr. Lindbergh while we made our way two blocks north. An imposingly large gentleman puffed on a cigarette in front of a promising red door on East 30th. Our guide paused and looked a little nervously back at the two of us.

"I forgot to mention one peculiarity of this establishment," he said. "I hope you don't mind, but it also serves Faust."

Aileen's nod froze halfway. She turned to look at me. "Zephyr?" she said, a plea.

The trouble was that I had spent all of my time recently buried in work for my latest cause—Friends Against Faust. We were dedicated to prohibition of the vampire liquor that had spread like wildfire across New York City in the six months since its introduction. My organization contended that Faust consumption had proved too dangerous for vampires and humans alike. Which explained why Aileen thought I would refuse to set foot in any establishment that served the brew.

But the truth of the matter was that I felt profoundly ambivalent about the wisdom of our cause. After all, if I allowed myself to indulge in the dubious pleasures of alcohol, who was I to declare that vampires were incapable of controlling their own impulses? The real trouble was Amir. The djinni had brought Faust to the city in the first place, and now I found myself unaccountably in control of his powers. An unscrupulous, spendthrift djinni with a penchant for playing practical jokes on humans would hardly be an ideal partner in the best of times. But I had become his vessel—the one human able to control his powers and make wishes. Guilt as much as anything motivated my participation in Friends Against Faust.

But right now, I didn't give a fig. I wanted a gin and tonic, and I didn't care who gave it to me.

"It's perfectly fine," I said, to both of their relief.

The inside of the speakeasy was low-lit and smoky, with a jazz band barely visible on stage and a shabby but glamorous clientele crowding the bar. As promised, vampires mixed with humans, seemingly without regard for social status. The vampires I easily identified by the dusty pallor of their skin and the unmistakable red flush around their cheeks and ears from a recent feeding. Some even flashed unretracted fangs, a taboo in other social situations. The bartenders alternated alcohol with shots of a thick liquid, so dark it appeared black in the low light. Occasionally, they would top it with a dash of real blood from a bag. Faust had originally been developed from pig blood, but it paradoxically caused vampires to go blood-mad. Presumably adding a bit of human blood helped ameliorate the effect.

Aileen and I took our drinks and settled into a booth in a corner of the room. The music was nice, but I wouldn't have been keen on dancing even if my feet weren't killing me. After relaxing into that peculiar burning pleasure of not-quite bathtub gin, Aileen gave me an appraising stare.

"Why won't you make a wish, Zeph?"

I coughed. "Why? Haven't I told you before?"

She lifted one corner of her mouth. "Not really. You talk about not wanting to be bound, but it seems to me that you're a lot more bound to Amir when he's desperate for you to make a wish than you would have been if you'd just asked for some rutabagas in February."

"But that's just it, Aileen! If I asked for rutabagas in February, I would have to ask for more in March and April and every other damn month for the rest of my life. The second I give in—"

"Zeph. You put your *blood* in his *mouth*. You bound yourself to him. Why cavil now?"

I took a big gulp of my drink and coughed again. "He was dying," I said hoarsely. Half a year before, I found out that Amir was slowly being poisoned by the bite of a vampire, and only my blood—which my daddy had somehow made immune to all vampirism—could save him.

"You still did it. Even I can see how desperate he's getting for you to make a wish. All his djinni relatives must be giving him hell."

I looked away from her frank gaze and slouched into the seat. She was mostly right, but her logic couldn't touch my inner conviction that I *had* to break the bond of vessel and djinni between Amir and me.

"I don't know, Aileen . . ." I said, and groped for some way to change the subject. "Lindbergh did have a very nice hat," I said.

She sighed. "Don't you feel anything for him anymore?"

"Lindbergh?"

"Zephyr."

I sighed and slouched even further into my seat. "I feel something," I muttered. "None of this would matter if I didn't."

"Then make a wish!"

"Aileen!" I said, bolting upright in sudden frustration. "Whatever I feel for Amir, it's complicated. He brought Faust into the city as a practical joke, for heaven's sake! I can't just forgive that. But I also can't . . . he means something to me, whatever it is, and how will we ever work anything out if we always have this horribly unequal, magically competing bond where I can force him to do whatever I want? Where even if I do make a wish, chances are it will backfire? If I make a wish now, it's like I'm giving up on . . . I don't even know, but something that might matter, something I might want. And if I don't want it, or if he doesn't want it, well, better that we aren't forced to see each other."

Aileen took a careful sip of her drink and rested it on the table.

"I'm sorry, Zeph," she said, worry in her eyes. "I didn't understand."

"So you agree?"

She laughed and popped a melting ice cube in her mouth. "No," she said. "But that's never mattered before."

∾

The next morning the proprietress of our boardinghouse was making the oddest noises in her attic chambers. Mrs. Brodsky was with her boyfriend, who we jokingly called Mr. Brodsky. The floorboards even managed a creak or two, and I could only admire her stamina in this bloody miserable weather.

"There has to be something we can do," I said to Aileen, who was practicing Eastern meditation beneath the window. My roommate even wore her lounging kimono—with more determination than comfort, I imagined, given the damp stains spreading at her armpits.

"Wish for Mr. Brodsky to turn into a frog. No, a water sprinkler. Or one of those newfangled refrigerators that Amir has. That would be lovely."

"We could go to his place," I said, trying to ignore the conflicting strains of anticipation and dread at the very thought.

"Brave the heat *and* listen to the bickering duo? I'd rather achieve inner peace, thank you very much."

I eyed the copy of *Harper's Bazaar* still open on her bed. ANCIENT MYSTICS REVEAL TRUTH AND BEAUTY was the promising headline. "You don't look very peaceful," I said.

"I haven't had much of a chance."

"I doubt Mr. Brodsky is going to give it to you."

Aileen sighed and opened her eyes with a speed that suggested she hadn't been quite so close to inner peace as she claimed. Above us, the floor creaked alarmingly.

"I think," said Aileen, "that we should climb onto the roof."

"The roof? It's filthy!"

Aileen's smile grew wider. "We'll bring a blanket."

"It's probably a hundred degrees up there."

"Then it must be a hundred and twenty in here. I swear, if I'd known back in Dublin about New York summers . . . and New York winters, for that matter. This city has some lousy weather, you know that?"

"Which is why we must atone by being the greatest city in the world."

"A city where no one will think twice about two girls taking the air in the midst of a heat wave."

She removed the damp kimono and searched through her trunk. I stayed put, eyeing her cream-colored lace teddy with not inconsiderable envy. I wore my habitual skirt and fitted blouse, clothes that had contented me for ages, but increasingly frustrated me now. That was Lily's influence, of course.

"Don't you have another one of those teddies?" I asked.

"Things heating up with Amir after all?" she asked, holding up a delicate little slip of navy silk and black lace.

I blushed and quickly plucked the teddy from her hands. Our discussion last night had been a necessary clearing of the air, perhaps, but I intended to quash any further investigations about myself and my djinni. "Things are heating up inside my blouse. If we're doing this, I mean to get properly cool."

Aileen looked at me like she knew precisely what I was avoiding. But we understood each other very well, and she left well enough alone. Not a day had passed that I hadn't relived that terrible experience of watching Amir die in his brother's garden, or heard his voice reciting a poem with such urgency in a language I didn't understand. And then I helped him live, with my blood staining his lips.

Take her home, brother, he had said. *Let her dream she never met me.*

I couldn't talk about it to either Aileen or Amir, but I had been investigating possible methods for a vessel to quit her djinni. Elspeth, the vampire leader of Friends Against Faust, had promised to help if she could. She said she might be able to find a *sahir*—a witch—powerful enough to solve my problem.

Aileen shook loose her thick black hair. "Shall we? If I'm going to die of this heat, let it at least be with a good view."

The rooftop was not so grimy as I feared, though the fire escape creaked and groaned like a graveyard revenant. Aileen laid out her blanket and we collapsed upon it, basking in the breeze and muggy open air.

Perhaps an hour later, when my skin had begun to turn unpleasantly red, I was startled to hear the sound of someone else banging on the fire escape.

"You!" shouted Mrs. Brodsky. "There are some men here for you, Zephyr Hollis! They say it is important!"

Aileen rolled on her side and peered at me. "Men? Sounds promising."

I groaned. "It's probably Amir again, damn him." I leaned over the edge of the roof. "I told you yesterday, Amir, I'm not making a wish—"

"Amir? No, no, it's not your Mohammedan, they say they're with the police though they don't look much like police to me—"

Mrs. Brodsky's strident voice cut off with a squawk, followed by the thud of booted, male feet greatly taxing the corroded metal of the fire escape.

"Zephyr Hollis!" called a voice I certainly didn't recognize. "Please come down immediately."

Aileen and I shared a panicked glance. "Did you bring a robe?" I whispered.

"It was *hot*, remember? Why would I?"

"I can't just go down there in this teddy! Why, you can practically see my nipples through the lace!"

Aileen squinted. "I think it's not so much *practically*, Zeph, dear."

I closed my eyes. "Oh, bloody stakes."

The fire escape rattled and creaked and groaned again, if anything more ominously than it had before.

"We hope you'll come peacefully, Miss Hollis," said the voice of a second man. "We don't want to use force, but we will if we have to."

"Force!" I said.

Aileen poked her nose gingerly over the ledge. "They're coming up, Zeph."

"No, stop!" I yelled. The footsteps paused.

"Miss Hollis, I suggest you make this easy for everyone."

"Who says I want to make this easy?" I said.

"I've heard you're a bit of a firecracker, but now is not the time to make a stand."

"Don't you think you could just . . . wait in the parlor for me to freshen up? I'm not at my best, at the moment. This weather, you know—"

"We're coming up, Miss Hollis."

Aileen scooted back. She looked around, peering at the neighboring rooftops and windows. "Do you think someone reported us?" she whispered. "Maybe they're arresting you for indecent exposure?"

"You're just as indecent as I am!"

Aileen looked at me dubiously. "You know, I'd never noticed that freckle on your left breast before."

"This is *your* teddy."

"Why don't you think I'm wearing it?"

A pair of hands made themselves visible just beyond the ledge. I looked longingly at the other rooftops, but I didn't have enough confidence in my vaulting abilities.

"Well," Aileen said. "Nothing else for it."

"What are you—"

But Aileen had already stood up on our blanket and was posing with her hand on her hip, as though she were a model for a particularly risqué *Harper's Bazaar*. A breeze passed over the rooftop, which lifted her teddy enough for a serious peep show before settling down again.

She had a point. I scrambled up and stood beside her, posing with perhaps less panache, but equal belligerence. *I'm a modern woman*, I had told my daddy back in January when he'd caught me in a similar state of dishabille, that time courtesy of Amir.

I grinned at the thought of what Daddy would make of me now.

The first man climbed onto the roof. He stopped short and stared until his partner pushed him forward.

"Ah . . ." said the first man, and cleared his throat. He was younger than I would have expected, mid-thirties at the most, and quite tall. His partner was a few inches shorter and even narrower, though I could hardly see his face behind his shadowy, wide-brimmed hat.

"What the devil is this?" said the shadowy one.

The first man blushed, much to my gratification. "Perhaps we should wait in the parlor."

"Oh," said the second. He clapped his gloved hands and I realized, with a shock, that he was a vampire. I doubted many vampires could claim the distinction of being officers of the law. "Taking your sapphic pleasures, Miss Hollis?"

Aileen gasped. The tall officer put a calming hand on his vampire partner's shoulder.

"Miss Hollis . . ." He nodded in our general direction without quite looking at either of us. "I trust we'll see you in the parlor in a few, ah, minutes."

And with that, they took themselves back down the fire escape.

"Well," Aileen said, after they'd left. "That didn't go so badly."

"You can keep the teddy," I said.

∝

The two officers were waiting in the parlor when I forced myself to descend ten minutes later, attired in my most conservative outfit. The vampire officer had removed his hat, revealing a thin, characteristically pale face with cheekbones that could slice pastrami. I could tell, from his expression of pinched disapproval, and his partner's awkward contemplation of the coffee table, that they were attempting to forget the view on the roof.

"I'm Agent McConnell," said the tall one, still addressing the coffee table. "This is Zuckerman. We're from the Other Crimes vice squad. We'd like to ask you a few questions about an ongoing investigation. We can do it here or at the station."

"Here, thank you," I said, trying to hide my surprise. Other Crimes was a special vice squad in the regular police department, tasked with investigating non-human criminal activity. Given the realities of our city, this mostly meant vampires, which made the presence of a vampire officer on the squad particularly interesting.

"What's this all about?" I asked, since they both seemed content to watch me in silence.

McConnell cleared his throat and took a monogrammed cigarette holder from his breast pocket. "Mind if I smoke?" he said, even as Zuckerman was lighting a match for him without so much as glancing at his partner. The effect was one of imposing harmony, a synchronicity of purpose between the officers that felt somehow intimidating. McConnell lit his cigarette and blew a long plume of smoke just barely to my left. I wrinkled my nose and pushed the ashtray conspicuously closer to his elbow. Mrs. Brodsky would blame me if any ashes dusted her precious table.

"Mort," McConnell said, slipping the cigarette box back into his pocket, "I think you had better explain matters to the young lady?"

Zuckerman's pinched lips receded even further into his face, so he looked like he had bitten a sour lemon. I wondered if he was annoyed with McConnell, but the glare he fixed on me as he leaned forward in his chair quickly made the object of his ire quite clear.

"We'd like to question you about a matter that occurred this past January."

I stopped breathing—just as well, since McConnell chose that moment to exhale his particularly malodorous cigarette into my face. January. The month haunted me, no matter how hard I tried to move on.

"What happened in January?" I asked, as calmly as I could manage.

McConnell tilted his head and shrugged at Zuckerman as he tapped his cigarette in the ashtray. Inexplicably, Zuckerman smiled.

"A major felony," the vampire officer said, in a tone dry as tinder.

"Felony?"

McConnell shook his head sadly. "Afraid so. We have reason to believe that you at one point harbored an underage vampire. A boy eleven years of age, according to our records. That's a class A felony."

"Minimum fifteen years," said Zuckerman, helpfully.

Harboring an underage vampire? Of all my less-than-legal activities this past January, saving Judah's life had risked the largest consequences, but I had barely spent a minute in the past six months worrying about it. I had assumed—stupidly, it appeared—that no one would ever find out.

"Mind telling me where you heard this, ah, scurrilous rumor about me and this boy?"

McConnell stubbed out his cigarette on the edge of the ashtray, liberally dusting the tabletop in the process. "Mort did. I don't have his contacts, of course. But he's sure."

"Sure?" I repeated faintly.

Zuckerman crossed his arms over his chest. "Your face is well-known, Miss Hollis."

"I don't understand," I said.

"Your type almost never do," Zuckerman said. "You didn't think about the stigma the rest of us suffer when an underage vampire gets loose. Now the only question we have is where you're keeping him now."

I cringed inside, but attempted to make a good show of it. "I've never had anything to do with an underage vampire! In this neighborhood, child vampires aren't so rare, anyhow. Surely you've heard of the Turn Boys?"

I might have missed my calling as a stage actress.

"True, we have heard of the underage vampire gang," said McConnell. "But Mort thinks this is a separate matter."

"And Troy Kavanagh's Defenders popped those boys in January," Zuckerman said.

"So maybe this boy died along with the others."

"Miss Hollis," McConnell said, "we dropped by to inform you that you are our primary suspect in this matter."

I swallowed. "So, are you going to arrest me?"

"Right now, you're just a suspect," McConnell said. "But we're going to be investigating extensively."

"Brilliant," I said.

Zuckerman made the sour-lemon face again, though he clasped his hands together in something like glee.

"We think so," he said. He and McConnell stood at the same moment, again without the slightest apparent need for communication.

"Good day, Miss Hollis," McConnell said, replacing his hat with that infuriatingly absent-minded, genial air. "We'll see ourselves out. Until next time."

I wished with all my heart that there wouldn't be a next time. It occurred to me that I could also wish on a djinni. But even with a felony hanging over my head I didn't take the possibility seriously. My skin tingled at just the thought of Amir. That was more than enough reason to refuse to contemplate any wishes but my own.

∾

A half-hour later, intending to clear my head with fresh air, I opened the door to find Amir waiting for me on the stoop. He held a letter and a bouquet of lilacs. I froze with my hand on the knob, and wondered for a fleeting moment if I could duck back into the hallway without him noticing me. My heart—already strained from my encounter with the detectives—seemed to stutter in my chest. Six months, and this fire-breathing, spendthrift, amoral djinni still had the power to do this to me.

And how he knew it.

Amir grinned and stood up. He held out the flowers. I caught my hands trembling and held them rigidly at my thighs.

"Are those . . ."

"For you," Amir said, "from the mayor, of all people."

I leaned against the doorjamb. My knees felt suspiciously weak. "The . . . what on earth, Amir?"

He shrugged, and his grin faded. "Far be it from me to question your choice of beaus. Though I must say, this doesn't read much like a love letter. In some trouble, Zephyr? You know, I could help—"

"Let me see that," I said, snatching both the flowers and the small note. My fingers brushed his for a moment, sending my stomach somewhere in the vicinity of my feet.

I, of course, gave no outward sign of my discomfiture. I was quite as cool as Amir as I opened the folded note on the mayor's personal stationery.

Miss Hollis,

You seem to be in difficulties. Should you like to get out of them, stop by my office—I'm sure you know where it is—around four tomorrow afternoon?

Regards,

James Walker

"I need a drink," I said.

"Before noon?"

"I'm sure it's midnight somewhere."

Amir settled against the doorjamb and held out his hand. "In Shadukiam, perhaps?" he said, a casual invitation. The strange otherworld that Amir and his djinni brothers called home had a certain appeal.

I considered—which is to say, I fought strenuously against my better judgment. "The Faust evidentiary hearings are at four. Friends Against Faust actually has a speaking invitation, I can't possibly miss it. This is our best chance to derail the vote next week."

"So we'll be back by four."

"There are two officers with the Other vice squad who are trying to throw me in jail. I'm not sure it's a good idea for me to be seen with you."

"Is that bigotry I smell, Miss Hollis?"

I twisted my lips. "No, it's prudence.

"You can't imagine the police would ever come after *me*."

"If there is any justice in this world—"

"Zeph, you naïve little thing."

I scowled. "You can't fight for justice unless you believe in it."

"And I can think of no better way to advance the causes of truth and justice than by going back to my place for a little judicious law-breaking."

"Please tell me," said Aileen, walking behind me in the doorway, "that this law includes the Eighteenth Amendment?"

"What else?" Amir said. "Like to come to Shadukiam with us?"

Aileen giggled beneath the force of his smile. "I've heard so much about it, how could I refuse—"

I turned on her. " 'No' would be a start."

"Why would I want to say that?" she said, all innocence.

I groaned. "I hope you have very good liquor," I said.

Amir brushed my fingertips with his. "Oh, *habibti*," he said, not quite smiling, "I should have known you were a natural."

I drew back so abruptly I nearly careened into Aileen. "A natural what? Drunk?"

He shook his head. "Lawbreaker. Now, shall we?"

Aileen was nodding and I was considering the very clear *not-goodness* of this idea even as he blinked and the world wobbled and faded and then I sank to my knees on a mosaic floor, with the smell of roses strong in my nostrils and fountains of water tinkling nearby.

A breeze blew over me, carrying with it the scent of oranges and olives and sun-kissed fields. I felt cool for the first time in a month and that, I decided, was worth the annoyance of spending an extended period of time with Amir.

"Zeph," said Aileen from a few feet away. "I cannot *believe* you didn't take me here before."

I grimaced and forced myself upright. Some trips were worse than others, but I'd developed a deep loathing for teleportation in the past six months. "I'll let you know when I open my other universe travel service, Aileen."

Though as far as I knew this was the first time she had teleported, Aileen didn't appear at all troubled. Amir had deposited us in a courtyard centered around a golden fountain. On the marble flagstones were two low-lying divans and large brocade cushions for relaxation. She was smiling up at him and arranging herself on the divan closest to the fountain. This was Amir's brother's palace, the only part of Shadukiam that I'd had the privilege to see. It was fantastically ostentatious, with a series of fountains and gardens, honeycombed with arcaded corridors and towers. Redolent pink and orange roses climbed arches inlaid with mosaic of lapis lazuli and jade. I took a deep, heady breath—I could never deny that wealth had its pleasures.

"So what refreshment suits you?" Amir asked, removing his jacket and sitting on the intricately inlaid mosaic lip of the fountain.

Aileen kicked off her shoes. "Sidecar," she said.

Amir turned to me, and I discovered that the sight of him stripped to a waistcoat and sharp-tailored pants had momentarily rendered me speechless.

"Same," I finally managed.

I didn't know if he noticed; he tugged a little at his lapel and then shook his head before walking away. I sat on the divan next to Aileen, and had just begun to relax into the cushions when he returned with the drinks.

"Did you make them?" I asked, surprised, as he handed me a frosted tumbler.

He smiled and sat on the edge of the fountain. Water spray beaded his slicked-back hair, but he didn't seem to notice. I took a judicious sip.

"Goodness, I don't mix the drinks, Zephyr. What do you take me for?"

"A wastrel?" I said.

"As you so often accuse me. But surely you must make allowances for a prince."

"He has a point," said Aileen.

I scowled at her, but without much conviction. Having gotten drunk for the first time not six months before, I was hardly what anyone would call an expert on spirits (well, not those kind of spirits). The only liquors I could identify by taste were cheap whiskey and bathtub gin, neither of which would dare offend the inside of such fine crystal. This smelled like the breeze from the orange fields outside his brother Kardal's palace; it tasted even better, with surprisingly pleasant hints of bitter and sweet. It hardly burned at all, which I had not known was possible.

"Well, your houris mix excellent drinks," I said, raising the glass to him.

He just smiled and waved his hand. A shot glass filled with deep amber liquid and a single cube of ice dropped with a slight clink on the mosaic tiles beside him.

"A toast," he said, taking his drink.

"To unearned luxury?" I said.

Aileen sighed. "Give it a rest, will you? Not *everything* has to be a suffragette rally."

"I was going to propose," said Amir, with such mildness that I felt, for a moment, quite churlish, "to pleasantly boring days. May we have many more of them."

"Amen," said Aileen fervently, and drained half her glass.

I licked some of the sugar off the rim. "We're too late for today," I said. "But perhaps it's not too much to hope for." I paused. "Providing Beau Jimmy can actually get the police off my back."

"Not to claim undue familiarity with the mayor of your fine city," he said, "but do you really imagine that his offer won't come with strings?"

"More like Promethean chains," I said dejectedly, "but I don't see many other options. How could they have learned about Judah! Six months too late, at that."

"I told you," said Aileen, "that was a bad idea."

"I told myself," I said to my nearly empty glass. "Several times. It didn't seem to stick."

Six months before, I had saved an underage vampire named Judah from being duly apprehended by the authorities and staked for the "good of the community." Underage vampires can be deadly when freshly turned—something about their brains can't handle the process. That one decision had led me into a criminal mess, which Amir and the notorious vampire mob boss Rinaldo had made between them. A mess from which I still had not fully extricated myself. I now seemed to be permanently bound to Amir—a side effect of saving his life with my vampire-immune blood. Judah had recovered (mostly) and was now living with my mama, siblings, and demon-hunting daddy in Yarrow, Montana. I'd had my doubts about this living arrangement, but according to my oldest brother, Harry, everyone got along just fine. Or about as well as they ever had.

"You could always make a wish," Amir said, setting down his drink.

I looked up at him and then away. He leaned forward, his eyebrows drawn together in a look so earnest and caring I could hardly stand it. I hated it when I could peek behind his mask—it was so much harder to view him with the necessary distance.

Aileen opened her mouth like she would say something, thought better of it, and took a long sip of her drink.

"Zephyr," Amir said softly, "you've seen what happens when a vessel takes too long between wishes. You've waited six months. It's getting . . . difficult."

Anxiety tightened, vise-like, around my middle. I *knew* we couldn't keep this up. I'd known it for months. But I'd persisted in my hope that some magical solution would reveal itself—some method by which

I could break the bond between us and leave all notions of mutual obligations and *wishes* safely in the past. I didn't think Amir relished the idea of being bound to me for life either, but he bore the obligation gracefully. Perhaps he saw it as recompense for saving his life. Or even his role in bringing Faust to the city. I didn't know, but the reasons I had given Aileen were as true now as they had been in January. Whatever Amir and I might have would never survive the pressure of a wish. Because a wish meant I owned his powers.

And yet I considered how easy it would be to wish my way out of my problems. *I wish for the police to never have suspected me of saving Judah.* That seemed safe enough. No rumors of an underage vampire, no vice squad catching me in a borrowed teddy on the rooftop. And maybe I could even have an extra: *I wish for the Faust vote to fail.* The Board of Aldermen was set to have their final vote on the full legalization next Monday, a week from today. I'd be a hero forever with Friends Against Faust and Elspeth. But the moment I made those wishes I knew that I would lose whatever chance I had to sever the bond between Amir and me.

"Could I wish to no longer be your vessel?" I asked, surprising myself with how meek I sounded.

Amir twisted his lips. "Only if you want to die."

This surprised a curse from Aileen. "Hell, really?"

"It's a permanent bond, so long as both parties are alive. And call me sentimental, *habibti*, but I'd dearly love for you to avoid suicide."

"How sweet of you."

"Is that what's behind all this? You think you can find some way to get out of the bond? I'll grant there are few fates worse than being tied to a wastrel for life, but one of them ought to be your early grave."

I took one look at his earnest eyes, tinged with humor, self-deprecation, bitterness, and just the smallest hint of literal fire—and stood up. I had taken one step toward him when Aileen started to whimper. The noise was small. She had dropped her sidecar to press her hands against her temples. Then the ground began to tremble.

I might have screamed—certainly, my throat felt very raw afterward—but the earth rumbled like a great bass horn in my ears and the marble cracked with deafening thunder. Amir reacted far faster than I. He plucked Aileen like a rag doll from the divan, turned to me with eyeballs of flame and yelled something I didn't understand. It took a long moment, while cracking stones showered me with powdered mortar and dust, to realize that he was speaking to someone behind me in a language I didn't know.

I turned to see Kardal as he placed a smoky, bilious hand on my shoulder. "My apologies," he said in that rumbling voice that merged with the sound of breaking stone.

And with that the world turned sideways, blinked, and then vanished entirely.

CHAPTER TWO

I spent ten minutes emptying good liquor into an immaculate porcelain bowl. When I decided nothing more could possibly leave my stomach, I stood and rinsed out my mouth as best I could. I wished for a lemonade or at least some food. But there wouldn't be time for that before the evidentiary hearing. I would probably be late, but no help for it.

When I returned to Amir's parlor, he and Kardal were still arguing. Aileen sat on a couch across from them, looking wan and ignored. I sat down next to her.

"Are you all right?" I asked. "What happened?"

"Fine," she said. "Just a touch of the Sight. Probably brought on by whatever that mess was."

"Seemed like more than a touch." I put my hand on her shoulders, but she shrugged me off.

"Can get like that sometimes. It's nothing I can't handle, Zeph, believe me."

Aileen had discovered an unfortunate inheritance in recent months. The visions of the future and past that had afflicted the women in her family for generations had hit her at a relatively advanced age. When in the grip of one, she lost the ability to see her surroundings and sometimes even control her body. At first she'd made use of her new ability by telling street fortunes, but for the last two months she'd found a far more lucrative gig: the New York Spiritualist Society. She brought on visions for rich ladies with a yearning for spirit photography, ectoplasm, and dead relatives. Considering how much the visions drained Aileen, I didn't think it a particularly good idea. But she paid about as much attention to my advice as I did to hers.

I sighed, and turned my attention to the screaming brothers. Things had escalated far enough.

"Boys," I said, with a deliberate drawl. "Do you think you could tell us what the hell just happened in there? Because we have places to be."

Kardal—so bilious he seemed like a cloud with flashing eyes— growled. "Tell her, Amir. Explain what she's done to my home."

"What *I've* done?" I asked. "I hadn't known you could cause an earthquake by drinking a sidecar. Prohibition must work a lot better in Shadukiam."

But Amir didn't laugh. He looked genuinely worried, which was never a good sign. "Too much power has built up from your unused wish. It's pooling in Shadukiam. I hadn't thought it would have reached that level—"

"You should have—"

"Fine, Kardal. I should have. I thought it would be safe enough to bring you there, Zephyr, but your presence created a kind of warp. It started to destabilize the forces keeping Kardal's palace together."

Kardal allowed himself to coalesce into a form recognizably human. "You must make a wish, Zephyr. Even now, it might be dangerous to release so much energy into the world at once, but if you wait any longer, the danger will be much worse."

I forced down a shiver. "I had no idea the situation was so serious."

He frowned. "Brother, the council has summoned you about this problem twice in the last month. How could you not have told her?"

Amir tapped his foot in discomfort. "It didn't seem fair."

"Fair! What's fair, then, destroying my home? Causing problems for all the djinni because of this excess power? Bad enough for you to have two vessels in so many years. Do you think our brothers do not notice? That our father doesn't?"

"Oh, Kashkash preserve us, Kardal—"

"Indeed, you had best hope he preserves you!"

I stood up. They turned to look at me with such a unison of surprise I had no trouble at all believing they were brothers. "Give me a week," I said.

"Zephyr—"

"It's too long—"

"A week," I repeated, firmly. "Give me that long, and then I promise to make a wish."

Give me one more chance to find a way to break this bond before Amir gets stuck with me forever.

Kardal gave me a long stare, and then nodded. "A deal, Zephyr. And Amir, I trust you will not be so foolish as to bring her back to my home before then?"

He didn't wait for Amir's answer, just burst into flame and left nothing of himself but a few ashes on the brocade couch.

"Well, that was exciting," Aileen said, her acerbic voice cutting the silence.

"I don't think your toast worked, Amir," I said.

He shook his head with a bitter smile. "You'd think I'd have learned by now," he said, "to beware making wishes in our city of roses."

———

Because Amir had used his previous worldly apartments as a storage facility for Faust, he had determined it would be prudent to move. Instead of finding another warehouse in which to install his flashy, opulent tastes, he'd instead opted to rent a suite of rooms in the Ritz hotel. We left Amir soon after Kardal's more flamboyant departure. The doorman let Aileen and I into the summer heat with barely a lift of his eyebrows, which was good of him, given our disheveled states. My roommate and I parted ways at Times Square.

"Got a séance tonight," she said.

"Are you sure that's—"

"It's fine, Zephyr," she said, with a look that said *are you one to talk?*

I subsided. "Take care of yourself."

Her face softened for a moment, and she hugged me. "You too. Make that wish, all right? I felt a bit of what was coming down on that place. It's nothing to trifle with."

I promised her I would, though of course I could only think about how I might still get out of the bargain entirely.

But right now, I was about to be late for the all-important hearing. I looked longingly at the passing cabs, counted the change in my pocket and then hurried to the subway. Elspeth, the head of our organization, had been invited to speak before the aldermanic council. This was a coup, both for advancing our cause and because she was one of the very few vampires allowed to speak in those halls of power.

I rattled along in the olive-green subway, grateful for the stale air that blasted through the windows and openings between the cars. I glanced at my watch and willed the train to hurry. I supposed I could have found more exciting activities (or at least more restful ones) for my two weeks of summer freedom. My night school classes for the Citizens' Council were on break until the start of August, and so I had thrown myself entirely into volunteer activities. I appeased Mrs. Brodsky with the small savings I'd kept from my share of the bounty from January. It felt like blood money, and so I tried not to consider the matter too deeply. More important that I keep a roof over my head and help stop Faust now than worry about the morality of my actions six months ago.

When I climbed out of the train station I was unsurprised to see people crowding City Hall Park, but I didn't understand why the newsboys seemed to be doing such a brisk business this late in the afternoon. I didn't take the time to look; my watch read three minutes after four, and I winced at the thought of what Elspeth would say about my tardiness. Thankfully, inside it appeared the evidentiary hearings had yet to start. The doors to the council chamber had been thrown open, but people still milled around the lobby. I spotted a flowered hat on an unusually tall head and I smiled to recognize a friend. Iris Tomkins had been widowed years before by her wealthy husband, and remained a marginal member of New York's elite society. She was godmother to Lily's sister, which is how I first met the deb journalist. Iris had devoted herself to causes in lieu of a man, and was one of my chief supporters, if not always the most subtle.

"Zephyr, you made it!" she called, when I had pushed my way closer. Iris, Elspeth, and a few others from the core committee of Friends Against Faust were waiting by the doors for the hearings to begin.

Elspeth frowned. "Late, Zephyr," she said. That was all; Elspeth had a talent for rigid disapproval. I flushed and mumbled something about the subway.

"There's news," Iris said. "Have you heard?" She waved one of the papers the newsboys had been selling out front.

I took her copy of *Evening Standard* and read the headline, at least an inch high: TEN VAMPIRES DEAD OVERNIGHT and then, in slightly smaller print beneath that, AUTHORITIES SUSPECT FAUST FROM LEGAL VENDOR.

"They're saying Faust *killed* vampires?" I said.

Elspeth wore a dark gray suit so severe it would not seem out of place at a funeral, but she still possessed a forbidding beauty that defied her efforts to bury it. Curly black hair, held back by a scarf, framed a dusky but still oddly pale face. She had been a vampire for five or so years, and could not have been older than thirty when she turned.

"They're speculating it's poison," Elspeth said, "though further down they quote a manufacturer on the possibility of it being a bad batch. The end result is the same, of course. Ten vampires dead on the spot. All from one drink sold by fully legal vendors."

"But Faust doesn't cause exsanguination," I said, baffled. "Could they have drunk liquor by mistake?"

Alcohol caused unwary (or desperate) vampires to bleed out, often fatally. Which accounted for Faust's runaway popularity in such a short time; vampires could indulge their need for inebriation without mortal danger. Unfortunately, Faust greatly increased their sensitivity to sunlight, so in the immediate weeks after its introduction, dozens of vampires had burned to death accidentally. It also appeared to make vampires dangerously rowdy—though I privately wondered whether it did so any more than plain alcohol's effect on a human.

Elspeth turned delicately on the ball of one foot and faced me with that direct, unnaturally bright stare that I had learned to dread. "There's been some suggestion that they died without exsanguinating. No one knows for sure; the police were apparently quick to cart the bodies back to the morgue."

I had never heard of a vampire who died without exsanguinating. And if it could happen, Daddy should have told me—my daddy is Montana's most famous demon hunter, though it's a fact I tend to keep to myself. "How is that possible?"

She shrugged. "Maybe it's a side effect of long-term abuse. Maybe it's a judgment from God. No one knows."

Even before she'd been turned Elspeth would have spent her life dealing with prejudice. Her parents had immigrated here from Syria when she was quite young. She still lived among that community of Christian Arabs at the far southern end of Washington Street, just a block east of the Hudson.

"It may be harsh to say so," Iris said with relish, "but this might be a great opportunity in disguise. Good people are dead, yes, but what better argument could we have for the dangers of Faust, of the absolute necessity of its immediate prohibition? You must make hay of this in your speech, Elspeth."

Elspeth regarded Iris impassively, then twisted her lips. "Perhaps before we rush to capitalize upon others' deaths for our own gain we could determine precisely how they died? It might not be Faust at all, and I'm not willing to make such a strong accusation without proof."

I was reminded again why I continued to support these efforts. Doubtful as I was about the efficacy of prohibition, I still valued Elspeth's essential honesty and clarity of purpose. She could be harsh, but she had a solid core that I could only admire.

Iris frowned, as though she wasn't sure what had just happened. "Why, Elspeth, I didn't mean—"

At that moment, the ushers began shouting for everyone to enter the chamber and take their seats. We hurried to follow Elspeth among the crush of people rushing inside. She had a seat reserved in a special block for evidentiary presenters. I called good luck to her, and she nodded briefly before walking away. Iris and I took ourselves to the public seats, where she secured two near the front by dint of heavy elbows and a gracious man who gave up his seat in my favor. We had a good view of both the speakers and the aldermen. The mayor did not technically have a vote in this council chamber, but he would of course be here for the hearings. Beau James had staked his political fortunes on the outcome of the Faust bill, for better or worse.

"I hope Elspeth sees sense about the deaths," Iris murmured. "Think of her persuasive force!"

I said something vaguely sympathetic, but I was more curious about the paper that Elspeth had taken with her. "They died last night?" I asked.

Iris nodded. "The ones who died were all drinking at two of those outdoor stalls near St. Marks Place," she said and shuddered. "What a filthy part of town."

St. Marks Place was famous for its speakeasies and otherwise easy access to the vices of modern life. Lately, outdoor Faust vendors using repurposed hot dog and pretzel stands had been doing a brisk business with the tenement dwellers. The murders must be wreaking havoc with Ysabel and her Blood Bank, so near the crime. I would have to check on her soon, perhaps help make some deliveries.

The room filled quickly. Few political spectacles of the past few years could equal the struggle surrounding the legalization of the "vampire liquor." Even Charles Lindbergh's successful traverse of the Atlantic the month before hadn't been enough to fully distract from the bill's contentious vote. Lindbergh's ticker tape had barely been swept from Broadway before the papers resumed running notices about the political infighting surrounding the bill. So no wonder that the news of Faust killing ten vampires overnight had caused a sensation.

"I wonder what happened to them," I said.

Iris sighed. "Zephyr, when you reach my age you learn there's no time to waste on niceties like that. Why, do you think we would have divorce today if Stanton hadn't been willing to fudge the facts now and again? We act in the service of a higher cause. Still, I suppose information is nothing to sneeze at. Say, Lily has turned into a fair reporter these days, hasn't she? Perhaps you could lure her away from the Hamptons."

"Certainly worth a phone call," I said. I smiled at the thought of

Lily's journalistic ambition bringing her back into the sticky Manhattan summer. She had started a new job at the prestigious *New-Star Ledger* two months ago, though she seemed to clash with the editor in chief with some frequency.

The ushers forced the doors closed. Jimmy Walker shared a whispered word with the board president. The volume in the room lessened in anticipation. In the presenters' corner, Elspeth held herself perfectly straight, her face a pleasant mask of polite interest. She had been an object of whispered innuendo since she had sat down. Apparently, not everyone approved that a vampire had been asked to present at this hearing. This didn't surprise me, but it made me furious to hear the snickers and whispered looks that Elspeth ignored out of necessity. Beside her sat Archibald Madison, the influential leader and founder of the Safety Council. Madison was her political opposite in every respect—except for the matter of Faust. He opposed it for vastly different reasons, but this had caused no small amount of consternation among our set. Madison was a tall, thick man of at least fifty, with gray hair and late-Victorian muttonchops. Among his followers he was considered handsome, but I found his pale blue eyes and habitually choleric expression profoundly off-putting. Madison had swelled the Safety Council rolls with his strident Other-hating vitriol at packed public events.

Iris nudged me, more out of excitement than anything. The board president was finally calling the hearing to order.

"Mayor, distinguished guests. Today the Board will hear presentations from many perspectives regarding the pending vote on Resolution 43, being the full approval of the drink known as Faust, heretofore approved under temporary license given by the Board of Licensure in January. Our first presenter will be Archibald Madison. You have the floor, sir."

The applause as he stood up before the Board surprised me; this wasn't a Safety Council rally, after all.

"Gentlemen of the Board," he said, nodding to them, "I am here to tell you, in all humility but with the truth of the Almighty behind me, that a plague has descended upon us! This plague cloaks its evil in the form and aspect of humanity, leading us to give these demons our sympathy and our love. Yes, love, I said. What wife would not love a husband, miraculously risen from the dead? What child would not love such a father? What brother such a brother? And yet these are but specters and apparitions, temptations of the devil and tests from God. We must exorcise these false creatures from our midst. The cleansing of vampires is our moral duty! And now Faust, that witch's brew of tainted blood, has compounded our problem. It emboldens the vampire, makes him reckless and strengthens his essential evil. We are in the plague's final stages if we believe for a moment that these creatures deserve anything more than a stake through their hearts and holy water in their eyes."

He smiled faintly at the ensuing applause, like it was the least he felt he deserved. Iris and I stared at each other.

"Good god," she said. "They invited *that* to speak?"

Elspeth sat as calmly as ever, but I could only imagine how it felt to be a vampire in the room at that moment—alone, facing a crowd who cheered your destruction.

⸎

Elspeth's speech went over fairly well, given the circumstances. In her quiet but forceful manner, she laid out the facts of vampirism in this city (vampires constituted only five percent of the city's population, as they had since the sixties), and the problem with Faust being one of vampire welfare and safety, not some existential danger to humans. Though you wouldn't know it from reading the press, the chances of being turned from a vampire bite are around one in two hundred.

Iris and I led the applause, such as it was. But one of the aldermen called her back before she could reach her seat. "Miss Akil, if you could please just answer one question?" It was Fred Moore, a negro alderman representing one of the two Harlem districts. "I trust you have heard of the latest incident involving this drink? Would you argue that Faust's implication in the matter of ten vampire deaths overnight gives a greater credence to the arguments for prohibition?"

A murmur went through the room. Iris gave my elbow a gleeful squeeze, as this was what she had encouraged Elspeth to say all along. But Elspeth, having paused a moment to consider her response, nodded. "It maybe so, sir, but the evidence is very thin right now. The bottles could have been poisoned, for all we know. Until the true cause can be ascertained, I am not comfortable making such a pronouncement, or capitalizing on these tragedies."

A wave of whispered conversation overtook the chamber as Elspeth retook her seat. Iris shook her head. "I should have known!" she said.

"At least she's consistent." I felt sure she had taken the proper route, though I saw Iris's point. If something about Faust *had* turned deadly, it would only strengthen our position.

The hearing concluded an hour or so later. Elspeth had tried her best to be persuasive, but I filed out of the chamber feeling discouraged. It felt more like a show trial than something designed to elicit information and debate.

The mayor and a woman I didn't recognize were speaking with Madison on the floor of the chamber. I tried to hurry past, but he caught my eye and nodded cordially. I blushed. Had Elspeth or Iris seen? On no account could I tell them of my letter this morning. I needed to see what exactly tomorrow's appointment with the mayor would bring. As I walked by, he was talking to Madison with a politician's false heartiness. "Well, my friend, you've got to at least make it to the banquet this Saturday. We're putting on quite a show—I just got word from Albany that Al might come down as well."

Madison's faint, supercilious smile didn't waver. "As I've told Mrs. Brandon, the invitation is flattering, but I can't say for sure. A man of my position must examine his affiliations very carefully . . ."

The drift of the crowd pushed me away before I could hear any more. The mayor really thought he could convert a demagogue like Madison to his side? Good news for us, then—such an improbable pursuit must mean he hadn't yet secured the necessary votes to legalize Faust. On the steps outside, Iris took a leaflet from a man passing them out and fanned herself. Elspeth had covered herself thoroughly for the journey into the evening sun, but she stayed with us for a little longer.

"Madison has too much support," Elspeth said, watching the earnest-looking young men passing out pamphlets to the lingering crowd. "He claims his Safety Council has doubled its membership in the last six months."

"Piffle," Iris said, "he would say so. The man thinks he's the second coming of our Lord."

"If only he would try to walk on water," Elspeth said and I laughed.

The man himself descended the steps a moment later, smiling and shaking hands. Iris grunted and lowered her makeshift fan. For the first time, I noticed that the leaflet had been issued by the Safety Council.

The bold text was lurid and explicit: TRUST MADISON! STOP THE VAMPIRE SCOURGE! JUSTICE IS IN YOUR HANDS. IF BEAU JAMES WILL NOT STOP THE SUCKER PLAGUE, YOU KNOW YOUR MORAL DUTY.

"Have you read this?" I asked, taking the damp paper. Elspeth leaned over.

"He would never have dared write this a year ago," she said. On the curb, Madison waved to the crowd and then climbed into a waiting sedan. For religious man, he didn't seem to have much trouble flaunting his wealth: his shining blue Packard probably cost what I made in five years of work for the Citizen's Council.

"Maybe his followers are the ones getting more radical," Iris said.

But I frowned over the paper, wondering at the childlike caricature of a long-fanged vampire sinking his teeth into a young, beautiful woman. Radical and violent. A stake was pictured beside the words "moral duty," and the implied message made me nauseous.

"Poison in the bottles could have killed those vampires," I said.

Elspeth looked at me sharply. "It could have. And you think someone had a motive to put it there?"

"I think quite a few someones might have been convinced to stop the vampire scourge."

"Murder!" Iris said so loudly that not a few people nearby turned. "But surely it's more likely the Faust itself killed them! Given everything else it does." Iris pouted, clearly frustrated by the possibility that these deaths might not help our cause as she had hoped. But I felt a pang at the thought of what such news would do to Amir. It sometimes seemed he felt guilty for bringing Faust into the city, but how much worse would it be if it turned out to kill vampires as well?

"Perhaps," Elspeth said quietly. "But you will allow, Iris, that every other side effect of the drug was witnessed very early. And even though I doubt most of Madison's followers are dedicated enough to take up this injunction . . ."

"Some might be," I said. "If not Madison himself."

"You don't think!" Iris said, clearly warming to the theory.

Elspeth shrugged. "I doubt he would so dirty his hands. He's far too savvy a political figure. But that doesn't preclude his involvement—if indeed these were murders. Zephyr?"

"Yes?"

"Would you mind looking into the matter?"

"Into Madison?"

"Yes. If he's involved in some way, it would be good to know. Even if he isn't, Madison is becoming a force to reckon with in the city."

"But wasn't I going to help you write letters and newspaper items?"

Elspeth waved her hand. "This is far more important. Iris and the others can help. But it seems clear to me that you have connections where we do not. The mayor knows you by sight."

I bit my lip. So she *had* noticed, drat it all. "I'm still not sure—"

"If you will just try, Zephyr," Elspeth said. "No one will judge you for failure."

"Of course, Elspeth. I'll do what I can." I didn't know how much good my sleuthing would do, but I admit the idea gave me a bit of a thrill.

"Well, I'm dead famished," Iris declared. "Would you like to dine with me, Zephyr? And Elspeth, of course," she added in hurried embarrassment. Elspeth declined graciously, claiming another appointment across town.

"But about that other matter, Zephyr," Elspeth said, her voice lower. "It's possible that I might have found a solution."

It took me a moment to realize she was speaking about Amir. "You have?" I said, shocked. I had first asked her about this months before.

"Yes. It is not safe to mention here, but if you come to the office tomorrow, I'll know for sure. Now, if you'll excuse me . . ."

She said farewell to Iris and then hurried down the steps to the subway entrance. The sun had descended considerably as we talked.

"I'm hungry myself," I said.

Iris laughed. "Zephyr, dear, if nothing else, your appetite can be relied upon."

∽

Iris took me to a wonderfully loud Italian restaurant on Mulberry Street, where we sat in the garden while Iris smoked and we both ate our weight in pasta. The whole place was packed with communists and anarchists, who periodically fired good-natured snipes at each other, like two pirate ships exchanging salutes. Iris procured Chianti and dessert, insisted on paying for everything, and hired a taxi to drop me off at Mrs. Brodsky's. The driver took me back through Little Italy, across Broome Street, and I noticed that the Beast's Rum—the speakeasy that had closed due its association with Rinaldo's now-defunct gang—seemed to have reopened for business. Under new management? I had not seen a trace of the child vampire Nicholas or his Turn Boy friends since January, but I knew they'd survived the fracas. Still, even half-mad Nicholas wouldn't have the gall to move right back into his murdered gangster daddy's old bar, would he?

We passed not a few Faust street vendors as well, all of whom seemed to be doing a brisk business, to my surprise. Perhaps these vampires hadn't heard of the strange deaths. Perhaps they didn't think they were likely to get the poison apple.

Maybe they just didn't care.

A message waited for me when I finally dragged myself through the door of Mrs. Brodsky's. Katya was cleaning the kitchen. A pot of soup sat on the stove, and when I indicated I'd already eaten, she handed me a letter.

"From your brother, I think," she said, in the thin voice that even now sometimes surprised me. For the first several months I had known her, Katya never spoke a word. We had attributed her silence to the shock from her husband's sudden death on a construction site, though now she thankfully seemed to be recovering. The young widow helped Mrs. Brodsky with the chores in return for very little thanks and even less pay. She had given birth to her late husband's child a few months before, and they both seemed to be doing well.

I opened the note, folded at a hasty diagonal on heavy water-marked paper, and recognized the handwriting as Harry's. As for the cream stock with the discreet filigreed monogram of E.H. in the lower corner, I assumed it belonged to another one of the rich society boys that Harry would leave brokenhearted in a week or so. When Harry first ran away to the big city to join Troy's Defenders, I hadn't anticipated that particular complication. But in the event, it did not come as much of a surprise to learn of his preference for pretty young men—and theirs for him. Troy might have cared had he known, but the only thing that really mattered to him was his job. And Harry did that well. None of Daddy's children were a slouch at demon hunting. Harry had made me swear on my life to never tell Daddy or Mama. *Like Mama didn't already know*, I told him, but I promised anyway. This was New York City, after all, the land of minimal social taboos and self-reinvention. If he was enjoying himself, then I wished him the best of it.

Though five years my junior, Harry had developed a slightly abashed sense of protectiveness toward me. He periodically checked to make sure I was "getting on all right." Like he had tonight.

Zeph—

Don't know if you heard, there's something strange happening to the suckers. Probably nothing dangerous, but I've heard the Faust's now got poison in it. Or maybe it turned bad on its own? I even heard they didn't pop. Be careful. I know you can take care of yourself, right, don't fuss at me I'm just saying be careful.

See me tomorrow if you can.

Harry

PS Mama called. Said Daddy's acting odd and keeps asking about you.

I stared at this letter while my thoughts chased each other like aging rabbits. If Harry said the Faust might be poisoned, then I had to take the possibility seriously. I would have to devise some means of investigating Madison. I sighed—the prospect looked daunting.

Elspeth thought I had connections with the mayor, but I wondered what kind of connection his strange letter represented.

Aileen hadn't yet returned when I climbed upstairs, but she was sitting on her bed when I returned from washing my hair. She was deathly pale, though the white dust on her collar told me the effect was due mostly to powder. But that didn't explain the dark circles under her eyes or her unusually bleak expression.

"Did somebody die?" I asked.

"Besides those poor suckers, you mean?"

I sat down beside her, still in my robe. "So you had a jolly time with the ladies, then," I said, forcing a smile out of her.

"Oh, much fun was had at the Spiritualist Society tonight," Aileen said, waving her hand theatrically. "Just not by their resident Spiritualist. Christ Almighty and spirits preserve me, but those ladies work me like a dog. Four separate séances, and they wouldn't be satisfied until the lights flickered and the room went cold and I channeled no fewer than *six* dead husbands. I felt like I was holding a jamboree."

"You mean you pretended to channel them?"

"Maybe," she said.

"Aileen."

"Bloody stakes, Zeph, what am I supposed to do? Go back to passing out on the floor in the bottle factory? The great ladies pay me to use my Sight. They don't pay too badly, either, so I'd rather use this blighted curse for real money instead of eking things out on Skid Row. If you don't mind."

She started pulling pins out of her hair and tossing them angrily on the floor. My heart felt like it was pulling apart in my chest. Hadn't I promised Aileen that I'd help her find a way to control her Sight? But instead it had just gotten stronger and more compelling as the months passed. It exhausted and traumatized her to use it, but I could see her point: if she had such a strong gift, why not use it to make money?

"Aileen, I didn't mean . . . You should do what you think is best. I just don't want it to hurt you."

Aileen laughed. "It's not my idea of a picnic, doing this all the time."

I wanted to promise that I would help her, but I knew better now. I just wrapped my arms around her waist.

"I'm tired," she said to my shoulder.

"Me too," I said.

CHAPTER THREE

I phoned Lily first thing Tuesday morning. I had awoken early, barely thirty minutes after dawn, overcome with nerves, the source of which I could not immediately identify. Then I recalled the *other* monogrammed letter that I had stuffed, along with the lilies, somewhere at the bottom of my clothes chest. The honorable Mayor James Walker had requested the pleasure of my company at four o'clock this afternoon. As I relished the thought of another encounter with agents McConnell and Zuckerman like I relished a fall in horse manure, I could not afford to miss it.

But until then, I had responsibilities.

I descended to the parlor in my kimono, my hair wrapped turban-style in a silk scarf that Harry had given me for my birthday. I had hoped that I might avoid the usual charade of asking Mrs. Brodsky for permission to use the phone by virtue of the early hour. But of course she was already seated in one of the chairs, reading glasses perched on her nose and correspondence laid out before her.

"Zephyr," she said, "a surprise to see you up so early."

"I merely wanted to appreciate the warm bounty of our rising sun," I said.

Mrs. Brodsky's lips twitched. "As you and Aileen did yesterday? A fine incident that was. If you get arrested, Zephyr, I'll have you know I won't hold the room for you."

I raised my eyebrows. "What if I pay my rent?"

She paused. "Well. In that case. Though I do not know what people will think of an establishment that houses a known felon!"

A known felon? Just the thought made me shiver. But I made my voice firm. "I assure you, Mrs. Brodsky, I am in no danger of arrest. The officers merely wanted some information from me regarding that incident last January. Now, if you don't mind, I'd like to use the phone."

"Information?" Mrs. Brodsky said. She shook her head. "I'll need a dollar for the phone."

This was extortion, pure and simple, but I refrained from arguing. The fees to call the Hamptons would be greater than calling within the city, and if I *did* find myself in prison stripes money would be the last of my worries.

I gave Lily's information to the operator and waited while the line rang.

"Hello, who is this?" said a woman's slow, sleepy drawl.

"Is Lily Harding there?" I asked.

"Isn't it a bit early? Lily, someone says they want to speak—"

"Who is it?" Lily's voice came over the phone after a brief struggle, sounding strangely eager for such an early hour.

"Zephyr," I said.

"Zephyr!" she practically cooed in delight. "Why, I believe I have missed your voice! How are things in our big red apple? Frightfully interesting, I'm sure. You must tell me everything."

"Lily?" I said. "Is that you?"

She laughed, but it had a high, brittle edge. "Who else would it be?

Have you forgotten me so quickly? I told you marching in this heat would addle your head."

"And clearly lazing about has done wonders for yours," I said.

"Oh, it's the berries, of course. Everyone whose anyone is up here. It's a social *whirl*, I'm telling you. Why just today I have no fewer than two lunch dates and a boat party with a very eligible fellow of whom my mother quite approves."

"That's *a* berry, at least."

"What? Oh, ha ha. Anyhow, Bill is terribly handsome. And rich— his daddy owns a manufacturing plant in Poughkeepsie, which he expects to take over. It makes him gobs of money."

I had never thought of Lily as especially prone to babbling, but I could think of no other description for this frenetic cataract of words tumbling through the receiver. Mrs. Brodsky glared at me from behind her reading glasses, but I had plenty of practice ignoring her.

"What does he manufacture?" I asked.

"Oh, some widget or other. I endeavor to avoid the subject, he can drone on so."

I laughed. "Sounds like a match made for a notice in the *Times*."

"Throwing stones, as usual? Or do I need to remind you what I caught your very handsome beau hiding in his warehouse this January?"

I winced. "He's not my beau."

"As you keep saying."

Lily had been the one to put together Amir's role in bringing Faust to the city, though in retrospect I should have seen the signs earlier. I only believed her when she came to me with photographs—stacks and stacks of frankfurter boxes, all filled with unlabeled bottles of a dark, thick beverage. Amir had asked for my help, but he'd been careful to hide the deal he'd made to distribute Faust. A deal that had gone very, very sour.

"You didn't spare the money for a chat," Lily said. "Does that mean I smell a story?

I smiled to hear her hard-nosed reporter's voice finally return. She must be dreadfully bored. "Faust is acting up again," I said.

"Really? Like in January? Are all the suckers going mad?"

I shuddered at the thought. But Amir promised no one else could access the "good stuff" once he had cut his personal connection. The goods on the street now were far less potent and dangerous than what had caused such trouble that first week. I hadn't told any of this to Lily, who knew too much already. "No," I said, "but they seem to be dying."

Lily's silence hung heavy on the line. "Dying," she said, flatly. "I thought at least the damn stuff didn't pop them like liquor. Wasn't that the whole point?"

"That's the trouble, Lily. No one knows, but those suckers are dead. And I heard . . ." I paused, remembering the strangest part of Harry's hastily written note. "There are rumors the vampires didn't pop."

"Suckers *always* pop. How else do they die if they don't exsanguinate?"

Lily had a point. "Maybe it's an effect of Faust we haven't seen before?"

"Well, bloody stakes," Lily said, and I heard her mother issue a sharp "*Lily!*" in the background. "I'm taking the next train into the city. I'm sure Breslin won't cry if I cut my vacation short. Oh, Mother, tell Bill I'll see him some other time. The whole city is breaking. Zephyr, I'll leave a message when I get there. And don't you dare talk to another reporter in the meantime!"

∽

Acutely aware of my impending meeting with Jimmy Walker, I hunted through my chest until I discovered Lily's cache of pity discards. Only one was remotely appropriate to the sweltering weather—a relatively simple day frock of blue cotton twill, lined in patterned yellow at the collar and hem. It wouldn't look particularly good with my faded green hat, but I decided that was better than the brown one or—heaven forbid—going bareheaded. I reasoned with myself that Beau James, punctilious dresser though he might be, could hardly fault a bluenose such as myself for her fashion sense. Though of course I had plenty of fashion sense. It was the funds that I lacked.

"Are you really going to wear that?" Aileen said, her voice drifting like a sleepy Irish ghost from the gloom.

"Do you have cat vision for clothes? It's darker than Hades in here." Aileen had purchased some blackout curtains a few months ago, prompting Mrs. Brodsky to suspiciously examine our skin and teeth until satisfied that we had not turned vampiric without prior notification.

"The door is open," Aileen said, rising on one elbow. The powder had rubbed off, but she still looked pale as a sucker, with a rasp in her throat. While sleep had revived me, she looked like she needed at least another twenty-four hours of it.

"How long were you at the Society, again?"

She sighed. "They do know how to keep an evening going. At least I don't have to regurgitate cheesecloth. It must be hell on your throat."

"Pardon?"

She laughed. "Ectoplasm, dear. The old-timers have learned to ingest yards of the stuff and regurgitate it on cue. It's all a farce—even what I'm doing for them, in some ways, I suppose. Who knows who I'm contacting when I'm deep into it, though they all seem pleased enough with my performances, which is all that matters."

"You look terrible," I said.

She shrugged. "And you look like you should be selling flowers in Times Square. Aren't you meeting his Honorable Mayor this afternoon?"

I swallowed. "It's not so bad. Is it?"

"Zeph." She shook her head and leveraged herself off the bed with the care of an old woman. I didn't smell booze or cigarettes on her—hangovers seemed easy compared to the effects of an evening using her Sight. She opened her own chest and pulled out a hat. A jaunty little thing of light blue, with a white flower attached to the band with a white ribbon. It matched my dress perfectly. I bent down to look at myself in Aileen's cracked dressing mirror and smiled. The hat seemed like the sort of thing Amir might comment on—perhaps I would see him today?

"Where did you get this?" I asked.

She yawned so wide her jaw cracked. "Oh, Lily gave it to me. She was bored of it, I'm sure. She gives me cast-offs all the time."

I swallowed back a childish bleat of jealousy. If Lily didn't feel I was worthy of her discards, I could hardly argue with her assessment.

Aileen did not sit so much as tumble back onto her bed. I made sure she hadn't fainted and then left her to her slumbers. Perhaps she'd feel better after a few more hours.

Outside was noticeably less sticky than it had been last night, and I even felt the rudiments of a breeze as I wrestled my bicycle out from the storage area beneath the steps. I pushed off and swung my leg over, wondering if Lily's dress perhaps rode a little too high up my legs. This suspicion was confirmed when two boys from down my block catcalled and whistled as I made the turn onto Houston. I gave them a cheery wave. Aside from periodic wobbles to wrest the handlebars straight and prevent the rusted gears from locking, I had a leisurely journey west to Greenwich Village. I wanted to know more about what Harry had heard about the Faust deaths. His letter was more than intriguing enough to warrant a visit before my meeting with the mayor. Troy's Defenders had relocated to a house on Bleecker and Perry, which contained not only a suite of rooms for him and his guests, but also a training arena in the basement. Troy had invited me to see it this past spring, and despite my loathing for his activities, I had admitted being grudgingly impressed. Troy gave Harry the attic room for very little rent, and I was content that my little brother was being well cared for. The Village was hardly a bastion of Defender supporters, but their bohemian neighbors tolerated nighttime activities far better than anyone might in a more upscale neighborhood. And the rent was a steal, Troy bragged.

The building was three stories of white brick, with bright blue shutters. It didn't open onto the street, but rather its gate led to a pathway through the garden and the side of the house. The gate was open, so I walked up to the side and knocked.

Derek opened the door a few seconds later. He grunted a greeting at me and wandered back to the front office. I did not take his laconic nature for rudeness—I might not approve of what the Defenders *did* (namely, the extra-judicial slaughtering of Others for whichever private citizens or public organizations could afford their retainer) but I occasionally felt some nostalgia for the gruff camaraderie of the lifestyle. Here, no one cared about my gender or the Montanan drawl that occasionally infected my speech. So long as I was handy with a blessed blade and didn't much mind the stink of a popped sucker, I was good enough for them.

Derek sat back behind the desk with a wince I pretended not to notice. He'd been hurt pretty badly during the fight with Rinaldo's gang and hadn't yet fully recovered. "Is Harry here?"

"Out back," he said. "Drinking lemonade with Troy and two officers from vice squad. I haven't seen many sucker police officers," he said, and shrugged. "I guess it takes all kinds."

I thought about running away, but some masochistic impulse led me to nod as though this news was of as little import to me as the Yankees score. I needed to know why they were here. I walked through a brightly wallpapered hallway to the open back door, which led to the courtyard garden. Troy was seated at a picnic table with my kid brother, glasses of lemonade nearly full.

And across from them sat the two men whose visages I had already learned to fear: agents McConnell and Zuckerman. McConnell hunched in his chair, alternating sips of icy beverage with a cigarette. Zuckerman had pushed his untouched glass closer to his partner, and I wondered at the awkward hospitality that would have prompted Troy to give a vampire lemonade. They were in the shadow of a large, shady umbrella, probably to ensure Zuckerman's comfort.

"We know you two were involved in that business with Rinaldo Sanguinetti in January," McConnell was saying, while Zuckerman took notes. "So you must have heard something about this child vampire. I'm sure I don't have to tell good Defenders like yourself of the seriousness of this crime. We just can't let this sort of thing slide, and, ah, your group is up for renewal soon, right? I think we could put in a good word with the licensing officer? What do you say, Mort?"

Zuckerman nodded thoughtfully. "I think we could. Provided co-operation."

McConnell smiled happily and downed his lemonade like it was a shot of triple-distilled whiskey. I heard the threat as clearly as Troy and Harry did, I'm sure. Rank corruption, and it made me furious. I stepped fully into the courtyard. "Well," I said, "at least no one can accuse you of inconstancy, Officers."

McConnell looked up and doffed his hat. Zuckerman just stared at me for an uncomfortable moment, then made a note in his book. "Too late, Miss Hollis," Zuckerman said, "if you were planning to warn your former colleagues."

"I rather thought I was going to save them from two bullies with police badges. But please continue. I was merely paying a social call on my way to a meeting with the mayor. I can wait." I made my way over to a wicker armchair and sat down. I smiled and waved my hand. "Go on," I said. "And Harry, if you're not going to drink that, mind bringing it over here?" I fanned myself. "Nothing like a New York summer, is there?"

Zuckerman still stared, immune to my powers of conversation. "You still deny harboring this child vampire?"

"Of course I do."

McConnell picked up Zuckerman's glass and shook the melting ice cubes like he could divine the truth from their motion. "Mort doesn't believe you," he said.

"Maybe *Mort* doesn't know everything," I snapped.

Harry stood awkwardly and walked over to where I sat, across the courtyard. He gave me a look of something close to terror and mouthed, *Judah?* I gave a slow, discreet nod and took the drink from him with loud thanks. I could only pray that even if the officers proved my own role in Judah's rescue, they wouldn't follow his trail back to my family in Yarrow. Harry knew the danger, but he acted unconcerned when he sat back down with the officers. *He might be young,* I thought, *but Harry learns fast.* A Hollis trait, perhaps, drilled into us by our crazy daddy.

The officers took their leave soon after, and I resisted the urge to stick my tongue out at McConnell's willowy back. Troy and Harry had been as one in their denial of any knowledge about any child vampire. As far as Troy knew, he only told the truth—I had not been fool enough to confide my involvement with Judah to him, and I assumed that Harry had been discreet enough not to mention the latest addition to our family.

"What the devil was that about, Zephyr?" Troy asked. He plucked a few ice cubes from the bottom of his glass and dropped them, with very little ceremony, down the back of his shirt. He practically groaned in pleasure; Harry gave him a lopsided smile.

"Beats me," I said, with I hoped convincing bafflement. "Those officers are convinced I'm guilty of some felony or other. Something to do with the Rinaldo affair, I think. But they don't have enough evidence to arrest me, so I'm just hoping it will go away."

With a little help from the Mayor.

Harry pursed his lips, looking, for a moment, much older than his nineteen years. I could not believe that the same brother who once dropped part of a hornet's nest down my knickers was now helping me avoid police investigation two thousand miles from home. How times change.

"You should steer clear of those two, Zeph. There's something about 'em I don't trust."

"Don't be daft, Harry," Troy said. "They're officers, even if one is a sucker. Our Zephyr can take care of herself, as she always tells me." Troy patted his dirty-blond hair in a vain attempt to reinvigorate the pomade, which seemed to have given up in the heat. Stray strands resolutely insisted on curling and sticking out in a fashion I had not seen since we were much younger.

I sucked down the dregs of Harry's lemonade and contemplated emulating Troy's idea for the ice. "Did you hear anything else about those deaths yesterday?"

Harry shrugged and sprawled on the grass beside my chair. "The bodies are at the morgue, but we'd have a better chance of getting into Grant's Tomb."

Troy nodded. "I've tried to call in favors with some friends in the Sixth Precinct. Professional curiosity. But the bodies are in a warded room and even the top brass can't get in. Zephyr, are you really meeting with the mayor this afternoon?"

"I think she means picketing in front of City Hall."

I glared at them both. "I'll have you know I will be meeting with him—at his personal invitation—at four o'clock."

Harry whistled. "I heard you were a little famous down here. Daddy said so."

"Daddy thinks famous is your picture in the paper. People knew who I was for a week, and I'm grateful for my return to obscurity."

It was getting hotter in the garden. Would the ice ruin Lily's dress? I settled for removing my hat and rubbing the ice along my hairline.

"Well, if you really are meeting Beau James," Troy said, with a curled lip that clearly said *which I doubt*, "then you might ask him about the bodies yourself. Rumor has it he's visited the morgue."

"If they're in a morgue," I said, "do you think that means they didn't pop?"

Harry chewed his lip. "Could be."

"They bring poppers for autopsies sometimes, too," Troy said. "As you should know, Zephyr. The police spent a week cleaning out Rinaldo's lair."

Considering that Troy knew I had spent most of that week huddled in my bed, I thought this was unfair. But I didn't want to tarnish Harry's image of his daring big sister, so I let it pass.

"I'll ask," I said, "but if none of your contacts have learned anything, I rather doubt he'll tell me." I stood. "Anyway, I must be going. Harry, would you walk me out?"

Harry scrambled up obligingly enough while Troy frowned after us like he wasn't quite sure what had just happened.

"Zephyr," Harry said, as soon as we were out of earshot, "what's all this about the mayor?"

I sighed. "I'm not sure. I got a visit from those two officers yesterday and before I can say striped pajamas I have a note from the mayor requesting my presence. He hinted he might be able to help me with my legal difficulties."

"Are you and Jimmy Walker *that* friendly with each other?"

I gave Harry a long look. "I really don't think he's my type," I said.

Harry blushed. "Zeph, you know, with his reputation . . ."

I laughed and kissed him on the cheek. "I will let you know of any startling developments, I promise. That one, however, is vanishingly unlikely."

I shook my head in disbelief as I retrieved my bicycle. An affair with the *mayor*! Amir would never let me hear the end of it. I'd sooner get head lice. I'd sooner vote for Faust!

⁂

I skidded to a stop at the corner of Chambers and Elm, digging my heels into the hot tarmac to aid my slowly declining brakes. Amir had offered to get me a new bicycle, but I had decaying for the same reason I refused to ask for a pair of dancing shoes. I was beginning to regret that now, when no fewer than two gear malfunctions had nearly sent me crashing into a streetcar and forced me to waste precious minutes realigning the chain. Despite my best efforts, I had smudged grease on the hem of the dress, and I did not even want to contemplate my fingernails. The street behind City Hall was quiet and strangely empty for a Tuesday afternoon. I muttered a stream of imprecations at bicycle manufacturers, the mayor, and reckless street-car drivers, in that order, as I checked my watch.

I hastily locked my bicycle to the tall wrought-iron gates that sur-round the grounds of City Hall. It occurred to me that this wasn't strictly legal, but it didn't seem likely that even the most enterprising police officer would bother with it at nearly the close of business on Tuesday.

The aldermanic chamber was shuttered this afternoon. In the main lobby, a woman with an armful of leather-bound books hurried up the stairs. I walked past a group of suited men having a quiet con-versation. One of them glanced at me, and I increased my pace. I was sure I looked painfully out of place. At least it was blessedly cooler, here among the marble and electric fans. A large hall branched off from the left side of the lobby, blocked by a young lady at a desk.

"Can I help you, miss?" she asked.

"I'm here to see the mayor," I said.

"Oh, you're Miss Hollis? Mrs. Brandon told me to expect you. Just wait here a moment."

I took the opportunity to discreetly straighten my dress and smooth my hair. The group of men went outside just as the secretary returned to her desk, accompanied by another woman. She seemed familiar, and as she drew closer I recognized her as the same woman speaking with Madison and the mayor after the evidentiary hearings yesterday. That implied a level of responsibility and power, which was certainly unusual for a woman in a place like City Hall. She wore a skirt and blouse nearly as conservative as my habitual attire, and despite the boiling weather outside, looked freshly starched and pressed. Her blunt features seemed friendly enough—she smiled when she saw me.

"Miss Hollis," she said. "We were hoping you would make it. I'm Judith Brandon, one of James's special advisors. Follow me, please."

We headed down a long marble corridor. She stopped in front of a door of inlaid mahogany and rapped three times. No one responded. She knocked again, then shook her head and opened the door a crack.

"Jimmy?" she called. "Miss Hollis is here."

A muffled shout emanated from somewhere deep inside the room.

"Oh," said Mrs. Brandon, "he must be changing. We might as well wait inside."

I wanted to ask what the mayor would think of us watching him undress, but when she opened the door fully I saw no trace of the man I'd come to meet. The mayor's office was masterfully appointed, with a large oak bureau, a leather couch in one corner, and two chairs facing the desk.

"He'll be up in a minute," Mrs. Brandon said, sitting down. "James must always be impeccable, as I'm sure you know. In the summer, he changes as many as four times a day."

I gaped. Even I hadn't imagined our mayor owning enough custom-tailored suits to change them four times a day! "And how much does this habit cost the city?" I heard myself asking. I winced. I had two police officers who would happily eat me for lunch and a mayor who had mysteriously offered to help. Now was not the time to interrogate his advisor about city finances.

But Mrs. Brandon just nodded approvingly. "Oh, it's not the city's money. Jimmy has enough friends to buy him a new suit every day of the year, if he wanted."

I felt chastened, and wished I could say something that might impress her. Her face was unlined and firm, but her air of self-confidence and poise made me think she had to be at least forty.

"You said you're one of Mayor Walker's advisors?" I asked. Women might have won the vote, but we were still a long way from equality. It heartened me to see a woman so close to a center of power, for all that I disagreed with her politics.

She nodded. "It says 'Special Assistant' on the letterhead, but I'm his unofficial advisor for Other affairs. I was the one who suggested he speak to you, in fact."

"About that," I said, "the note was rather cryptic. Why am I here, exactly?"

Something rustled and then a door in the back of the room opened. The mayor stepped out of it, much to my surprise. I had assumed the door led to a closet, but just behind him I could see stairs winding down.

"There's a basement?" I asked.

Judith Brandon leaned closer to my ear. "A tunnel to the catacombs beneath us. It's now his dressing room."

Jimmy Walker gave me a bright, insouciant grin and came over to shake my hand with an unmistakable politician's grip. "Miss Hollis," he said. "Delighted to see you again, in slightly better circumstances."

He released my hand and then inspected his own with some astonishment. It was surely a rarity for his guests to greet him with a liberal coating of bicycle grease. I attempted to apologize, but he merely lifted his handkerchief from his breast pocket and carefully wiped away the offending substance with a smile.

"Bicycle grease?" he said, to cut through my stumbling mortification.

"How did you know?"

"They were more of a childhood fascination, but I remember the smell well enough. Now, Miss Hollis," he said, pulling up a third chair in lieu of sitting behind his desk, "you must be curious about my rather terse invitation. I apologize, but my esteemed advisor deemed some caution necessary."

"Well," I said, forcing a smile. "You have my curiosity and my presence. What's this all about?"

"Forgive me for being so blunt, but it seems you've gotten yourself in a bit of trouble. Harboring a child vampire is a serious crime. But I'm sure you know that already—they do call you the 'Vampire Suffragette,' after all."

I winced. "Yes, I'm aware. But I assure you, I'm completely innocent—"

The mayor waved a hand lightly in the air, as though my guilt or innocence were immaterial. "I'm sure you are," he said. "But those rottweilers on the vice squad are another matter, aren't they? I appreciated your help regarding that business with the mob boss in January. Quite a few people in high places appreciate it, too. In fact, I heard about you from Joe Warren himself. Now, I don't know, but I think a word from Joe Warren might do a lot to convince those fellows on the vice squad to look elsewhere, especially as you're innocent."

"Why would he do that?" I asked, shocked.

"If I asked him, I daresay."

Joe Warren was our city's police commissioner, and a good friend of the mayor. If James Walker called in a favor and asked him to stop investigating me, I probably wouldn't have to worry about any more rooftop visits—or, even worse, striped pajamas.

Judith Brandon turned to me. "We have a proposition for you," she said.

"I see."

Jimmy Walker shrugged. "I think you'll find it's a fair arrangement," he said. "My request is simple enough. Several aldermen have informed me that they would be willing to change their vote if I could prove scientifically that the Faust being sold now is not as potent as when the brew was first introduced in January. We all remember that first week, and I can understand their reticence, frankly. But I am sure as I am of my name that Faust now is safe as liquor."

"And liquor is illegal," I said.

"Much to our frustration, Miss Hollis," he said, and I couldn't bring myself to object to the "our." "In any case, these four aldermen would bring the vote firmly in my camp. The trouble is that I've been unable to locate a single remaining bottle of the original substance. It seems to have vanished from the earth."

"And you want me to find it?" I hazarded.

He laughed. "Nothing so strenuous, Miss Hollis. Judith reminded me of the rumors that you tutored some of the Turn Boys gang in January. And according to the reports, the Turn Boys were quite involved in the initial Faust influx. So here is my proposal: you find the leader of the Turn Boys wherever he's hiding and convince him to come by for a nice chat about his distribution model. And once he does, I'll be happy to give Warren a ring."

He wanted me to find *Nicholas*? "I don't even know if he's still alive," I said. "If he is, he might not be happy with me. I did kill his daddy."

"I suspect he's alive. If he isn't, give me proof and I'll call Commissioner Warren anyway. And as for the danger—well, Miss Hollis, I have it on good authority that you can take care of yourself."

I rolled my eyes, but appeals to my vanity rarely fail. "And how do you expect to persuade him?"

He smiled and looked down at his desk, as though to indicate the massive wealth and power that his position commanded. And he was right: power like that could pay Nicholas's price as surely as it could mine.

What the mayor didn't know, and what I saw immediately, was that he was headed in the wrong direction. It was common enough to speculate that Faust had lost its potency. I happened to know for sure, because I knew the djinni who had brought the first batch from Germany. I would be shocked if Amir didn't have a few original bottles stashed somewhere—if only because of his decadent fondness for priceless human collectibles. But given the circumstances in which Nicholas and the few surviving Turn Boys had disappeared in January, I doubted that they would have been able to keep any of the evidence. So if I could find Nicholas, there would be no harm in my encouraging him to speak to the mayor. Commissioner Warren would tell the vice squad to look elsewhere, and Nicholas wouldn't be able to give the mayor anything useful for the vote. The mayor had given me the perfect opportunity to avoid trouble without troubling my conscious. But I couldn't appear to agree too easily.

"But you know I'm a supporter of Friends Against Faust. Why would I help you *pass* the bill?"

Walker leaned forward and spread his arms wide, palms out— a surprisingly disarming gesture. "I have a hunch, you see," he said, "that you don't support this new prohibition any more than you support the old. Not really."

I shifted in my seat. "And why would you think that?"

He stood and opened the sideboard, from which he removed two heavy, cut-glass tumblers and an even more imposing decanter. The liquid inside was amber, aromatic, and alcoholic. He poured about two knuckle-joints worth into each glass and handed one to me.

"Neat," he said. "Judith, would you mind going down to the pantry and fetching us some ice? And some tonic, too, in case Miss Hollis prefers it."

Judith Brandon nodded sharply and made herself scarce without another word. I had a flash memory of my time in Shadukiam yesterday—Amir sitting by the fountain, using his powers to fetch us drinks. Not even the mayor of New York City could top that kind of hospitality. When she had left, Jimmy Walker reached for his glass and cocked his head, his smile quizzical. *Well?* It seemed to say.

True, I had in the past enjoyed champagne in his presence at an exclusive party in The Carlyle hotel. There, he had laughingly enjoined me to sing with the band. I moonlighted at Horace's speakeasy on 24th Street, for heaven's sake—an establishment he might have even patronized with one of his vaudeville floozies. I would gain no points by pretending to abstain now, when the past six months had set me firmly on the side of alcoholic vice.

I lifted the glass.

"To accommodation," he said, lifting his.

"I'm not sure that's something I want to drink to," I said.

He leaned forward, his beau eyes trapping mine. "Then how about to freedom? Because I suspect, Miss Hollis, that you'll continue to improve your fashion so long as we can keep you out of a prison uniform."

I'd say this for the man: he had enough charisma for a roomful of people. And unlike a vampire's Sway, I wasn't immune to this kind of persuasion.

I took a sip and cleared my throat. Whiskey, not gin, and eye-watering strong. "I'll do it," I said.

The mayor smiled and drank. "I'm glad you've seen it my way, Miss Hollis."

I nodded absently. I wouldn't bother to tell Elspeth and the others of this request—it would necessitate too much explanation, and besides, I was doing my best to protect them.

Though it made me feel like the worst sort of hypocrite, Jimmy Walker wasn't wrong about my feelings on prohibition of all kinds.

True, Faust had dangerous side effects that had injured countless humans and Others alike, but most of those dangers had been greatly mitigated by six months of public awareness and the reduced potency of the drug. But I would never let Jimmy Walker learn that last fact. It was one thing to harbor private doubts and quite another to actively help the enemy of my friends.

"What about the recent deaths?" I asked. "Even you can't legalize Faust if it's starting to kill vampires outright."

Jimmy Walker swirled the liquor in his glass. "No one quite knows what happened to those suckers—"

"Did they pop?" I asked.

The mayor frowned at my interruption. "I'm not sure I can tell you that, Miss Hollis," he said. "The investigation is ongoing."

"Like the one about me harboring a child vampire?"

Walker gave a dismissive shrug. "However they died, I don't think it had a thing to do with Faust. We've had it for six months, so why would it start poisoning vampires now?"

"Maybe the effect is cumulative?"

"Perhaps. It might be too early to rule it out. But I'll make you a promise. If we find out that those suckers died because of something that Faust did, and not some other reason, then I'll argue for prohibition myself. And you won't get any more visits from the vice squad."

I felt my vague uneasiness melt away with the languor from the alcohol. I considered the almost shocking decadence of what we were doing here. Bargaining for the legality of one dangerous drug while enjoying another, all in the safety of the mayor's office. *I hated people like me, once.* But the moral lines seemed hazily drawn.

The mayor pulled out a cigarette from a case in his inside pocket and offered me one. I declined—Mama thought smoking was unladylike, and I'd never quite gotten the hang of breathing it in. I wondered about the slightly herbal hint in his cigarette. Probably something dreadfully expensive, just like his suits. If Mrs. Brandon had been telling the truth about the source of his pleasures, his friends must be rich *and* indulgent.

Just then, she returned with the ice and tonic. I plucked a few pieces of chipped ice with tongs and watched them melt into the whiskey.

"Miss Hollis has agreed to find our boy," the mayor said, quite pleased with himself.

Mrs. Brandon beamed. "That's excellent news."

"Try," I said. "You'll have to give me a few days."

"Just as long as you can find him before this Saturday," she said. "That's the day of the big supporters' banquet."

Yes, I remembered hearing the mayor invite Archibald Warren yesterday, and the latter's polite equivocation.

"Did you have any success convincing Madison to attend?" I asked, just to see how they would react. The mayor tilted his head, a querulous, bird-like gesture. Mrs. Brandon sat down.

"That's more the lady's department," he said, gesturing to his advisor. "She's been after Madison for months now. I think he's a lost cause, but sometimes Judith has a sense for such matters."

"I truly feel that he's on the edge, Jimmy."

"He's on the edge, alright. I'm just not sure it's *our* edge."

The indulgent weariness in the mayor's voice told me they had argued this many times before. Mrs. Brandon shook her head with a rueful smile and looked at me.

"I have a last-minute appointment to see the lost cause in just half an hour," she said. "So if we're done here, I can see you out, Miss Hollis."

I took this in the spirit of friendly dismissal and bid my farewell to the mayor.

"When you learn anything, you can leave a message for Judith," he said. "She'll make sure I read it."

Back in the marble hallway, I turned to Mrs. Brandon before she could hurry away.

"This is terribly forward of me," I said, "but would you mind bringing me to Madison's with you?"

"Madison! Why?"

"I want to ask him something," I said. "About the murders."

I hadn't thought this would be enough to convince her, but she considered for a moment and then nodded. "Why not?" she said. "Madison loves new disciples. You might even help."

∾

The Safety Council had offices on the top floor of a Fifth Avenue office building. It was a supremely appropriate location: vampires might be a common enough sight in my Lower East Side neighborhood, but up here they were rare as unicorns. Even the menial positions were entirely staffed by humans—immigrant or negro humans, to be sure, but to afford human labor was considered a mark of class. Human employment was governed by stricter standards than vampire employment, but it didn't matter on Fifth Avenue: Archibald Madison could afford it.

Mrs. Brandon had taken us here in one of the cars maintained by City Hall for such errands, complete with a driver to wait with the car during our meeting. An older secretary greeted Mrs. Brandon by name, and indicated we should sit in the reception area. The furniture was surprisingly modern—all clean, art deco lines and solid colors, like something from a Frank Lloyd Wright design. I attempted to study my surroundings without gaping at the luxury.

"Your question," Mrs. Brandon asked. "It's nothing inflammatory, right?"

I thought it was rather too late to be making sure of that, but I nodded. "I'm mostly curious. His rise to prominence has happened very fast."

"In certain circles," Mrs. Brandon said. "He's very well-connected."

"Ah," I said, a neutral acknowledgment of the delicacy of her reply. I would have heard of him long ago if I had any access to power, she meant. I gratefully acknowledged that I remained, in my Ludlow Street boardinghouse, quite far from that world.

Except now I was sitting in the Safety Council's inner sanctum, with the mayor's special Other advisor beside me. A few books and leaflets had been arranged on the long wood coffee table. A *Cleansed World* was the title of one well-produced pamphlet written by Madison himself. His old-fashioned visage stared straight ahead from a photograph on the last page. A glance through revealed it to be a paean to the halcyon days when vampires were staked on sight and humans had "very nearly won the battle against the greatest evil, cloaked in human skin." Then he called for righteous humans to recommence the battle, and destroy vampires once and for all.

"Charming," I muttered, and after a moment of consideration, squashed the pamphlet into my pocket.

"I'm sorry for the delay, Mrs. Brandon," said the lady at the front desk. "I believe his broker had just called about an urgent matter when you arrived."

"Oh dear. I hope it's nothing bad. The market has been so volatile this summer."

The lady spread her lips in a patronizing smile. "Not at all. One of his more speculative investments has taken off, as I understand it."

"How perspicacious of him," Mrs. Brandon said. "I'm hopelessly conservative in my investments, I'm afraid. My late husband had a keen eye for stocks, but I must labor without his insight."

If she was involved in the stock market, Mrs. Brandon was probably not doing badly for herself, conservative investments aside. The stock market was a rich man's gambling hall. My mind was boggled at the vast sums wagered and lost on Wall Street. On the other hand, these days everyone seemed to be winning. I'd even caught Mrs. Brodsky putting a few calls into a broker last month, which had given Aileen and me no small amount of amusement.

At long last, Madison himself entered the parlor with the air of a man expecting a standing ovation. Mrs. Brandon gave him one, rising to offer her hand. He kissed it and then turned to me with a quizzical expression. Feeling the disadvantage of his towering height, I stood as well.

"Delightful to see you, as always, Mrs. Brandon," he said. "And who is your companion?"

"Zephyr Hollis, Archibald Madison. Miss Hollis has been retained by the mayor in an advisory capacity."

"Limited advisory capacity," I said quickly. The last thing I wanted was for my association with the mayor to become public knowledge.

"Pleased to meet you, Miss Hollis," he said. "Shall we go to my office?"

Mrs. Brandon and I followed him past a series of open rooms, each of which looked more like a tea parlor than an office space. In the one closest to the entrance, two men discussed something from two plush armchairs. Otherwise the grand offices struck me as oddly empty. Why bother with so much space if you had nothing to do with it? Madison's office was at the end of the hallway, with tall windows that overlooked the avenue. His room actually contained a desk, but we instead sat on more of his modern parlor furniture.

"Miss Hollis," he said, "pardon my asking, but you look awfully familiar. Have you by any chance attended one of our Safety Council community meetings?"

I coughed. "I'm afraid I haven't, Mr. Madison," I said. "Though I'm very curious."

"I see," he said and stared at me for another moment before shrugging and turning to Mrs. Brandon. "I asked you here because I wanted to tell you, in person, how very much I appreciate your attention to me and my movement for the last several months. I feel like I have the mayor's ear in some small way, which can be heartening for a man such as myself. I believe that Mayor Walker and I see eye to eye on many issues. And I look forward to working with him on those. But after much deliberation, I'm afraid I must decline your invitation to the dinner on Saturday." He shook his head, the very picture of moral regret. "I simply cannot compromise my positions to such an extent. Even if I am only attending as an interested party, you know how these yellow journalists would cast it."

Mrs. Brandon took this blow with grace, though I noticed her right hand spasm briefly, clutching the wood beneath the couch cushion.

"I can't tell you how sorry I am to hear that, Mr. Madison," she said, her voice so gentle it was almost melodic. "But I understand. You are a principled man—that's why the mayor values your opinion so highly. Perhaps I might call on you again, if circumstances change . . ."

But Madison shook his head firmly. I could tell that beneath the pained regret, he was quite enjoying this exercise of power over the mayor, if only by proxy. I empathized with Mrs. Brandon; her position as mayoral punching bag could not be easy to bear.

"Well, then. I will not take up any more of your time. But Miss Hollis wished to ask you a question, I believe?"

"A question, Miss Hollis?" he said. "I am always delighted to see the interest of our youth," he said. "I'd be happy to answer whatever it is."

Ah, yes. I had considered many options on the ride up, and this seemed safest. "I had just wondered, Mr. Madison," I said, "what you think about the recent deaths from Faust? Given your position on the matter of vampires in general, perhaps now you have cause to celebrate the drug?"

His low chuckle filled me with disgust. But at least he was willing to answer. "You want to know what I think of it? I think it's merely justice, long-delayed. I think using Faust as the means of retribution is God's signal to all of us who toil on the righteous path. But I still cannot in good conscience celebrate the drink that makes the monsters more monstrous, even if it has proven to be their poison. Does that satisfy you, Miss?"

I nodded. "Quite."

Mrs. Brandon stood a moment later, clearly eager to vacate the office after her rejection. Madison stood with us, but as we walked out of his office I paused and turned to him, as though embarrassed.

"I'm terribly sorry, sir," I said, "but where is your washroom? Would you mind?"

He directed me to the one closed door next to his office. Mrs. Brandon frowned and told me she would wait downstairs, in a tone that suggested she wished my bladder had better manners. Madison was too puffed-up with his victory to notice much at all, and so I was soon left alone in the Safety Council headquarters. I ducked into the lavatory just in case someone was watching and then opened the door soundlessly. No one was there. Even the two men in the room down the hall seemed to have left. I heard Madison's rumble and Mrs. Brandon's softer echo from the parlor. Good, I had a little time left. I dashed into his office, which he had left open, and ran to his desk. I didn't know what I hoped to find. A bottle of Faust marked "poison"? I snorted softly. The top drawer contained ten or so fountain pens, neatly arrayed in cases. I bit my lip—just one of these would be worth a mint, and he kept them in an unlocked drawer? The Safety Council must have some wealthy benefactors. The second drawer seemed to have drafts of correspondence—hastily scrawled notes on letterhead and stacks of what appeared to be essays written in longhand. But none of it looked particularly interesting at first glance. "Vampire scourge" this and "reclaim our heritage" that, nothing that indicated a specific plan to kill vampires, just a general desire to see them dead. Was that enough?

Of course not. He said as much in the pamphlet I had in my pocket.

His ideas were hateful, but not proof of specific intent. The third drawer was locked, and the vein in my neck throbbed as I removed a pin from Aileen's hat and stuck it carefully into the keyhole. I still heard Madison's voice in the parlor, but it sounded as though his interlocutor was the receptionist, not Mrs. Brandon. He would be back soon. Luckily, the lock was simple, truly a rip for such an expensive desk. Books this time, a thick volume of the first half of the Oxford English Dictionary, with a magnifying glass on top. It was a handsome edition, but it struck me as an odd thing to lock in a drawer. So I pulled it out. The drawer was empty, but it didn't take much effort for me to find a latch in back, which released the false bottom.

I stared at a photograph of a young flapper wearing an ostrich feather, fox-head stole, silk shoes . . . and nothing else. Behind her, a vampire bit the back of her knee, though she looked more ecstatic than alarmed. Years of Aileen's erotic novels had not quite prepared me for the sight. I flipped through the others—more of the same, mostly young human girls and cruel, malevolent, darkly sexual vampires of either gender engaging in acts that would make my mother faint to hear about. I supposed I must be naïve for such a revelation to surprise me, but I was as appalled as a Victorian matron. How did these women keep from turning, if they regularly allowed themselves to be bitten by vampires? I had heard of scientists investigating prophylactic possibilities for vampirism transmission, but I doubted they had reached a stage where the practices depicted in these photographs could in any way be considered safe. I felt the old indignation rise up—if nothing laid bare the falsehood of Madison's moral posturing, this would. To rail against vampirism while supporting the exploitation of women and vampires alike in the production of this kind of sick pornography?

Unfortunately, my moral indignation was so acute, I had quite forgotten the imminent threat of detection. At the last moment, I heard footsteps hurrying up the hall. I cursed silently and replaced the false bottom and then the dictionary. I certainly had no time to lock the drawer before I stood. I pushed it silently shut with my foot.

A man stood in the doorway. Not Madison, thankfully, but a balding, hunched man who looked older than the robust demagogue. He must have been one of the men in the other office, and he stared at me with something like horror.

"What are you doing here?" he asked.

"I . . . I thought I left my compact here," I said.

"Behind his desk?" the man said. "Mr. Madison is coming back now." He said this with some urgency, as though it would harm him for me to be caught snooping in his employer's office. Did he know about the pornography? Perhaps it was his duty to guard it.

"I'm leaving now," I said, and hurried to the door. As I walked past him, he caught my wrist in a painfully strong grip.

"It's not safe," he said in a fierce whisper. His milky gray eyes, wide and intense, held me as firmly as his hand on my wrist. "You shouldn't have come. Someone might see." He spoke as though he knew me, but I had never seen him before in my life.

"I think you've mistaken me for someone, sir," I said, struggling to keep calm. Did Madison employ madmen in his office?

But the man just stared at me for a moment longer and then nodded, releasing me. "Right," he said, still whispering. "Good, Miss Hollis. But you must leave now."

To emphasize his point, gave me a hard push just in time to catch Madison coming back. He inclined his head to me and I thanked him before hurrying out.

I did not want to be here when he discovered his drawer unlocked. Hopefully he would dismiss it as an oversight on his part, but I couldn't be sure. Downstairs, Mrs. Brandon was seated in the backseat of the town car with barely concealed impatience.

"Where should I drop you off," she asked brusquely, as I climbed back inside. "I must get back downtown."

"City Hall should be fine," I said. "That's where I left my bicycle."

She wrinkled her nose, as though even the word carried a faint odor of poverty, but I didn't mind. Without the instant command of a hackney whenever one wished, a bicycle was as good a mode of transportation as any.

"Thank you very much for bringing me, Mrs. Brandon," I said, when the driver pulled up in front of the main post office across the street from City Hall.

"Then at least one of us got something out of this," she said. "I hope the next time we meet you will have good news for the mayor, Miss Hollis."

She drove away and I wondered to what extent her fortunes in this matter depended on my own.

CHAPTER FOUR

My bicycle had vanished.

I stared at the unencumbered gate for a very long time. I could almost imagine that I'd forgotten where I locked it, if not for the neatly printed note an officer had left on the fence where my bicycle had once rested.

> Bicycle, color rust and black, confiscated by the New York Police Department. For retrieval, please come to Headquarters (240 Centre Street).

"Goddamnit!" I said, and as that seemed entirely too mild for the occasion, concluded with the solid, venerable, "Fuck."

"I always know life is about to get interesting when Zephyr starts to curse," said a voice behind me.

My heart stuttered. I had wondered if he would find me today. "Did you come to gloat, o prince?"

Amir put his hand on my shoulder; I let it linger longer than I should. "Never," he said, with uncharacteristic solemnity. "You know I'd help if you would let me."

"How about I wish for a new bicycle?"

"Really?" He seemed torn between horror and amusement.

I snorted. "Not really. Something tells me that I'd end up crushed under a mountain of them if I wished now."

And I still have to find a way to break our bond, I thought.

"Entirely possible," he said. "I take it that's what the friendly officers were doing here a few minutes ago?"

Indignation made me draw myself up to my full height—still only about par with his shoulder blades, but I hoped my glare made up the difference. "You *saw them* and didn't stop it?"

Amir gave that throaty, low laugh that I so loathed (or, at least, it did things to me that I loathed) and leaned against the bars of the fence. "How was I supposed to know what they were doing, Zeph? I thought I'd catch you after your meeting with Mr. Walker, so I've been waiting for quite a while. I thought they were absconding with some other miscreant's broken-down bicycle. You're well rid of the thing, you know."

I scowled at him. "I have no funds to purchase another. It works well enough."

He ignored this obvious falsehood. "And that sorry little bicycle warranted officers from *headquarters*? I thought they seemed too energetic for traffic cops."

I closed my eyes against the obvious conclusion. "Oh, *damn* the vice squad."

"Is that a wish?"

I leaned against the fence, just beside him but not touching. "I am not making a wish, Amir."

"I know."

"I still have a week."

"For what, I wonder."

I couldn't tell him, so I changed the subject. "What did you want me for, anyway?"

"I need a reason?"

"Most likely."

He sighed and pulled a coin from the pocket of his impeccably tailored suit. If he and Jimmy Walker ever met, they could have quite the conversation about men's fashion.

"I thought I could feed you. Dinner at the Ritz? The chef there makes this incredible cold soup he calls a vichyssoise. No meat, he swears up and down."

"Really?" I said, stunned to sincerity.

"My word as a prince."

I needed to make a late-night delivery for Ysabel's Blood Bank, but I had an hour to spare, and with Amir transportation was never much trouble. I agreed.

∞

The vichyssoise was delicious as promised; Amir ordered a second bowl and an extra loaf of bread and butter without my asking. He ate himself, but daintily, picking at his food as though he could hardly bother.

"Do you need to eat?" I asked, considering the question for the first time.

He looked up from his plate with a delicately arched eyebrow. "How gauche of you, Zephyr. I've been playing human for months now."

Of course, Amir had two strikes against his full participation in our bigoted society: his status as an Other and his dark skin. Passing as human was, for him, a simple enough matter. But that still left the other, trickier question. I had wondered how a man I had once seen scorned for tea at the Roosevelt had landed the suites at the Ritz. But

I now realized it was a matter of presentation and money: a wealthy Arab prince of impeccable education was an interesting social object, even if his peers called him "nigger" behind his back. I considered how money could warp otherwise straightforward prejudice. As long as he masked his Otherness, he could swim in some very rarefied social waters.

"Answer the rube, then."

He shrugged. "Of course. In Shadukiam the definition of food gets a tad wider, but I need some form of sustenance."

"Maybe we should get you some frankfurters on the street corner."

He grinned at me, and I couldn't help but grin back. Ten-cent hot dogs: Amir's secret weakness. We shared that moment—happiness, with the promise of something more—until someone approached our table. I recognized Mrs. Brandon with a shock, one compounded by the friendliness with which she greeted Amir.

"I'm just on my way out," she said. "I wondered if I might see you here."

"Official duties?"

She laughed and shook her head. "Personal, thankfully. I'm on my way to the Society. That young friend of yours is doing another reading—speaking of which, I see you know Miss Hollis as well?"

"Small world," Amir said, with a certain tone in his voice that made me suspect this acquaintance was not mere chance.

"Nice to see you again, Mrs. Brandon," I said. "You said you were going to a society?"

She reached up to touch the high collar of her dark blue dress— she had changed for the evening, though to my eyes the effect was rather severe.

"Yes, that's where I met your friend Amir last week. We were attending a séance at the Spiritualist Society."

I hid my surprise as best I could. Why on earth would Amir have attended one of Aileen's readings?

"Oh, I've heard they employ quite powerful mediums," I said, wondering if it was rude to ask who she was trying to reach on the other side.

"It's true. Amir knows their newest medium. I have very high hopes for her—she has, I don't know, a special air. An aura of power I haven't quite encountered before." She smiled apologetically. "One can ramble so about one's hobby. I'm afraid I must leave now if I'm to arrive on time. But it was delightful seeing both of you."

As soon as she had passed through the doors, I leveled Amir with a glare.

"You *have* been up to something," I said.

He shrugged innocently. "I'm not allowed to have friends?"

"Why were you at one of Aileen's readings?"

"A desire to see another world?"

"You can probably see a dozen of them by blinking your eyes."

Amir laughed. "You overestimate me, *habibti*. It has a certain charm."

I shivered and discovered a sudden fascination with the precise shade of green of my soup. My dealings with Amir were always so disconcerting. He disarmed me completely, yet I always anticipated seeing him again.

"Aileen never told me you dropped by," I said to my soup.

Amir brushed my fingers with his. Just a touch, but my hand snapped back with enough force to send the soup spoon clattering against the bowl. "I asked her not to," Amir said.

"Why?"

"I hoped she would help me convince you to make a wish. She refused, and rightfully so, I suppose. It was foolish of me to ask her."

Warmth pooled in my heart and settled somewhere in the vicinity of my stomach. I looked at his dark, rueful eyes and sighed. "And in the meantime, you made a useful personal acquaintance?"

He shrugged. "You can learn many interesting things if you spend enough money in the right places. I thought it might be useful to count an aide of the mayor as a friend. Perhaps even do my part to help Friends Against Faust?"

"You *want* to help?"

"If *I* could make a wish . . ." he said, and the mingled frustration and wistfulness in his voice made me lose my appetite entirely.

"You'd wish for January to never happen? Tempting." But my breathless joke was met with silence.

"Do you want the rest of your soup?" he asked, finally.

When confronted with the principle, my appetite reasserted itself and I slurped down the bowl.

It was only as we were leaving the restaurant that he turned to me and said, "I'd rather you never make a wish than ask for that."

∞

At this time of the evening, St. Marks Place began to show its true character. The street-corner Faust vendors replaced the rapidly departing hot dog and pretzel stands, and already the vampires had begun to stand in line. The regular speakeasies would be opening soon, also, though they couldn't be quite so overt about their activities. At a time like this, I would have expected the St. Marks Blood Bank to be packed with vampires needing their weekly drink. But the windows were shuttered and the door closed.

"Was she expecting you?" Amir asked.

I frowned. "I thought so." I rapped on the door. When no one answered, I tried the knob. It was unlocked.

"Ysabel?" I called, poking my head inside. Through the gloom, I could barely make out the open supply closet door and their golem standing placidly at the entrance. If the golem hadn't moved, I decided, things couldn't be too bad. I opened the door fully and walked into the waiting room. Amir followed me, though I'd asked him to wait outside.

Ysabel didn't like him much. I didn't tell him to leave, though—it felt comforting, I confess, to have his warm, watchful presence at my back.

From inside the supply closet came a crash and a stream of Yiddish invective. I rushed forward, feeling for the silver knife under my skirt even as I contemplated how to best disable a very ornery piece of animated clay. But the golem let me through—maybe it even recognized me—and I found Ysabel sitting amid a pile of fallen blood bags, hands in her hair and an expression on her face that seemed close to weeping.

"Zephyr," she said, sadly. "*Bubbala,* what are you doing here?"

"I came by to get the delivery for Elspeth and the others. Are you alright?"

She laughed, though it took me a moment to recognize it as such. I'd never seen Ysabel so distraught. "Oh, fine, fine," she said. "Just some family trouble, you know how that can be. Here, I set aside a box for you."

She pushed aside the fallen bags and made her slow, methodical way to a box in the corner of the room. I hefted it before she could.

"Do you want me to come back after to help you clean? Is Saul all right?"

Saul was her husband, and his health hadn't been the best of late. But Ysabel just shook her head. "Saul is the same as ever. No, no, Zephyr, you go. I'll deal with it in the morning. You should go."

I almost protested, but something about the finality of her tone made me duck my head and quietly retreat. Amir had stayed in the waiting room, where he and the golem continued to eye each other warily.

"Should I come back tomorrow?" I called back, when Amir opened the door to leave.

Ysabel shook her head with some vigor. "No! I have to close for a few days. Just to deal with the trouble, you understand."

"Oh," I said. I wasn't sure what else to do, Ysabel looked so determined and closed-off that I knew she wouldn't welcome any more prying. "Good night, then. Good luck with everything."

"Yes, you too, Zephyr." I had almost left before she enveloped me in one of those great hugs that I always associated with her presence. She said nothing else, just closed the door behind me.

Amir took the box from my numb fingers. "Is she always that emotional?" he asked.

I shook my head. Amir maintained a tactful silence until we reached the First Avenue building that served as the temporary headquarters for Friends Against Faust. The local Temperance Union had loaned us the use of their space, after much lobbying on the part of Elspeth and Iris.

The room allotted us was only slightly larger than Mrs. Brodsky's parlor, and oppressively stuffy despite the open windows. Elspeth worked alone at a desk in the corner, writing what looked like the dozens of last-minute letters urging aldermen to take our side during the vote.

She looked up when we walked in. "Zephyr, you got the delivery? Wonderful. I was worried when I saw the Bank closed earlier."

"Ysabel says she has to close for a few days," I said, taking the box from Amir. "Some kind of family trouble."

Elspeth nodded abstractedly. "Put those behind the desk, if you would."

Amir stayed diffidently by the door, and I had a belated pang of remorse for letting him accompany me. Elspeth had said to ask her again today about my djinni problem, and I had inadvertently brought him with me. I wondered why, but the answer seemed to have too much to do with enjoying his presence. I put down the box.

Elspeth stared at Amir like he might eat her at any minute. "That's the trouble you were telling me about?" she said to me, in a whisper that he could surely hear.

"His name is Amir," I said.

She lifted her chin and sniffed, nostrils flaring. "Frankincense and fire. That's how my mother always described the djinni smell. I'm not entirely sure I believed you until now."

Amir sighed. "Its ears are also in perfect working order, *sayidati*. A prince of the djinn at your service." He placed his hand over his heart and bowed low from the waist. The gesture didn't have as much mockery as I would have expected. I had never seen him behave like that with a human before, but then again, I'd never seen him with a human who knew more than a few things about djinn.

After a moment of uncharacteristic shock, Elspeth closed her mouth and nodded. "It's dangerous to play with a djinni, Zephyr," she said, very softly.

"Hence my attempts to rectify the situation," I said.

Amir cocked his head to the side, as though he was studying me for some later purpose. I felt a rush of heat before I realized he looked more regretful than lascivious.

"I see I've overstayed my welcome. I'll leave so you can better discuss my failings."

I felt ashamed and then furious with myself for the sensation. Did Amir expect me to be *happy* he'd imported Faust? "Don't sulk, darling," I said, stepping too close. "It's unbecoming of royalty."

"Don't preen, sweet," he said, leaning forward. "It's unbecoming of peahens."

I opened my mouth—either to gasp or in some automatic, damnable expectation of a kiss. But he didn't wait to see. Without the slightest warning, he vanished in a shimmer of heat.

"I hope you know what you're doing, Zephyr," Elspeth said, after a moment.

I shook my head. A *peahen*! "Will you help me now?"

She sucked in a breath. "I have found a *sahir*. The most powerful in the city. She has agreed to try, Zephyr, but it won't be for free. How much can you pay?"

I could still smell him. "I have forty dollars saved up," I said.

She sighed. "It might be enough. We can see. Meet me tomorrow morning at eight. There's a little pastry shop on the east side of Washington Street, between Morris and Rector. It will say Aleppo in the window with a red awning. Sofia is the baker."

It seemed from her demeanor that Elspeth must have gone through much trouble to arrange this meeting. "Thank you, Elspeth," I said. "I can't tell you how much this means to me."

She turned back to her desk. "No thanks, Zephyr. I can't let a friend get mixed up in such business and not try to help."

I tried not to remember in whose office I had spent my afternoon. No harm would come of it, I told myself. Somehow, I would make it all turn out right.

∞

The next morning was Wednesday. I sat up in bed and watched the sunrise through the tenements across the street. I felt exhausted, yet somehow disinclined to sleep. Too much to do, too many threats and looming deadlines and not nearly enough time to accomplish everything. Eventually, I washed and dressed and left Aileen still snoring in her bed. I didn't know when she had gotten in last night, but it had been hours after me. Judging by the perfume-soaked pile of clothes on the floor and the makeup she had smeared on her pillow, I gathered she had enjoyed a festive evening after her reading at the Spiritualist Society, possibly in Lily's company. My favorite lady reporter had left me a note with Mrs. Brodsky the night before, indicating her triumphant return to the city and her desire for me to drop by the *New-Star Ledger* office this afternoon. She had written the address on the note, so I stuffed that in my pocket and hurried out the door. I was running late for my appointment with Elspeth.

I spent a long minute searching for my bicycle before I remembered: my best friends in the vice squad had taken it into custody. I could have attempted to retrieve my main means of transportation, but I suspected that Zuckerman and McConnell had a nasty surprise in store for me. I refused to give them the satisfaction. No subway was convenient, so I walked, arriving on Washington Street half an hour late.

I'd been past the Syrian neighborhood on Washington Street a few times before, but never taken the time to explore it thoroughly. The pastry shop Elspeth had told me to find this morning was one of a dozen tiny shops in the center of the block. On the street, a few men wearing fezzes smoked hookahs and drank coffee from little cups. I found Elspeth seated at a table inside, reading a newspaper. She'd sat in the far back, closest to the ovens. It felt like walking into a hot pudding; no wonder Elspeth and the woman baking in back were the only people here. But when I sat down across from her, she looked as cool and composed as ever. A wide-brimmed hat and draping overcoat were slung over a chair behind her, but I supposed one of the benefits of vampirism is being relatively unfazed by temperature extremes.

"You're late," she said, as I sat down. "I was wondering if you'd forgotten."

"The vice squad has stolen my bicycle."

"That piece of junk? You should thank them for the favor and get a new one."

I thought of telling her that Amir had been saying much the same thing for months, but decided that I didn't want to muddy the issue at hand. Elspeth had finally agreed to help me, and might not appreciate any hint that Amir and I could be friendly. Or more than friendly, on occasion. I dabbed at my forehead with a handkerchief.

"It's hot in here," I said.

Elspeth turned to the woman tending pastries in back. She rattled off something in Arabic, which I recognized from conversations between Amir and Kardal. The woman called back and a moment later placed a tall icy glass before me. I stared at Elspeth.

"Drink," she said. "You look like a stewed prawn."

The drink was bright green. This put me off for a moment, but my thirst was too great to resist. Luckily, it turned out to be deliciously strong lemonade mixed with fresh mint. Elspeth slid the paper across the table while I gulped.

"Have you seen this?"

It was the *New-Star Ledger*. I read the headline: MAYOR'S OFFICE CONDEMNS VAMPIRE "MURDERS"; VOWS TO CATCH KILLER.

"Well, that's new," I said.

Elspeth waved at the paper. "Keep reading."

An official close to the mayor has confirmed to this reporter that the mysterious deaths of ten vampires this past Sunday night are a source of ongoing concern for Mayor Walker. Speaking on condition of anonymity, the official called the controversial deaths—occurring after the individuals consumed Faust from a Lower East Side street vendor—"possible murders," also referencing the long-term Faust consumption in the German cities of Dresden and Berlin. "Vampires in those cities have had access to Faust for several months longer than here in New York, and they have had no similar incidents. Therefore we are pursuing the possibility that the drink was deliberately adulterated," said the official. Mayor Walker himself declined to comment, but the medical examiner's absolute secrecy regarding the remains of the deceased vampires speaks to the priority this issue has taken in the administration.

Neither the official nor the Mayor would speak about the upcoming Board of Aldermen vote for making Faust legally available.

*But many other commentators have not been shy about noting the
curious timing of these mysterious murders just days before a vote
that many expect will take all of Mayor Walker's considerable powers of persuasion to push through.*

I looked up from the paper, my mouth suddenly dry. "So he's
admitting it's murder?" I said. "But it doesn't say how."

"I doubt they know," Elspeth said. "My best guess is poison or
tainted blood."

"A taint? I've never heard of one that could kill a suck—vampire
outright." I blushed at my slip. "Sucker" wasn't exactly a pejorative, but
I still felt uncomfortable using the slang in Elspeth's presence.

Elspeth raised an eyebrow. "Neither have I," she said. "But what
better place to test how much humans can poison their blood than
New York City?"

Some human donors were so ill that they passed on that illness—
or "taint"—to unsuspecting vampires. I remembered an indigent I
had met while investigating Rinaldo. The man had lived in the subway and had a line of needle marks up his arm from injecting alcohol.
He'd smelled of rot and death; Judah had said he wouldn't drink the
man's blood. Laudanum, alcohol, cocaine, illnesses like tuberculosis
and syphillis . . . Elspeth was right. Who was to say that some combination of these taints—which were known to sicken vampires—
might not actually kill them?

"But the Banks screen donors," I said. "Anyone whose blood was
so tainted must be near death. How could it have gotten past them?"

Ysabel was always very careful about who she would let give blood
to the "bruxa," as she called vampires. But Elspeth dismissed this
objection. "Banks are hardly the only place vampires obtain blood,
Zephyr," she said.

I knew richer vampires had other means of obtaining their vital
sustenance—often through an arrangement with one or two willing

humans, carefully vetted and well-remunerated. But even that didn't make sense. "But why would anyone take obviously tainted blood?"

"To kill vampires?"

I took a deep breath. "I don't know if it's Madison," I said. "Honestly, I would be surprised if he did it himself, or even directed someone to do it. He would approve of the murders, I think, but he's interested in political power."

"Fanatics can do irrational things. You don't deny the man's viciousness?"

"Goodness, no. I managed to speak with him yesterday and do a little snooping, well, look at this." I handed her the pamphlet I had taken from his office. I wondered if I should also mention the graphic pornography I had found stashed in his desk.

Elspeth flipped through the pamphlet, her eyebrows furrowing into a deep frown. Eventually she slammed it down with a snarl. "The man's a danger to society! Even if he's savvy as you say, Zephyr, I can't believe that he wouldn't have a hand in this. He has men who would die for him, strays he picks from the lines in soup kitchens. They'd certainly murder for him."

I nodded slowly. Perhaps this explained the strange, wild-eyed man who worked in his office. But still, I wondered if Madison would risk sending even a loyal servant for such grisly work. Getting caught could end all of his political ambitions.

As would an intrepid journalist discovering his stash of vampire bite pornography. Elspeth was right—anyone could act irrationally.

"But still," Elspeth continued, "if it is one of his strays or someone else, I want to know how these vampires died. Taint or poison or both . . ."

"Could the mayor be lying?" I asked suddenly. "It would be a blow to his designs on Faust if the drink itself turned out to kill vampires."

Elspeth smiled ruefully. "You and Iris can be remarkably tenacious, really. Yes, I know it would be best for us if it turned out to be the

Faust itself. But wishing doesn't make it so. The article is right, Faust has been available to vampires in Germany far longer than it has here. If the effects are cumulative, there should be dozens dead across a dozen cities, not ten dead from one Faust stall on one night."

Murder, then. It was the most likely possibility, as Elspeth said. I sighed and sucked down the last of my lemonade, leaving the chunky mint leaf pulp in the bottom.

"How do they get so much mint in there?" I asked.

"Mortar and pestle," Elspeth said, not meeting my eyes. "That always tasted of summer to me, when I was alive."

"You're still alive."

She snorted. "And all my mother's food now tastes of rust and dirt. You don't know how lucky you are, Zephyr, to be human. No, don't argue, of course I still believe in the cause. We want equality—both for those who embrace this life and for those like me."

Those like who? I wanted to ask, but I had never seen Elspeth quite so contemplative or raw before. I knew that many vampires lived with the regret of their condition. Elsepth was right: this didn't diminish in any way the need for their fight for equality, but it did sometimes fill me with this aching sadness. Thanks to whatever my daddy had done when Mama was still pregnant with me, I was immune to all vampire bites. That fact had saved Amir's life, but had also turned me into his living vessel, a bond that would last until my death. Unless I found some unorthodox means of breaking it.

"So you said a woman here could help me?" I asked.

Elspeth blinked as though I had startled her. "Sofia," she said. "She made you the *limon nana.*"

I turned around to study the woman pulling a tray of pastries from an oven. Sofia was younger than I'd imagined a famous *sahir* would be, a robust woman of around fifty, with wiry arms and sun-baked skin. Her smock was liberally coated with flour, and she had a streak or two in her dark hair.

Sofia looked reassuring. I had a hard time distrusting anyone who baked. Memories of my mama's kitchen, I suppose. As though she could sense our topic of conversation, Sofia looked over. Elspeth nodded and waved her hand at me.

"This is the one I told you about," she said.

Sofia came over a moment later with a plate of pastries. I recognized none of them, but just the smell made me painfully conscious of my lack of breakfast. She smiled and gestured to the plate.

"For you," she said. She spoke with a thick accent, but her meaning was plain enough. I grabbed the nearest item: a triangular layered wedge, sticky to the touch, that crunched with some unidentifiable nut and melted with honey and a hundred other flavors on my tongue. I might have groaned.

She laughed and clapped her hands. "Good," she said. "My baklava is best, I always say."

Baklava. I filed that word away for future use. Perhaps I could ask Amir to magic me an entire box of them the next time we were in Shadukiam. Then I swallowed the last of the baklava and remembered that until I made a wish, my presence in Shadukiam would cause seismic disturbances.

Elspeth regarded the pastries with a twist to her lips that could be construed as derision, but I suspected was regret. She and Sofia spoke for a minute or so in their own language while I tried another pastry: this time a honey-soaked confection that resembled a bird's nest.

"Sofia asks why you would capture a djinni you don't want."

"I didn't mean to."

More conversation. "How could you do such a thing by accident? Djinn don't often reveal themselves to humans willingly."

I flushed—the heat, of course. "It's complicated. I helped him out of some trouble and now I am his vessel and I would very much like to get out of the obligation."

I watched Sofia take this in—both my own words and Elspeth's translation. "You make wish?" she asked, without waiting for Elspeth.

Her direct gaze made my skin prickle. "No," I said hoarsely. "It's been six months, but I haven't yet."

She nodded. "Then is possible. Hard. But possible."

For the first time since the vice squad found me in my unmentionables on the roof, I felt the tonic of pure relief. Perhaps I would find a way out of all this, after all.

"What do I need to do?" I asked.

The two women conversed, their voices low though no one else could possibly hear or understand them. Finally, Elspeth nodded. "She says to come here this Sunday night. She will need that much time to prepare. She asks for fifty dollars—which is much less than what she should charge for something like this. Can you get it?"

I had exactly forty-one dollars in my steamer trunk and no chance of earning any more for another week, but I nodded. Aileen was flush these days from her work for the Society ladies; she would lend me ten dollars if I asked. "I can, I promise," I said.

"And Sofia says you must know that this will be a summoning. She will call on a power—a demon or something like it. The demon will ask you for something in exchange, and you must have things to give it. Otherwise, it could destroy you."

I knew a little about this from Daddy. Enough to be afraid. The older woman trained her clear gaze firmly on me, as though she was judging my suitability for market day. I halfway expected that she would cluck her tongue and shake her head and say, "No, no, that one's too skinny—you take fifty cents?" But she leaned forward, elbows on the stained wood table, and raised her dark eyebrows.

"Always need same thing," she said, her English perfectly clear. "The thing you not want to lose."

Elspeth cleared her throat. "Your offerings must be precious to you, otherwise the magic will go badly awry."

As quickly as the relief had come, it vanished again, replaced by the now-familiar churning in my gut. "And then the demon will take it away," I said.

Elspeth twisted her bloodless lips, and didn't bother translating. "Wouldn't be much of a spell if it didn't."

Another customer entered the shop and Sofia stood with a nod in my direction. "Remember, Sunday," she said. "Fifty dollars!"

"I'll be here," I said. All I had to do was find something to offer a demon.

Elspeth stood soon after and I followed suit. I waited until she was safely attired in her long, dark coat and gloves. Her hat resembled those worn by beekeepers, with a modest brim and layers of gauze draped over the face. Only once she was safely attired did we depart.

"You'll tell me if you learn anything about the dead vampires?" she said.

"Of course," I said. Though I suspected that my avenues for investigation were limited.

"Good luck, then. If Madison is responsible, I hope you find some evidence. You'll be there for the Monday City Hall picket? Iris says that so far we've collected three thousand signatures."

"That many? Admit that her tenacity can be useful," I said.

I thought she smiled, though I couldn't quite see her face. "You both can be useful," she said. "I must get back. I'm drafting a letter to the Harlem aldermen. Keep me informed, Zephyr."

I thanked her again for her help with Sofia, but she merely waved a brusque hand and walked north on Washington Street, toward Rector. Swaddled as she was, her status was unmistakable. I ached to see how people stared and avoided her before she disappeared from view, but Elspeth never gave even the slightest indication that she noticed.

CHAPTER FIVE

The offices of the *New-Star Ledger* occupied the southern half of the fourteenth floor of the Fuller Building, colloquially known as the Flatiron in recognition of its peculiar wedge shape. The newsroom made do with the layout, with desks haphazardly abutting the walls of a series of increasingly narrow corridors. They ended at the point where two desks could fit with just enough space for a person turned sideways. The terminus was a wooden door with two opaque glass panels and an open transom through which I supposed journalistic hopefuls could throw their screeds. But I wouldn't envy any transom-thrower at the moment, as the editor in chief himself was engaged in a loud argument to which the entire office seemed to be paying studious attention.

I looked around and caught the eye of the newsman at the desk closest to the door. He had his reporter's notebook open before him, but didn't appear to be looking at it.

"Hello," I half-whispered.

"You want the chief, this isn't a good time."

"Lily Harding, actually."

He leaned back in his chair and nodded his head at the door. "I'd give it another ten minutes," he said.

Oh dear. It didn't sound like things were going well in there. The yelling continued.

"If I'd wanted a puff piece on sucker marriage, I would have called the Bowery Mission. You're supposed to be reporting on the murders—"

"Rodney Kilpatrick's wife—"

"Doesn't matter a fig to anyone with a pulse! Get back out there, shake down your sources and find me a *story*. More blood and fewer grieving widows, got it? My officer down in Battery Park says a few others got taken into the morgue last night."

More murders? I thought. I remembered, with a shudder, Archibald Madison's words to his followers: *whatever it takes.* Had someone followed his advice?

"They're not letting anyone into the morgue, chief. It might just be a rumor."

"Then find someone—some*thing* who watched them die! Find a witness—heck, find me some popper skin, and I'll forget you ever turned this in."

"There's a rumor the vampires didn't pop," Lily said, her tone an odd mixture of defiance and deference.

The man gave a bark of a laugh. "If *that's* true and you can prove it, I'll give you Billy's desk."

The reporter to my right jerked, nearly crashing into the wall. "Hey!" he said.

"Back to work, Billy," bellowed the voice from the office. "And you, Harding, twenty-three skidoo. You got this job because of your sucker sources, so you had better make them sing."

The door opened a second later. Lily clutched a few typewritten pages, her face nearly as white as her knuckles. She stopped short when she saw me.

"Zephyr," she said. "You're early." I couldn't tell if this was an annoyance or a relief.

I opened my mouth, then paused. "Just got back from meeting with the mayor," I said, loudly enough for all interested parties to overhear. "Heard a few things you might want to know."

Lily's eyes widened ever so slightly, but she gave no other indication of her surprise. "Great news. Shall we go someplace quieter?"

I nodded and followed behind her while the other reporters in the office stared after us, the speculation about my identity and what business I could possibly have with the mayor practically written on their foreheads. Lily headed straight out of the office and into the elevator before she allowed herself to relax against the wrought-iron and mirrored backing.

"Now I remember why I'd escaped to the Hamptons," Lily said. "I just can't tell what Breslin wants some days. How much of that did you hear?"

"He doesn't approve of widows?"

Lily sighed. The elevator operator pulled open the doors to the lobby and we stepped out. "He doesn't approve of *sucker* widows."

"Where are we going?" I asked.

"Coffee. I need a drink and there's a place around the corner."

Unsurprisingly, given the types that tended to rent office space in the Flatiron, the shop on Twenty-third Street was genteel, discreet, and perfectly happy to add a shot of whiskey to any drink for a bill slipped under the table. Lily drank her hot toddy like it wasn't ninety-five degrees outside, while I opted for a cool drink and more pastries.

Lily relaxed with something closer to her usual grace against the chair. "Meeting with the mayor, eh? Nice one, Zeph."

"I actually did, would you believe it. Yesterday."

"A picket line does not an appointment make."

"I had a handwritten invitation!"

"Let me see it, then."

"I'm not carrying it around like a love-token. The Hamptons really did turn you screwy."

"What would Gentleman Jimmy want to do with the vampire suffragette?"

"We negotiated an exchange of services," I said. "I, ah, ran into some trouble with the law and he offered to help me in exchange for an introduction."

This explanation nearly made Lily's eyebrows shoot up into her forehead. "A speakeasy raid?"

"Nothing that exciting," I said. "Just a misunderstanding related to that matter in January." I hadn't told Lily about rescuing Judah, and this did not seem like a good moment to explain. "In any case, it turns out the mayor wants me to introduce him to Nicholas."

"No! Is the devil-boy still alive?"

I shrugged. "He got away," I said. I didn't add that I had saved his life so he could do so.

"And now Walker wants you to find him again. Whyever for?"

Now came the tricky part. "He wants to see if Nicholas has any of the original bottles of Faust," I said. "He suspects that the original brew was more potent than the one currently on the market."

"And he wants Nicholas," Lily repeated, flatly. "Why not give him Amir?"

Either out of kindness or a sense of self-preservation, Lily had declined to identify Amir as the original distributor in her big article last January. She had referred vaguely to a well-placed international investor, mysterious to everyone but Rinaldo himself. "I'd rather not," I said firmly. "I'm attempting to break the bond between us, and any further complications would only muddy things." I didn't bother to explain that I also was disinclined to sabotage my friends' campaign.

"So the mayor doesn't know you know the original distributor?"

she said. "An intrepid reporter could get quite a scoop with that information."

"Lily Harding, if you tell Jimmy Walker anything at all, I swear I will never give you another story again in my life."

Lily leaned forward. "All right, no need to get the vapors. Do you want the whole place to hear you? Never mind, I'm bluffing. I can't mention Amir now any more than I could last January—I'd sooner claim the Tooth Fairy brought Faust over than a genie. I'd be laughed out of the office."

I slumped over in my chair. "The myopia of your peers is a profound relief," I said.

"Still, do you think Nicholas has the original bottles?"

"No."

"Then why do you think the mayor will help you?

"He did promise."

Lily gasped. "You don't *want* him to find it!"

"What if my help wins him the vote this Monday?"

"I doubt you'd manage very well in prison."

"There's just so much . . . The issue isn't simple, that's all. Look at me, I'm hardly the mascot for temperance. Who am I to declare that vampires have to follow an example I can't even keep?"

"Nuance? From the vampire suffragette herself? I think you might have revoked your radical credentials."

"That is a gross caricature," I said.

Lily shrugged. "I'm a reporter."

"Your forthright moral stance, Lily, it's why I like to keep you around."

"Likewise, darling."

We raised our half-drunk glasses in an ironic toast. "Speaking of which," I said. "Did your troll of a boss mention something about *more* killings? Faust, again?"

"I can't confirm it. Something definitely happened in a blind pig in Little Italy last night, but right now all I have are reports of a fight. The police scraped a few poppers off the tarmac, sure, but officials aren't talking and I can't tell if that's because something strange happened or because everyone's still gone mum about what happened on Sunday."

I shook the ice at the bottom of my glass. "Little Italy . . . where?"

Lily pulled out her reporter's notebook and flipped through it. "Broome Street, according to Breslin."

I had a flash of the Beast's Rum, unexpectedly resurrected. "That's where Nicholas and the others used to drink, you know."

"And St. Marks is where they used to deliver," Lily said.

"That's one heck of a coincidence," I said.

She tapped her pen on the table. "Not neighborhoods I'm inclined to nose around in myself, but shall we try together? By gum, I'll give old Breslin a story he can choke on."

∞

In the cab ride on the way over, Lily told me everything she'd already learned about the incident on Sunday night. She'd managed to gather more concrete information than any of the reports I'd read so far, but didn't want to publish until she found something really damning. "Like the coroner's reports," she said. But since at the moment the basement of the Pathological Wing might as well be Grant's Tomb, she was willing to pursue other angles.

Ten vampires died that night, all after after drinking Faust that came from a single bottle delivered earlier that evening to a stall that was seedy even by that neighborhood's standards. Its clientele were mostly Jewish, with a smattering of Irish and other immigrants. Several of the dead vampires had been identified, including Rodney Kilpatrick, whose unfortunate widow had been the proximate cause of Lily's row with her editor.

Sixth Street was bustling—street hawkers fought with bums for the attention of passersby, and they all avoided the packed mess of jalopies and streetcars. The summer stink was high and almost overpowering; Lily untied her scarf and clamped its fringed end tightly to her face.

"Now I remember why I avoid this place. Ugh, there's a *turd* on the *sidewalk*."

I gave her a sideways smirk and shook my head. "Be grateful you don't live on Ludlow."

"I don't know how you can stand it."

"I'll let you know when I come into my family fortune, Miss Harding. Now, where exactly was this Faust stall?"

"The city closed it two nights ago," she said, as we weaved through the crowd, "but it ought to have been . . . right here."

I looked around. We were standing under the awning of a haberdashery, with men inside haggling over the price of a beaver fur hat. The sidewalk was fairly deep here, which made it a reasonable location for a portable storefront. Just a few feet away, a vendor with a wheeled tin cart sold knishes under a tattered umbrella. Formally, vendors had to apply to the Board of Licensure, but in reality the rules governing their placement depended much more on the local beat cop, the neighborhood association, and the general popularity of their wares.

"I don't suppose the Faust cart had a license," I said to Lily.

"I think there's a total of five formally registered with the city."

"Of course. Do you have a quarter?" I asked.

Lily sighed and pulled out her change purse. "You can be quite the shameless beggar, Zeph."

"Only when I'm around the shamelessly wealthy," I said, and tossed her quarter in the air. "Just a moment."

I walked over to the knish vendor fanning herself in the sweltering heat. "How much?" I asked.

"One for a dime, three for a quarter."

I plopped down the quarter. "One of each," I said. Her three flavors were potato, kasha, and onion. As she wrapped each one in a bit of wax paper I leaned forward casually.

"Do you sell here often?" I asked.

"For the past year," she said, without looking up.

"So did you know the one who set up after you? At night?"

Now she paused, twisting the paper over the last knish. "I leave at sundown. I don't talk to nobody. Not to those damn blood sellers. Why do you care?"

"Those murders everyone's talking about," I said, quietly. "I heard they happened here, that's all. I was wondering if you knew how they died."

She frowned as she handed me the fragrant dumplings. "I told you, I keep my head down. You really want to mess with this, a *maidel* like you? I wouldn't. You know what I saw? I saw one of them dead with rosy cheeks. I saw him breathe his last like a true man."

"He didn't pop?"

She shook her head, but refused to say anything more. "Take my advice, stay out of this one. You'll live longer and eat more knishes."

I took a bite of the first: potato, fresh and salty and chewy with yeast and grease. "That would be a good thing," I agreed.

I walked back to Lily, seemingly frozen in place several feet away. Two boys whistled at her from the back of a truck. Her shoulders went rigid, but she ignored them.

"I hate this place!" Lily said, her voice edging to shrillness.

"Endure," I said. "Do you want the story or not? Here, have a knish."

"A what?" Lily said, taking the greasy paper like it might bite.

"Try it," I said. "Guaranteed to delight."

I relayed my conversation with the woman while Lily took steady, dainty bites from her onion knish. She looked like she enjoyed it, but I pretended not to notice.

"We have *got* to get into the morgue!" she said, when I finished.

"What in blazes is Walker trying to keep from us, anyway? If they didn't pop . . ." She frowned, opened her mouth, and then closed it without saying anything.

"What?" I asked.

She shrugged. "Nothing. It's crazy."

"So are these murders. Tell me."

She sighed. "I had a thought . . . what if the vampires didn't pop because they didn't die as vampires? What if whatever was in the Faust turned them *human*?"

I stared. "It's impossible."

"I know," she said, but I was remembering what the knish vendor had said: *breathe his last like a true man.* What if something *could* cure vampirism? Even if only for a moment? Even if it were deadly? The power of such a serum would be incalculable.

Lily and I maintained a contemplative silence on the way to Broome Street. I didn't think it was a particularly far walk, but she insisted on a taxi with a sniff that indicated what she thought of people who had to walk everywhere. Before she hailed it, I dashed a block ahead, to check on Ysabel's Blood Bank. It was dark and shuttered, to my disappointment but not to my surprise. There was a sign on the door in Yiddish, English, and German, tersely explaining that the Bank would be closed for the next week. I sighed. I hoped Saul was okay.

The address on Broome Street did indeed correspond to the newly reopened Beast's Rum. Lily took one look at the laughing vampires spilling out the doorway and crossed her arms stubbornly over her chest.

"*That's* where you spent so much time this January?" she said. "I'm surprised you're still alive."

"So am I. You won't go inside?"

"Those suckers would bite me to say hello!"

"Not even for the sake of a story?" I asked, just to tease her.

She shuddered. "There are limits, Zephyr Hollis."

I patted her on her shoulder. "Wait here. If I look in danger of expiry, do not hesitate to call the appropriate authorities."

Lily raised an uncertain eyebrow and I grinned before sauntering into the maw of the Beast's. I wasn't terribly nervous, but I did make sure to keep my knife in my pocket. My interactions at the Beast's Rum had never been particularly safe, but they had been manageable. The vampires at the door stopped their conversation to stare at me, but they let me through. I didn't bother to ask them any questions; if I could find Nicholas here, then he would do nicely. If not, the person most likely to have information would be behind the bar.

Inside was as dark as I remembered, though Faust's signature smell of cloying rot seemed to have impregnated the floorboards. At the time of my visits in January, the Beast's Rum had been a true blind pig, slinging illegal hooch to humans and vampires willing to dare the risks. The Faust had been an afterthought, a new taste brought in by Rinaldo's entrepreneurial gang. Now the Rum had been reborn as an entirely aboveboard establishment, serving licensed Faust to a strictly sucker clientele.

There were fewer than a dozen people inside, all male, having somber, low-voiced conversations. A few puffed slowly on cheap cigarettes while drinking a thick, dark beverage. I didn't recognize Nicholas or Charlie, the two Turn Boys of my personal acquaintance. Everyone here had been turned well into adulthood. Their eyes followed me as I walked in, but no one said anything. The Faust here seemed to have given them a strange lassitude, quite different from the caricatures of Faust-mad vampires so common in the papers. The bar looked mostly the same, except that the back room where I had tutored Nicholas had been replaced with a small performing stage. I had a hard time imagining a vampire cabaret in a dive like this, but this was New York City.

I walked to the bar and sat gingerly on one of the cracked leather stools. I recognized the bartender—a favorite of Nicholas and the

Turn Boys. Bruno must have recognized me as well, because he nodded before turning to the sucker who had walked up beside me.

"What'll it be?" Bruno asked.

"Devil's Advocate." The vampire plunked a half-dollar on the table. This struck me as a little steep, and I watched in fascination as Bruno pulled out a bottle of Faust and two smaller bags of blood. They didn't look like the standard-issue bags from charity Blood Banks, which probably meant the mob. Not Rinaldo's obviously, but perhaps someone else had quickly taken his place. Bruno poured blood from one bag in first, then layered in the Faust and topped it off with the other. A much fancier operation than what I had witnessed with Aileen back at that speakeasy Sunday night. A possible source for a killing taint?

"That's the last of the O," Bruno said, sliding the glass across.

"The show still on for tonight?" the vampire said, taking a sip.

Bruno looked at the stage and shook his head. "I haven't heard," he said. "Doubt it, though."

Bruno leaned forward, his elbows resting against the edge of the bar, close enough for me to have a very good view of the almost scale-like scars that marked the right side of his face. Bruno was human, but none of the vampires here seemed to fault him for it.

"I don't think you'll like what I'm serving," he said to me.

"I have a question," I said.

"You did the last time you showed up in this joint."

The twist of his mouth said clearly: *and look what happened then.* I tried to look confident and unthreatening, which mostly meant an uncertain smile.

"Did some vampires die here last night?"

"Could have."

"Brave bunch you're serving this afternoon."

He shrugged. "These bottles are from an old crate we ordered months ago. As safe as anything in the city, and anyway, times like these a man needs a drink."

"Even when it kills him?"

"Everything kills you eventually."

"The ones that died, did they pop?"

"You ask more questions than the cops. They just wanted the bottle."

"Did they get it?"

He straightened. "Disappeared," he said with the flicker of a smile. "Cops took away the bodies. Poor old Kevin."

I realized that he had answered my question. No one would ever confuse poppers with bodies.

"What's the show?" I asked, nodding at the stage.

Bruno gave me a long look. "Dancing girls," he said, finally. "But mostly people come for the singer."

"And who's that?"

"Never comes on stage," he said. "Just an angelic voice with a piano."

He said this deliberately, but even without that cue I would have realized the significance of his description. Nicholas's father had turned him at the age of thirteen in order to preserve his perfect young boy's soprano. Nicholas had never fully recovered—even after the initial, lengthy period of madness after awakening. He was prone to strange mental attacks and in general seemed to lack a functioning conscience. I didn't know if the mayor truly realized how dangerous the request he had made of me would be. But like he said, I could take care of myself.

"I'll be back," I said, and hurried outside. Lily was waiting across the street in front of a bakery.

"Well?" she said, when I approached her.

"Curiouser and curiouser." I plucked her reporter's notebook from her hand and ripped out a page.

"Zephyr, what—"

"You have a pen?"

Lily handed it to me. I uncapped it, considered, and then wrote a few judicious words. Kept it simple, since I knew that my intended recipient wasn't terribly good with his letters.

NICK, CHARITY DO-GOOD WANTS TO TALK

Reasonably safe, I decided. If he was really singing in the Rum, he'd get the message. If not, no harm done. Nicholas might not be the most savory of my vampiric connections, but given that I'd saved his life this past January, I had reason to believe myself fairly safe from him. Even in his less stable moods.

I took the message inside and handed it to Bruno. "For the singer," I said.

He slid it inside his pocket, which was all the acknowledgment I could ask for.

∞

Lily took a cab back to her offices while I walked the few blocks home. I had promised to let her know if Nicholas got in touch, or if I learned anything more about the deaths that had taken place at the Beast's Rum. Lily wondered if the mayor's office (or, at the least, Judith Brandon) might not have something official to say about them soon. In which case she would want to be near the newspaper's phones.

For my part, though I had not seen my hateful officers since early yesterday, I had hardly forgotten their dedication to uncovering my crimes. As soon as Nicholas contacted me, I would send him to the mayor and make sure Beau Jimmy knew I had done so. I just hoped Nicholas didn't take too long—the mayor's dinner on Saturday was just three days away.

In the meantime, I didn't know if McConnell and Zuckerman's silence should worry or reassure me. Maybe they couldn't actually find any hard evidence of my connection with Judah? Maybe they'd only been trying to frighten me into incriminating myself? In that case, I might be able to dispense with the mayor's charade entirely. But how could I be sure? They still had my bicycle, but that seemed a small price to pay for never seeing their faces again.

Ludlow Street stank in the summer, and despite Mrs. Brodsky's best efforts, there wasn't much she could do about it. Less conscientious tenement owners and residents tossed their offal into the streets when the pipes proved intractable (often), and refuse when the garbage bins overflowed (daily). Among the dubious benefits of winter was that these presents did not smell. But in the high heat of summer, I pitied the children playing so blithely among pools of stagnant water and hunting for treasures in the piles of trash. I couldn't stop them. I'd learned that quickly enough. I'd learned to ignore them, though what that said about me I wasn't sure I wanted to know. A few summers ago I'd heard a rumor that a poor girl in a tenement on Orchard Street had been dared by some heartless friends into drinking the stagnant sewer water. She'd died in agony just a few days later. I shook my head: and here I was, worrying about *Faust*?

But I couldn't ignore a problem that I'd helped to create.

At first I thought some of the boys from the neighborhood were sitting on Mrs. Brodsky's immaculate steps, but as I came closer I recognized Kardal and Aileen. They were playing a board game, so engrossed that they didn't seem to have seen me at all. Kardal was at his most human, though still an unusual sight in this neighborhood: dark brown skin, finely embroidered clothes that looked like they belonged to another century, and perhaps another continent. Even Aileen looked a little wild. Her hair hung in lank strips, as though she hadn't washed or combed it for days. She wore a dress I'd most often seen her sleep in, though I supposed it met the basic requirements of modesty. Kardal moved a piece across the board—inlaid lapis lazuli and ivory, as far as I could tell, with pieces of jade. Aileen cursed good-naturedly. To my shock, Kardal smiled.

"I believe I have won, dear," he said.

"I still have a few moves!"

"Yes, but each of them ends with me winning."

He said this with his typically inscrutable imperiousness, but Aileen just bit her tongue and smiled ruefully. "I can see the future, you know," she said.

"I do," said Kardal, solemnly. "One of my brothers can, as well. It is a burden."

Aileen sighed, closed her eyes. "Isn't that the buggered truth," she said slowly. "You might as well show me how you'll win."

She moved a piece—a knight, I guessed, from its L-shaped progression, though this chess set had the oddest figurines I'd ever seen. It took his queen—I knew that because I'd stepped closer, and could see the somehow feminine sweep of her robes and bracelets up and down her arms. For a moment I could have sworn that the figurine closed her eyes and *fell*, but Kardal scooped it up and it looked ordinary enough.

"Here," he said, and moved his bishop (though it looked far more like a minaret tower than any bishop I'd ever seen). Freed by the death of his queen, he had a clear shot at her king. Which he took, with due reverence.

Aileen clapped. "Well played," she said. "You're even better than my da."

He inclined his head.

"Does Amir play?" I found myself asking. Aileen looked up, startled, but Kardal merely shrugged. He'd known I was there.

"When he thinks he'll win," Kardal said.

"Does he?"

For the briefest of moments, Kardal's punctiliously human form seemed to billow. "Not always," he said.

Aileen leaned back against the doorjamb. "He's been waiting for you," she said, unnecessarily. "I invited him in, but he said he liked it out here."

"Is Amir all right?" I asked, though I swear I meant to say something else.

"Well enough," he said. "We've had to call council. It seems Kashkash is displeased."

I remembered hearing that name before. "Your father?"

His expression didn't change, but he still seemed dismissive. "A human could not understand. Every djinni owes Kashkash fealty. Both good and . . . unreformed."

Unreformed? That was as accurate a depiction of Amir as any. "And Kashkash wants me to make a wish?"

Kardal's eyes turned just the slightest bit orange—a hint of glowing coals. "You have promised to make a wish. I have told them so. I am here to warn you."

"Warn?" A jolt of terror shook my stomach. My familiarity with Kardal had made me forget how utterly menacing he could be when he wished. I half expected him to intone a prediction of my imminent demise. I took a step backward.

He was implacable. "I know what you have been attempting, Zephyr Hollis. I know of the woman you spoke to, and the thing you wish to accomplish."

"How . . ."

"That woman, the *sahir*, she is known to me. I suspected you might try such a thing. I made sure I would know if you approached her."

My heart was hammering too fast and hard for coherent thought. "But, I had already *promised* you . . ."

"Much too glibly," he said. "After all these months, you finally agree? You forget I know you a little. Yours is the stubbornness of a rock: it holds until it shatters."

I swallowed with difficulty. "Does Amir know?" I asked.

Kardal shook his head. "If he does, not because I have told him."

"Why haven't you?"

"Because he would let you try," Kardal said, enunciating each word with the voice of rumbling stones. "He knows how little you want to be tied to him. Do you know he could have compelled you? Months ago, when the council first started to be concerned, there were a dozen ways he could have tricked or cajoled you to do his bidding. You humans might be our vessels but you are rarely our masters. And yet here we sit, months longer than any human vessel has ever waited since the days of Kashkash himself. Do you know how this looks to others? The embarrassment Amir has caused our whole family?"

"I'm sorry—"

"Are you?"

Fear compelled honesty. "A little?"

"Then accept your lot and make a wish! You endanger more than yourself and Amir the longer you wait. This power we wield is not entirely in our control. There are too many paths it can take out in your world."

"Kardal, you say I've held out the longest of any vessel. But am I the first to try to break away?"

He held himself still, even for a djinni. "No," he said.

"Did any succeed?" I asked.

"One," he said. "He lived a long, happy life."

I felt relief like blood returning to a sleeping limb. "And his djinni?"

Kardal looked unmistakably bleak. "The hundred and fortieth son of Kashkash, and my brother two before me, has not returned to Shadukiam in the five centuries since his exile, and none of us remaining may speak his whole name, nor remember his fire lest we risk the same fate."

I felt as if someone had slapped me. All I could hear was a high ringing. All I could smell was Kardal: smoke and ash and charred earth—not nearly so sweet as his brother.

"Consider carefully, vessel," said Kardal in my ear. "Perhaps you don't see him so very differently from how he sees you?'"

Kardal vanished before I could summon the courage to ask what he meant. I half fell on the highest step, my legs shaking too badly to hold me up. Aileen had pressed herself into the door.

"Those brothers!" she said.

I forced myself to take deep, calming breaths. "He knows about the *sahir*!"

"The witch? What are you going to do?"

I stared at her. Forcing Amir into a lifetime of exile seemed like a harsh bargain. Assuming Kardal was telling the truth. "God, I don't know," I said.

Down on the sidewalk and to our left, something metallic crashed against the basement fence. I dragged the back of my hand quickly across my eyes.

Agent Zuckerman gave me a cold nod. With the sun on its way down, he could have passed for human in his wide-brimmed fedora and suit. I could barely move. Would he arrest me now, with a vampire murderer on the loose and two angry djinn demanding my fealty?

But his hand was on the rear tire of my bicycle, and his expression was rueful, not triumphant.

"Special delivery from the vice squad," he said, nodding at the bicycle.

"You're . . ."

"Giving it back," he said. "And informing you that our department is following other leads." He gave me a speculative look.

"Apart from me?"

He shrugged. "You're still high on our list, Miss Hollis. Good day."

He started to walk away and then paused. "You do keep interesting company though. Having business with certain kinds of Others isn't always a good idea."

Consorting with a djinni? Surely that couldn't be illegal. "Don't sound so excited," I said.

He fixed me with that intense, abstracted stare, as though I were more statue than human. "Oh, I'm going to get you for something, Miss Hollis. The way you do business." He tipped his hat at me. "Be seeing you," he said.

He had a spring in his step as he ambled back down the street. I closed my eyes.

"Maybe I should make that wish," I said.

"Haven't I been telling you so!"

She had. And it was time I decided what to do about it, once and for all.

∽

Something rapped at our window. Aileen snored on, but I hadn't been able to sleep very well in the heavy, wet heat. And there was something else—a smell that lingered in the still night air that hadn't been there a moment before. Like a wet cave and metal and rot. I knew that smell; it kept me quiet on the bed, my breathing steady as I ever so slowly reached for the blessed blade that I had lately kept beneath my pillow.

The rapping came again, quiet but deliberate. Then the smell grew just a little stronger, and I knew that it had climbed over the sill. I turned on the bed, restlessly, as though in sleep. The vampire knelt beside me. For a kiss, for a peek of my breast through the lace of an oversized teddy? I didn't wait to find out. I sat up and lunged forward in one smooth motion, surprising the vampire into staggering backward against the wall. I snapped open the silver blade, pressed it into his neck, rubbed at my sleep-fogged eyes with one hand—

"*Nicholas!*" I said.

The very same grinned, a familiar expression that both pleased me and reminded me to be wary.

"You're a little violent for charity, you know that?" he said. "You want to put that down? It might make me excited."

I moved my arm as though I'd been burned. I sheathed the knife in a quick motion and tossed it on the bed. Perhaps not my smartest idea, but I'd asked him to find me, and it would be a poor show of confidence to keep a knife between us. To my left, Aileen jerked upright and cursed.

"What the hell is he doing here?"

The last (and first) time Aileen had met Nicholas, he'd been dueling with his father while she cowered in a corner.

"Your Zephyr asked me," Nicholas said, and laughed. Nicholas had the voice of an angel condemning you to death—inhumanly beautiful and terrifying.

"Zephyr—" Aileen's voice held a warning.

"We'll go to the hallway," I said quickly, and Nicholas allowed me to push him out the door.

"What's this about?" I whispered. It was dark, but I could see him clearly in the moonlight. He looked just the same as I remembered him: apple-red cheeks, too-bright eyes, light brown hair in a deceptively boyish cut. He was several inches shorter than me but I never felt the advantage. When Rinaldo turned Nicholas, he did more than just preserve a beautiful adolescent voice. He warped his son's adolescent mind, twisted it into a shape that was part madness, part genius, and all dangerous.

It was lucky that Nicholas liked me.

"I liked your note," he said. "I read it myself."

"That's great, Nicholas! Has someone been teaching you?"

He shrugged. "Charlie and me've been practicing. He knew a bit more, so."

It was strange that I even cared. After all, I'd only started to tutor Nicholas in an effort to spy on his gang of child vampires, and, by proxy, his mob-boss father, Rinaldo.

"So, Charity, rumor has it you've been nosing around Faust again," Nicholas said, leaning with cat-like grace against the wall.

"People have been dying."

"*Suckers* have been dying. You care?" He laughed again. "Of course you do. Even if you and your Defender friends kill a few of us yourselves every now and then."

"You *wanted* me to kill your—Rinaldo."

"Of course I did."

"So do you know anything about this? Did more die last night at the Rum?"

He shrugged. "I know plenty, I know nothing. How much will you give to find out, Charity? What's it worth?"

Careful now. "What do you want?"

His mouth twisted and he leaned forward—just close enough for me to smell the hint of Faust on his breath. "A working dick and somewhere to stick it," he said.

I froze. I would have choked, but I had that much self-control. I wondered if he was having another one of his fits—succumbing to a madness that took him into another world. But no, he grinned, perfectly lucid.

He giggled and slapped his thigh. "See your face!" he said. "You should see your face, Charity!"

"Nicholas, tell me something useful or go," I snapped. "I need to sleep."

He nodded and leaned back against the wall. "The poison caught two of us drinking at the Rum last night. One died right there—oh, you should have seen it, Charity. Shook like a doll in a dog's mouth. Then he started to upchuck, blood and blood and something tar black. Then he fell into the mess and died."

"You mean he exsanguinated?"

"*Exsanguinated,*" Nicholas mocked, exaggerating my diction. "No, the sucker didn't pop, and yeah I'm sure he was a sucker and yeah I'm sure he's dead. Just lost it all over the floor and his skin turned the color of a gravestone and he died."

My skin felt the shock before the rest of me. Hot and cold chased each other down my arms and stomach. Blood rushed to my cheeks. I thought, *So it's really true. They are turning human before they die.*

But I couldn't be sure of that on just Nicholas's word alone. Not yet. "And the other?" I asked.

"Dead too. Just took longer. Long enough to get an ambulance to take him. City won't say nothing about them now."

"So how do you know he's dead?"

For a moment Nicholas looked like the thirty-year-old man he probably was. "Because he was one of mine, Charity. He escaped that pit of hell with your crazy daddy and Defenders, but he gets caught by a bad bottle of Faust. I trailed the ambulance. They only take corpses to that part of Bellevue."

I couldn't quite bring myself to offer condolences. I remembered what the Turn Boys had done to this neighborhood, back in their heyday. Still, his grief was real.

"I got the bottle," he said. "Something funny about it."

"You drank—"

"I'm not stupid, Charity. Just smelled it. Something funny. I gotta know who did this. Me and Charlie, we gotta know. This isn't right. A fight, that's one thing, but you can't go around poisoning people's liquor, killing whoever happens to drink it. That's wrong and I'm going to make them pay."

I shuddered. I doubted Nicholas would leave much when he was through with his revenge.

"I'll help you catch them," I said, "if you just do me one favor."

"A favor?"

"Do you have any of the original bottles of Faust?"

His bright eyes widened. "Why, you want some?"

"Just tell me."

"Nah, I don't. Nobody does, far as I know, except maybe that nigger genie."

In the interest of civility, I overlooked the slur. "So I need you to go to the mayor and tell him that."

He whistled. "The mayor! Next you'll be asking me to drop in on Hoover! Flying high, are you, Charity?"

"Even you can't be ignorant of the vote this Monday. The mayor wants to know about the first week of distribution. If you go to him and tell him that you don't have anything, then I'll help you."

"Why not just send him your genie?" he asked.

Damn. I'd been hoping that Nicholas hadn't quite figured out my relationship with Amir. "He's not my genie," I lied. "I haven't seen him since I last saw you. You're the one I can find, so you're the one who I need to meet the mayor."

He looked away from me and out the soot-encrusted window at the end of the hall. "And what do you get out of this, Charity?" he asked softly. "Beau Jimmy made you his beau?"

"Beau Jimmy has offered to help me out of some trouble in exchange," I said. I couldn't possibly explain that I was in danger of being arrested for saving the life of the same young boy that he and his gang had turned in the first place.

But Nicholas just shrugged. "If you say so," he said. "I can do that. But I want something too, Charity."

"I already said I'd help you!"

"I don't give a shit. Only thing I care about is getting into that morgue. You help me do that, I talk to the mayor. I gotta see Kevin with my own eyes."

"Why, Nicholas?"

"He talked before he went. He vomited like the other one, but not so much, and then he turned to me and I held him and he was *breathing* all in and out and I swear I felt his heart beat. And he said 'Got turned back, Nick,' and then his eyes rolled back and he didn't speak no more. And here's the thing: I've never heard of a sucker ever dying without popping."

"Maybe this poison is different," I said, though I didn't really believe it.

"Maybe they ain't suckers when they die," he said. "You can ask the mayor to get us in."

"Maybe I could ask Mrs. Brandon," I said slowly. "But you have to talk to the mayor tomorrow, got it?"

"How do I know you'll keep your word?"

"You call me Charity, don't you? I promise. And I want to see those bodies, too."

My curiosity, if nothing else, convinced him. "Then I'll give Jimmy a big surprise tomorrow," he said. His mouth twisted. "And if you're lying . . ."

From the look in his eyes, I wouldn't fare much better than the actual killer. I backed away. "I promise. In the meantime, could you give me the bottle you stole? I'll see what I can learn."

Nicholas gave me that childish smile that was anything but innocent. "You'll get it tomorrow," he said. "Good to see you again, Charity."

"You too, Nick," I said, and surprised myself by meaning it.

I showed him to the roof since I didn't want Aileen to start screaming. I hoped she would be asleep, but when I came back inside, I found her sitting on my bed.

"Strange friends, Zeph," she said, balefully.

"If someone's poisoning vampires, I have to know."

She sighed. "You know Judith Brandon?"

"Were you listening?"

"Of course I was."

"Judith met me with the mayor," I said. "She mentioned something about the Spiritualist Society."

Aileen yawned and toddled back to her bed. "She's one of the regulars at my readings."

"Really?" I feigned surprise, remembering Amir's abashed confession over dinner yesterday.

"Don't sound so surprised. There's lots of respectable ladies at my meetings."

"And she wants to talk to the dead?"

"Don't they all?"

"Anyone in particular?"

"Her husband."

"Has he said anything?" I felt awkward even asking. Aileen and I had a tacit agreement not to talk about the details of her work at the Society.

"Not a bleeding word. I'm starting to think he's left her for his mistress in Mallorca and she just comes to keep up appearances, but I do what I'm told."

I tried to keep silent, but the words came out anyway. "Aileen, have you thought you might—"

"I'm having my biggest night yet, tomorrow. 'LEGENDARY IRISH SEER PEERS THROUGH THE MISTS TO ANSWER LIFE'S QUESTIONS,' or so say the flyers. I know Judith will be there, probably a few other people who might know a thing or two about these dead vampires. You want to come?"

I smiled, though I felt like I'd lost. "Sure, Aileen. That sounds like a great idea."

I had a hard time falling asleep. I rehearsed all the possibilities for the next few important days until I felt exhausted just thinking of it: Aileen's séance Thursday, the mayor's dinner Saturday, Sofia's summoning Sunday, and—of course—the Faust vote Monday.

I didn't fall back asleep until dawn, and when I did it was to dream of rose gardens, and fountains that filled the air with the gentle sound of water falling onto marble tile.

CHAPTER SIX

"Zephyr," said Harry, entering my room early the next morning without so much as a knock, "I found something in your cellar."

Right on his heels came Mrs. Brodsky. "Miss Zephyr!" she said, shrill as a shrieking cat. "This is the last straw! How many times have I said, no males allowed? First those police, and now this! This is a clean establishment—"

I fumbled for a robe. "Mrs. Brodsky, I assure you—"

"No, Zeph, you should come look," Harry said. He grabbed my elbow and Mrs. Brodsky actually smacked him.

"Off, off!"

Aileen groaned and put the pillow over her head. "Zephyr, if your life must be insane, does it *always* have to wake me up?"

I grimaced. "Harry, you couldn't have waited downstairs?"

"The cellar, Zeph," he said, tugging again. "You've got to look."

"This man . . . your *beau* cannot just waltz—"

"He's my brother," I said, at the same time Harry rolled his eyes, turned around and said, "She's my *sister*, you old prude."

"You have a brother?" she said.

Harry took off his cap and bowed far too extravagantly. "Harold Hollis at your service, ma'am."

Mrs. Brodsky looked between us, her expression a hilarious mixture of relief and annoyance. She pursed her lips. "This is very improper, Zephyr," she said at a thankfully more tolerable pitch.

"Well *I* didn't invite him. Harry, what is this?"

"Will you come downstairs already? The cellar—"

"What on earth is in the cellar!"

Mrs. Brodsky frowned. "Yes, what do you mean? I went to the cellar last night, there was nothing improper in it."

"Maybe it's rats, Mrs. Brodsky," said Aileen, sepulchral tones muffled through her pillow.

"*Rats!*"

I put my hands over my ears. Harry, at least a head taller than Mrs. Brodsky, put a solicitous hand on her shoulder and stared directly at me. *Sucker*, he mouthed.

"Oh," I said. "Let me get my slippers."

"Rats!" Mrs. Brodsky said, shaking her head in something like despair. "How could this be? I keep everything so *clean* . . ."

I choked on a laugh. "I'm sure you do, ma'am," Harry said soothingly. "It's probably a stray one that got stuck down there. Zeph and I will have it out in a jiffy."

"Zephyr knows how to kill rats?" Mrs. Brodsky asked, some suspicion returning.

I had found one slipper, but the other had lodged itself among the dust bunnies far under the bed. I sighed and knelt on the floor.

"Oh, she's a natural, ma'am," Harry said. "One of the best I've ever seen."

"Are you an exterminator?"

I sneezed.

"Something like that," Harry said.

"Got it!" I said, emerging from beneath my bed with the slipper triumphantly aloft. Aileen, having given up even the pretense of sleep, raised her eyebrows at me.

"You have dust in your hair," she said.

I shrugged and shook out the slipper. "The better to hunt . . . ah, rats with," I said. "Lead on, Harry."

"You will tell me when you catch it?" Mrs. Brodsky was asking as we went back down the stairs. "If there are many of them . . ."

She shuddered and for a moment I thought she might cry. Harry was very adult and reassuring, which spared me the task of being sympathetic.

We left her in the parlor without much of an argument while Harry and I went out the back door to the small alleyway. Harry had secured the metal doors of the cellar with a blessed blade and a chain.

"The sucker's still alive?" I whispered.

Harry pulled out the sword, handed it to me and tossed open the doors. "When I left him," he said. "He swore he knew you, so I thought I'd check."

"Please tell me that you did not just threaten to kill a law-abiding vampire who happened to be coming by to pay me a visit? And that you definitely did not lock him in my *landlady's cellar!*"

He led the way down the steep stairs. "Well, I don't know, Zeph," he said, looking over his shoulder with a disconcertingly appraising look. "I'm the last one to tell you not to do whatever you like with yourself, but I thought it was possible you didn't want a sucker with a gun in his pocket climbing up your fire escape to crawl through your window."

Nicholas, again? "That's . . . ah . . ." I smiled awkwardly at my suddenly all grown up younger brother. "Thanks, Harry."

The cellar was crowded and dark, filled with enough canned food to last us a winter and piles of bric-a-brac it would take a miner to uncover. Harry had tied the sucker quite neatly in a far corner. He was gagged, which explained the eerie silence. I so expected to see Nicholas once again that I nearly yelped when Harry lit the oil lamp Mrs. Brodsky had given us.

"Charlie!"

Charlie met my eyes and then looked at the floor, so embarrassed even his muffled greeting sounded like a bleat.

"It's okay, Harry," I said. I put down the sword and set about prying open Harry's thorough knots.

"Zephyr, I'm sorry, Nick said I could go through the window, I didn't mean nothing by it!" I could have sworn he was blushing, except vampires didn't really blush. Blood near the skin indicated a recent feeding.

I knelt and untied his feet. "Nicholas shouldn't have gone through the window, either," I said. "You're lucky that my brother has such forbearance."

Harry grinned and ruffled my dust-filled hair. "I'm my daddy's son, but my sister's brother."

I stood up. "You mean you didn't buy all of Daddy's tripe about me ruining the family name?"

"Of course not, Zeph. Look at you! You're living like a pauper just so you can do what you believe in. That's really something. And I think you're right, to a point. When they're not evil, suckers can be all right."

Charlie sat up a little straighter. "Course we can," he said.

"Just like humans," I said carefully.

Harry shrugged. "A sucker's a little more dangerous than your average person."

I thought about Archibald Warren and whoever had decided to start poisoning vampires. "Maybe," I said. I stood up. "So, Charlie, what's so important that you had to come crawling up my fire escape to tell me?"

"Nick said you needed the bottle. I got it in my bag, but your . . . friend here took it."

Charlie looked at me hopefully. "Harry," I said, "give him his stuff back. Charlie, Harry's my brother."

"Glad to meet you, Harry." He held out his hand and after a moment Harry shook it.

"So what's this bottle?" Harry asked, taking the dark glass from Charlie's bag. Harry handed it to me, and even though the cork had been firmly replaced, Faust's unmistakable stench leeched through.

"You don't recognize it?" I asked. "The scourge of New York's undead?"

Harry wrinkled his nose. "Don't know how they can drink that stuff. Smells foul."

"S'not so bad," Charlie said defensively. "But don't let anyone drink that one. It's got the poison, whatever it is."

I nodded. "Listen, I need you to deliver this for me. Take it to Lily Harding, at the *New-Star Ledger* offices in the Flatiron Building. In person, okay?"

Charlie nodded. "They're not always so friendly to suckers round there, Zephyr, but I'll figure it out."

"Thanks, Charlie." I scribbled a note telling Lily what was in the bottle and suggesting she find someone who could analyze it. Money and contacts could work miracles my goodwill couldn't. I folded it in half and handed it to him. "Tell Nicholas I'll see what I can do."

Charlie beamed. "Okay, Zeph. I'll . . . be seeing you around, then. Nick says you're going to get us into the morgue? I want to see if Kevin really got turned back before he died. That's what they're saying, you know. Some of us are even trying to *find* the poison. You know, like it might not be so bad being dead, if you got to be human one last time."

He looked almost wistful, which scared me in a strange way. "Charlie, you're not—"

"Oh! No! Not me, Zephyr, no way. Nick needs me and besides, this isn't so bad. But maybe I can just see the logic, that's all."

He shrugged and pulled a heavy cloak from his bag. "Bye, Zephyr," he said. I waved as he put the hood over his head and climbed carefully back into the sunlight.

"That's one way to start a morning," I said, after he had left. "Want to share breakfast with me? Mrs. Brodsky probably won't mind, given that you've saved her from uncleanliness. I must warn you, however, that the porridge is always lumpy."

Harry put his hand on my arm. "I think you should come back to headquarters with me."

"I'm wearing slippers!" I said, still laughing, though I saw something oddly serious behind Harry's eyes.

"I'll wait for you to dress."

"What is this, Harry? Why are you here so early, anyway? And without a note?"

He sighed. "It's Mama," he said. "She says that Daddy's gone crazy."

∾

"What exactly constitutes crazy?" I asked, drinking surprisingly decent coffee in the Defenders parlor. "Because it's not as though our daddy is some paragon of mental hygiene."

Harry took a tactful bite of toast. He was too loyal to agree with me, and too honest to argue. "She didn't want me to tell you," he said, after a moment.

"Mama? Why not?"

"Because she thinks it's got something to do with you. Why he's gone crazy."

I put down the cup, forcefully enough to splash my fingers. "Christ, Harry, what is he doing? Running naked down Main Street?"

Harry swallowed. "Mama says . . . he burned down his shack,

Zeph. Soaked it in kerosene and stayed to make sure the whole place had turned to a cinder."

"His *weapons* . . ."

"Mama said he saved a few of those. But everything else. All his hunting notes, the trophies—"

"Good riddance," I said, recalling Daddy's grisly collection of tokens from past hunts: strips of fur, taxidermied hands, teeth, and odd bits of jewelry.

"He *loves* that collection."

Which was true. Even if it made me shudder to step through the door of what I had privately referred to as Daddy's "lair," that didn't make him love it any less. I couldn't imagine him allowing Mama to clean the place, let alone burning it to the ground.

"Did he say why?"

"He won't talk about it. But Mama said he's been acting more paranoid since this rabbi came to Yarrow a few weeks ago."

"A rabbi? Are there any Jews in Yarrow?"

"I didn't think so. But he wasn't setting up shop. He was asking questions about some sort of grimoire, like Daddy has anything to do with those. Mama didn't hear any more than that, but afterward Daddy started acting strange. He keeps asking if you've come to your senses."

I blinked. "He does? He's not still hoping I'll rejoin the Defenders?"

"That too," Harry said, and looked away.

"Why," I asked, taking too long to put this together, "were you underneath my window to catch Charlie in the first place?"

"To tell you about Mama—"

"Knock on the door, then. You were skulking under my window!"

Harry blushed red as his hair and twisted his empty coffee cup in his hands. "Daddy would kill me if anything happened to you. He made me promise when I came out here."

"He doesn't think I can take care of myself?"

"He doesn't think you'll bother," Harry said, blush fading. He looked straight at me. "And, frankly, Zeph, I agree with him. Charlie—he was one of those Turn Boys, wasn't he? Troy told me about them. The police were bad enough, but now you're nosing around these murders—"

"How do you know that?"

He rolled his eyes. "Is it a secret? I swear half the Lower East Side has heard of you. It doesn't take much effort to follow your tracks. For me, or anyone else interested."

My scalp prickled. I finished the last of my coffee, lukewarm and bitter. "Has anyone else been interested?"

Harry started to speak, paused, and put his cup firmly on the table. "Archibald Warren, I think."

"What?" That was the last name I had expected to hear.

"I saw one of his acolytes at that blind pig in Little Italy. You know, the one on Broome Street."

"Why do you think he was after *me*?"

"He was asking around the whole place. Trying to find out if you'd been there and what you might have known about the two dead suckers."

I sucked in a breath and let it out slowly. "How do you know he was with Warren?"

Harry blushed again, but more modestly—just in his cheeks, and there was something self-satisfied in his smile as he leaned back in his chair. "I, ah, have a passing acquaintance with another one of Warren's associates."

"Passing acquaintance."

"Uh-huh."

With one of Archibald Warren's inner circle! I could only imagine the reaction if that got out. "The monogrammed letter kind?" I asked, just to be sure.

Harry nodded. I whistled. "And Daddy's worried about *me*?" I said.

My younger brother—who was most certainly, absolutely, no longer the child who had once put a beehive in my knickers—gave a delicate shrug. "What Daddy doesn't know," he said, "can't hurt him."

∞

I loved my bicycle. Maybe the gears jammed, maybe the brakes caught, perhaps the front wheel had been bent ever so slightly to the left, but as soon as I pushed off from the curb, I felt like I'd come home. Two days of walking in this sticky heat had felt like an eternity. Now I glided past the teeming mess of my neighborhood streets with verve.

Thursday was still young, so I mapped out who I most needed to see today before Aileen's séance. If I was to keep my bargain with Nicholas and get into the morgue, Judith Brandon was my best chance. But before I could do that, I had to check in with Elspeth. She would want to know of my latest discoveries, particularly about events at the Beast's Rum. I bought a paper from a newsboy on my way over and checked it for any news about the recent deaths. Thankfully, it looked like no one else had died but those two vampires at the Beast's Rum on Tuesday night. An anonymous official in the mayor's office offered sympathy for the most recent deaths and confirmed that they suspected a killer—not Faust itself. No less a personage than Police Commissioner Warren had vowed to *"not rest until we've found who is responsible."*

He might even mean it, I thought, but I still didn't trust anyone associated with the mayor to give vampires a fair shake.

I found Elspeth exactly where I expected—toiling without pause in the dark, stuffy upstairs room on First Avenue. She was alone, and seemed startled when I entered.

"Have you found something?" she asked, putting down a pen with ink-smudged fingers.

She looked tired, though it was a difficult thing to judge in a vampire. They didn't sleep in any way I could recognize, though they could only go so long without resting. I'd seen vampires at rest upright against a wall with their eyes open. Most at least feigned the appearance of sleep, but it always disturbed me to see someone who looked human maintain that uncanny stillness. I imagined that Elspeth had not managed even a short rest for the last several days.

"I have the bottle of Faust that might have killed the latest two vampires," I said.

"Really? That's marvelous! I take it you've seen this morning's paper? They're vowing to catch the killer, now. Do you think they're serious?" Elspeth asked.

"They might be. I can ask my journalist friend what she thinks." I picked up Elspeth's copy of the *New-Star Ledger* and fruitlessly scanned the stories for Lily's byline. She hadn't managed to get any column space. I hoped that didn't indicate anything too dire.

"If you think the police can be trusted, you should give them that bottle. It's vital that Faust's role in this be clear to the public, one way or another."

"You wouldn't rather use the ambiguity in our favor?" I said.

She shook her head. "In the long run, Zephyr, the truth is always best."

As usual, Elspeth had made me feel very small-minded. "Mind if I ask my friend first? I don't trust the police in this town to find Times Square with a Baedeker."

Elspeth nodded brusquely and retrieved her pen. She started writing, then paused and looked back up at me. "You came for something else?"

"I have a question. About the . . . djinni matter."

"Have you changed your mind?"

I grimaced. "That's the trouble. I've, ah, been informed that it's possible that, ah, *breaking* from my djinni like this might hurt him.

That he might be exiled from Shadukiam for the rest of his life. Which is, let me tell you, a very, very long time."

Elspeth frowned. "Why do you care if the djinni is exiled? Surely that's one less to worry about."

I might have to worry about this one anyway, I thought. "I just want us to be *separate* from each other. But I don't want to ruin his life."

"Zephyr, just how well do you know your djinni?"

"He *is* mine," I said, with an awkward laugh. "It would be hard not to know him a little." I had a sudden flash of Amir's hot hands popping the buttons from my blouse, tipping me over the balcony of his brother's palace in Shadukiam . . . kissing me. . . .

"I really don't know," Elspeth said. "I can ask Sofia, if you like. I don't think there's been many attempts to do this sort of thing before."

"Thank you!" I said, backing away quickly. "You can send me a note, if you like. Or I can stop by later. In any case, I must run. I might have a lead on the murders."

Elspeth didn't even acknowledge me. Sighing as though she had better things to attend to, she picked up her pen and resumed writing.

City Hall was bustling again, some sort of legislative session having just released for lunch. I pushed through the throng to reach the hallway I remembered from my first visit. The secretary at the entrance to the back offices frowned up at me when I asked to see Judith Brandon. However, she agreed to see if Mrs. Brandon could speak to me, though "we're all terribly busy today, as you can see."

She returned a few minutes later and indicated that I should follow her. I hurried behind, through the hallway that I recognized, around several corners that I didn't, and then down two flights of stairs.

"You're not taking me to the dungeon, are you?" I said, attempting a smile.

"Not quite," she said.

There were no windows, just a few sparse lights that gave off a hazy orange glow. Most of the rooms appeared to be storage spaces, but two offices capped the end of the hallway. One looked empty and the woman stopped by the second: a plain door with a green beveled glass window and a placard reading: BRANDON.

The woman nodded at the knob and left, as though she thought something unpleasant might happen if she lingered. I hesitated, looked up and down the deserted hallway, and knocked.

"Come in," said a voice.

I entered. Mrs. Brandon was seated behind a small desk that took up most of the room. She had organized her space carefully: books lined the walls, paper sat in neat, if overlarge, piles on her desk. She was perusing one now—a short paper with a rough scrawl that I couldn't hope to read upside-down.

"You've heard already?" she said.

"Well . . ."

She sighed. "Jimmy will have to speak to the press. It's gone too far for anything less."

"Another death," I hazarded, and Judith nodded grimly.

"Stranger this time," she said. "Whose interests could this possibly serve? I don't suppose you have any theories, Miss Hollis?"

"I just heard a rumor," I said, putting my best face on it. "I'm a little hazy on the details."

Mrs. Brandon gestured to a wooden folding chair, the only other seat.

"An officer," she said. "A specialist on the Other vice squad."

"A *vampire* officer?" I didn't need the clarification, but I asked regardless.

"An unusual situation," Mrs. Brandon said. "He was turned in the course of duty. He didn't wish to leave the service, and his partner fought for him to stay on."

"But," I said, "I just saw him last evening."

She looked up sharply from the scribbled missive. "You knew Officer Zuckerman?"

"He was investigating me. For the other matter. The child vampire. He and his partner. He's really dead?"

She pursed her lips and stared at me long enough for a bead of sweat to migrate from my temple to my chin. I didn't dare reach up to wipe it away. A small electric fan whirred away in one corner, but it didn't dissipate the stale, muggy air so much as move it around. Better conditions than my room at Mrs. Brodsky's, perhaps, but that didn't seem appropriate for one of the mayor's special advisors.

"His partner found Officer Zuckerman early this morning in his apartment. He was dead, with a bottle of Faust beside him."

I wiped the sweat from my forehead. I could hardly feel my fingertips, but I was aware of every sticky inch of my shirt collar.

"I was at home all night," I said softly.

Mrs. Brandon frowned. "Goodness, you can't imagine that I suspect you, Miss Hollis. Though . . ." She trailed off. "You're right, to an outsider the situation might place you under some slight suspicion. Best for you to make sure that someone can confirm your alibi, just in case."

I was surprised I hadn't seen McConnell already. The news of Zuckerman's death made me feel physically ill—what would his partner do without the friend who seemed able to read his thoughts? And what would he do if his suspicions fall on me? But at least Mrs. Brandon had dismissed the notion out of hand. I could do worse than having her on my side.

"Did he pop?" I asked, after a moment.

Mrs. Brandon pursed her lips, considering her answer, then shook her head briefly. "I'm not authorized to discuss details, but . . ."

So he hadn't, just like every other vampire killed this past week.

"He was murdered, too?"

"Officer Zuckerman was well known for his opposition to Faust," she said.

"He'd hardly be the first person to privately practice what he publicly condemned."

Mrs. Brandon laughed abruptly and then stopped. "No. Indeed not, Miss Hollis. I'm sure you have much experience with that."

I did, but it surprised me that she would have guessed such a thing. "I imagine you see even more at City Hall."

She smiled. "Speaking of which, do you have any news about that other matter for me to pass on to Jimmy?"

"I've talked to the former leader of the Turn Boys. He's agreed to meet with the mayor."

She dropped the letter in a pile on her desk and hurriedly flipped to a clean sheet in her blotter. "At what time?" she asked. "Does he have the original material?"

"I don't know," I said, and wondered when I had gotten so accomplished at lying. "And Nicholas isn't the type to keep to a schedule. He said he would contact the mayor soon. Today, I hope."

Mrs. Brandon looked affronted at the idea, but then shook her head and dashed off a note. "Once he contacts the mayor, I'll make sure James puts in a call," she said.

"Even if Nicholas doesn't have the original?"

She frowned. "Do you have any reason to expect he won't?"

"Oh, no. I just want to make sure I've fulfilled my side of the bargain."

"As long as the mayor gets to talk to the original distributor, he will consider your obligation fulfilled."

I shifted. But Jimmy Walker couldn't possibly get to Amir. I would be safe. "Thank you," I said.

It struck me that the mayor would be calling in a very big favor in exchange for my help. But for all I knew, such derailment of legitimate police investigations were de rigueur in this administration. I felt thankful to have Mrs. Brandon as an intermediary—at least she understood the political waters that seemed to be crashing far over my head.

"Mrs. Brandon," I said, "it seems strange to me that you—and the mayor—are so concerned about these particular murders. Pardon my bluntness, but you haven't evinced much concern for vampires before."

"Vampires are a vital part of our city's population," she said, with surprising passion. A flush stained her cheekbones. I remembered how Jimmy Walker had once admonished me during a demonstration for vampire rights: *"For heaven's sake, they're not people."*

Perhaps being the mayor's Other advisor was a more thankless task than I had previously appreciated. Certainly, looking around Mrs. Brandon's cramped office, it was hard not to come to that conclusion.

"I can't tell you how glad I am to hear you say so," I said. "The mayor is lucky to have you on his side."

She leaned forward. "You must understand that I would never work for this bill if I thought that Faust itself posed any threat to the well-being of any vampire who consumes it."

Elspeth and the others would argue that Faust did, in fact, harm the well-being of vampires. Though it probably didn't murder them. "But I wonder how a murderer would poison the drink?"

I hoped this might prompt her into giving me something specific to look for in Nicholas's bottle, but she just put her hands flat on her desk and sighed. "We're investigating several possibilities," she said. "I can't say more than that for now. With some luck, the mayor will be able to give many answers to the press this evening."

This made me recall my original purpose in coming here, made even more urgent by the news of Zuckerman's death. "Actually, I was hoping I might persuade you to let me see the bodies."

"You mean visit the morgue? I'm sorry, Miss Hollis, but that would be quite impossible," she said, with such regretful finality that I saw it would be fruitless to argue. I shrugged.

"I understand. I appreciate you telling me what you could."

"It was the least I could do. Such a terrible situation . . . Miss Hollis, do remember to confirm your alibi. I would hate to see you mixed up in another investigation."

I bit my lip at the thought. "I will, thank you."

I stood, but with so little room to maneuver, I accidentally knocked the folding chair to the ground. As I knelt to pick it up, I caught sight of a tiny photograph of a young man nestled in an antique keepsake frame at the far corner of Mrs. Brandon's desk. She'd arranged it so it was only clearly visible at eye level.

She caught me staring. "My late husband," she said, before I could ask. "He used to be Mayor Walker's Other advisor. He grew quite ill and had to resign. He died a few months after. James was kind enough to offer me the substance of Michael's position."

"I'm so sorry," I said, inadequately.

"Don't be," Mrs. Brandon said, reaching for a newspaper at the top of a pile. "It will all work out in the end. I've become quite indispensable to James over the years. I believe—"

Someone rapped sharply on the door and pushed it open. It was the mayor himself, his hair unaccountably mussed, sweat beading his forehead, and his cheeks flushed red. He gripped the edge of the door like he would rip it from its hinges.

"Judith," he said, his raspy voice hinting at a quaver. "I need you to see something. In my office. Now, if you please."

Mrs. Brandon's eyes widened and she scrambled from behind her desk. "Of course, Jimmy," she said. "What is it?"

He stared at her bleakly. I wondered if he was even aware of my presence. "It seems my father has come for a visit."

∽

The mayor's office was dark as twilight. At first I thought storm clouds had gathered outside, but the sun was clearly visible through the windows. It was just dark, like the light existed but couldn't pass through an invisible barrier. Mrs. Brandon and I had entered the room, but the mayor hovered on its threshold. He grimaced as though he couldn't quite bear to approach and was furious at himself for his weakness.

He had my sympathy. Billy Walker had been our mayor's role model and a consummate Tammany politician to the end, but anyone dead for eleven years had no business paying his son a visit.

"Where did the spirit show himself, James?" Mrs. Brandon asked.

Mayor Walker took a shaking breath and stepped into his office. "The Boss spoke to me from the fireplace."

Mrs. Brandon fearlessly approached, while I forced myself to remember everything Daddy had ever taught me about hauntings. Not much, as it turned out—there hadn't been much opportunity for personal experience in Yarrow.

"You built a fire in this heat?" Mrs. Brandon asked.

Jimmy Walker shook his head in frustration. "Heavens, Judith, of course not! The thing just lit up, and the rest of the lights went down."

Even now, however, the strange gloom was receding. Light streamed through the window, dissipating the haunting that had prompted the mayor's mad dash to the subterranean office of his Other advisor.

"The grate is cold," Mrs. Brandon said, running a finger through the ash in front of it.

"I assure you, I didn't imagine this."

"I would never dream of suggesting such a thing, Jimmy. The spirits work mysteriously, though I must say it's rare to hear of one so . . . forcefully entering our world."

The fireplace had been as immaculate as the rest of his office when I'd last visited. The fine layer of ash that seemed to have settled in a perfect radius around the grate struck me as unnatural.

I knelt beside Mrs. Brandon and ran my own finger through the muck. Sulphur and scorched earth. *The aroma of hell?* I wondered. But there was a hint of something else, something less like brimstone and more like the inside of a cathedral, a censer swung by a priest, trailing a fog of myrrh and frankincense and burnt oranges—

I knew that smell. Bloody stakes, but I knew it too damn well.

I sneezed. Mrs. Brandon and the mayor, thankfully, were too focused on the mystery of the apparition to note my discomfiture.

"He's gone, isn't he?" The mayor sank into the nearest chair and buried his face in his thin, pale hands. He looked so unguarded and lost at that moment I looked away in embarrassment. Now that it appeared the danger had passed—dubious though I suspected it to be—I wondered if I could make a discreet exit. Mrs. Brandon had invited me to come along because of my "history with such matters," though I wondered if that referred to the affair with Rinaldo or my unusual upbringing.

But the only way out was past the mayor, and indecision kept me in place.

"Whatever spirit was here has departed, James," Mrs. Brandon said, walking over to him. "Did he say his reason for contacting you? Even with the aid of a medium experienced in such matters, it can be quite difficult for a spirit to contact someone among the living. For your father to have found a means of haunting you himself . . ."

Mrs. Brandon looked down with a jerk of her head and bunched her skirt in her hands. Aileen had said Mrs. Brandon always tried to contact her husband but never succeeded. That explained the grief and frustration that flashed across her face.

"He wanted to talk about Faust, Judith. He said I'd been making a hash of things, that there are these poor souls of the dead vampires there with him . . . 'down *here*,' he said. Oh God—"

The mayor's hands trembled; his Adam's apple bobbed, but he couldn't seem to force out another word. Mrs. Brandon hesitated, then rested her hand on his shoulder.

"I wouldn't read too deeply into it, Jimmy," she said, softly. "I believe our conceptions of heaven and hell to be misleading descriptions of the spirit world. Perhaps he meant 'down' just as you would say you went down to Washington, D.C."

Jimmy Walker sat up straighter in his chair, palpably relieved to hear her sensible, matter-of-fact explanation. "The Boss didn't *sound* tortured," he said slowly. "Though he did sound rather far away, like I was talking to him through a subway tunnel."

Mrs. Brandon turned back to look at the fireplace, with me frozen beside it. "Just stunning, Jimmy. The Society has been keeping records of visitations and hauntings, but I have never heard of such a strong event before—"

"I don't want this public, Judith," the mayor said, sharply.

Mrs. Brandon blushed. "Of course not, Jimmy."

"The ghost . . . your father was telling you about Faust?" I asked, because if I was going to be the third party to this uncomfortably intimate conversation, I might as well learn something for myself.

Jimmy Walker blinked several times, like he had mistaken me for a chair. "He said I shouldn't go through with the vote. And I asked why not, and he said the ghosts with him, the dead vampires, had died in agony and it was too dangerous for the city."

"He said all that?" I asked.

The mayor managed a shade of a smile. "He was very specific, Miss Hollis. I daresay you agree with him."

But Mrs. Brandon looked all the more worried. "The spirit said the Faust itself had killed the vampires?"

"I'm not sure. He wasn't terribly clear at that point. He just kept repeating it was dangerous, that the ghosts had told him so . . . then his voice faded and I went to find you."

Mrs. Brandon smoothed out the wrinkles her hands had bunched into her skirt.

"This is just *so strange*," Mrs. Brandon said, as though part of her longed to use a more pungent adjective.

"Perhaps the dead vampires begged him to intercede," the mayor said, gloomily. "Just what I need right now—the Boss reprising the role of my conscience."

Someone ought to do it, I thought, but just barely refrained from saying aloud.

"Anyhow," the mayor continued, "I can't just ignore him. If the vampires died because of the Faust . . ."

Mrs. Brandon shot a look at me. "You know that's unlikely," she said, widening her eyes at the mayor. Hinting about the autopsy reports?

"But the ghosts said—"

"Ghosts aren't always accurate!" She clapped her hands together and stalked to the slightly ajar door. She slammed it home. "It's the nature of their distance from us. We can't just change policy based on . . ."

"A visitation?" the mayor said, and gave Mrs. Brandon a strange smile.

"I've never heard of vampires having ghosts," I said. "I thought that was part of what turns."

This observation made both Mrs. Brandon and the mayor stare at me for a long, uncomfortable moment. "I'm hardly an expert, of course," I said, just to cut the silence.

But the mayor was shaking his head, the sunlight and conversation apparently dispelling his terror. "No, you're quite right, Miss Hollis. Now that I think of it, the idea of vampire ghosts is quite odd. But intriguing. Do you think it's possible, Judith?"

Mrs. Brandon gasped. She stared at the mayor and then gave one jerky nod. "I do."

The mayor grinned now and clapped his hands. "Well, then. Thank you, Boss," he said, nodding his head at the ash-filled grate. "I believe I know what we will do."

"Jimmy, what?" Mrs. Brandon looked a little terrified at the gleam in his eyes, and I didn't blame her.

"You always worry so, Judith. Don't—it ages you prematurely. Would you mind showing Miss Hollis out? I'm afraid I've neglected a bit more work than usual this afternoon."

Mrs. Brandon and I shared a long, worried glance, but there was nothing either of us could do but comply.

∞

"Amir!" I called from the fountain in City Hall Park. A few dozen pigeons fluttered away from me and an old man feeding them stale bread fixed me with a baleful glare. "Amir," I said, "if you don't show up right now, I'll—"

"Refuse to make a wish? Lecture me on moral laxity?"

He had somehow come up behind me, startling me so much I yelped and stumbled. I would have fallen into the fountain if not for his arm gently putting me upright.

"Oh!" I said, breathlessly. "You're here!"

He drew his lips in, like he was puckering for a kiss or suppressing laughter. "You were screaming my name to the pigeons a moment ago."

"You heard me?"

He sighed. "I was just on the other side of the building. As I assume you knew."

"I guessed." I had hoped I was wrong. My conjecture of what had really taken place in the mayor's office didn't say anything good about a certain djinni's continued penchant for practical jokes.

"You guessed," he said in that deadpan way of his, at once self-mocking and despairing. "Because you happened to choose this exact moment to visit Beau James."

"The ghost of his *daddy*, Amir? Who knew your taste in pranks ran so literary."

He took my elbow and steered me away from the fountain and the curious old man. "I thought it would be effective," he said.

"I'm surprised you left out the rattling chains."

He laughed bitterly. "You know me," he said. "I abhor excess."

He looked so miserable that my frustration and anger stopped short, like I had prepared myself for a plunge in an icy lake and ended up in a wading pool. He had played a practical joke on the mayor, true, but he didn't appear particularly happy about it. And the joke itself had been strange, to say the least.

"Amir," I said slowly, "are you conning the mayor into throwing the vote on Monday?"

"An attempt. Hardly a con. A con ought to work, after all."

We were ambling down a side street, but at this I stopped short. "Why would you even bother?" I asked.

"Forty-two reasons," he said, and didn't look at me.

"What?"

He laughed. "The vampire suffragette doesn't know? Forty-two. The number of vampires killed in Faust-related incidents since January."

"Oh." My hand flew to my mouth, but something about my reaction terrified me even more than Amir's bleak memorization of that number. I gripped my elbows instead.

"Could you actually care?" I said, half to myself. "After what you did in January?"

"For a charity worker, you seem to have a remarkably thin belief in repentance."

"I believe in human—well, *person* nature. Did you get a Ming vase in the bargain?"

He gave me a look that I could only describe as withering and continued walking without a response. I had the uncomfortable feeling that I had behaved badly, which was never pleasant, but trebly so because it necessitated an unflattering comparison between myself and the amoral djinni who had inflicted Faust on New York City.

I hurried after him, though I suppose I could have let him walk away. But we hadn't seen each other for a few days and his absence had begun to gnaw at me. I had wondered what he was doing—plotting a practical joke, as it turned out—but even now something made me want to prolong our encounter. His long legs moved deceptively quickly. By the time I decided to jog after him, he was a block away.

"I wanted to ask you something," I said, panting a little.

Amir stopped and turned around. For a moment his eyes flashed the orange and umber of dying coals. I wondered if he was still angry, but he just smiled and brushed a sweaty curl from my forehead. "Yes?" he said.

"Do you know what happened to your brother two before Kardal?" This question had lingered in my thoughts since Kardal's visit, and it seemed safer than exploring the extent of Amir's Faustian regret. Or, perhaps, just safer than what I felt when he spoke of it.

Amir stared at me like I'd asked him to fly to the moon. "Aban?" he said. "What would you know about him?"

"Was he exiled?" I asked.

"That's the story. It happened before I was born. Kashkash desired a woman in the world, but Aban took her instead. So he was exiled. I think it expires in another hundred years or so. I might meet him, then."

"A woman?" I said, dumbfounded. "It had nothing to do with his vessel cutting the bond between them?"

"Zephyr, it's practically impossible to cut the bond between a djinni and his vessel."

"Practically? You mean except through death."

135

His eyes flared, briefly. A few dark flakes of ash drifted to the ground like dirty snow. "Yes. So tell me, how *would* you like to die, since you seem to be so keen on breaking free of me? Fire? I can make it painless."

I winced. "But what if it is possible, Amir? What no one has ever tried?"

This made him laugh. "People have tried. My brothers aren't all very nice. Odious as you find me, you'd find some of them much worse."

I forced myself to breathe. And yet, looking at his dark skin under light dappled by a nearby tree, I couldn't help but wonder what might happen without this artificial obligation between us. If it were possible, shouldn't we know? "But let's say that it did work. And I didn't die. Would you be in trouble? Would the djinn council exile you?"

Amir ran his hand up the bark of the tree, each touch of his fingertips leaving a small black singe. But he seemed abstracted from his agitation, a man torn between different sides of himself.

"I can't imagine why," he said, finally.

I sighed in deep relief. "Your brother," I said, "is almost as rank a liar as you."

"Runs in the family, dear."

I started walking again, but I didn't make it very far. Amir pulled me back, very gently, by the wrist. I faced him with about as much conscious thought as a leaf falling to the ground. He lifted my chin with one hand and twined his hand in mine with the other. My lips burned. I nearly closed my eyes. But he didn't kiss me.

"If you're planning to kill yourself," he said, "could you at least give me a few hours notice?"

"I'm not planning to kill myself."

"Or break free, however you're planning to try. Will you tell me?"

I wanted to say no. I fully intended to say no. "If you want," I said. "But you can't stop me."

"Could I ever?" He laughed. "Do you promise?"

"Okay," I said.

He let me go. I stumbled on the sidewalk. I wondered if he would reach down to catch me and then touch my bare skin and perhaps raise my chin again—

But he let me pick myself up. Left alone, I recalled the other request that Mrs. Brandon had refused, but I had to manage somehow. "I need a favor," I said. "I need your help getting in somewhere."

"If it's the moon, I can't help you."

"Almost," I said. "The morgue."

"You're never boring," he said, and took my hand.

CHAPTER SEVEN

"Aileen," I said, "you look like you're going to a funeral. In your own shroud."

"The ladies expect a certain dignity." Aileen secured the edge of her black headscarf with a pin. Though I stood right beside her vanity in the tiny dressing room, I felt as though she were not so much a person as a floating head. Every inch of skin besides her face was covered in a severe, shapeless black dress that resembled a nun's habit. Though an evening rainstorm had finally brought the temperature back to something bearable, it was hardly cool enough outside or in to warrant such enthusiastic body covering. I fanned myself pointedly.

"They think you'll be better able to contact the other side if you overheat on stage?"

"They trust me more if I look ethereal and otherworldly. Not like a flapper. Here, be useful and help me powder my face."

I sighed, and knelt so I was eye level with her seated at the vanity.

I had to admit that I was impressed by the sumptuousness of the Spiritualist Society headquarters. No wonder Aileen ran herself ragged for them. Tonight's Thursday evening séance was, she claimed, her biggest event yet. They must be paying her handsomely. Not that I had seen much evidence of Aileen *spending* the money, but perhaps she was saving it for some big purchase.

Aileen closed her eyes and I dusted the brush lightly over her face. I stopped.

"What's the matter?" Aileen said.

"You look hideous. What is this, flour?"

"Talcum powder," she said, sighing. "For heaven's sake, Zeph, I'm not trying to catch a beau. Hurry up."

"You want to look like a ghost?" I said, whitening Aileen's already pale face.

She smiled thinly. "Or like someone who could have a conversation with one."

A sharp rap on the door startled me into dropping the brush. Aileen cursed. "Christ above, is it time already?" she muttered, and then, in a louder voice, "Come in!"

But the intruder wasn't the young and portly woman who served as under-secretary of the Spiritualist Society who had greeted Aileen so warmly at the door a half hour earlier. It was Lily, red-faced and dripping wet.

"Goodness, did you run here from the Flatiron Building?" I asked. It was still raining outside. I couldn't imagine what would have possessed Lily to ruin her clothes in this weather.

Lily slammed the door. "I just heard back from the chemist," she said, ignoring my question. She slipped off her jacket and then her blouse. "Do you have anything dry lying around, Aileen?" she said. "Not that fearsome habit, though. I'd rather be wet."

"There's a dress in the closet," Aileen said, picking up the brush and finishing the powder herself.

Lily pulled out the dress—well-cared-for, at least a few years old. She sighed. "Better than nothing, I suppose."

Aileen shrugged. "Take me shopping if you want to borrow better clothes."

"Just as soon as I solve the crime of the decade, darling." She kicked her skirt to the corner of the room, nearly missing me.

"So you ran here because you heard from a chemist?" I asked, moving into what I hoped was a safe corner of the room.

"You wouldn't *believe* the traffic on Broadway. Anyway, I admit I was a little put out by the vampire delivery boy—the doorman nearly had a fit—but the bottle was worth it, Zeph."

I'd nearly forgotten I had told Charlie to give it to her a million years ago this morning. My pulse sped. "There's something in the Faust?" I said. "Some vampire poison?"

"I don't know about poison, but there's something. He said he'd run more tests, but right now it looks like the Faust has been spiked."

"Liquor?" I hadn't expected that. The manner of the deaths hadn't resembled alcohol poisoning.

She pulled the dress over her head. "No, no," she said, her voice muffled by the fabric. "Why would a vampire spike Faust with liquor? They spike it with *blood*."

"Of course!" I said. "So it's tainted blood, then? Something bad enough to kill them?"

"That's his best guess, though it turns out no one knows much about sucker body chemistry. It's hard to say what a human would have to do to their own blood to kill a vampire."

"Could it have been an accident?" If the blood came from mob sources, a bad taint didn't much surprise me.

She shrugged and knelt next to Aileen in front of the vanity. "Once, maybe," she said. "But it's happened too many times, with different bottles. And now with that poor police officer . . . Aileen, what have you done to your face? It's not 1920 anymore. You can afford a little color."

"She wants to look like a ghost," I said.

Aileen sighed. "It's just talcum powder."

"You look like a cadaver," Lily said, "but I suppose if that's what they want."

"Thank you, Lily," Aileen said, looking pointedly at me. "For displaying such an uncharacteristic empathy for the realities of earning one's keep."

"There's earning your keep," I said, "and practically whoring yourself for a bunch of old ladies who don't know the first thing about the Sight."

Aileen whirled around, so pale and colorless that the red of her unstained lips looked like blood. "And you do, Miss Vampire Suffragette? You said you'd help me find a way out of this, remember? Back when that sucker swayed me and my whole world went to hell? Well, it's been six months, Zeph. Where's the help? Where's my way back to normal? Because if you don't have that, then stop treating me like one of your bloody charity cases for the bloody Citizen's Council! If I have to have the Sight, then this is how I'll use it, and I'll thank you for not always looking at me like I'm about to fall apart."

She turned back to the vanity.

"Aileen . . . I . . ." I didn't know what to say. I knew I had behaved badly, but felt put-upon and defensive all the same.

Lily had the look of a woman who hadn't meant to step into a snake pit, but she gamely put a hand on Aileen's shoulder. "I'm sure she didn't mean it like that," Lily said.

"I take it you haven't been on the receiving end of Zephyr's disapproval."

"I wouldn't say that."

"I didn't meant to disapprove of you, Aileen," I said.

"What would you call it, then?"

I paused. "Concern," I said.

"Of course." She stood. "Well, this has been lovely, both of you, but I have a veil to part."

Someone knocked on the door. Aileen opened it, moving with the grace of a true ghost.

"What are you doing here?" she said, sounding none too pleased.

I peered over her shoulder and was startled to see Amir. "Looking for Zephyr," he said, and sighed.

"You too?" Aileen stepped back to let him in.

Lily checked herself in the vanity mirror, decided that she looked well enough and gave him a practiced smile. "Fancy seeing you again," she said.

"Lovely as ever, Miss . . . Harding, was it?" he said.

I would have rolled my eyes, but Aileen was close enough to hit me.

"How did you get backstage?" I asked.

Amir leaned against the wall and his sleeve brushed my arm. I swear he meant to do it, but his face was bland as butter. "You're pulling quite the crowd out there," he said to Aileen. "I think I caught sight of the mayor's Duesenberg outside. No one paid me much attention."

"The mayor?" said Lily and Aileen in unison, one with excitement and the other with terror.

"What would the mayor want to do with me?" Aileen asked.

Amir's smile wobbled. "I suspect he wants to contact a ghost," he said.

I groaned. "His father?"

"Not exactly." Amir glanced at Aileen.

"Who, then?" Aileen asked.

He looked away from both of us, unaccountably abashed. "It seems . . . I ran into Mrs. Brandon outside. He wants to contact the dead vampires."

Lily dove for her bag and pulled out a slightly damp reporter's notebook and a pen. "The mayor wants to contact *vampire* ghosts? Just to be clear."

Aileen drilled her fingers against the doorframe. "Why would he want to do that?"

"To ask who killed them?" Lily hazarded. "But I didn't think vampires could have ghosts. Is it possible, Aileen?"

"I didn't think so. I don't think I've ever talked to one, but that might not mean anything."

Amir's countenance had turned so dyspeptic I would have suspected him of a stomach upset if he were human. But I understood his expression very well—it mirrored my own, realizing how badly awry his scheme from this afternoon had gone.

"You just had to mention vampire ghosts!" I snarled. "So much for listening to Daddy's advice!"

"This is amazing," said Lily.

"Fuck," said Aileen.

Someone else knocked on the door. I opened it.

"Harry!" I said. My brother stood in the doorway, and the undersecretary came into view right behind him. "Aileen," she said. "Aileen dear, they're calling for you."

"Break a leg," said Lily.

Aileen gasped. "What?"

"It's theater slang," Lily said airily. "It means good luck."

"Zephyr," said Harry, pulling me out of the dressing room and into the hallway, while the others went to the stage. "You have to be careful."

"Have you been following me again? Wait until I tell Mama—"

"Listen," he said, bending down until his mouth was by my ear. "Archibald Madison is here. And guess who's with him? That other fellow, the one I've seen snooping around after you."

"How did you know I'd be here?" I asked.

"I followed Madison's guy. Which meant I followed you, I guess."

"Christ," I said.

"Do you have a gun?"

"Of course I don't have a gun, Harry! When do I ever carry a gun?"

He nodded. "What I thought. Here." He reached into his pocket and pulled out a pocket pistol. "Keep it."

I backed up. "Not a chance," I said.

"Papa'll kill me—"

"Papa's too crazy to kill you! Just leave me alone. I've got too much—"

Lily waved frantically at me from down the hall. Aileen's performance must be starting. "Just, talk to me after, okay? Nothing will happen here."

I left Harry standing in the hall while I caught up with Lily and Amir, who were watching from the wings behind the stage. Directly in front of us, heavy black curtains blocked our view of the small stage. Further curtains remained bunched above, but if I moved carefully to the far right, I could see Aileen's silhouette and the packed throng that had come to see her tonight.

"I'm the only reporter here!" Lily whispered. "Breslin will give me the front page for sure. And look over there—isn't that the partner of that vampire officer who got killed this morning?"

I followed her finger automatically, but I should have known even without looking. Of course McConnell would be here. If he'd heard the rumor that Aileen—the darling of the New York Spiritualist Society—was going to attempt contact with the dead vampires, he would have had to come. But the sight of him turned my formless dread into something hard and difficult to digest.

Amir wasn't looking at the audience. He was looking at Aileen, settling herself on the single chair in the middle of the stage. Perhaps he wouldn't have appeared upset to anyone else, but I had spent the past several months in his company and I knew that face.

"Yes," I whispered angrily. "This is your fault. Vampires don't have ghosts! What's going to happen when she can't contact them in front of all these people!"

Lily looked at us intently, though I was fairly sure she couldn't have heard me. Still, Amir pulled me into the hall. "How was I supposed to know he'd find a medium!"

"Maybe," I snarled, "because you *impersonated* a *ghost*! Who was he supposed to ask, the electrician?"

"Aileen isn't a dumb Dora," he said, more worried than angry. "If she can't contact a vampire, she'll make something up, won't she?"

"She can't always," I said. "When she gets deep into the Sight, sometimes she can't control anything." That, I thought, was why I'd so disapproved of her using it for money. The Sight was too dangerous. I ignored the voice that told me such danger was her decision, and surely she would understand it better than I, regardless.

Inside the auditorium, the audience clapped enthusiastically.

"Oh, God," I said.

"I didn't realize this would happen," he said.

I sighed. "You never do." I left him and walked back to the side stage, where Lily watched the proceedings with giddy fascination.

"I'm delighted to present, to such an illustrious audience, the woman who seems poised to become the greatest medium of our generation." That was the head of the Society, I gathered, sounding far too pleased with herself. *Aileen's doing all the work*, I thought crossly. Aileen glanced up at the ceiling, as though distracted by something beyond normal sight. At least she put on a good act. I felt terrible about our fight; I wished I'd had a chance to apologize before her performance.

"Please be aware that the mastery of a gift as prodigious as hers sometimes requires time. I request that you keep complete silence while she contacts the Other Side. And now, may I present the great Lady Cassandra."

Lady Cassandra? I snorted, but thankfully another round of

clapping covered the sound. Anticipation permeated the room like a low-lying fog.

Aileen lowered her gaze and spoke, her Irish accent measured and uncanny. "Who among you wishes to speak to the dead?" she asked.

∞

In the end, McConnell made the request. I'd half expected Jimmy Walker himself to rise and make some irritatingly charming speech, but he sat in the far back, as though he wished to avoid notice. This did not deter everyone in the audience from periodically turning their heads, as though curious about a piece of lint on their shoulders. New York's most flamboyant mayor ignored the attention. Mrs. Brandon had seated herself near the front, as close to Aileen as possible. She looked at the short stage with almost devotional intensity. I recalled the photograph of her late husband: he had earnest eyes, even in faded sepia. Determined and yet slightly ill-at-ease in an old-fashioned suit. I knew she must have loved him very much, to hope for a contact during every one of Aileen's sessions.

When Aileen had asked her question, she was greeted with murmurs and silence. She didn't seem perturbed by this, merely waited on her wooden chair, still as a nun contemplating God. Then McConnell rose to his feet. He wore an evening suit a few years out of date, clumsily patched by the shoulder. Though I had every reason to fear and loathe him, I could only muster an overwhelming pity. He seemed dazed, still reeling from Zuckerman's death. I hoped that, despite Amir's thoughtless prank, Aileen *would* be able to contact a vampire ghost. The whole city would benefit if we could actually catch the killer so quickly, even if it didn't help swing the votes against Faust.

"Mort Zuckerman," McConnell said clearly. "If you think you can find him, I'd be much obliged."

Aileen nodded thoughtfully, as though the name meant nothing to her. I had to smile—she knew her audience. Even her unnaturally white face seemed appropriately haunted in the low glow from the surrounding gas lamps (the building was fully wired, of course, but I gathered the flickering orange light was better for ambiance).

"Do you have an object of importance to the deceased?" she asked.

McConnell nodded. "His notebook."

"Bring it to me."

McConnell pushed his way to the aisle and handed a square object to one of the waiting attendants. Aileen handled it carefully, as though the soul of the deceased might reside in the object itself. I recognized that notebook from my encounters with Zuckerman—he had chosen odd times to write things down, as though his notes had remarkably little to do with our conversation.

Aileen rested it on her lap. "I will see if the spirits provide," she said.

McConnell stared plaintively. The rest of the audience leaned forward with a rustle of clothes and indrawn breaths.

"The medium requires absolute silence," said the head of the Society, quite unnecessarily. Lily tugged at my shirtsleeve, as though I were in any danger of looking away.

In the ensuing silence, Aileen began to sway, like a mother rocking a baby. Her eyes opened and closed at seemingly random intervals—too long for blinking and too short for sleep. She spoke on occasion, but the sounds were nonsense, or at least not any language I recognized.

"Think she's on the level?" Lily whispered.

"I think so." Just observing her slow sway raised goose bumps on my arms.

The gas lamps flickered, though the air in the room remained stiflingly still. Aileen's voice grew louder and higher, though no more intelligible than before. The lights flickered again, almost guttering in an absent breeze. The few strands of Aileen's hair not secured beneath the black scarf floated in a nimbus around her face. She seemed to glow with electricity instead of light.

"Mort," she screamed, as though over a howling wind. "Will you come? Will you speak?"

It could have been a room full of vampires, so little of our breath moved the air. She rose, so fluidly it seemed she floated. Her eyes were wide and unblinking, but she held her hands before her as though moving through a thick gloom. "So far under," she said, as though to herself. "Where have they hidden you?"

In the audience, someone whimpered. There was no way to know who; I think perhaps the same fear ran through all of us. What I was seeing here made the uncanny reading she had done for Lily the night they first met in our parlor seem like a child's game. I might have spent the last six months avoiding my potential power, but Aileen had clearly embraced hers. I knew at once that the head of the Society had not exaggerated in her praise. It shocked me that she could have grown this powerful and I hadn't even noticed.

"Mort," she said, again. "Are you there? Can you hear me?" She paused and drew herself up. "He is between the veils. The one I can part, the one I cannot. But I can hear him. He has not gone too far beyond us."

"Mort!" McConnell shouted, entirely out of order. "Who killed you? Who gave you that damned bottle, just tell me and I'll—"

"Quiet in the hall!"

A few rows down from McConnell, Archibald Madison whispered to the man sitting beside him. With a start, I recognized the strange man who had caught me in Madison's office and behaved so oddly— was *he* the one who had so worried my brother? The man nodded and left quickly through a side door. I looked behind me for Harry, but both he and Amir had vanished.

"Do you hear us, Mort?" Aileen said, ignoring the commotion

entirely. Silence fell again, absolute. Aileen stayed frozen in a half crouch for nearly a minute. Then she jerked upright. The movement disturbed me, but I didn't understand why until she spoke.

"McConnell?" she said, with a sharp laugh I had never heard her make. "This is something. Your voice sounds different in her ears. You know I'm dead?"

McConnell coughed and wiped his dripping forehead. "Sure I know," he said. His voice shook perceptibly. "But I don't know who killed you."

That was not Aileen on the stage. It looked like her, even spoke with her voice, but she had been inhabited by someone else—a dead police officer who shouldn't even have a soul, let alone conversational ability. But Aileen even mimicked some of Zuckerman's mannerisms, like the way he scrunched in his lips as if he'd bitten a lemon. Lily kept scribbling, but her hand trembled so violently I doubted the script was legible.

"The informant gave me the bottle," Aileen-Zuckerman said. The audience gasped—I did, too, though I had no idea who "the informant" might be.

"He forced you to drink, right?" McConnell said.

But Aileen-Zuckerman shook her head. "I tried Faust the second week it hit the streets. Everyone did. You never guessed. But McConnell, follow up with the Blood Bank—"

A commotion in the audience interrupted her. Judith Brandon, of all people, stood with a frantic expression. "Someone's on stage!"

I caught a shadow at the edge of my vision. I turned, but it was too late: with a sharp crack, the backstage electric lights turned off, rendering me temporarily blind. Then a gunshot and a small cry and the unmistakable thump of a body hitting the floor. I ran without a thought for anyone but Aileen. The front stage curtains had fallen about halfway, so even the hazy gas lamps couldn't illuminate the scene.

I bumped into a body with my shins and dropped to the floor. When I looked down, I could barely make out Aileen's white powdered face.

I called her name, but she didn't respond. I put my finger to her cloth-enshrouded neck, and was unspeakably relieved to find her pulse steady, if weak. Unfortunately, given Aileen's taste in performance clothing, it would be difficult for me to find evidence of a wound even in good lighting. And I had not forgotten the shadowy figure from just before the lights went out.

"Zephyr!" Lily screamed. Just that, but it was enough for me to throw myself over Aileen's body. A blow that would have hit my head connected instead with the floor beneath me. I couldn't see my attacker very well even now—just that he seemed stocky and strong and bent on harming either me or Aileen. Neither was acceptable. I dove for his legs, hoping surprise could overcome his superior strength. He toppled to the floor like a carnival dummy, with a crash and a curse. This satisfied me even as I pressed my advantage, giving him a solid blow to the stomach. I wondered if my knife was sharp enough to do much damage to a human assailant. But I didn't have time to hunt for it beneath my skirt. With a grunt, the man wrenched out of my one-handed grip and walloped me on the side of my head. I fell to the floor, barely retaining consciousness. From my position beside Aileen, I saw the hazy figure of a man lurch to his feet and spit perilously close to my face.

"I had to," he whispered, and I finally recognized him as the man from Madison's office. "She would have said everything. Didn't mean to hit you." I stared, baffled, and attempted to get my arms underneath me. I flopped uselessly to the ground a moment later, but thankfully my assailant refrained from further violence. He just turned around and loped away. My third attempt to rise succeeded. Almost immediately, I wished it hadn't.

My head ached and my vision wobbled like a jelly mold. "Catch him!" I rasped.

I wouldn't have thought anyone had heard me—especially over the screaming, shouting racket coming from the auditorium behind the half-fallen curtains. But another shadow detached itself from the wall and set off after my assailant at a dead run with a whoop.

I *definitely* knew that voice. I smiled. Lily, apparently having decided she was in no immediate danger, ran over.

"Are you all right?" she said.

"I think you have a scoop," I said, gingerly touching the swelling at my temple. It didn't feel as bad as I'd feared, though Lily was still in danger of getting vomit all over her haute couture. I decided it was best not to tell her.

"Ha!" Lily said, her voice shaking a little. "I think I have twenty. Is Aileen . . ."

We both looked over. "Aileen," I called gently. She was breathing and her pulse was steady, but she didn't respond to us at all. Deep in the hallway backstage, someone shouted.

"Who in the blazes was that?" Lily asked, gripping my elbow.

My smile widened. "I think we're about to find out."

The Society under-secretary poked her head beneath the curtain, her cheeks flushed apple-red. "Are you . . . Has it . . ."

"We seem fine," I said, hoping my assertion made it true. "I heard a shot, but as far as I can tell, Aileen wasn't hit."

The woman raised her eyes heavenward and put a doughy hand over her chest. "Thank the lord," she said. "The police are on their way. I'm sure they'll catch whoever—"

The backstage lights as well as those in the auditorium flickered and then came back on with a high-pitched whine. I had never been so grateful for illumination: Aileen still hadn't regained consciousness, but at least I could be sure she wasn't quietly bleeding to death.

A few seconds later, Harry came bounding back through the hall, a man slung across his broad shoulders.

Lily's eyes went wide as she saw him: a picture of youthful vigor and beauty, a dashing curl across his forehead.

"Got him, Zeph!" Harry proclaimed, tossing the man to the floor with somewhat vindictive force. He groaned, which reassured me—I didn't want Harry locked up for murder, even in self-defense. Daddy would cover the legal fees, but how he would complain.

The curtain was still half-fallen, but from my vantage point I could see quite a few waists drifting closer to the stage. I contemplated standing, but decided it was far more comfortable down here. The room still rocked in a manner that might have been pleasant had I been drunk.

The mayor poked his head beneath the curtain, a mere foot away from me. "Miss Hollis," he said, a little breathlessly. "I always find you in the most fascinating situations. Is that man . . ."

"The culprit," Harry said, nudging the man in the ribs with the toe of his leather boot. I wondered, idly, how Harry had managed to afford such well-tooled shoes. They were probably a present from some monogrammed letterhead or another, I decided.

The man rolled over, allowing me to see his face clearly for the first time. I had never seen him before that day in Madison's office, and yet both times he had behaved as though he knew me. I wondered why, but the faint, shimmering haze that seemed to have settled over my vision made it difficult to concentrate.

"How hard did that bastard hit me?" I muttered.

The mayor raised his eyebrows. "Such language, Miss Hollis."

"Such prudery, Mr. Walker," I said.

Judith Brandon's head joined that of her well-placed employer. "Isn't that Madison's man? What's his name . . ."

Jimmy Walker's sudden smile held more than a touch of schadenfreude. "Why, aren't you right, Judith? It's one of his foundling puppies. And it seems he assaulted a famous medium in public just as she would have divulged the identity of the vampire killer."

I swear Walker was about to lick his well-formed lips. He raised his eyes heavenward. "My thanks, Boss," he said, quietly.

"Mayor," I said, aware my words were slurring and not entirely inclined to care, "you seem to like your ghosts."

"I confess to being a convert," said the mayor, his eyebrows raised in arch innocence. "What information the dead possess! And I have a suspicion, you see." He ducked his head back under the curtain. "Madison!" he called, his stentorian politician voice booming like a foghorn through the continued din. "The proceedings on stage might be of interest to you."

I looked back at Madison's assistant, now groaning his way back to consciousness beneath Harry's expensive shoes. I did not worry that he posed a further danger to me or Aileen. Harry was a Hollis, after all, and could do our daddy proud without my assistance.

By the time Madison himself poked his head under the curtain, the mayor was clearly not the only one wondering about his relationship with the man on the floor. But only my favorite deb reporter had the guts to say so.

"Mr. Madison," Lily said, flipping to a fresh page in her notebook, "did your associate kill officer Zuckerman and the other vampires?"

Madison's ruddy face turned the shade of pickled beets. I giggled.

"How dare you imply such a thing, young lady!" His voice was very loud, and a few drops of foam-flecked spittle sprayed my cheek.

Lily wiped her forehead. "Well, he did assault the medium just as she was about to reveal the identity of the killer."

"It's all fraud and nonsense," Madison said, with quite unnecessary vigor.

I turned to him. "You spat in my ear."

He stared at me like I was a statue that had inexplicably begun to talk. "I beg your pardon?" he managed.

"It wasn't very pleasant."

"Why . . . I'm quite sorry."

From deep inside the hallway, I heard the sound of several booted feet running toward the stage. I looked between Lily and the mayor.

"Who do you suppose that is?" I asked.

"The police, I hope," said the under-secretary.

"I'm sure they'll sort this all out in a jiffy," said the mayor. He pulled out a gray pocket square and dabbed at a sheen of sweat on his forehead. "I'm afraid, however, that I must depart. I have a prior engagement—"

"At the Ziegfeld, I'm sure," I said. Judith Brandon glared at me, but the mayor just blinked in surprise and laughed.

"Everybody stay right where you are!" That was McConnell—to my surprise, I'd quite forgotten about him in the confusion. But he was at the head of a dozen of New York's finest, crowding the stage and pointing their firearms quite indiscriminately.

"Who fired the shot?" McConnell asked no one in particular.

My brother, who has always been lacking in common sense, stepped forward. "I did, sir," he said.

McConnell trained his gun on Harry, who didn't look nearly as perturbed as he ought. A few feet away, the man groaned and his eyes fluttered.

"Which of them did you shoot?" McConnell asked.

At this, Harry bristled. "Neither, of course. He attacked the medium and I fired into the ceiling to scare him off."

"Will Lady Cassandra be all right?" McConnell asked.

I checked Aileen hopefully for signs of consciousness, but she remained prone and insensate. Worry clamped my chest, and I wondered how much of her pallor could be attributed to cosmetics.

"I don't know. I think perhaps she needs a doctor," I said, and swayed.

Lily caught me. "Zephyr, what's wrong with you?" she whispered.

"Just a . . . head thing," I said. "Used to happen all the time in Montana. It'll go away in a day or so."

McConnell put away his gun and walked closer to Aileen. "Perhaps she'll remember what Zuckerman was going to say?"

"I certainly hope so," said Jimmy Walker. "I'm afraid the city can't stand much more of this. But perhaps, officer, your culprit has already revealed himself?"

The mayor nodded toward Madison's man, who blinked in the manner of one unwillingly roused from a deep sleep just as a police officer cuffed him.

"Yes, Mr. Madison," Lily said, a hound with blood in her nose. "What about the crimes of your associate? Did you encourage him to kill unsuspecting vampires, including Officer Zuckerman?"

"I deny it completely!" he said, and wriggled awkwardly under the curtain from the theater floor until he was able to get his legs beneath him on stage. "If he committed any crimes in this matter, they are his own."

McConnell stood his ground before Madison's bluster. "I seem to recall you telling your followers that it's God's calling to do anything to beat back the vampire scourge," he said. "And now someone in your employ appears to have killed them. That's a remarkable coincidence, Mr. Madison."

"I encourage no one to break the law," Madison said angrily, but he looked at the crowd around him like I imagined a fox might watch the approaching hounds. "I merely advocate that we do all we can to keep our city safe from *them*."

"In that case, I'm sure you'll have no objection to us searching your offices for any evidence relating to the crime?"

"You may search Brad's desk, of course. But much of my work is of a sensitive and confidential nature, and nothing of mine would be of use in your investigation."

Remembering what I had found in the false bottom drawer of his office desk, I could well understand his discomfort with the idea.

"We'll see, won't we?" McConnell said, and turned around. The man, Brad, had sat up, staring like he was more or less awake. "And what do you have to say for yourself?"

Brad blinked slowly. He surveyed the attentive crowd with a deliberate, burning hatred that made me shudder. I suddenly had no doubt that he had killed those vampires. "I don't say anything."

"Did you kill Mort, you—" McConnell choked back what promised to be an epithet too colorful for polite company.

Brad's eyes darted around the room—landing on me, the mayor, Judith Brandon, and Madison before finally settling on his accuser.

"I won't talk," he said.

McConnell sighed. "Take this one back to the station. Get her a doctor," he said, gesturing to Aileen. "The rest of you are free to go. We might need to speak to you for questioning later. I haven't forgotten about you, Miss Hollis."

I groaned, just a little. "I never thought otherwise, officer."

The crowd dispersed as soon as the officers hauled Brad away. I stayed by Aileen with Lily.

"We should get her back home," I said, though the thought of managing such a complicated matter was exacerbating the nausea caused by the blow to my head.

"Yes," she said. "I'll call a doctor. I'll need someone to get her into the taxi, though."

"That's a good idea," I agreed, and surged to my knees.

"Will you . . . Zephyr, what is a head thing?"

"You should move your shoes," I said.

Lily jumped back like I had shown her a snake. And good thing, as I proceeded to vomit all over the stage.

———

Harry took me out back. We determined that further evacuation of my stomach was best conducted away from the Society head, whose shrieks still echoed behind us.

"Remember that time in the Black Hills? Those revenants?"

I groaned and laughed at the same time. "Barely. I couldn't see straight for a week. Daddy said it served me right for not hitting soon enough."

"Never made that mistake again though, did you?" Harry said.

I gulped the relatively cool night air and gratefully rested against my brother's side. "Guess not," I said. "I should have seen that blow coming."

"You're out of practice," Harry said. "How often do you train?"

I attempted a glower, but it ended in a second, less violent, purging. "I'm attempting a higher good," I said, wiping my mouth with a shaking hand. Harry handed me his handkerchief.

"You still oughtta train," he said. "What would Daddy say if he saw you back there?"

I smiled in the face of his concern. "I don't know, Harry. Rumor has it he's gone crazy." We were silent for a moment, listening to the cars trundling past the alley that now reeked of vomit in addition to garbage and piss.

"You should have been born first," I said, suddenly. "You'd give him less grief."

Harry drew himself up and cocked his head. "I doubt that, Zephyr," he said, and I recalled the not quite secret about the nature of his love life.

"Let's go out front," I said. "It stinks in here."

"I can't imagine why," Harry said, and kept a firm grip on my elbow. A few people milled about outside, but I noticed one immediately.

"Amir!" I said, yanking my arm from Harry's grip and stumbling toward him. "Where on earth have you been! You missed all the excitement!"

He looked angry as he turned, though that didn't worry me because I was always doing something or other to annoy him. It was part of the charm, really. But then his eyes widened and his face took on a rather disturbing greenish tinge.

"Zephyr, what—"

Harry caught me before I fell. "Sorry," he said, blushing. "She's a little . . ."

"Splifficated?"

The two people with whom Amir had been conversing with turned to me. I gasped. "Elspeth! Sofia! What are you—it's not Sunday, is it?"

Sofia smiled. "Thursday," she said.

"Zephyr Hollis," said Elspeth, "have you been drinking?"

"I have not!" I said. "Though it sounds like a swell idea."

"I don't think so, Zeph," Harry said.

Amir leaned down to look in my eyes. "Did you hit your head?"

I giggled. "We have a winner! But it wasn't my fault. Madison's man hit *me*."

Harry shrugged helplessly. "It was a mess in there."

"Is she all right?" Amir asked.

"I'm fine!"

"I'm a little worried," Harry said.

I leaned toward Amir and caught myself on his waistcoat. "He's just afraid of Daddy," I whispered.

Amir set me back upright with careful, warm hands. "*I'm* afraid of your daddy," he said. "I take it this is your brother?"

"Harry Hollis," Harry said, extending his hand. "And you are?"

Amir's mouth twisted a little. "Amir al-Natar ibn Kashkash, youngest prince of Shadukiam, the great city of roses, at your service." He executed an ostentatiously formal bow, mostly directed at Sofia and Elspeth.

"You never told me you knew a prince, Zeph," Harry said.

"He's just showing off," I said. "Amir is my genie."

Amir sighed. "And Zephyr is my cross," he said. "Though apparently she means to be rid of me on Sunday."

Elspeth shifted uncomfortably. "You *told* him?" I said. Indignation didn't agree with my stomach. I swallowed back bile.

"He seemed to know already," Elspeth said. "We were trying to find you, but—"

Sofia said something in her language, to which Amir responded with a shrug.

"Sofia says she understands now why you want to be rid of him."

For some reason, this made my nausea even more acute. The world deepened its greenish hue. "She does?"

Sofia interrupted Elspeth's dutiful translation with a wave of her hand. They argued for a brief moment and then Elspeth shook her head.

"This one," said Sofia, in her perfectly intelligible, if limited, English. "Too hot. No control. You," she said, pressing one finger against my chest for emphasis, "need control."

I opened my mouth, sure some suitable protest would emerge. "That's . . ."

Amir's laugh did not sound very mirthful. "Entirely accurate?"

He said something to Sofia, who beamed at him like a proud mother. I scowled. I should have guessed Amir would charm her. Control, Sofia had said. Well, perhaps she was right. Was it such a sin to desire to steer the boat of one's own life? And how could I, with Amir burning and observing and aggravating me every day? How could I, if I always had to care about him?

"Why did you want to talk?" I asked Elspeth.

"Sofia did," she said. "I asked her about the story you told me—the djinni whose vessel broke free."

"And?" I asked.

"Zephyr," Amir said, "I already told you—"

"It's true. The last djinni whose vessel broke free was exiled for life."

It was *true*? I hadn't expected this. It felt like more of a blow than it ought, like Brad had hit me with a billy club instead of his fist.

I whirled on Amir, squinting against the glare of electric lamps flickering greenly behind him. "You are a rank, shameless, unprincipled liar!"

Harry put a tentative hand on my shoulder, as though to steady me, but I wrenched free. "How dare you! Especially about something so important?"

Amir had looked vaguely guilty, but now he drew himself up, every inch a prince. "Why? So I could use guilt to make you remain in a situation so clearly untenable to you? Perhaps I'm shameless as you say, but I have more pride than that."

The lights flickered greener. My body felt light, as though it might come up off the sidewalk itself, but if I kept my gaze straight on Amir's dark eyes, I could keep myself from swaying. "You've been trying to convince me to make a wish for *months*," I said. "Why stop now?"

"It's my greatest desire, darling," Amir said angrily, but with an undercurrent of something like tenderness. He took my elbow and led me a few feet away from the others. "But Kardal crossed a line in telling you that story—yes, of course, I guessed from the moment you asked. It reeks of Kardal. He didn't tell you the full tale, you know. Just enough to manipulate you."

"Then tell me now. I should at least know the truth before I decide."

Amir smiled. "No," he said.

"I have the right to make my own decisions, Amir!"

"Of course you do," he said. "But you don't have the right to all the details of my life."

"Shouldn't I know if this will hurt you?" I hadn't meant to sound so plaintive, but it was all I could do to keep the unspoken *again* from damning the end of the sentence.

"You've already decided," he said. "I just hope you pick your payment wisely."

"Payment?"

"Whatever power ends up taking your bargain," he said, "will demand a great deal in return."

The demon's price. I had avoided thinking of that all week. Now the reality of the choice weighed on my shoulders like a lead mantle. Or an albatross. Amir thought I had already decided, but I didn't feel very sure anymore. The world glowed green and Amir smelled of roses and Sofia's pastries. *Magic*, I thought.

"Amir," I said, "you'll still get me into the morgue, won't you?"

"Of course, *habibti*," he said, and caught me when I floated to the ground.

CHAPTER EIGHT

I awoke on a bed of honey and spice, the humming drone of bees warm in my ears.

"Could I have the one with the pistachios?" I murmured. Perhaps one of the houris of this paradise could dash to Sofia's bakery.

"I'm afraid I only have water at the moment," said a voice that most emphatically did not belong to a houri. I still held out the possibility that I might be in paradise.

The buzzing faded and I opened my eyes. Amir, looking down at me, his skin once again a healthy brown.

"You look much better without green," I said.

Amir shook his head and handed me a glass of water. I had a horrible taste in my mouth, now that I thought on it. I gulped it down, spilling a good deal on my blouse.

"Where are we?" I asked. "Where did everyone else go? Did you say you can get into the morgue?"

I felt better than I had in front of the Spiritualist Society, though still woozy.

Amir propped me upright against silken pillows and put the empty glass down on the side table. "The Ritz," he said, ticking the answers off on his fingers. "Various directions. You were quite insensible and your brother had a previous engagement, so I elected to bring you here rather than learn of your untimely demise in your garret on Ludlow. And yes, but perhaps we had better postpone illicit murder investigations until you can stand unassisted? In any case, from what I heard, the murderer himself walked onstage and hit you on the head."

I snuggled deeper into the deliciously soft pillows. He slept like this every night? "It does seem likely," I said. "But he didn't admit to anything."

"And those bodies . . ." Amir trailed off, his smell briefly flaring with sulphur. "I did some reconnaissance at the morgue this evening. You should see them. They weren't vampires, whatever they were."

"Human?" I asked, heart pounding.

He looked at me very frankly. "I'm not sure."

The moment held, and changed. Midnight pupils sparked, flint against hard stone. I held my breath, watching him watch me, wondering at the look in those inhuman eyes and understanding it completely. I thought, it's my head, nothing more. Amir had hardly touched me for six months, after all. I hadn't encouraged it; we were better off without such treacherous, heady thoughts. At least until I broke the bond. At least until I forgave him.

My lungs betrayed me; I breathed in deeply, the unbearably rich scent of him far too familiar and far too welcome. He leaned forward. His hair needed to be cut—the pomade had long since lost its grip and dark locks fell over his eyes. He didn't seem to notice, deliberately closing the distance between us. I reached out and brushed back his hair. My hand stayed there, buried in its luxurious thickness as though trapped.

"*Habibti*," he said, "may I kiss you?"

I felt nearly as light-headed as I had after my blow to the head, but I knew I wouldn't faint. There was clarity in this moment. Clarity and fear and the barest outline of something like a decision.

"*You wondered at my ills, but my health was the wonder,*" I said, a whisper from another world.

Amir froze. "*The Bearer of Love?* You read Arabic poetry?"

"You said it to me, right after I killed Rinaldo. Kardal told me what it meant."

"*Each time a bond broke, through you a new bond came . . .* so my brother is good for something, after all. Should I thank Abu Nuwas for my life, Zephyr?"

My hand was still in his hair. Carefully, I removed it. And yet, somehow, the gesture moved us even closer, mere inches apart— painfully aware of the other's presence, and yet never touching.

"No," I said, and realized it was true.

"Then why?" he asked.

For some reason, I thought of Sofia and our bargain. To break the bond, I would have to offer a demon something I would hate to lose. I felt so close to understanding it now, like I was waking up from a dream in which I had learned the secret of life, but couldn't quite recall the wording.

"Perhaps . . ."

Our noses touched. I closed my eyes.

A telephone ring startled us apart.

He flung his hands in the air and stalked into the other room. He answered with a churlish, "What is it?" but his voice grew immediately quieter and more conciliatory. "Why, yes. Of course. I'd be happy to receive her."

The receiver clicked and he poked his head into the bedroom a moment later. "Judith Brandon is on her way up," he said.

"Mrs. Brandon! I'd have thought her a little old for an assignation."

Amir pursed his lips and made no comment. Even I had to squirm at the outburst—I must have had quite a knock on the head to be jealous of a middle-aged widow.

She rapped on the door a moment later. "I'll be back," Amir said. "I wouldn't advise you show yourself if you'd like to maintain your reputation."

"What reputation?" I muttered, but only the silk sheets heard me. "He sleeps on *silk*," I groaned. I suspected my indignation had not found its proper target.

From inside I heard Amir welcome Mrs. Brandon.

"I'm so sorry to trouble you, Amir. I've had some disturbing news, and I realized I had no one else to turn to in this matter."

"It's no trouble, Judith. I'm happy to help in any way I can. Has something happened to Ail, I mean, Lady Cassandra?"

"No, no, not as far as I know. It's about the man who assaulted her—Madison's associate? He's certainly the murderer. I just got word from Jimmy."

"Really? Shouldn't that be good news, then?"

Mrs. Brandon paused, as though choosing her words judiciously. "There's an accomplice, it seems. The police raided the man's quarters a few hours ago. They found dozens of anonymous letters exhorting him to follow Madison's advice and rid the world of vampires."

Even frustrated passion and the lingering effects of a severe blow to the head could keep me on the bed no longer. I stood carefully, reassured myself that I was in no immediate danger of collapse, and peered through the crack in the door.

Mrs. Brandon sat in one of two filigreed chairs upholstered in red brocade. Amir paced a circle in the middle of the room, like he had recently vacated the other.

"So it's Madison, then?" Amir asked.

Mrs. Brandon, still dressed for the evening, clutched her purse. "Well, that's just the thing. It's all very preliminary, but from what Jimmy could tell me the letter writer doesn't sound like him. In fact . . ."

Mrs. Brandon shifted a little in her seat and fidgeted with the gold lion's head at the end of one chair arm.

"In fact?"

"That's why I came to you, Amir. I want to help Miss Hollis, but given all I know I can't be seen near her tonight. But you're a friend of hers, and I realized that you could help convey to her the gravity of the situation."

I gasped, but thankfully Amir's reaction was sufficiently theatrical to cover the sound. "Zephyr? What could she possibly have to do with this?"

"I tell you this strictly in confidence, you must understand. No one has spoken to the press. But apparently there were some indications in the letters that they may have come from a woman closely involved in the anti-Faust movement."

Amir's frown could have chilled lava. "I'm shocked I even have to tell you, Judith, but there are a good many women involved in the anti-Faust movement. Has the man himself admitted to anything?"

"Everything, once they confronted him with the evidence. He says he used tainted blood to lace the deadly bottles. He's quite the fanatic."

"Shocking, with Archibald Madison as his mentor."

Mrs. Brandon smiled thinly. "Indeed. But he was used, Amir. By someone else, someone with an agenda that could benefit from this past week's headlines. A week, might I remind you, that comes right before the final vote."

"Are you really suggesting that Zephyr or someone of her sympathies could have deliberately used Faust to kill at least twelve innocent vampires as a *political* maneuver?"

But Mrs. Brandon shook her head with reassuring vehemence. "Of course not, Amir! Why do you think I've come tonight? I simply can't believe Miss Hollis capable of such a calculation. But I'm afraid the police won't be as perceptive. I'm afraid that with such pressure to find a culprit, they might focus on Miss Hollis without adequate investigation. So I realized I must tell you what is happening in confidence, so you can inform Miss Hollis. Forewarned is forearmed."

"Do you have any copies of the letters?" Amir asked.

Mrs. Brandon opened her clutch purse and pulled out a square of paper, folded multiple times. "I was able to copy out one of them. I'm sorry I can't show you more. They date back to February."

Amir took the folded sheet and read it for a long, silent minute. "I see," he said. "I understand your concern, now. Do you mind if I give this to Zephyr?"

Mrs. Brandon closed her purse with a satisfied snap. "Of course, Amir. And please tell her I will do all I can to encourage the police to look at other possibilities. At the least, I can assure her that Jimmy would never let this go to the press with anything but a solid case. Her name won't be sullied."

"I'm grateful to you for telling me," Amir said. He folded the letter and set it on a coffee table. I longed to dash in and retrieve it, but I had the feeling that my reputation could use the forbearance.

"Aside from encouraging him to do the deed," Amir said, "did the letterwriter provide any material support? A weapon?"

Mrs. Brandon frowned. "They found a bag of blood in his room, along with the letters. The writer sent it, apparently."

"Poisoned blood? So she provided the murder weapon," Amir said, and his frown was a little too deep, his worry a little too obvious, for a man who believed in my innocence. He was afraid I *had* written Madison's assistant those letters to further my political cause! I seethed, but of course I had to keep my rage to myself. Of all the unmitigated gall—to have brought the plague of Faust to this city and then to believe *me* capable of murdering for it. I felt quite glad that I hadn't kissed him. He didn't deserve it.

"The blood came from a Blood Bank," Mrs. Brandon said. She paused as though she had said something shocking.

"Isn't that where blood generally comes from?"

"No, you don't understand. The blood was tainted—not from a poison, as the police originally suspected. And certainly not from Faust. The blood *itself*. Someone with tainted blood gave it to a Bank with no trouble. If this gets out, who knows what could happen? Vampires who don't trust Blood Banks . . ."

"Might turn to other sources," Amir finished.

∞

Mrs. Brandon had hardly shut the door behind her before I toddled to the living room, snatched up the letter, and collapsed none-too-steadily into the nearest chair.

"I'm sorry—" Amir began, but I shook my head.

"Quiet," I said. "I'm reading."

He waited. I squinted. "Does it generally take you this long?" he said.

"You are an ass."

"I can read it aloud if you'd like."

I closed my eyes and leaned back in the chair—not as comfortable as I would have wished, given how much money seemed to have been wasted on its appearance. To be honest, I had forgotten the way blows to the head tended to hamper one's vision.

I scowled and squinted at him. He was kneeling in front of me, with a look of far greater concern than I had expected from his voice.

"Oh, read the blasted thing," I said.

Amir responded graciously to my gracelessness.

"From letter May 30th, 1927. 'It's low season at the Blood Banks, Brad. Those who can give in the summer, but not all of their blood can nourish. Some hurts. Some kills. Did you know that? Faust kills, too. It kills humans and makes vampires mad, just as Madison says. But what if you could get rid of them all? What if you could kill them with the blood they need, through the drink they crave? This blood will kill the scourge, which is your mentor's greatest desire. And if you poison the drink, even the mayor won't be able to push through Faust's legalization. I don't want Faust on the streets, Brad. Madison doesn't. I don't think you do, either. Will you take up the mantle? Will you mete out justice? I used to defend my fellow humans, like you and Madison. I was raised to do so by my father, but my path has changed. I can do more good in disguise. This blood is a weapon, but a woman cannot wield it. Only you.'"

Amir's face was damningly blank. He put down the note. I stared at it. The room seemed to tremble. I realized it was me.

"Christ," I said. "Bloody Christ."

"Zephyr," Amir said, very carefully, "if you perhaps did something ill-advised, in the heat of entirely justified anger at Faust or . . . or myself and the responsibility I bear for it, I . . ."

His eyes implored me—to do what, I wasn't sure. Though he clearly tried to hold himself in check, emotion gripped him so strongly that a slight haze of smoke drifted over his shoulders.

I wasn't inclined to sympathy.

"You *what*, Amir?" I asked.

He took a deep breath. "I will do anything in my power to help you," he said.

I laughed. "You get your wish at last!"

"You think that's what matters to me? You wouldn't want your wish anywhere near this. You've waited too long to make it, Zephyr. I couldn't possibly control the outcome. I have other, more mundane, skills. I'm inviting you to use them."

I was surprised by his answer, but too angry to let it show. How could he believe me capable of such ugliness? "To spare me the consequences of inciting murder for political gain? What will you do, haunt all of City Hall? Such lengths for a murderous hypocrite."

Amir winced. "If so, only because she was desperate."

"You mean you aren't sure?"

"I'll help you either way. I owe you that much, after what I've done."

I suppose it should have reassured me that Amir felt such guilt for bringing Faust to the city, but it only fueled my anger. But infuriating or not, I needed his help. Confused as I was, I knew I hadn't written that letter. Which meant only one thing.

"Someone is trying to frame me for the murders," I said.

"Someone would have to hate you very much. They would have planned it very far in advance. Mrs. Brandon said the letters dated from February."

"A month after the affair with Rinaldo," I said.

"And Faust," he said.

Amir and I looked at each other. We didn't have to say it out loud: if they knew what had happened in January, too many people to count might hate me just enough.

∞

I had every intention of going back to the boardinghouse that night for news of Aileen, but my exhaustion betrayed me. No sooner had I realized the truly frightening number of people who might wish me ill than I was taking such cheery thoughts into my dreams. I roused to warmth and a gentle bobbing sensation—Amir had plucked me from my uncomfortable slouch on the brocade chair.

"How undignified," I murmured into his chest. Something beat inside, but it didn't sound like the other hearts of my acquaintance.

In addition to pounding, it produced the occasional hiss and rattle, like a cranky steam engine. In my somnambulant state, I somehow found this comforting.

Amir lay me on the bed. The sheets felt as marvelous as I remembered, but I forced myself to sit up.

"But I have to get back," I said.

"Whatever it is can wait till morning."

I squinted at him. "Are you trapping me in your bower?"

"I wouldn't dream of it. But your brother made me promise to keep an eye on you tonight, so your toddling back to that puritan boarding-house would pose certain logistical constraints."

I yawned. "Mrs. Brodsky could use the excitement," I said, and fell asleep again with his laughter in my ears.

When I awoke, sun streamed through a crack in the heavy red curtains. Amir was gone. I indulged a moment of pure disappointment—all the more ridiculous for having no plausible basis—and then took deep, calming breaths. A murderer had been caught last night, but unfortunately the person who had goaded him to do it seemed to want my head on a stick. I wouldn't give it to them without a fight.

I was in my slip—a fact which seemed to not have registered last night, indication enough that I had been in no fit state to go anywhere. Amir had draped my clothes neatly over the chair of the vanity. I dressed and checked myself in the mirror.

"Goodness," I said, fingering the purpling bruise on the right side of my head. That certainly justified this morning's headache, though thankfully sleep had taken care of the wooziness and nausea. It looked a fright, however. Not as though I ever looked precisely smashing, but this seemed a little much even for my usual state of disarray. I pulled my hat down very low, and then carefully arranged the curls that stuck out. Not perfect, but at least I was unlikely to be pointed at on the street.

Suitably attired, I opened the bedroom door.

"Amir?" I called. I looked in all the rooms—one bathroom, another bedroom, and the foyer and kitchen. He was absent from them all. Only after my second time through did I discover the note he'd left for me on the parlor table.

Zephyr,

I am pursuing a lead, but will find you in the evening. I believe I promised you a trip to the morgue? In the meantime, I hope to present you with something useful when next we meet.

I hold my tongue lest I make it known.

Amir

(Sorry, habibti, that last is Nuwas, another part of that poem you knew)

I held the note far longer than necessary. I stared at it as though into a well, or the stars on a clear Montana night. I didn't understand why, only that I was furious. For his leaving when I had woken up with the thought of him. Furious for his poetry, for his contrition, for his surprising conscientiousness in the face of what I realized was extreme provocation. If Kardal would say what he had to *me*, I could only imagine the family dinners in Shadukiam. Amir had probably gone off to do something else to help me, but instead of being grateful I could only process my fury at his presumption.

Typical Amir, of course. Half the disastrous mess of this January could have been averted if he had managed to overcome his pigheadedness and tell me the truth of his dealings with Rinaldo. But apparently princes of the djinni weren't taught to admit bad judgment or confusion. It never occurred to him to *talk* to me about his problems. He much preferred to bumble ahead on his own, and use me to get out of the sticky aftermath.

"Damn you, Amir!" I said, with much satisfaction.

I nearly tore the note, but my hands froze.

I hold my tongue lest I make it known.

I didn't know what it meant, but my breath caught just the same.

I would see him this evening. I could yell at him then. In the meantime, I had more than enough to do without worrying about him. I tucked the note into my pocket before I left.

∽

It was just as well that I'd slept on Amir's silk sheets, because Lily had spent the night on mine. She and Aileen were both awake by the time I made it back, and if I was surprised to see Lily looking more or less at home on the worn chintz of Mrs. Brodsky's living room, I didn't say so. I owed her for taking care of Aileen after the séance—Lily possessed greater depths than she preferred to let on.

Aileen noticed me first, standing awkwardly in the entrance to the parlor. "Why, hullo. We were wondering when you'd return. Is that frankincense I smell?"

I grimaced. "Purely innocent frankincense."

Lily looked between the two of us, confused. "Is that some new slang?"

Aileen leaned back in the armchair. "Yes," she said gravely, "for handsome djinni who are angling for a certain suffragette's bloomers."

Lily was aghast. "You wear *bloomers*!"

"I do not! Well, not unless I'm too busy to do the laundry—"

"Zephyr has perfectly respectable undergarments, Lily," Aileen said, patting her hand.

"So did you make it with your djinni?" Lily asked.

I blushed and made a fuss sitting down on the ottoman across from them. "I *told* you," I said. "I've been chaste as a preacher's daughter."

Lily arched her brows. "Pity," she said.

"When did you wake up?" I asked Aileen. "Are you all right?"

Aileen smiled thinly. "As I ever am," she said. "I woke up as soon as that doctor started prodding me. I hadn't really been asleep, besides. Just in too deep. It took me a while to crawl back out."

"Crawl out?" I said.

Lily sighed. "I don't understand either. However, as I'm not a famous medium, I have taken her word for it. She seems okay."

"I *am* okay," Aileen said. "And in the room, in case you didn't notice."

"I'm so glad!" I said. "I was worried, of course, but with so much happening at once . . ." I leaned forward and embraced her. She returned the gesture, then froze.

"Christ, Zeph, what's that on your head?"

Whoops. I'd forgotten it would be visible without my hat. "War casualty," I said. "After the man knocked you out."

"And I thought *I* had a bump! Did he use a billy club?"

I squirmed. Harry was right—I was becoming as helpless as a civilian. "Oh, you know," I said, "it was dark. More importantly, what do you remember? You got stopped at a nail-biter."

Lily sighed theatrically. "She's not saying."

Aileen bit her lip and shook her head. "Lily doesn't understand. It's not that I don't want to tell, it's that I'm not *sure*. I wasn't parroting what Zuckerman said to me, I'd allowed him to, well, inhabit my body. It's not very pleasant!"

I shuddered. "Doesn't sound like it."

"I could hear him a little," she said, her eyes staring into a place I couldn't follow, "but it was muffled. Distant. I had to focus so much just to hold myself together, to make sure that I could push him out when the time came. Then I felt something like an earthquake and Zuckerman spoke to me. To *me*, I mean, not to the audience."

"And what did he say?" Lily had pulled out her notebook. This struck me as crass, though I understood the impulse.

Aileen frowned at her, her eyes returning to sharp focus. "Not for the paper, Lily."

"After last night, you're a news item whether you like it or not."

"Not about this," Aileen said, drawing herself up with a dignity that surprised me. "And if you think so, you're free to leave."

Lily pouted. "You'd kick me out? *She* was the one who left you unconscious. I stayed with you all night!"

"And I'm grateful for it, but this *isn't news*. Or at least, I won't be the one to make it so. Besides, I don't see you with a bruise the size of a goose egg on your temple."

I beamed at her. "You are my dearest friend, you know that?"

"You aren't going to like this, Zephyr," she said.

I sighed. "I haven't liked much since Zuckerman and McConnell caught us on the roof. But in current circumstances, forewarned is forearmed," I said, echoing Mrs. Brandon's dictum from last night.

With a distressed sigh, Lily put her reporter's notebook and pen down carefully on the coffee table. "Off the record," she said, and then looked at me sharply. "Current circumstances?" she repeated. "Has something else happened?"

"Oh, just that the murdering spree had an anonymous mastermind, and apparently top brass is betting on me. Someone wrote Madison's man very particular letters, and that someone seems to have an uncanny knowledge of private details of my life."

"You're being framed?" Lily said, inching toward the notebook as though she were hardly aware of it.

Aileen smacked her hand away. "No quotes," she said, biting off each word.

"About Zuckerman, not Zephyr's latest headline!"

"You will see," Aileen said, "that the one seems to be the other."

My scalp tingled and my head gave a single, bell-like throb. "What did he say?" I asked.

Aileen cleared her throat. "He said . . ." She closed her eyes. "He said that he remembered me from the roof. He said that I should watch out for you, Zephyr, and I said yes, she's in danger and he said no, watch yourself around her. 'She's been cursed,' he said. 'I'm almost positive of it.' "

I hadn't expected that. I didn't know much about curses—or any spell working at all, since I was incapable of performing them. "Who would have cursed me? What kind of curse?"

"He didn't say. Maybe he didn't know? He said 'Tell McConnell to look up the Nussbaum murder file from oh-three. There's blood in the Faust and it isn't normal.' "

"He was right," I said. "The blood in the Faust was tainted. The police found the bag and the man confessed to as much."

Lily clapped her hands. "Well then," she said, "that seems the place to start. Someone has acquired deeply tainted blood. We find out how and perhaps we can exonerate Zephyr and I can have my headline."

"I'm so grateful you'd deign to not destroy my life for newspaper inches, Lily."

"And I'm grateful you'll let me save your reputation and future liberty by helping you solve this crime, Zephyr."

"Good!" Aileen said, cutting through the tension with well-timed obliviousness. "This Nussbaum case is clearly the place to start—"

The doorbell rang. Aileen cut herself off.

"I will get it," called Mrs. Brodsky, and then, "You! What do you want with her now? No, you cannot come in today. Later, when she feels better."

We all looked at each other. "I don't think I want to meet whoever is at that door," Aileen said.

"I'm sorry for the intrusion, ma'am," said a male voice I recognized.

"You don't," I said, sinking so low I nearly fell off the ottoman. "But McConnell won't care."

❧

"So," McConnell said, alone on the large couch beneath the window, "what do you remember?"

Lily had wanted to stay, but he recognized her as a reporter and sent her off with the same frightening intensity that had gained him entry to the parlor. Lily made some cryptic references to research before she left, and I hoped she would uncover something useful about whatever this Nussbaum case had been. In the meantime, Zuckerman's partner was eyeing me and my roommate like he wished to impale us on tiny pins for a museum exhibit. It would have been disconcerting even if we hadn't had so much to hide.

"Nothing," Aileen said, wisely.

McConnell nodded. "I understand it must be difficult for you. But it's of utmost importance to our investigation that you tell me what you know."

"I know I found your partner. He was in a strange place . . . I'm not sure, I've never encountered a vampire spirit before. I asked him if he would speak to the living one last time and he didn't seem too bothered by it."

"And then?"

"And then I let him enter my body. I don't remember a thing he said, officer. When possession occurs, I enter a different state. The next thing I knew, I was lying in my bed with a hot water bottle on my feet and a doctor poking me."

I was duly impressed. Aileen took a sip of cold tea while Officer McConnell stared at his hands. I felt momentarily guilty that Aileen was refusing to give a departing soul his final wish in order to protect me. I was sure that Zuckerman wouldn't approve of her collusion, but

Zuckerman hadn't liked me very much, and whatever he had uncovered, he was sure to see it in the least flattering light. McConnell would learn the truth just as soon as I did—and in the meantime, he couldn't put me in jail for something I didn't do. Or something I did do, for that matter.

"Would it be possible to try again, miss?" McConnell asked. "I could compensate you for your efforts."

Aileen's fingers turned white around the teacup. "I'm not sure I could . . . vampires are strange souls. I've never seen one before your partner and it was . . . I mean, I don't believe—"

"*Please*, Lady Cassandra," McConnell said, leaning forward.

"Leave her be!" I snapped. "Can't you see she's shaken up from her ordeal? You'd put her through that again?"

McConnell rounded on me. "If it will help catch a murderer," he said.

"You've already caught one!"

"The real murderer, Miss Hollis," he said, his voice—and his anger—quieter now, and all the more frightening for it. "As I believe you well know."

I opened my mouth and closed it. *Tread carefully, Zephyr.* If I admitted knowledge of the letters, McConnell might very well arrest me on Mrs. Brodsky's ottoman.

"Real murderer?" I said, as innocently as I could manage. "Do you mean that informant Zuckerman mentioned during the séance?"

Aileen looked startled and I recalled that though she'd been inhabited by the ghost, she knew nothing of what he had said.

"No, no." McConnell gave a tiny, frustrated shake of his head. "The informant Mort referred to was Brad, the man who assaulted you."

"You had an informant in Madison's office? Your *own* spy killed . . ." I fumbled to a stop, realizing it was perhaps impolitic to state it so baldly.

McConnell looked away, his grief suddenly quite clear.

"So what do you mean *real* murderer?" Aileen asked. "It sounds to me like you've caught him."

McConnell shifted uncomfortably, but he answered readily enough. "It appears Madison's man had an accomplice."

"An accomplice?" I said, with what I hoped was adequate surprise. "In that case, I hope you'll start with Madison himself."

McConnell tilted his head, examining me. "We don't think it's Madison," he said.

I tried to swallow, but my mouth had gone too dry. "Didn't Zuckerman say something about a Blood Bank?" I said, flailing but unable to stop. "Aren't there plenty of leads to investigate? You can't imagine that I . . . I mean . . ."

"Miss Hollis," McConnell said, leaning forward. He regarded me so intently I half-expected him to pull a quizzing glass from his suit pocket. "Whyever would you imagine we suspect you?"

Normally, fear helped me focus. My reactions grew swifter, my aim inerrant. But now I felt as helpless as a trapped mouse. It was all I could do not to panic, but my flush must have looked damning.

"I don't know why you would," I said.

"You can rest assured, Miss Hollis, we will be investigating *every* possible lead." McConnell smiled pleasantly and stood. "Good day, Lady Cassandra, Miss Hollis. I'm sure you'll be hearing more from me."

"Delighted to hear it," I said, in tones considerably less so.

"Oh, one more thing," McConnell said, pausing on his way to the door. "It seems this accomplice was the one who told Brad to kill a vampire officer. The letter—there were letters, you see—used some odd language. Something about 'furthering the cause'?"

Oh, Christ. Mrs. Brandon hadn't told Amir *that*. McConnell let himself out.

CHAPTER NINE

I should have been plotting ways to prove my innocence, but instead I wandered around the city in a daze. My disastrous interview with McConnell ran through my head like a toy train on a looped track. I was in bigger trouble than ever, and I had no idea how to save myself. I had less than a day to go until the mayor's dinner on Saturday—if Nicholas didn't contact him by then, who knew what McConnell would do to me. But perhaps Nicholas already had. If I was lucky, Jimmy Walker had already called Commissioner Warren and told him to halt the investigation regarding Judah. That would be one less worry, but I had a nagging feeling of uncertainty. What if Nicholas told the mayor about the original supplier and Walker demanded an introduction? Impossible, I reassured myself. Since Nicholas didn't know about my continuing relationship with Amir, he couldn't betray me. And Mrs. Brandon thought Amir was an Arabian prince, not a djinni.

On the other hand, while a phone call from the mayor might convince the police commissioner to drop the investigation into Judah, I doubted even a call from the Vatican would stop McConnell and the other vice squad officers from investigating the murders. I was incalculably grateful to Mrs. Brandon for taking the trouble to forewarn me about the letters, and touched by her faith in my innocence. The letters were damning. I hadn't sent them, but someone had gone through a great deal of trouble to make it seem like I had. Who would do such a thing?

Eventually, old habits reasserted themselves and I recalled my obligations for the day. First among them, I needed to tell Elspeth about the developments in the murder investigation. Perhaps she would have some idea of who might want to frame me.

She wasn't in the office, but a note on the door said she'd return in ten minutes. I had waited half that long when I heard her climbing the steps. "Zephyr!" she said. "I hoped I'd see you! How is your head?" She unlocked the door.

"Better," I said, though just her question reminded me of the throb at my temple.

I followed her inside, unsure of where to begin.

Elspeth sat behind her desk. "That's quite a bruise," she said. "I'm impressed you came at all." She paused. "I trust you know more than the papers?"

I hesitated, but I couldn't in good conscience not tell her. "They think the man had an accomplice," I said. "There's some implication that the person might be someone politically motivated to oppose Faust."

"How?"

I explained about the letters, but didn't name Mrs. Brandon specifically as my source. "But I didn't—"

Elspeth sliced her hand through the air, emphatically cutting me off. "How absurd. You're the last person I'd believe capable of such a thing. No, someone is trying to frame you—or all of us. Someone,

I imagine, who wouldn't himself mind if Faust went down along with
his enemies."

"Madison?"

She gave a tiny shrug. "It seems plausible. But without knowing his
method, his guilt is hard to prove. They're saying that he used some
sort of tainted blood. The Faust itself has been ruled out." She looked
oddly disappointed.

"Would it be better if it had been the Faust?"

"No, you're right, of course. It's a horrible thought. Much better for
all of us that this man is behind bars. It's just—well, you must see,
Zephyr, how much easier our task would have been if Faust itself had
proved to be deadly after long exposure."

"But when Iris suggested we say so—"

"Iris suggested we say so as propaganda! She wasn't interested in
the truth of the matter, only the uses to which we could put a plausible fiction."

I understood now that I had misunderstood Elspeth's position
entirely. She had wanted Faust to be poisonous, but she hadn't been
willing to lie to make the case. She'd asked me to investigate the possibility of murder in the hope that there wouldn't be any.

"I'm sorry," I said.

"Don't be," she said. "It was a shameful desire. However much I
might disapprove of Faust, no one deserves to die for it."

I looked into her eyes—clear and alert, a sign of a recent feeding.
I wondered where Elspeth got her blood. Probably a Blood Bank.
I doubted she could afford the private delivery services and human
volunteers I'd seen advertised in the *Times* for the genteel undead. I
wondered if she was afraid of the possibility that tainted blood had
made its way into the public supply.

"But they deserve to go to jail?" I said.

She narrowed her eyes. "That's the argument of an opponent,
Zephyr."

"Even if you don't approve of Faust—"

"Approve? How could I? It's destroying our community, one drink at a time. It makes the humans hate us, and it makes vampires lose all judgment, all sense of safety and proportion. It puts us *all* in danger. Or have you already forgotten the dozen perfectly innocent vampires shot with silver bullets last January during the first Faust scares?"

I swallowed. Of course I hadn't forgotten—I'd nearly been crushed to death by a human mob that was desperate to rip a wounded vampire to shreds. "But jail?" I repeated, though the question felt asinine even as I said it.

"If it protects the rest of us? If the threat of jail stops us from succumbing? Then yes, I do support that."

"But it . . ." Elspeth's expression was harrowing enough that I nearly swallowed my words, but something made me press on. Stupidity, probably. "It hasn't worked out quite that way with alcohol."

"What is this, Zephyr? Alcohol and Faust are two very different beasts. Yes, I'm sure there will be some illegal trade, but there are far fewer vampires than humans. A ban will be much easier to enforce."

"But shouldn't we be trying to help them? Teach about drinking safely and promote responsible behavior—"

Elspeth laughed. "Responsible behavior? With Faust? I appreciate all of your efforts on our behalf, Zephyr, I truly do, but sometimes your human hubris is staggering. Faust makes vampires *blood mad*. I know you think you understand what that means, but you clearly don't. Imagine the worst hunger you've ever felt. Imagine you haven't eaten for days and days. Imagine how desperate you'd be for something, *anything* to eat. Now make it twice as bad. *That's* blood madness, Zephyr. An uncontrollable hunger, only for other sentient beings. And you think it's wise to let something that causes such madness flow freely on the streets?"

I felt clammy and cold, though the air in this tiny, darkened office was stifling. Elspeth had an uncanny ability to make those who disagreed with her feel smaller than a snowpea. "But they do resist," I said. "If all the vampires who drank Faust felt that way . . ."

Well, there wouldn't be a human left in the city who hadn't been bitten by a vampire.

She sighed. "They've found ways to mitigate it. Drinking Faust with a blood chaser. Or keeping a few bags of blood around the speakeasies and stalls to help someone who's coming down with the madness. Some people stepped in—the gangs, mostly, if you can believe it—and put some safety mechanisms in place after that first disastrous week. They say the brew itself is less potent now, though you know how little I believe it. But yes, before you say so, Faust has become far less dangerous."

"So why . . ."

Elspeth glared at me. Her eyes glowed for just a second. Not a Sway, but a sign of surging emotion. "Because this cannot happen again! We have to show that we will police ourselves, that we won't let any foreign drug destroy the progress that we've made integrating with society. What happens when someone invents the next Faust, Zephyr? What happens when we get as many drugs as you humans enjoy? When we can be demonized as a group because so many of us are already so persecuted and poverty-stricken that any momentary release might be enough? So we come down on this now, with as strong of a blow as possible. We educate each other and pressure the government for civil rights and better living conditions. *That* is the way forward. Is it unfair to an individual vampire who might go to jail for being desperate enough to drink Faust? Of course it is. Don't imagine that you've brought up some moral dilemma that I hadn't yet considered. I have considered it. And I think it's worth the price."

I took a shaky breath. I couldn't argue with that, and I wouldn't if I could. I wasn't a vampire, and I didn't live with that prejudice every day of my life, as Elspeth did. If the thought of going to jail for a drink made me feel slightly ill, that wasn't much of an argument given my circumstances. Maybe in different ways both of us could be right.

Some of the fervor seemed to leave Elspeth; she closed her eyes briefly and leaned against her desk, piled with books and papers.

"Was there something else, Zephyr?" she asked.

"You must really hate the one who brought it here," I said.

"You mean the gangs?" She seemed surprised.

"No, the original distributor. The one who brought it from Germany."

She shook out her dark, curly hair and rested her chin on her hand. "You mistake me, Zephyr," she said. "Faust is an evil, but I would never fault its creation. It's the uses to which we put those creations that pose problems. How many drugs do humans have? Dozens? Impossible to destroy them, but we can try to mitigate the effects. No one person is responsible for Faust—we all are. If your apocryphal original distributor hadn't brought it here in January, someone else would have in March. What's important is for vampires to show that we can police our own borders."

I was startled into silence. I would never have guessed Elspeth would defend Amir, even unknowingly. And I was surprised, as well, that her pragmatic argument had never once occurred to me. Of course someone else would have brought Faust to New York—it had been making the rounds in Dresden for months before. I suddenly realized Amir had been willing to shoulder all the blame, just as I had been willing to give it.

"Oh, Zephyr, I nearly forgot. Sofia wanted me to ask you if you still wanted her to try the spell. She seemed to think you might like that djinni more than you let on."

I blushed. Elspeth raised her eyebrows. "Could I let her know Sunday? I have to make him tell me the truth about what it might do."

"What if he doesn't know?"

"I'll decide by Sunday, I promise."

"Why not? I'm sure Sofia won't mind. She likes the djinni too."

She sighed. "Humans."

∞

I'd harbored a faint hope that Ysabel might have reopened the Blood Bank, but it was shuttered and dark with the sign now slightly yellowed and wrinkled from rain. I stared at it for too long, disappointment giving way to fear. The tainted blood had come from a Bank, Mrs. Brandon had said. There were hundreds in the city, but I couldn't shake the coincidence from my thoughts. Ysabel had been so clearly worried when I last saw her. I had believed her story about her family, but now I wondered. Had a tainted bag slipped through? Had she panicked?

But no, Ysabel was always so careful about those she allowed to donate, and a taint of the kind that could kill a dozen vampires would cause a deathly illness in a human. The St. Marks Place Blood Bank was well known for its drug-free, healthy donors. It was impossible for her to have distributed tainted blood. She was just having family trouble, like she said. I released a slow breath and fanned myself with my hat. Panic about the murder investigation was making me see conspiracies everywhere.

I left a note for Nicholas with Bruno at the Beast's Rum, informing him that I could get us into the morgue tonight. I realized this meant reintroducing him to Amir, but at this point I imagined that was the least of my problems. Either the mayor would help me or he wouldn't, but I doubted he would be inviting Nicholas back for drinks anytime soon.

It took me another forty minutes to walk to Twentieth Street, by which time gnawing fear, withering heat, and overexertion made me feel likely to faint on the steps of the Spiritualist Society. I unchained my bicycle from where I had left it the night before and wondered if

I had enough energy to take it back home. A heat shimmer radiated from the sidewalk and I drooped painfully over the handlebars. My head began to throb.

"That's it," I muttered. "Find someplace to rest."

So I wobbled over to the Flatiron Building, which was the only likely spot I could think of in the area. I might as well see if Lily had made any progress investigating Zuckerman's final words to Aileen. I found her at her desk, staring balefully at some papers.

"You look like Marie Antoinette on her way to the guillotine," I said, pulling up an empty chair and flopping down beside her.

Her dolorous expression deepened. "Give me a few more days and I might follow her. *You* look oversteamed."

I closed my eyes. "Water."

"Am I your maid?"

"Please?"

Lily huffed, took pity on me, and came back a few moments later with a glass. It even had ice in it. I sipped its glorious chill and eventually my headache receded enough to allow me to open my eyes.

The papers that so perturbed Lily were an article she had written, now covered with furious scrawls in heavy black ink. "Editor not fond of your latest story?"

"My editor," she said, looking daggers at the only person near enough to hear us, "is not fond of vampires. Which is a problem, given that he hired me as an Other reporter."

I pursed my lips and nodded. "That could be an issue." I felt badly for her, though I knew she didn't need my pity. Lily had been ecstatic about this job when she'd received the offer. I think she liked the Other beat and wanted greater recognition for her efforts. But it looked like the *New Star-Ledger* wanted the same kind of Other reporting the big journals did: pro-human.

She sighed and put down her paper. "Why are you here? Did someone else try to kill you?"

"Nothing too serious," I said. "Find anything interesting about Nussbaum?"

"If I found the right case. In oh-three a man from Spuyten Duyvil killed his infant son. He confessed immediately and killed himself in custody. It caused a minor scandal at the time, as you can imagine, but I don't know what it has to do with Faust."

"Maybe there's another case you missed?"

She shrugged. "And maybe Zuckerman is dead and Aileen was not precisely lucid. Who knows what he said. I need those letters, Zeph."

I glared at her. "Pardon me for continuing to enjoy free air."

"Fine," she said. "Then go off somewhere else and enjoy it. I have work to do."

She proceeded to demonstrate her utter indifference to my presence by uncapping her pen and scribbling on a clean sheet of paper.

"What would you do in my situation, Lily?" I asked.

"Give my reporter friend all the details so she can publish an exposé."

"No, really," I said, my words somewhat garbled by an ice cube in my mouth.

Lily tossed her pen with enough force to splatter ink and swiveled to face me. "Well, if I knew a nice lady who liked me and happened to work in the mayor's office, I might just ask her for help instead of bothering the overworked reporter you won't give the story to anyway."

I crunched down the last bit of ice and grinned. "Now that," I said, "is why I so value our relationship."

"Glad to be of service," Lily said. "Now, leave."

∞

The secretary guarding City Hall's inner sanctum took one look at me and shook her head.

"Mrs. Brandon's left for the day," she said.

Already? It was barely four o'clock on a Friday. Perhaps she was busy running errands for the mayor's dinner tomorrow night. "Maybe I wanted to see someone else?" I asked.

The woman tilted her head. "Like who?"

"The mayor?"

I had meant this mostly as a joke, but she jolted upright and looked down at something on her desk. "Oh!" she said. "He gave me a note to send you."

"He did?"

"I haven't sent it yet."

"Oh? I had a feeling he might want to hear from me," I said.

She looked at the note again and shook her head. "Give me a moment. I'll let him know you're here."

Not two minutes later, she ushered me into his office. He was adjusting his tie in the mirror and gave me a suspiciously friendly smile when I sat down.

"I'm glad to see you, Miss Hollis," he said. "Darned good luck for you to have come just now. I've been booked solid all day. But you had some business of your own, I'm sure?"

I should have left as soon as I learned Mrs. Brandon wasn't in. There was a world of difference between asking a sympathetic ally for help and playing political games with the mayor.

"I'm afraid I was wondering . . . did you call the commissioner?"

He nodded gravely. "I see, I see. Well, I can grant how you would appreciate that, Miss Hollis, but I'm afraid it isn't possible."

"It isn't?" I felt as though he had slapped me.

He turned from the mirror and walked over to his desk, though he did not sit down. "The trouble, you see, is that you haven't kept your side of the bargain."

"You didn't talk to Nicholas?" I said. "He promised that he would come!"

His lip curled in remembered distaste and he dabbed at his mouth with his pocket square. "I spoke to the vampire boy, yes. He's a piece of work, that one. But not much help to me. And he was curiously emphatic about one thing, Miss Hollis."

"What's that?" I prayed I didn't already know the answer.

Mayor Walker leaned against the edge of his desk, close enough for me to get a good look at his gray spats and the white carnation in his buttonhole. He looked like a man about to make the social rounds, and yet he had happily made time for me.

"Your Nicholas, it seems, is not the original distributor."

"Well, Rinaldo's dead."

"That's the curious thing, Miss Hollis. Your Nicholas said he didn't have an original bottle, but that you know a genie who might."

I laughed, perhaps a little too forcefully. "A genie? Like one who lives in a lamp? How could I have managed that?" I imagined all the responses Amir could make to this statement and had to force back a giggle. In other circumstances, I would have loved to see Amir and the mayor face off.

"Improbable, I grant you," he said. "But you strike me as an improbable lady. And Nicholas was sure that a genie was the original distributor."

I cursed Nicholas ten different ways in the privacy of my thoughts. I had *told* him I knew nothing about Amir! Had he known I was lying? I decided to go on the offensive. "Even if a genie was the original distributor, I certainly know nothing about him. I know Nicholas, and that's who you asked me for. So keep your word."

He frowned. "But I doubt you've kept yours, Miss Hollis. If you know this genie—"

"A practically mythical creature—"

"If you know him," the mayor continued, unperturbed, "and you sent me Nicholas instead, then you haven't kept your side of the bargain. I think you knew full well that Nicholas wouldn't have the original Faust. I think you are hiding the genie from me so as not to hurt your bluenose friends."

I glowered. "*If* genies exist," I said, "I doubt there's more than two people in all the world who know one. What you are accusing me of, sir, is absurd. I'm sorry your hopes were disappointed in this manner, but you asked for Nicholas. If you insist on breaking your promise, then tell me so. I will leave you to it."

I felt quite proud of this performance, and it seemed to give the mayor pause. He walked back over to the mounted mirror and examined some minute imperfection in the lining of his suit jacket. Finally, he turned around with a rueful smile.

"My sincerest apologies, Miss Hollis. You are entirely right. I had pinned too many hopes on your Nicholas. But we had a bargain, and I would never let it be said that Gentleman Jimmy goes back on his word. I will call the commissioner within the hour and clear up that pesky business about the child vampire. Will that satisfy you?"

I wanted to ask him if he could also put in a word about me not murdering anyone. But that would reveal knowledge that I shouldn't have, and possibly hurt Mrs. Brandon.

So I stood. "It certainly will," I said, as though I had no idea I was under suspicion for murder.

"Brilliant," the mayor said. "Oh, and here," he said, reaching for a small envelope resting on his desk. "It would delight me to see you at the banquet tomorrow evening. It's my big event before the vote on Monday."

I took the invitation, inked by hand on thick cream paper. My ticket to the most exclusive social event since Lindbergh's banquet. I had no doubt the mayor had some political purpose in mind for giving it to me—perhaps he hoped I might still give him the "genie"? But I was thinking about Lily and how much she would owe me if I brought her as my guest.

"I just might attend," I said.

———

There were only a few people loitering in City Hall Park, but to my surprise I thought I recognized one of them. Someone whose presence here was so odd that I had to get very close before I was sure it was her.

"Ysabel?" I said. She was sitting on a bench, a scarf pulled tight over her silver hair and tapping her foot anxiously. She nearly jumped when she saw me.

"Oh, *bubbala*! Why are you here? Are you in trouble?"

She seemed agitated. I sat beside her. "Of course not," I said, blithely ignoring the last week of my life. "Why would I be?"

"You know, this whole mess, the shibboleth with the dead *bruxa*. Such a shame. It must stop."

She looked away from me, her throat working.

"But didn't you hear? They caught the killer last night. He won't be able to hurt anyone again."

I had hoped this would comfort her, but she turned to me with such intensity I nearly backed away. "It is not the man that kills," she said. "It is the blood."

Blood from her Bank? But I couldn't ask. "The police have the blood now. It can't kill anyone else."

"And what if the killer finds more, Zephyr?" she said.

"Ysabel, there are rumors . . . I've heard the tainted blood came from a Bank. That the blood supply might be compromised. Are you saying . . ."

"No! I am saying nothing. How could I? There is too much blood, too many *bruxa*, too many mensch, how can we tell if blood is good or blood is bad? We cannot. Unless it is too late."

"Is that why you closed the Bank?" I asked.

Her eyes widened. "I closed the Bank because of some family

trouble, like I said. I will open as soon as I can and I will make *sure* that the blood is safe."

Nearby, someone honked their horn with jarring force. Ysabel sprung upright like a jack-in-the-box and looked around frantically. A sedan with a dented fender idled in front of the giant post office. The driver honked again, loud enough that the only other person in the park—a man leaning against the clock tower with a cigarette—lifted his cap and frowned.

"I'm coming, I'm coming," she muttered. I took her elbow and helped her stand. "So late," she said, straightening her scarf and gripping her bag more tightly. "Always too close to Shabbos."

"Will you tell me when you open the Blood Bank again?" I asked.

Her eyes focused on me again and she smiled, a little sadly. "Of course, *bubbala*. In the meantime, you keep from trouble."

She pecked me on the cheek and then paused.

"Do you know that man over there?" she said, quietly.

She was referring to the gentleman smoking by the clock tower, who looked away as soon as I glanced over. "I've never seen him before in my life," I said.

She shook her head. "I think he is police. I saw him talking to an officer before you came. And he has stared at you ever since you sat here."

I held my breath and looked, ever so carefully, over Ysabel's stooped shoulder. Sure enough, the man was staring at me from under his cap. A coincidence? But I couldn't discount that the police might have decided upon a more active form of investigation.

"Oh, God," I said.

The car honked again, a loud and sustained racket that caused the pigeons to fly away. "Stay safe, Zephyr," she said and hurried to the car, the owner of which seemed to be in danger of breaking his horn. She started lecturing in Yiddish the moment the door opened and had not stopped by the time the car turned down Park Row and away.

I stared after her for a moment. Clearly Ysabel suspected the St. Marks Bank might have distributed the tainted blood. I hoped she was wrong, but I was afraid. I took a deep breath and turned back to the possible police officer. He was conspicuously ignoring me now, lighting a second cigarette and admiring the towering post office building.

I stood up and took a leisurely turn around the park. At first he didn't move, and I was about to ascribe my and Ysabel's suspicions to overactive imagination. But once I ambled out of his line of sight, I soon discovered that he kept a distance of no fewer than twenty yards between us. Bloody stakes. I wondered what to do about it. Despite the fact that I grew up with a stake in my hand, Daddy never taught us much about tailing.

City Hall proper shared building space with the Third Precinct. As I completed my circuit, a uniformed policeman just exiting the precinct hailed my unwanted companion and they began to chat. My man looked around nervously, so I pretended blithe ignorance and sat down on a nearby bench, leaning back in feigned exhaustion. As I suspected, the man relaxed and continued his conversation. As soon as I judged his attention sufficiently diverted, I moved.

With a swiftness that would make Harry proud, I dashed across the street to the gaudy victorian monstrosity of our main post office, and headed behind a truck loading its final mail delivery. A man in a postal uniform smoked on the loading bay and looked at me curiously.

"I'll give you ten cents for your cap and jacket," I said.

He laughed. "And I'll give you twenty for a look under that skirt."

I rolled my eyes and dared a glance back in the park. My shadow was looking frantically up and down the street.

"A dollar," I said. "And that's all I have on me, so that's all you'll get."

"What you want with—"

"Will you take it or not?"

"All right. More than I paid for 'em." I took the coins from my pocket while he removed his clothes. I tried not to notice that the jacket had stains in the armpits and the cap was ripe with hair grease.

"I wasn't here," I said, and grabbed an empty mail bin from the back of the truck.

I couldn't help that I wore a skirt instead of trousers—and I didn't imagine that too many women worked to deliver the mail—but I walked swiftly and with purpose down the east facade of the building. I didn't want to enter in the public lobby, but the delivery entrance suited me just fine. I didn't dare look behind me to see if the officer had discovered my ruse. I passed a few postal workers in the basement corridors, but I kept my head down and if I seemed unusual, apparently it didn't worry them enough to stop me. I made my way down a central hall, hoping that I would find a door leading out the other side.

I had nearly made it through when I realized that I hadn't lost my tail.

Ahead and to my left, a smaller hallway branched off of this main one. For once, I had cause to appreciate the atrocious architectural sensibilities of my Victorian forebears. If not for their dedication to crowding perfectly good spaces with unnecessary passageways, I would have a much harder time leaving the man behind. I turned left, made sure no one was ahead of me, and broke into a dead sprint. This was all over if the hallway dead-ended, but no, there was another turn to the right. I slid on the worn soles of my boots and plopped the empty mail crate bottom-up on the floor behind me. This new corridor led into a wall, but that didn't matter much. I ducked into the deep shadow of a recessed doorway and waited.

Footsteps, louder and faster, approached. A male voice cursed under his breath.

I recognized it, but didn't have time to shout a warning before he came barreling around the corner, hit the overturned mail crate and fell with a rather sharp smack onto the tiled floor.

I knelt to assess the damage, but my brother didn't seem too bad off. "I wish you wouldn't follow me around like that," I said.

Harry rubbed his elbow, aggrieved. "Duly noted. So you knew about the police officer?"

"Why else would I be down here, wearing this? Speaking of which . . ." I pulled off the grimy cap and jacket and tossed them to the floor. "I would love to find a bath."

He sniffed. "I can see why. Come to my place? We need to talk."

I helped him up and we set off down the hall. "Are letters too good for you, now?" I asked.

"They're too dangerous for *you*, Zephyr. You wouldn't believe the rumors I've been hearing! And now the police . . ."

"If that's what you came to talk to me about, I have the situation well in hand."

Harry rolled his eyes and opened the door to the west facade. He poked his head out first, then motioned for me to follow. He slipped his arm around my waist, and I automatically leaned into his broad shoulder—a perfect impersonation of a young, loving couple, out for a stroll. Sometimes the best disguises were the simplest.

"I highly doubt that," Harry said, his voice carefully pleasant. "But that's not why I'm here. We need to go back to headquarters. There's a message from Mama."

"You couldn't have brought it with you?"

Harry pursed his lips. "Well, I could, but I imagine he would only increase your troubles."

I paused. "He? What is going on, Harry?"

"It's Judah. He's in my room."

CHAPTER TEN

Harry lived on the top floor of the Defenders' newly relocated head-quarters, though I imagined that he could afford something better and more private. He had been working for Troy for nearly six months, after all. Odious as I found him, the man did know how to find well-paying work. But Harry didn't seem to have bothered. I suppose it made sense: why worry about finding a nicer place when you could just rotate among the poster beds of your wealthy lovers?

"You kept him *here?*" I whispered, while he unlocked the court-yard gate.

"Where else could I put him? In my pocket?"

"But Troy—"

Harry sighed. "Troy is the least of your troubles, Zeph. For Christ's sake, you're not still sweet on him, are you?"

"Perish the thought." Troy had been my first beau back in Mon-tana, and we were well rid of each other.

Harry grinned impishly and tugged at one of my damp ringlets. "Zephyr has a crush," he said in the singsong tone of our childhood.

There were no observers here in the garden courtyard. I stuck my tongue out at him.

Inside, the headquarters were silent and dark, and we encountered no one until we reached the landing of the third floor. Troy sat in front of Harry's door, a sword across his knees and a pistol by his side. Several wisps of dirty blond hair had escaped the rigid cage of his pomade, which told me more about his mood than his flat expression.

"There is an underage vampire in your room," Troy said, with the sort of calm that presaged violence.

Harry took a step back. He seemed to consider many responses—thankfully, none of them involved the pistol I knew he kept in his vest pocket. Finally, he settled on, "Yes."

"And how did you intend to manage the situation?"

Harry darted a glance at me. "Have a conversation with him?" he said.

"A conversation." Troy didn't reach for the gun, but his hands tightened on the pommel of the sword.

Harry flushed, highlighting his freckles and ginger hair. I recalled that I had rescued Judah all those months ago because of his resemblance to my brother at that age.

"Troy, I know the kid, he's—"

"An underage vampire," Troy repeated, in about the same tones one would use for "plague-ridden corpse" or "Boss Tweed."

It was time to attempt to defuse the situation, though I doubted Troy would listen. I stepped forward. "His name is Judah, I rescued him this January and our parents have been caring for him ever since."

Troy looked dumbfounded enough to put down the sword. "Your . . . your *parents*!"

"Yes. And by our parents we also mean our daddy."

Troy scrambled up, his righteous indignation in full flower. This was a relief—when Troy engaged in theatrics, no one could be in serious danger.

"How in seven hells did you ever get the great John Hollis to *live* with an underage vampire? Has he gone mad?"

Quite possibly, I thought.

Harry's throat worked, and he looked down in embarrassment. "Ah, the kid's not that bad once you get to know him."

"Get to know him? Underage vampires are dervishes of destruction. There's a reason why we have the laws we do, Zephyr. No wonder the police were interrogating us! You made me lie to an officer of the law!"

I rolled my eyes. "No, Harry lied. You were merely ignorant. And you would have *remained* ignorant if you hadn't gone around poking your nose in my brother's possessions."

Harry looked startled. "Yeah, Troy, what are you doing here?"

"I heard something! I have the right to inspect my own property, and in any case, you must admit, Harry, some of your late-night escapades would make anybody wonder . . ."

Troy's face was getting redder than a bowl of borscht. I raised my eyebrows at Harry, who gave me a pleading look. I took pity.

"My brother has become quite the libertine," I said. "Have some understanding, Troy. You were young once."

This had the desired effect. "I only turn thirty next year!" he said. "In January."

"I am not *old*," he said peevishly. "But I suppose you have a point. I enjoyed myself quite a bit at nineteen, I must say," he must said, and *winked* at me.

I hoped Harry appreciated the lengths to which I would go for him. "So now, Troy, unless you would like to mire yourself further in our illegal affairs than you already have, perhaps you should go downstairs, polish your weapons, and attempt to forget everything you have just seen?"

Troy seemed to agree with this plan, as he picked up his sword and started back down the stairs.

"He will be gone within the hour, Harry, or I dock your cut!" he called, when safely on the second landing.

Harry sighed. "Yes, sir." And then, under his breath, "Nosy bastard."

∞

Judah sat cross-legged on Harry's narrow cot. He had been looking out the window at the twilit street, but turned around when we came in.

"The gold-hair man is gone?" he asked. Harry nodded. "Good," he said. "Mama wouldn't have wanted me to speak to him." Something about his voice seemed odd to me, but I couldn't quite place it.

"What did Mama want you to say?" I asked.

"Hello, Zephyr," he said, rather solemnly. "Mama said I should speak to you, though Harry should know also. Mama wants me to tell you that Daddy is missing," he said.

Harry frowned. "Missing! Is he out on a hunt?"

"Mama doesn't know, but I think so. He took his gun and his grimmer."

I looked at Harry, his worried expression mirroring mine. "Grimmer?" I said.

Judah nodded solemnly. "Yes, the book with magic words."

"Oh, a grimoire," Harry said and sat on the bed. Judah scooted next to him and lay his head on Harry's shoulder. *Like a real brother,* I thought, and then understood what had seemed odd about Judah's voice. When we'd first met, his accent had hinted of the Italian of his stepfather. But now he sounded like a true Montana boy, down to the slight twang with which he said "Daddy." I should know—years of living in New York hadn't eradicated it from my speech.

"Daddy has a grimoire?" I said. "I've never seen him do spell-work."

In fact, when I had discovered that I had no aptitude for it at all, he'd comforted me by saying that spells didn't matter to a real hunter, and most of them were useless anyway. I'd had the impression that he disdained the use of anything that wasn't blunt, physical force.

Harry looked at me oddly. "Well, he never did it around *you*."

"What do you mean?"

"Forget it."

"Harry, answer the question!"

Perhaps I should not have sounded so imperious, because Harry's lower jaw took on that characteristic jut of mule-headedness that I recognized all too well.

"I'm an adult," he said. "You can't just order me around like we're back in Yarrow."

"I'm not ordering you around. Just tell me since when has Daddy became some great spell worker."

"That sounded like an order."

"It's not a bleeding order, it's a *request*."

"Then, in that case," Harry said, settling back against the wall. "I'll consider it carefully."

Judah looked between us with clear-eyed fascination, though he said nothing.

"Judah," I said, attempting to sound calm. "Do you know anything about Daddy's spells? Why wouldn't he use them around me?"

Something like worry flitted over Judah's face. "Because you're dangerous, Zephyr," he said.

Harry straightened abruptly. "That's—"

"Dangerous? To Daddy?" Daddy could outfight me blindfolded.

"*Judah*," Harry said, with a quelling look. Judah fell silent. Harry bounded off the bed and took my hands, peevishness forgotten.

"It's the magic," he said. "It goes strange around you. It always has. Not that any of us are much use at witchery—though Mama says Sonny is showing some aptitude—but if you were nearby something would always go wrong. Daddy never cast much, but he always did it in the shed. He told us to work away from you."

I gaped. "*All* of you?" I tried to imagine my thoroughly non-magical family gathering speckled toads by the new moon—and the hundred other ingredients even simple spells required—all to secretly cast little charms without my knowledge.

"Betty? Vera? Tess?" He nodded as I named each of my sisters. "And Sonny, too!" When I left home, Sonny (his real name was John Hollis, Jr.) still took most of his meals from Mama's breast. He couldn't be older than six, now.

Harry wouldn't meet my eyes. "Daddy made sure we could do the basics. He said you never knew when it could save you, because sometimes the hunt goes wrong."

I had to sit down. My heart beat too fast; I could hardly breathe. The bed creaked a little beneath my weight. Judah gave me a worried look.

"It's okay, Zephyr," he said, with such unusual gravitas for a child his age that I had to smile. "You have too much, that's all."

"Too much?"

Judah blinked, as though it were obvious. "Magic," he said.

"But I don't have any magic."

Harry rolled his eyes. "You're *immune* to *vampires*, Zeph. Have you really never wondered what that means?"

"Of course I did. You know I tried asking Daddy and Mama for years, but they would never say. I guess I . . ."

Harry looked a strange combination of amused and peeved. I was realizing that while my immunity had become part of the wallpaper of my life, my siblings had probably spent a good portion of theirs wondering about it.

"Forgot about it?" Harry said.

"No. Maybe a little. Do I ask why I have curly hair? Brown eyes?

There are things that make up who I am, and that seems fine. The immunity is a little unusual—"

"Have you met anyone else with it?"

"I haven't asked! I tend to keep it a secret, after all."

"And why is that?"

"Because—" I cut myself off. He deserved more than the glib answer I felt at the back of my throat. *So, why, Zephyr?* I thought, and had a sudden image of myself no more than five years old, sitting on my daddy's knee. We were in his shed and I had a small knife in my hands. He told me that my immunity is our secret, that it can never go past our family. I asked why. He said, *"Because they will hurt you for it."*

"Zeph?" Harry touched my hand. I nearly jumped.

"He told me to," I said, softly.

The three of us were silent for several minutes, while the dying sun sucked the light from the room.

"So," I said, finally, "you think Daddy cast a spell on me that made me immune? And that's why I can't use magic?"

Harry shrugged. "That's what we all reckoned," he said. "But it's not as though Daddy gave us a talk about it."

"What kind of a spell would make someone immune?" I asked.

Judah had maintained an eerie stillness up to this point—so much so that I'd nearly forgotten he was in the room. But at this, his head snapped up. He looked me straight in the eye. "A bad one," he said.

I shivered. "Judah," I said. "Where do you think Daddy's gone?"

"There was a preacher who asked about you. Not a Bible preacher, the other kind. With the caps and beards."

Harry nodded. "The rabbi Mama told me of. Do you know what he said to Daddy, Judah?"

"I couldn't hear," he said. "But after, Daddy found his grimmer and he left."

To make another bad spell? But I didn't ask the question aloud. I didn't know if I wanted the answer.

Harry stood, massaged his temples, and pulled the string for the ceiling light. I groaned and covered my eyes; Judah didn't react at all.

"But why spend so much on the Fairie Transport to send you?" Harry said. "I talked to Mama yesterday and she didn't say anything about this."

"She couldn't," Judah said. "The preacher left a little clay man on the roof. It will tell him if we say anything about Zephyr or Daddy."

Harry looked baffled, but I recognized that description. "A golem," I said.

"So the rabbi is spying on Mama. And Daddy left!"

I wrapped my arms around my waist. I felt ill. The situation at home sounded worse than I'd ever heard it. "Maybe he didn't have a choice?"

"Maybe not," Harry said. "But I have a feeling that nothing good is going to come out of that grimoire."

"But the fairies didn't send me, Harry," Judah said.

We turned to him. "They didn't?" I said, a slightly hysterical laugh bubbling up like champagne. "How did you get here, in that case? Flight?"

"I can't fly," Judah said, smiling as though he didn't quite get the joke. "Uncle Amir brought me."

"Amir! Where's he now?"

"At home. He's helping Betty kill the golem."

Harry threw up his hands and flopped bonelessly on the bed. "Heaven help us," he said.

My headache was returning. "Amen," I agreed, and slid to the floor beside him.

———

My head throbbed like it had taken residence inside a bass drum. One would think that somewhere in the Defenders' headquarters one might find the remedy for such a situation, but the closest I discovered was a ten-year-old bottle of Dr. Beechman's Magic Cure-All Tonic. As I imagined that such quantities of laudanum might knock out far more than my headache, I regretfully replaced it next to the ipecac in the woefully out-of-date medicine cabinet. I entered the kitchen in search of a more robust solution, but had only made it as far as the ice closet before being startled by a voice from the door.

"Would you like me to turn on the lights?" Amir asked.

I groaned. "Only if you would like me to stab you."

This startled a laugh out of him. "I've had better greetings," he said.

Head in hand, heart in throat, I turned to face him. His teeth gleamed, but the rest of him was slightly bedraggled. It looked like he had come in from wrestling a pig. "I've had better greeters," I said. "So, who won? You or the golem? And I do hope my sister made it out better than you did." Betty was only seventeen, but she had more natural athleticism than either Harry or myself.

Amir shook his head ruefully. "Your sister finally cornered the blasted thing. I had the honors of delivering the final blow."

I released a slow breath. I hadn't known until this moment how worried I had been about my family. "Who do you think left it?" I asked.

"A rabbi—or, at least, someone acting the role. Someone clearly thinks your family will provide them with some useful information. Any idea why?"

My head hurt so badly I had to squint to see Amir. I wondered if I would be sick. I cast about for someplace to sit and then decided that the floor was as good a place as any. "I'd ask Daddy if he hadn't run away," I said.

Amir knelt. "Zeph, are you—"

"Perfectly fine," I said. "Why were you at my parents' house, Amir? I thought you said you were following leads."

Amir started, but he recovered quickly—smiling and patting my knee. "I was," he said. "I'm afraid that one didn't quite pan out, but I'm sure you'll agree it was lucky I arrived when I did."

"Quite," I said, enunciation brittle. "So what else have you been doing on my behalf? Rescuing old women from burning buildings?"

"Scaring away that police officer who was lingering across the street? Illegally breaking you into the morgue?"

I pursed my lips. Perhaps I was being just a smidge ungrateful. "That officer found me again?"

"It would appear."

"How did you scare him away?"

Amir smiled like a cat. "I turned into smoke and whispered in his ear that his woman knew his secret."

"What secret?"

"I have no idea," he said, "but you humans all have them."

I recognized the way Amir said "humans." That mix of imperious disdain and incurable fascination, the way I imagined a scientist might refer to his laboratory animals. Needless to say, it infuriated me.

"So you threatened a poor man just because you could? Will you never stop manipulating us? Yes, Amir, humans have foibles, but perhaps not quite so many as your average djinni."

I was in high dudgeon, but it still surprised me to see Amir look so deflated. I had expected him to argue with me (perhaps I had hoped so), but instead he bowed his head. "I hadn't meant it that way."

"How reassuring for the rest of us," I said, but without much venom. I rubbed my head and wished he would look at me again. "Judah is waiting for you upstairs," I said. "Harry is with him."

Amir nodded and left without another word. I wondered what I had done to make him act so strange and contrite. I knew he regretted his actions this past January. I knew, and yet I never missed an opportunity to harangue him for it.

And well I should! But I couldn't quite escape the sensation that my moral high ground had eroded over the past several months. Someone else would have brought Faust if he hadn't, Elspeth had said. But I wished that someone else had. A few minutes later Amir returned, alone.

"Where's Harry?" I asked.

"At the family estate," Amir said, with a smile. I couldn't help returning it. "He was worried about your mother. He said to tell you he'd come back tomorrow with any news."

"You're a regular courier service, Amir," I said, painfully dragging myself back upright. First morgue, then liquor, then sleep.

"Only for you, dear," he said, and pulled a tin from his pocket. "Here," he said. "It will work better than whatever swill you had in mind."

"What is it? Fairy dust?"

"Aspirin," he said, laconically.

I blushed, and took two.

∝

Given that I was about to be crucified for instigating these murders, I wanted any details to have a public viewing. It seemed to me that the mayor's office was exercising far too much control of the public perception of this case. And that perception was skewing in a direction decidedly *not* in my favor. All together, our merry band numbered five: Charlie, Nicholas, Lily, Amir, and myself. Charlie and Nicholas because I had promised them. Lily and her notebook for my own protection. Lily had the jitters around the two vampires. We had first stopped at the Beast's Rum to get them, interrupting the end of a surprisingly chaste performance of dancing girls. Bruno had been right—the vampires and humans mostly seemed to care about the otherworldly voice emanating from beneath the stairs. The fact that Nicholas had been the one making such beautiful music hadn't reassured Lily. I couldn't blame her for being worried about the two surviving members of the notorious Turn Boys gang. Still, she didn't complain. Lily was getting her promised scoop, and she'd probably spend the evening with Lizzie Borden if she had to.

Once we arrived at the south side of the Bellevue Hospital Pathological Wing, Amir told us to wait and then disappeared. I felt exposed and conspicuous, but hardly anyone passed us by.

"He's been in a long time," Lily said, looking around nervously. "Are you sure he can do this?"

"Yeah, Charity," Nicholas said. "I don't know that I trust your smoke belcher."

"He *said* he can get us in, he can get us in." I spoke with such authority that they both backed down. It was odd, I thought, that I wasn't more worried. But I trusted him. Sure enough, after twenty-one minutes we caught his signal: the on-and-off flash of lights in the corner windows.

Charlie grinned. "I knew you were right, Zephyr!" he said. Nicholas cuffed him on the back of the neck. Lily sighed and brushed passed all of us. The office windows were behind a short balcony a little over five feet from the ground. Amir shut the lights and stepped onto the balcony while the rest of us slunk into the bushes and trees below. He lifted Lily to the balustrade while Nicholas and Charlie scrambled up with little difficulty.

I stayed on the street to make sure that no one saw us entering, and so I was the last to get inside. Amir lifted me with an ease that would have been uncanny had I given it much thought. I lingered in his arms longer than necessary.

"All clear, *habibti?*" he whispered.

I nodded, dry-throated. He put me down.

The others were waiting inside what appeared to be a medical library. In the moonlight coming through the window, I could just make out the shapes of thick leather-bound volumes with long, incomprehensible titles printed in silver foil.

"I don't see no bodies," Nicholas said, so loudly that I winced.

"You were expecting them in the library?" Lily said, dripping with disdain.

"Maybe I'm *expecting* smoky here to keep his bargain, eh, *baldracca?*"

I doubted Lily understood Italian any better than I, but the gist seemed clear. She reddened and turned away, her reporter's notebook buckling from the force of her grip.

Charlie looked alarmed. "Nick, Nick, I'm sure the genie's got it all figured out. Let's just follow along and we'll see Kevin. Right, Zephyr?"

I nodded vigorously, but Amir forestalled my response.

"Listen to your friend, Nicholas," he said from the library door. "And speak easy. I make no promises if the police get called."

Amir turned and left. Nicholas looked for a moment like a real thirteen-year-old boy floundering in the wake of a thorough set-down. But Amir was heading away without any apparent worry for the rest of us. Lily hurried behind him and Charlie took Nicholas's arm to propel him out the door. Nicholas didn't look very happy, but he didn't argue.

"Goodness," I muttered under my breath. I made a quick check again through the windows to the street: no one loitering nearby and certainly no one who looked like a police officer. I dashed back into the hall and hurried to catch up with the others.

We went through the main corridor and then turned left at a large framed photograph of the pathological wing from what must have been the sixties. Two long rows of white beds with thin, emaciated patients and a few hard-faced nurses. Probably tubercular, I guessed, given how common the diagnosis had been in the slums back in those days.

"Zephyr!" Lily's harsh whisper echoed like a shout in the grand hallway. She stood before an open door to a staircase leading down. We were alone on the first floor.

I looked over my shoulder. "This place makes me nervous."

"It's a building full of dead bodies," Lily whispered, though it seemed unlikely anyone would hear us. "Were you expecting the Ritz?"

I smiled wryly. "That place makes me nervous too."

The basement was dark and cool. Amir had stopped at a door not too far from the stairs, but that was all I could make out. Nicholas and Charlie weren't too bothered by the darkness, of course, but Lily and I bumped into each other and made the best of it by linking elbows.

"Do you think you might spare a light, Amir?" I asked.

I thought I saw his head come up, as though he had been bent over. "I didn't know you smoked."

"To *see by*," I said, and Lily giggled.

Amir muttered something—a curse, I thought, though it might have been a djinni equivalent of a spell, for a moment later a crown of flames burst alight around his head.

"Holy shit!" Charlie said, stumbling back into Nicholas, who did not so much curse as growl like a mad dog, which made Lily shriek (though it might have been the vulgar language) and me sigh.

"You *know* the effect that has on people," I said, though perhaps I meant the effect it had on *me*. "Showing off is a sign of ill-breeding."

Amir gave me a small smile. "Consider it payment," he said, and turned back to the door. In the light, I could see that it was clearly the bar to our goal: every inch of the iron door had been branded with warding sigils, and—in case those didn't work, no fewer than five locks and deadbolts.

"Are you trying to break the wards?" I asked.

"Broken," he said, absently. "I'm trying to pick the locks."

I was duly impressed, though I wouldn't dream of saying so. Amir might be young for a djinni, but three hundred years would give any-one ample time to learn useful tricks like lock-picking.

"Zephyr?" said Charlie. "I'm sorry I used such foul language in your presence."

I nearly laughed. One does not spend any length of time working for the Defenders without developing a healthy tolerance for such idiom. I'd been known to employ it myself, but I supposed there was no need to dull my halo by telling him so. "I quite understand, Charlie," I said.

"It's me who deserves the apology!" Lily straightened her hat, obvi-ously trying to regain her composure. "Zephyr spends all her time among the coarser set; I'm sure she's quite used to it."

"I apologize, ma'am," Charlie said.

Nicholas cuffed him. "She don't deserve it, Charlie," he said.

Lily drew herself up and for a moment I thought she'd storm out, but journalistic ambition eventually won.

"Amir," I said, under my breath. "Please tell me you're almost done? We are developing a situation."

"Control the cats for another moment," he said. "I've almost got it."

"Why can't you just, I don't know, smoke yourself and unlock it from the other side?"

"Wards," he said. "I could only crack the ones keyed to humans and vampires. And . . . there!"

With a gentle click, the door released its locks and glided inward. Amir's fire cast enough light for us to see more than a dozen gurneys with bodies under white cloth.

"Christ," Nicholas said, and for the first time it occurred to me that his particular testiness this evening might be a cover for undue emotion. Kevin had been his friend, and now Nicholas could finally pay his respects.

Lily, Charlie, and I followed Nicholas into the room. He pulled back each sheet until he reached the tenth gurney.

"Kevin," he said, his voice somehow melodic with grief. "I swear, I will kill that bastard. I will crucify him that did this to you."

Lily flipped open her notebook and started scribbling. I felt the need to restart my heart. Did Nicholas know about the letters? Did he know that someone else was involved besides Madison's man? But no, his fury was such that he wouldn't fail to mention an accomplice if he knew about it.

And I certainly wouldn't tell him.

"The murderer will have a trial," I said. Danger to myself aside, I didn't like the idea of Nicholas on a quest for vigilante justice.

"Good for him," Nicholas said, not taking his eyes from Kevin's face. I shivered and left the matter alone.

Amir waited from the doorway, following us with his eyes. "Didn't you say you broke in before?" I asked.

He shrugged. "I should have guessed they would change the wards. I probably left a trace. In any case, there might be an alarm on them, so let's hurry?"

I nodded. Nicholas, Charlie, and Lily had taken all the available spaces around Kevin's body, but I was interested in a different victim. I pulled back the sheet covering the last body. Zuckerman, naked in death as I had never seen him in life—curiously appropriate, given our first encounter. Other details assaulted me, but none so forcefully as the single, bare fact of his presence on that gurney.

Occasionally, the morgue did take on poppers, but the exsanguinated remains of vampires could all fit in a box about a foot square, and their investigation was more the provence of forceps and tweezers than scalpels and scales. Each of these bodies had been vampires. I had seen Zuckerman multiple times and been sure of it, and of course Nicholas could hardly have mistaken his friend. And yet here they were, the first vampires I had ever known who didn't exsanguinate upon death. I peered at Zuckerman's face again, frustrated by the dim light. The same generous nose and narrow mouth. I suppressed revulsion and used my forefinger to push up his stiff lip. His small fangs were retracted, but unmistakably present. So, a vampire. Dead. With a body to dissect.

What kind of tainted blood would stop a vampire's exsanguination, but kill him anyway? It was almost like he'd turned human. "But he's not human," I whispered. In the chill air of this grim storage room, the words carried.

"None of them are," Lily said. She was looking at the other two victims and flipping through the papers attached to the side of each gurney. "But they're changed, somehow."

"Yeah," Charlie said, "they smell kind of funny."

"Maybe that's cause they're dead, *idiota*," Nicholas said. "Dead and poisoned."

"That's what I mean, Nick! The poison makes them smell funny. Not like a regular popper. They smell . . ."

Lily looked up from her perusal of the first gurney's clipboard. "Half popper, half human," she said.

Nicholas stared at her. "What do you mean?"

Lily's hands were shaking, but from excitement or terror I couldn't tell. "It says here: 'subject's central cavity liquefied, gonadal region to third rib. Anterior and posterior, however, definition of organs remains. Heart present but badly damaged and nonfunctional. Portions of extremities also internally liquefied, all consistent with the normal presentation of exsanguinated vampires. No known cause, pending further investigation."

Absolute silence. From outside came a distant crash of lightning from a summer storm. I understood what this meant. We all did, but perhaps someone had to say it.

"They were turning *back*," I said. "And halfway to human, it killed them."

Torrential sheets of rain sliced through the streets in merciless wave after wave. First Avenue was deserted as ever; which gave me ample opportunity to admire nature.

At least, as best as I could while being soaked in it. There had been one umbrella in the stand by the entrance door. Amir had given it to Lily, who promptly used it to dash into the street, hail what must have been the only on-duty taxi in a twenty-block radius, and sail off without so much as inquiring whether we needed a ride. Nicholas and Charlie had left soon after our grisly discovery. Nicholas had gone so silent and furious I wondered if he might be having another one of those strange dissociative attacks. I didn't ask—Nicholas wasn't particularly safe at his most genial and lucid, let alone moments after he had looked upon the dead body of his friend and vowed revenge.

Which left Amir and me, alone in a summer thunderstorm.

"You really can't teleport us back?" I asked. Water had overflowed the gutters, leaving it ankle-high at many points on the sidewalk. I sloshed through, refusing to think about the filth. Amir turned to me at the exact moment a bolt of lightning flashed across the sky. For that split second, I took in both his uncanny beauty and his harrowed, drawn expression. He seemed overworked and exhausted—an odd thing to think of a djinni, especially this one.

"Even I have my limits, Zephyr," he said. "Though it's flattering that you think me indefatigable."

"I just thought your djinni business was, well . . ." I snapped my fingers and fluttered my hands.

Amir gave a short laugh and shook his head. "More like running up a very steep hill for several hours. One's capacity does give out after a while. So if you'd like your brother back tomorrow, we have to walk."

I shrugged waterlogged shoulders and forged ahead. I was bothered by Amir's frank admission of weakness, but I couldn't quite place why. Perhaps because he had exhausted himself on my behalf? But of course

I couldn't know what other business he'd attended to all day. For all I knew, he'd spent the afternoon in a Shadukiam harem before flitting to Yarrow for the evening entertainment. Indeed, I had to be vigilant around Amir, exactly *because* his presence always seemed to disarm me. When I saw those coal-dark eyes with their thick lashes, when I heard that gently amused voice and smelled that particular banked-fire-and-oranges smell, I quite frankly lost the good sense God gave me. It was absurd: Amir had lied to me practically since we met. It was almost certain that he had lied in some manner about the fate of his older brother and there was no reason for me to believe that he wasn't lying now. Of course he *looked* tired, but there was no reason for me to believe it, or even if I did, to think that all of his travels today had been for my sake.

Yet, Amir had undeniably been attempting to atone for his actions in January. He had even haunted the mayor to help the anti-Faust cause, though the plan had backfired. I recalled how he had stated the exact number of casualties—*forty-two*, a grim figure so tellingly memorized, as though guilt had branded it on his thoughts. Could I forgive him? Could I at least look past his failings in light of his change of heart? It frightened me how much I wanted to. It frightened me, because in so many ways he hadn't changed.

"You look nearly as stormy as the weather, Zephyr," Amir said.

"Merely taking stock of my situation, Amir."

He wiped the water from his eyes, sober and watchful. "And have you reached a conclusion?" he asked.

He stood very close. Enough so that I became aware of the gentle cloud of steam rising from his exposed skin and wet suit. The smell of him, that very intoxicant against which I had just girded myself, seemed to radiate like a bodily object, filling my nose and throat and pores, sliding down my spine like the hand of a lover, long denied.

I shivered and nearly sobbed. Amir frowned and cocked his head—entirely unaware, it seemed, of his uncanny effect.

A rolling thunderclap shocked me to my senses. I stepped away from him and shook my head, suddenly relishing the cold, clear rain.

"To beware of dangerous things," I said, to which Amir made no response at all.

CHAPTER ELEVEN

"You can't possibly mean to go back there!"

Aileen scowled at me over her toast. We were taking our Saturday-morning breakfast in Mrs. Brodsky's kitchen. "Not this again, Zeph."

"You nearly died the last time," I said. "Of course I'm concerned."

"You shouldn't be," she said, "because I did not nearly die. I was firmly on this side of the veil, Zeph, and surely you can grant that I ought to know."

I took a deep breath and a long drink of milk. "I bow to your expertise," I said. "But it *was* hard on you this Thursday. Perhaps it's time you finally changed your situation? Found a steadier method of utilizing your talents?"

Aileen gave a bitter laugh and bit off her crust with too much ferocity. "Steadier?" she said, while chewing. "Like what, Zephyr? Please, tell me, what *other* gainful employment might your average Irish girl with a bit of Sight find in this town? Because as I see it, either I read on Skid Row or I tell fortunes for rich ladies with lettuce to spare."

I wanted to tell her to give it up entirely, but I knew that the consequences of her ignoring her Sight were even more debilitating than those of her using it. The last time she tried, she had passed out on the factory floor after being accosted by an unwanted vision.

"You don't have to *try* so hard," I said. Aileen raised her eyebrows, but she didn't interrupt. "Couldn't you fake them most of the time? Tell a real one now and then to keep the hounds at bay? What difference will it make to the biddies anyway?"

Aileen looked down at the stale crust in her hand, shook her head, and tossed it unceremoniously on her plate. "The difference," she said, with more weariness than anger, "is the ten clairvoyants who read for the Society on other nights. It's the hundred other charlatans on Skid Row. It's that the occupation of a Seer is one with a great deal of competition, and if I don't try, then others will. Those 'old biddies' know their way around the Other Side."

"At least you could tender your regrets for *this* appointment? Just relax for a week to recover?"

Aileen slid her plate over the counter to Katya and pulled a defiant cigarette from her case. "I'm perfectly recovered," she said, standing to demonstrate the point. "And this client pays well enough not to accept regrets."

I knew I should just leave well enough alone. Aileen was as stubborn as myself—it was perhaps a reason why we made such good friends. But she looked so worn, lighting her cigarette with a jerky motion. She was nearly pale enough to not need talcum powder. "This isn't smart," I said.

"Then you'll just have to let me be dumb."

"At least tell me you won't contact Zuckerman."

She hesitated, then shrugged. "I won't contact Zuckerman."

"You don't sound very sure of that."

"I'm—what right do you have to know everything I do?"

"Friendship?"

"Nosiness?"

I sighed. "Nosy friendship? *Please*, Aileen?"

Aileen ashed her cigarette in my cold coffee, but she gave me a rueful smile. "I should have known that one day you'd go do-gooding on me. If you must know, I'm reading for Judith Brandon. While it's *possible* she'll ask after the officer, something tells me she will want me to do the same thing I've done for her the past ten times."

"Contact her husband?" I asked.

"Or try, anyway."

Mrs. Brodsky poked her head into the kitchen. "The phone is for you, Zephyr," she said.

I started. I hadn't even heard it ring. "Who is it?" I asked.

Mrs. Brodsky frowned and waved her hand. "How do I know? Some woman. Come, you pay for the extra minutes."

I sighed. Aileen waggled her fingers at me. "Ta-ta, darling," she said, in a slightly hysterical imitation of Lily's posh New England accent.

I snorted. "I'll say hello for you," I said, and followed Mrs. Brodsky into the parlor.

But much to my surprise, it wasn't Lily calling.

"Zephyr?" she said.

"Mama? Did something happen to Harry?"

"No, no, he's fine, sweetie. Everyone's fine except your daddy. That's why I called."

Somehow, I'd managed to not think about the mess at home all morning. Mama's voice brought back all the stomach-churning anxiety that I'd felt last night after seeing Judah. "I don't know what's happened to him, Mama," I said.

The connection wasn't the best, with crackles and pops and a distant echo, but I was still sure that I heard my mother sobbing on the phone. I had seen Mama cry before, but not very often. Not in years. "You have to help us, Zephyr. I think your daddy . . ." She sniffed and hardened her voice. "Listen, dear, I know this won't sit well with you, but you've got to do it for the sake of your family. We need your daddy. I don't know where he is, I don't know how much trouble he's in. But no matter what he did, we have to do something to get him back."

"You want *me* to do something to get him back? Mama, I'm no Leatherstocking. I can't track him across Montana." Not to mention that I had plenty of my own problems right here in New York.

"It's not that kind of help," Mama said, a little faintly.

"I'm sure he'll be back," I said. "He's always come back before, hasn't he?" I said it to reassure her, but in truth I believed it. My daddy is John Hollis, most famous demon hunter in Montana, and I suppose a part of me has always thought him invincible.

Mama stared to cry again. "This time is different. We need your help."

My diffuse anxiety turned sharp as a knife. I had never heard my mother this upset. Something had gone very, very wrong.

"But what do you want me to do?" I asked.

She took a deep, shaky breath. "Honey," she said, "I need you to make a wish."

∞

Amir had told my mother.

Not everything, perhaps, but enough for her to realize the potential of my unused wish. Enough to have reasoned her way to the perfect solution to her problems, never mind that they might be the ruination of mine. I could kill him. Indeed, after hanging up the phone, I stormed incoherently around the parlor until Mrs. Brodsky announced that I either use more ladylike language or take myself outside. I went outside, though not very far. To the end of the block and around, past children playing in the standing pools from last night's rainstorm and old women watching the day from their stoops. It felt like home, and I was possessed of a painful, wistful longing—as though someone had already taken it from me. But who would finally do so? The mayor? The police? My family?

Amir?

How could he have used my own mother, clearly at her wit's end with my father's antics, to manipulate me into making a wish?

"Of all the crass, manipulative, selfish—" I paused and gave a bitter laugh. This was Amir, after all. Had I really expected him to perform courier service for my family—fight a *golem* off of a goddamned *roof*—without any personal benefit? I had, perhaps, but then I was a naive fool who deserved what she got. Perhaps next week I'd learn that he'd helped me get into the morgue to help cover up some other crime he'd committed.

I wanted to give him a good piece of my mind, preferably with invective of which Mrs. Brodsky would wholeheartedly disapprove. I marched back down the street to retrieve my bicycle. I wouldn't let him get away with this, and I was less inclined by the minute to give two figs about the consequences of performing the ceremony with Sofia.

The temperature seemed to climb a degree for every block I traversed, and my entire back was damp by the time I reached the Ritz. I sighed. Perhaps I should have taken the subway, but I hated to waste a fare just to avoid the heat. I shook myself out after locking the bicycle, hoping that the damp patches wouldn't show too easily on the burgundy blouse (itself perhaps a mistake in this heat, but everything else needed laundering). The doormen paid me no mind, however, and I studiously avoided eye contact with the concierge. I directed the elevator operator to the fourteenth-floor apartments.

"You'll be seeing the prince, ma'am?" he asked, hesitating with one hand on the grate.

I nodded. *The Perfidious Prince,* I thought, and stifled a dark laugh. We went up smoothly, but upon arrival we were assaulted with the unmistakable sounds of two men in loud argument. I looked down the hallway, but I needn't have bothered: I recognized Amir's voice, even muffled through a wall.

The elevator operator looked around uncomfortably. "Perhaps miss would rather wait in the parlor while the concierge rings up?" he said.

In other circumstances, I might have given Amir the courtesy. Instead I waved my hand. "Oh, it's quite all right," I said, smiling. "He's expecting me. I imagine that he's going on again about the Yankees game. Baseball overexcites him," I said. The man nodded vaguely, as though this didn't seem quite right, though he couldn't remember why. I did not wait for him to figure it out; I waved again and set off firmly down the hall.

I paused before Amir's door, my hand frozen before a knock. I recognized the other voice, now. Amir and Kardal were engaged in another of their voluble arguments. The language and tone would have told me so, even without the smoke drifting under the door.

I shook my head. "Bleeding djinn," I said. "What do they want to do, bring down the fire department?"

I rapped three times, firmly. "Let me in, Amir!" I called.

Abrupt silence.

"Zephyr?"

"The very same."

"This isn't exactly a good time, Zeph," he said. "You couldn't have rung first?"

"Funny you should mention it," I said. "Because my mother just called to make the most interesting request."

"Ah, did she?" Amir's voice came more clearly through the door, as though he was standing just on the other side.

"Yes," I said. "It seems you and she had *quite the conversation.*"

Amir opened the door. He looked tired, though less so than last night. "You might as well join the fun," he said, and waved me into the sitting room.

Kardal was seated with precise posture in one of the red brocade chairs. I nodded at him.

"You haven't made a wish," he said. His rumbling tones had now ceased to faze me at all, even when he, as now, made not the slightest effort to appear human. Smoke tumbled from his head and shoulders in dense waves that puddled around his feet like fog. His eyes smoldered blue and white. I had learned through past interactions to better read his moods, though today's didn't take much deduction. Kardal was very, very angry.

"I've been having second thoughts," I said, and crossed my arms over my chest.

Amir settled against the wall and looked heavenward.

"You made a promise," Kardal said, "to make a wish within a week."

"It's only Saturday!"

"You really mean to wait until Monday?"

"In any case, I don't know that your brother's recent behavior"— I glared at him—"is providing a particularly good argument for my keeping that promise."

Kardal barked a laugh, blowing fire from his nostrils like an agitated dragon. "Humans! Your word is as good as your dung," he said.

"My word was based on the understanding that I had no other choice in the matter. But as it seems that I can free myself from Amir entirely, you will have nothing to worry about."

This caused Amir to step away from the wall. "Zeph, you can't mean to go through with this," he said. "Not now. Your father—"

"Yes, Amir!" I stood, without quite deciding to do so. "Tell me about my daddy. Tell me all about how you manipulated my poor, overwhelmed mother into sobbing over the phone, begging me to make a goddamned wish!"

Amir couldn't even look at me. He stared at a vase to my right, his eyes shifty as the damned. "I didn't mean to upset her," he said, quietly.

"Upset her! She made it sound like you told her Daddy had killed someone!"

Amir sat down abruptly on the coffee table. He looked down at his hands, as though in search of some inscrutable answer. Then he released a stream of what I could only assume were Arabic curses and looked straight up at me.

"Your brother," he said, clearly.

I forgot to breathe. "Harry? But I just saw—"

"Not Harry," Amir interrupted. "And not Sonny."

"I don't have any other brothers," I said, though I was remembering that once I had.

Mama raised six children, but she'd given birth to eight. I'd had a sister who died in her crib when I could barely walk. Her name had been Lilah and Daddy dug her a tiny grave in the backyard.

Right beside another one. Older, with just an unmarked cross and wild grass to cover it. My twin brother, Daddy said when I asked. He wouldn't tell me any more, and Mama just cried.

Amir waited for me to figure it out. Patiently, I would have said, had I not been overcome with incalculable rage.

"That child was *stillborn*," I bit out, "and Mama still grieved for him years after. What, did you see that sad little grave in the backyard? Did your mean-spirited, self-interested, morally bankrupt excuse for a mind hatch the clever plan? Use a mother's grief to solve your problems?" I laughed, high-pitched and not a little hysterical. Amir looked frozen in place. He didn't even try to argue. How could he? "And here I'd fooled myself into believing you. Like every other woman in the world, I suppose. He might be a selfish cad for three hundred years, but oh, for *me* he'll change in six months! You unleashed Faust on the world," I said. "Why would you balk at some petty emotional blackmail?"

Amir seemed shaken, but I didn't credit it. "That's not how it was," he said.

"Are you saying you haven't lied to me?" Amir winced. I laughed. "At least you have that much decency."

I brushed past him on the way to the door. I felt Kardal's eyes follow me, but Amir didn't so much as lift his head. Had the confidence man finally lost his confidence?

It wasn't until I'd turned the brass handle that I heard his voice.

"You're right," Amir said. I wondered if I could smell him from even this far away—fire and sulphur, like he was agitated. But when I turned, he looked cool enough. "I lied to you and your mother."

"About my brother?" I said, just to be sure.

He nodded and gave a faint smile. "Seemed like a good idea at the time."

I could hardly contain my disgust. "You puerile, amoral—"

"He's lying."

Amir and I turned in unison to stare at Kardal, who up till now had seemed content to watch our argument with distant interest.

"He's . . . what?"

"Kardal!"

"He's lying about lying," Kardal said.

"So . . . you're saying my father *did* kill my brother?"

"Kardal, you will stay out of this, or I will make you."

Kardal gave Amir a look that said, quite eloquently, what he thought of this threat. "Yes," he said to me.

Amir shook his head. "Kardal is lying. He wants you to make a wish, that's all, so he's trying to salvage the situation."

I looked between the two of them. It was like that old riddle, where one guard is cursed to always lie and the other is cursed to always tell the truth, and somehow you had to figure out which was which before the banshee came and ate you.

Or something like that. Unfortunately, I've never been particularly good at riddles.

"I think you're both untrustworthy bastards," I said, "but I know my daddy and I know that whatever his faults, there's no power on earth that could make him hurt his children. Amir, Kardal, good day. I would very much like to never see you again in my life."

"Zeph!"

I slammed the door in his face. He didn't open it again, even though I dithered for almost a minute before calling the elevator.

I cried on the way down, but they train the service staff very well in such places; he pretended not to notice.

∽

I had not known it was possible to convey superiority while wearing nothing but hair curlers and silk stockings, but Lily managed. "You really haven't heard?" she asked.

"I haven't read the papers today," I said, looking morosely into Lily's vanity. My hair had grown hopelessly frizzy in the day's humidity; it flared about my scalp like an ochre halo. Lily had rouged my cheeks and done my eyes, but the effect struck me as more sinister than beautiful. I looked like a corpse with two shiners.

Lily clucked her tongue. "If it were *my* freedom at stake, I'd manage to drum up some interest in current events."

We had been talking to each other's reflections in the vanity's oversize mirror, but at this I turned around. "Oh, out with it already!"

Lily shrugged and handed me a copy of the *New-Star Ledger*.

"ANTI-VAMPIRE LEADER APOLOGIZES FOR MURDERS; VOWS SUPPORT FOR INVESTIGATION," I read, and then paused. "By James LeRoy? Scooped by your own paper, Lily?"

"More like robbed," she said, fists clenching. "Goddamn LeRoy and Breslin. This is my beat and I'd done half of that reporting, but I don't even get a credit." Lily sighed and collapsed onto her modern couch. "It's because I'm a woman," she said balefully. "Breslin just doesn't trust me to 'do it right,' as he says. He says my womanly empathy makes me bad at hard-nosed reporting. I said I did hard-nosed reporting, just as I saw it, and did anyone else have my connections? And do you know what he told me?"

"What?"

Lily drew herself up. "He said, 'That's why we took you on, Harding, so they'd better start earning out our investment.' And I said, 'I'm a reporter, not a darned *stock option*!'"

I gasped. "What did he say?"

"Nothing. He kicked me out. So you see why I have to go to this party."

I did. I had offered to let her come if she let me borrow a dress, a more than fair arrangement.

"I'm sorry the *New-Star Ledger* has become such a trial," I said.

I'd been perfectly sincere, but Lily just pouted. "Don't gloat," she said. "Read the article, damn them."

I shrugged. The paper's ink had smudged where I gripped it with sweaty hands. Lily's apartment was on the top floor of a white-brick building in the Upper Sixties by Lexington. She had electrical outlets in every room, but in this weather even two fans did not provide much relief. The article in question was perfectly legible, fortunately.

Archibald Madison has publicly apologized for the murderous activities of Bradley Keck, the man currently in police custody for the alleged murders of thirteen vampires, including a decorated officer of the vice squad. Mr. Madison, founder and president of the Safety Council, the most prominent organization opposed to the existence of vampires, had employed Mr. Keck, a former indigent, for seven months at the time of the murders. Since the arrest, many have suggested Mr. Keck indiscriminately murdered the vampires at the instigation of his employer and mentor. Early this morning, Mr. Madison roundly dismissed any such inference as "baseless scandal-mongering."

"I unreservedly condemn the actions of my former employee," Mr. Madison said. *"I have never, by word or deed, encouraged anyone to harm other creatures, even abominations such as vampires. I have only ever sought legal means for the amelioration of the demographic threat to our city, and I will only continue to do so."* He went on to add, *"The Safety Council has a simple mission at heart: to promote a better, human-oriented society, where Others have their proper place."*

I snorted. *Proper place.* Under his boot, no doubt.

When asked whether he still supported the anti-Faust forces opposing the council's vote on Monday, Madison declined to comment.

The article went on for a few more paragraphs, about the influence of Madison's Safety Council and its reaction to the "Faustian menace."

"I wonder what he's up to," I said. "Declined to comment? Do you think he'll change his mind?"

Lily was applying lipstick, but paused halfway through. "Oh, you can bet the mayor is trying. Madison is in a bad position. Either he looks like a hypocrite because he changed sides or he looks like a murderer because he stuck to his convictions."

"But he *is* a murderer," I said.

Lily rolled her artfully smoky eyes. "Zephyr, I know you don't like him, and I'm not saying he hasn't said some rather incendiary stuff, but it hardly amounts to murder. Bradley Keck murdered those vampires because someone encouraged him to. And I doubt it was Madison."

"Well, why not?" I asked. "Someone meant to frame me."

Lily puckered blood-red lips and blotted them on a tissue. "I doubt he gave you a thought in his life before this week. I think your letter-writer must be someone familiar with your past, Zeph."

I took an extra tissue and attempted to wipe at my eyes. They were still puffy from the hour I'd spent crying earlier today, and the charcoal did them no favors. "That seems rather like no one and everyone, doesn't it? Next you'll be suggesting Troy wrote them. Or Harry! Or Daddy!" I choked a little on the last word, remembering Amir's horrible accusation. My hand slipped, smearing charcoal eyeliner down my cheek.

"Zephyr!" Lily abandoned her rouge brush and dove for my hands. "My sixteen-year-old cousin takes making-up better than you! No, leave it alone, I'll fix it." Lily knelt and used a wet cloth to wipe the lining from my eyes before starting again.

"Well, whoever is the culprit," she said, moving the pencil with a steady hand, "you had better find out soon. For both of our sakes. Breslin said the morgue story was old news—he buried it in the middle of the paper. I need to give him something big, and that's definitely the ticket."

"Do I actually look like a person to you, or just walking newsprint inches?"

Lily finished and leaned back on her heels. "Newsprint inches," she said, with raised eyebrows, "don't wear Lanvin."

CHAPTER TWELVE

The Tammany Wigwam on Fourteenth and Irving had recently been slated for demolition, so the organizers had moved the event to the glittering opulence of the Hotel Vanderbilt's banquet hall. We arrived punctually, despite Lily's none-too-subtle inferences that I was a rube for doing so. I didn't tell her my real reason: a vague unease about the mayor's reasons for inviting me here. He'd seemed to accept my denials about knowing Amir, but now I wondered if he'd done so too easily. I was a mediocre liar, and Beau James was a born politician—had I really convinced him so easily? But as long he didn't put Judith's acquaintance together with Nicholas's hint of a genie distributor, I didn't see what even our wily mayor could do about it. Even so, I decided to arrive early. If something seemed amiss, I would hopefully be able to leave quietly.

I had to admit, Lily hadn't held back on her side of the deal. She had draped me like a dressmaker's doll at the positive bleeding edge of fashion, in a she-swore-original Jeanne Lanvin delivered by her mother from Paris just last month. Rust red chenille silk with a swooping back and a flared skirt layered with black. She gave me a bandeau with a white flower and short red gloves with the wrists folded down. I said I looked like a robber bride, or like those girls who pretended to be vampires for certain men in certain brothels.

"Fashion," Lily said, with her particular emphasis, "is just something you don't grasp, Zephyr. Trust me. This will make an impression."

Lily had decided upon a more subdued ensemble for herself—crushed velvet in midnight blue with a high neck and a long rope of pearls—though I had no doubt it was every bit as modern. Lily looked smashing in everything she wore, a trait I had come to accept philosophically.

Heads turned when we stepped into the hotel lobby. Lily regally took this as her due. We were accompanied by a dozen or so other early arrivals, none of whom I recognized. We were easily the youngest of the group and far more fashionably attired. Velvet ropes and smartly attired attendants directed us to the ballroom. I tried to appreciate the surreptitious, whispering attention as we glided past, but any pride I might have taken in my appearance was tempered by overwhelming panic. I looked around, relieved to see no evidence of the mayor.

"Maybe this isn't a good idea," I whispered, while we waited in the receiving line.

Lily raised her chin. "Get me in and you can do whatever you please. But there's no need to let irrationality spoil a good time."

This seemed like a good mantra, so I repeated it several times before we reached the doorman. He took my invitation and waved us through after a check of my name on the list. As though we had passed through a magic portal, my vague worries about being trapped this evening evaporated. I took a glass of punch from a passing waiter's tray, tingling with a feeling of being young and beautiful and carefree.

"Is *this* what it's like to be Lily?" I said softly.

Lily laughed. "Hardly. I don't make a habit of attending dry parties. Dreadful dull." She sipped her drink and made a face. "And *sweet*."

I sipped mine and realized she was right: the punch had no kick at all. It hadn't even occurred to me, but the mayor could hardly serve illegal hooch at an official dinner—even if his regular consumption of liquor was an open secret.

I surveyed the banquet hall. The space could have fit Mrs. Brodsky's entire boardinghouse, and quite possibly the smaller tenement beside it. From the cavernous ceilings hung crystal chandeliers the size of two grown men, bathing the room in a fractured, sparkling glow. I felt as though it had lit my dress on fire, while I stayed within it, serene and devastating.

"Not many people, yet," Lily said, looking around with significantly less enchantment. "I knew we should have come later. Ah well. There's Marlowe, from my old paper. Society beat. I might as well say hello."

Lily departed before I could so much as nod. I didn't mind. Lily wanted her picture in the paper; I wanted the canapés that had lain untouched on the refreshment table since we arrived.

As usual, I hadn't managed to eat much beyond the toast from this morning's breakfast. I could have tried, but my argument with Amir had made me feel vaguely queasy for hours afterward. I had passed a hot dog vendor on the way to Lily's apartment and nearly burst into tears—which I had sworn would be the last of my sentimental effusions. I was well rid of him. Or I would be, once Sofia was done.

I was on my second canape when I heard—faintly, but unmistakably—a woman say, "I can't believe she *dared*!"

I stiffened, the pastry frozen halfway into my mouth. In my mind, a frantic litany of *I knew it, why did I come* ran in merry circles. But then the man with her laughed. "Nothing we can do about the old bird if she wants to make a fool of herself with a married man."

They walked off, still gossiping, while I blushed. *Get a hold of yourself,* I thought sternly. *No one here gives two figs about you.* I looked around and saw that this was true. The room was slowly filling with guests, everyone dressed to the nines, and they had more important people to pay attention to. I laughed a little and popped the rest of the canapé into my mouth. I was sure we would be served plenty of food for dinner, but I didn't imagine I'd run out of room.

From my position between the snack table and a listless piano player, I could watch the room unnoticed. I recognized the ancient, stooped figure of John Voorhis, the Grand Sachem of Tammany Hall, surrounded by aldermen, Tammany sachems, and other functionaries of the political machine. For the people invited to this party, there were connections to make, deals to attend to. In the end I was just a pawn, not a player. Lily sauntered back over a few minutes later, her cheeks flushed with excitement.

"What a shindig!" she said. "Everyone's here. Just wait till Breslin sees my article tomorrow. He spent an hour trying to get an invite yesterday."

I laughed. "Don't rub his nose in it."

"I wouldn't dream—oh!"

As one, all heads in the room turned to the doorway. I didn't understand why, at first. The object of admiration was a little too far away, at the center of a bobbing mass of people who blocked my view. But I heard someone nearby whisper his name: Al Smith. New York's recently elected governor had his sights on the president's seat, it was said, and his chances were considered good. He was a Tammany man, just like Jimmy Walker, and the ripples from our city's struggles with Faust had made themselves felt in Albany. The state senate had abstained from passing its own legislation on Faust so far, preferring to let the city bear the brunt of public scrutiny. Faust hadn't made inroads elsewhere in the state the way it had in New York City. Still, I'd read that Al Smith and the Tammany democrats supported Jimmy Walker. If the antiprohibition faction won here, it would probably win in Albany.

But not without a fight, if I knew Elspeth.

"Look at that," Lily said. "It'd be the berries if I could get a few quotes out of him."

But in lieu of elbowing her way to the governor, Lily gave me a running commentary on the other unworthy journalists jockeying for his attention.

"And look, there's Bill Oliver in a tuxedo even older than he is! I think I can smell the camphor. Oh, of course, he and Al Smith are pals, are they?"

Lily tossed back her glass of punch like she wished it could make her drunk and gave Bill Oliver, rival reporter from *The Sun*, a polite smile. He was chatting with Al Smith in what I admitted was a friendly manner.

"Oliver has been with *The Sun* since the nineties," I said. "You'd expect him to make some connections in all that time."

"I expect he's got more connections with headstones than live bodies. Al Smith!" She straightened her shoulders and made eye contact with a roving waiter. When he approached, she started to take a glass and then paused. "You know," she said, "I'm just feeling so terribly dry. Do you have something else back there? A little kick?"

"I could get you some tonic water if you'd like, miss."

"That's a start," she said, and leaned forward until her lips were a mere inch from his ear. "I'd really appreciate it," she said. "Two, if you don't mind."

The waiter froze for a moment before nodding and hurrying back to the kitchen. I stared at Lily.

"What was that about?"

Lily gave a very self-satisfied smile. "I slipped a five into his cummerbund," she said.

When the drinks arrived, Lily gave me one, much to my surprise. "My gift to you," she said. "Use it wisely. Fend for yourself for a while, hmm?"

I watched her dive into the crowd, pushing her way forward with a single-minded intensity toward Al Smith and his circle of admirers. I looked back down at my drink. The grain alcohol wafted from my glass, clearing my nostrils in a bracing fashion. I shrugged and took a sip. Smoother than Horace's bathtub swill, that's for sure. I gave a secret little smile; I was getting more glamorous by the minute.

"Zephyr Hollis?"

I looked up to see Mrs. Brandon, frowning like she'd caught me sneaking out after bedtime.

"Why, hello there," I said. "Lovely party."

But she just shook her head like my compliment was a horsefly. "What are you doing here? I mean, I don't mean to be rude, but the guest list—"

"The mayor invited me," I said, flustered. I didn't understand why my presence would perturb her.

She looked away. "I . . . my sincerest apologies, Miss Hollis. Please excuse me. As you can imagine, the last few days we have truly been inundated with work. I'm afraid exhaustion has made me thoughtless."

I waved away her apology. "I completely understand," I said, "if you didn't expect to see me." I lowered my voice, perhaps the alcohol helping me say aloud what I had previously only thought. "I can only imagine how draining all this must be for a woman in a position of power."

Mrs. Brandon gave me a grateful smile. "Some days it truly is," she said. "But the vote will be over soon enough. If it goes his way, I'm sure Jimmy will be generous."

Perhaps he could start with giving her a new office, I thought, but was not tactless enough to say. We shared another nervous smile while I wondered how to effect a graceful exit from the conversation. But it turned out to be unnecessary; a ripple went through the room again, as it had when the governor entered. This time it was the mayor, accompanied by two other men.

I vaguely recognized one of his advisors. The other . . . I gasped.

"What is *he* doing here?"

Mrs. Brandon turned back to me and narrowed her thin eyebrows. "Jimmy requested that I invite Amir," she said. "I'm surprised he didn't tell you."

She set down her half-eaten plate and hurried to intercept the mayor. I stayed where I was, contemplating hiding under the table skirts if it meant I could avoid a confrontation with my djinni. He whispered something to the mayor and they both laughed. My jaw clenched. Irrational as I knew the sentiment to be, I felt each of his smiles as a blow, every carefree laugh as a knife to my back. How *dare* he carouse and hobnob with the elite of the city while I fought for my freedom with the city police? A horrible suspicion gripped me: had Amir *told* the mayor? He had promised he would keep his role with Faust a secret, but at the moment I didn't value his promises very highly. I took a thick gulp of my drink, mostly for the distraction of its burning warmth. What would the mayor do if he knew I had lied to him? Ring up McConnell and declare open hunting season?

Or even worse, would he do nothing—because Amir's cooperation had been all he needed to corral the last of the swaying aldermen to his side? Despite my best efforts, had I delivered the death-blow to any hope of Faust prohibition?

At that moment, Amir—still smiling—looked up. From opposite sides of the room, our eyes connected with a snap that nearly made me spill my drink. He looked devastating; dark eyes in a suit so sharp it could cut. Maybe everyone here thought he was human, but I knew the truth like a catechism. *Make a wish*, it said. Like I had since January, I refused.

After a long moment, Amir nodded. I raised my glass. He was the first to look away—as though nothing had happened.

Because nothing did, I told myself fiercely.

∽

I avoided Amir. This was easy, as a circle of admirers followed him wherever he went in the crowded room. Whether this was due to his proximity to the mayor or the basic attraction of his exoticism, I didn't know.

"You two fell out again?" Lily asked, astutely interpreting my expression.

"For the last time," I said, and she patted my arm with something resembling sympathy. Perhaps the mayor's invitation had been a trap, but he had so far refrained from springing it. He and Mrs. Brandon were engaged in an intense, quiet conversation by the piano. They were both quite good at controlling their expressions, but they still seemed to be arguing. This surprised me, given that they had always gotten along so well in my presence. But then Mrs. Brandon nodded and said, just loud enough for me to catch:

"I'll phone his office now, Jimmy. Perhaps he's been delayed."

"He's been delayed the past half year, Judith. I don't know why I ever listened to you about him. Especially tonight. I *told* Al to expect him! You're making me look like a fool in front of sachems."

"He promised, Jimmy," Mrs. Brandon said, desperately.

Mayor Walker's smile could have withered fruit. "You're the fool who believes him. And I'm the fool who believes you."

Mrs. Brandon's face went rigid as a plaster statue. "I'll phone him now," she repeated and hurried away—past Lily, who was busy engaging a young gentleman. I hoped that Mrs. Brandon succeeded in finding her tardy guest. Perhaps the mayor respected her abilities, but not enough to treat her with decency in a crisis.

Lily's young gentleman had been joined by one other, more familiar to me. I couldn't quite make out their words over the general din of the crowded banquet hall, but Amir's deep laugh rang out like a bell. I felt vaguely betrayed that she would talk to him, but of course I hadn't told her what he had done.

"Marvelous to see you here, Miss Hollis. May I refresh your drink?"

The mayor gave me a self-deprecating smile, nearly dripping with charm. I looked down, surprised to see the puddling icy remains of my gin and tonic.

"The punch would be fine, thank you," I said. Best to sober up. I felt Amir's proximity like a hot stove, and I wanted no drunken burns.

"I'm afraid Voorhis wouldn't approve if I gave you anything else," he said, signaling a waiter. "Though I commend you for your ingenuity."

I thought of telling him that it had all been Lily's idea, but it couldn't hurt for the mayor to think me worldly.

He took my empty glass and replaced it with the pink punch that everyone in the room was struggling not to regard with overmuch distaste. "Fascinating party," I said. "I caught Mrs. Brandon on her way out. Will she be back?"

Mayor Walker waved a manicured hand. "I can't imagine what would keep her away," he said.

Given what I had overheard of their conversation, I felt offended on her behalf, but didn't say so. We each had our own battles to fight.

"Quite a lot of aldermen here," I said, looking around with a small smile. "Why, isn't that Fred Moore? I thought the Harlem aldermen were against you last week."

The mayor gave a friendly nod to the negro council member, who had noted our attention.

"Politics, my dear, is all in the negotiation."

"You mean bribery and corruption." I winced internally as soon as the words left my mouth. I certainly *had* drunk that too quickly.

He laughed—a short, hard bark. A few people glanced over, including Lily and Amir. I ignored them. "Try running the largest city in the world, Miss Hollis, and see how far that purity takes you. If you must know, Mr. Moore of the nineteenth district will be getting funds in the next budgetary meeting earmarked for new school texts, which the Harlem schools sorely need. I managed to convey to him that increased revenue from Faust taxation could go a long way to improving the lives of his *human* constituents. You'd be surprised at how well the truth works sometimes."

I took a long drink, hoping to tame my blush. "Then it's not such a tragedy that my . . . contact couldn't locate the original supplier for you. It would seem you have other persuasions at your disposal."

"It would seem," the mayor said, with a calculating expression I could not hope to decipher, but made me shudder regardless. He raised his glass. "To other persuasions," he said.

I felt as though the surreptitious stares of the people around us would burn me alive. I had no other choice but to smile grimly and return the toast.

"Ah, there's Miss Harding and Mrs. Brandon's princely acquaintance!" he exclaimed, as though noticing them for the first time. "You and the prince are acquainted, if I'm not mistaken?" He ambled over, much to the delight of Lily. Amir was pleasant as ever, though I wondered if I detected a hint of discomfort.

"Mind if I quote you for the paper, Mayor?" Lily said, with reassuring directness.

"Not at all, Miss Harding," he said. "But perhaps you could give me just a few minutes? I had wanted to show our young prince here an item of interest."

Amir's eyes locked with mine in a flash of worry that I hoped only I had seen. Then he took one of my red gloved hands and raised it to his lips.

"You look enchanting this evening, Miss Hollis," he said. I pulled my hand away and made a show of finding a place to put my half-empty glass. My hands shook too badly to hold it. Why did he still have the power to charm me when I *knew* the rot beneath the surface? To Amir, humans and vampires weren't individuals worthy of consideration and care; we were playthings, fascinating walking automatons that he could manipulate to his will. His recklessness was the reason we were all here in the first place, no matter what Elspeth said.

But why had the mayor invited him here? Did he suspect Amir of being a djinni—*the* djinni who had originally supplied Faust to the bootleggers?

I tilted my head toward Walker. "An item of interest?" I said.

"Why, yes," he said. "A historical object an adventurous friend of mine brought back from Syria. I believe you hail from the area, Prince?"

"The general vicinity," Amir said. "But I'm afraid I'm no expert on antiquities."

Lily sighed and put her pen back inside her jeweled handbag. "Mind if I see it too?"

Jimmy Walker looked among us with a bland smile. "I wouldn't dream of spoiling your fun. Perhaps we could step into the hallway? My friend tells me the object is valuable and I wouldn't want to make a spectacle."

My suspicions were ratcheting up by the second, but I would rather spontaneously combust than stay behind. This dinner was the mayor's major opportunity to woo supporters to his cause before the vote Monday afternoon. For all his reputation as a man-about-town, I very much doubted he would spend time chatting with Amir if he didn't think it would serve some political end.

Lily gave me a look of *what is he up to?* as we stepped into the porters' hallway behind the food tables. I shrugged and shook my head. Amir, for his part, chatted amiably with the mayor about his antiquarian friend, never giving the slightest hint that he was anything more than what he said: a well-cultured Arab prince, recently relocated to New York.

The mayor made sure we were alone and then reached into his inside suit pocket. "It's a tiny little thing," he said. "My friend is quite the scholar, but he claims the old Arabic script is beyond him."

Amir nodded as the mayor removed a tiny scroll from a gold-inlaid case. "So you were hoping I might be able to decipher it? I have some familiarity with the old texts. I'll do what I can."

Everyone leaned in until our heads nearly touched. The scroll looked like what Mayor Walker had claimed: a tiny piece of antiquity, written and illustrated in ornate calligraphy. Somehow I had ended up beside Amir, his ear grazing the top of my forehead. I longed to catch his eye and see if he understood what sort of trap this might be, but there was no way to do so discreetly. Whatever the mayor's plans, we had no choice but to see it through.

"Well," the mayor said. "You can read it?"

He had backed away, regarding Amir with a half-smile and eyes wide with anticipation. I didn't understand why. Amir seemed exactly as he had been. But as I looked at him, my vision started to go light and hazy. The image of him and Lily wavered and then split in two. A sharp pain, like a hammer blow, went through my skull. I held back a moan. Could that blow to my head still be affecting me?

Amir didn't look up, but I felt his hand rest, steady, on my back. The pain receded a little.

"It's quite simple," Amir said, his words clipped. "It says: I am the djinni of the lands beyond the moon, and I will obey the wishes of whosoever compels me to read these words."

I felt another, fainter, pain ricochet through my skull. My vision failed entirely. Amir's lips were the last thing I saw before the world faded to white. I wondered if I had died, though I could still hear voices, distant and distorted.

"Zephyr, are you all right?" It was Lily, her hand on my elbow, giving me a quizzing look. I turned my head with effort—the pain had gone, leaving a giddy exhaustion in its wake.

"I'm not sure that gin was the best idea," I said to her.

"And what a strange artifact," Lily said to the mayor. "Are ancient texts in the habit of discussing genies?"

Amir replaced the scroll in its surely priceless case. He did not even look at me. "It's not entirely uncommon," he said. "There have been legends for millennia about how to bind the djinn to humans. It seems your adventurous friend has happened upon a fairly common trick in past centuries. Disguising the trap in a gilded apple, as it were. I can't imagine many of the djinn have ever fallen for it, but it's certainly a curiosity."

Amir's smile held only quizzical friendliness as he handed the scroll back to the mayor. Jimmy Walker was far too good a politician to let his disappointment show, but I saw his moment of surprise and hesitation before he took the case and replaced it in his coat pocket.

It had been a trap, I thought. And somehow, Amir and I had escaped.

"Miss Hollis," Amir said, ignoring the mayor entirely. "Would you allow me to procure you another drink? And you, Miss Harding?"

The mayor blinked and then shrugged. "So much for divergences. I must get back—I'm sure the papers will print that I missed the necessary votes for the bill because I was too busy carousing in back hallways at my own supporters' dinner!"

"Those quotes, Mayor?" Lily asked, retrieving her notebook. He gestured for her to follow him and they walked back into the banquet hall.

Which left Amir and I alone in the porters' hallway.

"What was that?" I whispered.

He shook his head, though I don't know who he thought would be listening. "Will champagne do?" he asked.

"No one will believe it's punch."

He clenched his jaw, revealing, for less than a second, a deep, roiling fury. "If you think I give a shit what those ignorant humans believe, you don't know me at all."

And I did know him. Perhaps I wished I didn't, but I could no more remove my awareness of him than I could my own skin. He had known what the mayor planned; he had held on to me so I wouldn't fall.

"Champagne will do," I said.

∽

Archibald Madison arrived dramatically, just as we were sitting to dinner, with Judith Brandon scurrying in his wake like a seagull after a ship. I admit I gasped a little when I saw his towering figure stride directly to Jimmy Walker and shake his hand.

"I'm glad you could make it, Archie," Jimmy Walker said mildly, and gave a respectful nod to a breathless Mrs. Brandon. "Why don't you sit beside me?"

This displaced Mr. Miller, the Manhattan borough president, but given that he'd been firmly in the mayor's camp from the beginning, he was more than happy to give his pride of place for the prospect of securing this final coup. Though I despised the dirty politics that governed this city, I couldn't help but feel fascinated by the jockeying and gamesmanship on display at this most political of social events. I could easily see how some people got so seduced by the game, they entirely forgot the purpose for which they played.

Lily and I had been seated at the far right end of the table, with the other journalists and third-tier guests. She was talking excitedly about the quotes she'd gotten from the mayor and Al Smith about the

Faustian menace. She'd tried to talk to Sachem Voorhis, but even her vivacious smile couldn't induce him to give an interview. I was still a little shaky from the incident in the hallway, and merely nodded at appropriate intervals while Lily chattered on. In her own way, she could be quite restful.

I expected speeches, but Jimmy Walker seemed perfectly inclined to talk with his neighbors and let the rest of us eat in peace. Lily induced the bribable waiter to bring me a plate of cucumber sandwiches in lieu of the beef bourguignon. Amir and I glanced at each other from time to time, though he was seated clear on the other side of the table with most of the aldermen and Tammany officials. Seeing him here had been bad enough—especially after I had declared my intention to never see him again just this morning. But after the incident in the hallway, my emotions had revealed themselves as intractable and conflicting. With each look, I remembered his hand on my back. Regarding my dessert, I furiously recalled the lies he had told my mother so she would lobby on his behalf. He was my Janus, possessing a beautiful face and an ugly one, and I never knew which side was real.

I was taking a listless bite of strawberry parfait when Bill Oliver, three seats away, put down his napkin and leaned forward over the table.

"Miss Hollis?" he said. I looked over in surprise. "Would you mind if I asked you a question?"

"On the record?" I asked.

Lily smiled like she wanted to kill him. "Now, Bill—"

"You can't stop her from talking, Lily," he said. "And yes, for the paper, if you wouldn't mind."

Lily gave me an entreating look, but it felt churlish of me to refuse to speak to another reporter at what was, after all, a press event. "What would you like to know?"

"I'm rather wondering," he drawled, lifting the pen that had heretofore lain idle by his dessert plate, "if your presence here tonight means you've changed your tune about Faust. I'd be much obliged to know why—I recall the sensation of Miss Harding's story this past January. I believe you were involved in taking down the gangster who originated it."

A discreet cascade of pens had been readied while Bill Oliver asked his question. Lily, seeing the tide turned against her, sighed and picked up her own notebook.

"Well, Zephyr?" she said.

Panic welled in me, though of course I should have anticipated this question. I could hardly tell them the real reason for my recent contact with the mayor. And I owed too much to Elspeth to publicly reveal my ambivalence about Faust prohibition.

"I don't," I said, "I'm not—no, I mean to say, I'm most emphatically not in the mayor's camp on the issue of Faust. I'm here tonight at—because of my general interest in the issue given, as you say, my past involvement."

A younger reporter to Bill Oliver's left leaned forward. "Well, honey," he said, "in that case, how'd you snag an invitation?"

I looked to Lily, but she was clearly reveling in schadenfreude, and would be no help. "I don't know," I said. "You'll have to ask the mayor."

This elicited some good-natured laughter and scribbling. I hoped I wouldn't sound too absurd in the morning dailies. Thankfully, I was spared the rigors of further questioning by the chime of Mayor Walker's spoon against a glass.

"Ladies, gentlemen, I'd like to thank all of you for coming out tonight. It's been a terrific showing in support of an issue which, as you all know, has come to mean quite a bit to me and what I hope to leave as my legacy to the city of New York. This has been a tough fight, but tonight I want to tell you, as my friends, closest supporters— and best adversaries—" he gave a friendly nod to the press, though I imagined this category included Archibald Madison foremost, "that I firmly believe we have the votes to fully license and tax the vampire liquor known as Faust."

Some reporters joined in on the applause, which struck me as being in bad taste. I wondered if the mayor truly did have the votes to pass the bill. Last I had heard from Elspeth, there were still enough holdouts that defeat was possible. But perhaps Madison's defection had tipped the scales.

"Now," said the mayor, when he could be heard, "you might have noticed our very special guest. It's been my great pleasure to talk to him tonight, but I know the rest of you haven't yet had the opportunity. So I thought I'd give him a chance to say a few words to everyone here. Especially my boys in the press, since I don't know that you'd let me leave the room otherwise."

Laughter and clapping. Lily's pen hovered over the page, trembling with her eagerness to record what would surely be tomorrow morning's top story. For my part, I felt a curious unease as Archibald Madison thanked the mayor and stood up. He had that same fanatic gleam I recognized from his speech during the evidentiary hearing. His zeal had made him influential; I supposed he had a certain charisma. But he disturbed me. His hatred of vampires ran so irrationally deep that I couldn't help but shudder every time I looked at him. He thought of them as vermin, whether or not he had agreed to side with the mayor out of pragmatism.

"I'd like to tell you a story, if you'll permit me. The relevance will come clear soon enough. This story is about a youngster, never mind who for the moment, who grows up learning that true justice can sometimes only be found in hatred. This youngster knows, or has been told, about those who look and act just like real people, but who have dangerous lusts, unnatural desires. They are not people, they are Others and they must be killed. The youngster learns to kill, taught by a father who learned this lesson in blood and fire and pain. The youngster's father is a hero, and a hero is a hard man to look up to."

From the other side of the table, Amir caught my gaze and frowned. He jerked his head ever so slightly to the right. I turned around in time to catch a faint movement by the grand doors, the hint of a whisper. Had someone else arrived? But no one entered the room, and I focused again on Madison's odd speech.

". . . And so this youngster came up in the world, learned to kill and then learned to be shrewd. To repudiate killing these Others in public while effecting means to eradicate them in private. The youngster sought justice through hate, but what she didn't understand—"

A gasp went through the room and landed on me like a bucket of icy water. *Oh God no,* I thought. I couldn't move.

"What *she* didn't understand—" Madison continued, louder now, "was that which her hero father had never taught. There might be justice, and there might be virtue of fighting abominations, but there is a third pillar that supports these two, one that *must* support them, if we are to value ourselves as men over beasts, as humans over Others. And that third pillar is the law. Human and imperfect though it may be, it must be obeyed or broken at one's own peril. This youngster broke the law, and sought to blame it on someone far less capable than herself. But I am grateful to her, in my own way. I'm grateful because it caused me to see how my own teachings have neglected this important pillar, this separation of man from beast. Yes, vampires are abominations. Yes, I will fight until I die for their eradication from society. But I will never advocate the breaking of the law. Given that alternative, we are better off with Faust in the hands of the sinners who will suffer its taint."

Whispers ran through the room. I looked at my plate, struggling to keep my face neutral. A few of the sharper journalists gave me long, speculative looks. I wondered if I should leave, but surely fleeing the scene would only confirm everyone's suspicions.

Madison looked around the table and, apparently satisfied, pulled a folded sheet of paper from his breast pocket. I couldn't help it;

I looked at Amir. He stared back at me, a mirror of my own shock and helplessness. His hands didn't move, his face didn't change expression, but I felt his offer: *make a wish.*

I looked away. Even if I made a wish now, I didn't see how I could undo the disaster unfolding with such choreographed precision before me. What would be equal to this devastation? I might as well wish I had never been born.

"I will read you a letter, sent to my associate one week before the killings began. 'My father'—"

"Mr. Madison!" To everyone's utter astonishment, Judith Brandon bolted upright, nearly knocking over her chair. "You will refrain from reading classified material from ongoing police investigations in this public space!"

The mayor looked significantly less apoplectic than his advisor, but he nodded. "Yes, Madison, what's this all about?"

Madison looked up from his paper. "It's about bringing to justice the true perpetrator of these crimes. It's about exposing a hypocrite and a fraud to the world." He raised a trembling hand, like the finger of a vengeful deity.

"Zephyr Hollis," he said, "before God, man, and law, I declare you a murderer."

I found myself on my feet, my chair on the floor behind me. "I have done nothing!"

"Do you deny that you wrote letters to my associate for months encouraging these murders, and then provided him with the means to do so?"

"Of course I deny it! I have dedicated my life to improving conditions—"

"A clever disguise of your true purpose, revealed here in this letter." Abruptly, before Mrs. Brandon could stop him, he strode to the reporters' side of the table and tossed the paper in front of Bill Oliver.

"See the evidence for yourselves," he said.

"Mr. Madison!" Judith Brandon looked on the verge of tears.

The mayor stood up, but didn't walk over. He seemed disappointed and amused at the same time, though this stunt of Madison's had surely dealt his plans a body blow. "I take it you haven't actually changed your position on Faust?"

Madison laughed. "The devils don't need their own brew, Mr. Mayor. Now, if you'll excuse me . . ."

Something hard and cold snapped around my wrists. I didn't even have time to turn around. Harry would say I needed more training, and perhaps I did. But I can't berate myself for not realizing that McConnell had stepped behind me with a pair of handcuffs.

"You're under arrest, Miss Hollis," he said, his lips like a lover's against my ear.

"You've probably heard this one before," I said, "but I've been framed."

"Of course you have," he said. I was almost grateful that he led me from the banquet; with all the flashbulbs in my eyes, I could hardly see at all.

CHAPTER THIRTEEN

"My sister plays harmonica," I said, "but I could never be bothered to learn. Seems such a shame, now."

Across from me, separated by a grubby card table and an ashtray with a dozen cigarette butts, McConnell rubbed his temples. "I would take this more seriously in your place, Miss Hollis."

"I'm serious as a silver bullet," I said, bravely tamping down a hysterical giggle. "But you can't blame me if these farcical charges prompt some levity. It's all a girl can do to keep from screaming."

"I don't think the murder of thirteen vampires—one of whom was a decorated officer—is a farce."

"I don't think so either. And yet here I am, the innocent accused." I grimaced. "You can bet the mayor wasn't anticipating *that* for dessert."

McConnell gave me a long look. We had been in this room for several hours at least. I could not know precisely, because they had relieved me of my pocketwatch along with most of my other possessions. I attempted to take heart from the fact that McConnell seemed so keen to wring a confession from me. It implied that the case against me was not as solid as he wished.

He stood up and stretched his arms high above his head, so they brushed the low ceiling. "I'm going to get tea, Miss Hollis. Would you like some?"

I wondered at his sudden change of mood. Perhaps his kindness now was meant as a shock to my system, after the relentless questioning of the last few hours. Perhaps he thought I would start blubbering into my tea and confess my sins.

His lips twisted in a sardonic half-smile. "I won't poison it, Miss Hollis."

"With milk and extra sugar, if you please," I said.

Alone in the small interrogation room, I looked around idly for some means of escape. McConnell's pen might have a point fine enough to tumble a lock. It wasn't long enough, however, and I wouldn't make it very far even if I could leave this room. I wrapped my arms around my torso, fingering the smooth silk of Lily's dress. Probably my dress now—I couldn't imagine her wearing it after my ignominious performance. At this very moment the presses would be running images of the vampire suffragette being dragged away in handcuffs. At least McConnell had condescended to remove them once we reached the safety of police headquarters. I took a strange comfort in the resplendence of my clothing; as though the aura of just-from-Paris Lanvin might shield me from the worst depredations of my situation. I had asked for a lawyer, and McConnell informed me that none could be sent up before tomorrow morning. And I expected no help from the mayor's quarter.

So I talked. My only hope was that somehow I could convince McConnell I was telling the truth. But even I had to admit the evidence against me appeared damning.

Soon enough, McConnell returned, bearing a tray with the full tea service. He'd even cut lemon wedges, which surprised me. I busied myself with pouring the hot water and adding liberal amounts of cream and sugar. My hands did not tremble, but only with great effort.

He drank his black with lemon, and sipped it like penance. "Why don't we talk about the juvenile vampire."

A little tea splashed over my fingers. I took a careful sip and scalded my mouth. "Why?"

"Do you still deny it?"

I closed my eyes, and saw Judah pressed against Harry's window, looking down into the street. Had my police shadow seen my juvenile vampire in an attic window?

And what reason did I have to lie now? Perhaps telling the truth in this smaller matter would convince him that my denials of murder were truthful.

"Are you charging me?" I asked.

He pursed his lips. "We have been instructed not to," he said.

"By whom?"

"Top brass."

Good old Jimmy Walker kept his promises, much help they were to me now. "But you're sure I'm guilty?"

He set down his cup. "Yes, Miss Hollis."

"Do you have evidence?"

"Enough, I think."

"How odd that you hadn't brought me in already."

He nodded. "I thought so. But I was told it would 'muddy the waters,' in the matter of the current charges."

"So here we are," I said. I liked the tea: it was strong and sweet, and I hadn't had real cream in at least a month. I felt fortified, better than I had in hours. "Tea for two and two for tea."

McConnell laughed. "Indeed, Miss Hollis. But you must realize how hopeless your situation has become. I can make sure things go better for you if you confess now."

"Confess to what? Judah or the murders?"

"The murd—Judah?"

I finished the tea, the dregs sweet enough to hurt my teeth. *Time to play the ace.* "That's his name, the underage vampire I saved."

"You admit it!"

"Yes."

But his triumph quickly muted to anger. "And so you want only endangered the lives of countless people all for—what? You might as well have set off a bomb in Times Square."

I rolled my eyes. "You'll note the complete lack of a body count."

"That I know of—"

"Give yourself some credit, officer. I'm sure you've looked quite thoroughly."

He put his hands flat on the table. "However you managed to avert disaster, the fact remains that you committed a felony, endangered lives and, perhaps most importantly for our purposes here tonight, risked hurting the cause of genuine vampire supporters more than some poor patsy like Bradley Keck ever could."

"Mr. Keck might be a patsy, but he's not mine. I never wrote those letters."

"Why did you save the underage vampire?"

"Because he's just a boy! A scared, traumatized little boy, of no greater danger to you or I than the newsboys down the street."

"I've witnessed it, you know. When I was a boy in Raleigh a juvenile vampire drank dry two of his former playmates before the cops could take him down."

I shuddered. No wonder McConnell despised me. "The trouble," I said, softly, "is that at first they have less control than adults. If you can hold them for long enough, they come to their senses. Perhaps there's some . . . damage to their mental processes, but nothing to make them any more dangerous than you or me."

"I think you're quite dangerous," he said.

"I gathered."

"How did you hold him?"

I decided against mentioning Amir. "In a locked basement."

"The boy didn't hurt you?"

I couldn't tell him about my immunity either. I shook my head. "He had barely Awakened when I locked him in."

"How did you decide it was safe?"

"When he asked me for his mother."

This shocked him, I could tell, but he pressed on. "Where is he now?"

"I can't tell you."

"Miss Hollis, do you understand the danger—"

"He *speaks*. We have conversations. He is no more blood mad than you."

"I don't believe you."

"Then believe this, Officer McConnell. You can imply all you wish that I'm some Trojan Horse, meant to infiltrate the cause of vampire rights. But I saved Judah because of how deeply I believe in them. Imagine if a human child came down with an illness that caused him to temporarily lash out at his caretakers? Even hit them in his insensate fury?"

"Human children are harmless. Vampires are not."

"Is that their fault? Are we helpless before them? I should think not, given the vast number of suckers laid to rest each year. We rush to kill when perhaps we shouldn't. We act out of fear. If Judah's blood madness had proved intractable, I would have staked him myself."

"If you're telling the truth, then you're a fool."

"But I'm not a murderer."

McConnell sighed and shook out his shoulders. He reached under the table and pulled out a folder. Inside were a few dozen pieces of paper, covered in neat handwriting.

I sucked in an involuntary breath. He smiled. "Recognize them?"

"Not specifically. But I know my own noose when I see it."

"It resembles your handwriting," he said.

"True." I wrote in a careful cursive without flourish—a simple, elegant style drilled into me by my mama through painstaking effort. It would not have proved a great challenge for a person with a steady hand to forge. I did not bother to say so. McConnell picked a letter from the top of the pile and began reading.

" 'I believe Faust was a gift. The moment I heard of it, I understood that I had found the means, finally, of striking a blow against the evil among us.' Dated three weeks ago. And tonight you attended the mayor's dinner." He looked up expectantly.

"Not because I support Faust!"

"So you oppose it?"

"I'm not sure, if you must know. I've come to believe prohibition is a mistaken solution to social problems."

"You're still an active member of Friends Against Faust. That makes you a hypocrite by your own admission. Perhaps you're hypocrite enough to publicly support vampires while secretly murdering them?"

"If you're so sure, then why are we speaking? Because you only have those letters, flimsy enough without other evidence. And have you asked yourself why you have been unable to find other evidence, despite, I'm sure, herculean efforts?"

"Because you manipulated someone else into doing the dirty work."

"But *how* did he do it, officer? With tainted blood. Which I don't have, and have never had, and certainly never sent to him. If you can't prove that, I don't see how you have a case."

Honestly, I was far from sure of my accuracy on this point, but his eyes widened with a kind of frustrated self-doubt that heartened me. I was all bluster and fire now; the bravery of a woman with nothing left to lose.

"We have other evidence," he said softly.

"You—"

"We've determined the Blood Bank where the tainted blood originated."

My stomach squeezed so tightly I tasted the remains of my tea. Déjà vu overpowered me, as though I knew precisely what I would ask and what he would answer, and yet I did so anyway. "Which Bank?"

He watched me very carefully as he said, "St. Marks."

I closed my eyes and took several deep, calming breaths. I remembered Ysabel's strange behavior over the past week; the cryptic conversation, the worried looks. *Family trouble,* she had said. Or perhaps trouble of a deadlier kind? Of blood improperly sorted and given out?

"But how would the killer have known it was tainted?" I asked, mostly to myself.

"I imagine she had some familiarity with the Bank, having volunteered there for several years. She had probably learned the owners' system of marking the bags to be discarded. One Hebrew word, discreetly chalked in the corner. Forbidden."

I had never known this about Ysabel's operation, and the knowledge that she had shielded me from something so potentially dangerous frightened me. I started shaking and I couldn't stop. I had thought she trusted me. I regarded her as I would my own grandmother.

"Something else is going on," I said. "There's more to this. No, I don't know what, how could I! But consider it from your perspective, officer. Your friend and partner has been murdered. You're almost sure I did it. But there's doubt, I've seen it in your eyes all night. Why would I write so transparently about my family life? How would I know about the tainted blood when I've never seen Ysabel quarantine a bag in all my time there? What if by arresting me, you let the real killer go free?"

"You can't always be sure in this business, Miss Hollis. I think I've got a solid case."

"You're still talking to me."

He slammed his fist on the table, knocking over his teacup. "I wanted your confession!"

"I didn't do it," I said.

"You did!"

"The more you say it, the less you believe."

"You are a goddamned whore."

His swearing surprised me more than the overturned china. Had I pushed him too far? Had I lost? I tried one last time.

"Officer McConnell, do your job and ask. I didn't write those letters, so they're bound to get plenty wrong. If you dig a little more, you'll uncover something different. I know you hate me. I know you think I murdered your friend. But I didn't, and if you don't ask, you'll never be sure."

A long, tense silence. McConnell didn't even look at me, he just buried his head in his hands. Finally, he stood up. "I'll have an officer escort you to a cell, Miss Hollis," he said, the veneer of polite conversation painfully reapplied. "Good night."

And with that my last, best hope walked out the door and did not look back.

※

I fell asleep on a cot so hard it made my bed at Mrs. Brodsky's seem like the king's repose. I shivered inside the cocoon of my red dress, tears splashing on my hand when I could no longer keep them back. I knew hopelessness then, as though he were sitting in the cell with me and whispering my failures. Eventually, even my misery had to give way to sleep.

Not many hours later, I was roused by a vigorous banging on the doors of my cage. I leapt to my feet before I could focus properly, and fumbled for a knife before I remembered they had taken it.

"Do you do that every morning?" said the blurry figure from beyond the bars. McConnell.

"Only when threatened," I said.

"Set your mind at ease, then. I've come to ask your parents' telephone number."

I rubbed my eyes. "Why?"

"There are several mentions of them in the letters."

This seemed encouraging. I was not in the habit of divulging details of my family life, so perhaps the mysterious letter-writer had gotten something wrong. "Yarrow, Montana, 2R221."

He wrote this down and then nodded. "You'll see me again before long, Miss Hollis."

"My lawyer?"

He had turned to leave, but now paused. "In court on your behalf. It might take him some time to see you; it's a zoo out there."

I had conveniently forgotten that I had surely spawned the scandal of the . . . well, week, at least. Deep into the doldrums of late July, even Lindbergh's ticker tape would be looking a little yellow around the edges. I hoped that at least Lily was getting some newspaper inches out of this. She would owe me for years, so long as I stayed out of prison.

Alone again, I paced up and down the six by six room. There was a tiny metal lavatory in the corner, which I used only after a great internal struggle. My hair felt like straw, my mouth tasted like day old wine. I had never longed for Mrs. Brodsky's clean, lemon-scented floors more in my life. And to think, McConnell had kept me in relative luxury, in one of the few jail cells actually inside the police headquarters. Had he taken me to the Tombs, or worse, the alimony jail on Ludlow Street, who knew what indignities I would be suffering!

I wondered what Daddy would do in my place. Jailbreak? More likely yell down the hall for some beer. I started to laugh, but then remembered that Daddy had left the family for parts unknown, Betty had helped kill a golem on our roof, and Mama had cried on the phone yesterday for the first time in my adult memory. Were they all right? I wished Daddy would just come home and sort things out—I didn't believe Amir's murderous insinuations for a minute, but how could anyone relax until Daddy explained himself? I hoped that my family would stay safe, even if I ended up in the dock for multiple vampire homicides.

But I wished . . .

"Just one wish," I whispered to myself. "One to take away this whole horrible week."

I had spent so long avoiding making a decision about Amir that the ambiguity of our relationship had come to be a perverse comfort. I couldn't bear to push him away entirely, but I didn't dare pull him close. His crass manipulation of my family proved that he had not reformed in the least. He still thought of humans as interesting talking animals, to be turned and twisted according to his whims.

But today was the fateful Sunday, and I supposed I had made my decision. Sofia was my only option. Amir and I would be free of each other once and for all, assuming I managed to get released before this evening. I continued to pace until the pinched toes of Lily's borrowed shoes proved too much for me, and I sat back down on the cot. I did not consider walking in my stockings. The floor of this cell looked like its previous inmates had not bothered to aim for the lavatory. I desperately wanted a drink and some food, but when I shouted down the hall, no one came. To distract from thoughts of starving to death in a police oubliette, I contemplated who could possibly have written those letters to Bradley Keck. The letter-writer possessed a disturbing amount of knowledge about my life, but had twisted everything to fit a perverse mold. The reinterpretation of my every move as that of a secret vampire hater indicated a methodical vindictiveness that was nearly as impressive as it was frightening. It felt personal, but if I had done something to make anyone hate me this much, wouldn't I know it? Shouldn't I be able to point to my mortal enemy and vow revenge? I could name plenty of people who didn't like me, but enough to spend months carefully orchestrating a series of murders, with the apparently sole purpose of using me as a fall guy?

Maybe Nicholas had grieved more for the death of his father than I knew. It was possible; often victims of horrible abuse came to love the ones who had hurt them. But such a slow, methodical plan seemed entirely unlike him. If he wanted revenge, he was far more likely to crawl through my window and rip my throat out. He had been raised with little respect for the law; he'd hardly rely on it to mete out revenge.

Madison himself seemed far more likely. Indeed, looked at in a certain light, it was ingenious. He wanted vampires murdered systematically, but could not be seen doing so or encouraging it himself. So he adopts a gullible, easily manipulated former indigent, and grooms him with anonymous letters studded with enough references to an innocent person that anyone reading them would assume her to be the real culprit. *But why pick me?*

Ideologically we were completely opposed, but I was hardly the most prominent proponent of vampire rights in the city. I certainly wasn't of a stature to match his dominance of city politics, and I doubted that he had even heard of me before meeting me in his offices.

But Bradley Keck had acted as though he knew me during both of our encounters, I recalled, though I could have sworn I had never met him before. Perhaps that meant Madison had singled me out months before our formal meeting. Keck could have met me at a rally months ago and I wouldn't necessarily have recalled his face.

But I could be overcomplicating matters. Surely it was just as likely that Keck had acted as though he knew me because he *believed* that he did—through the letters he thought I was sending him.

Madison could be hateful and Keck could be ignorant and someone else could still be plotting my downfall.

At this moment in my thoughts, a harried police officer arrived, bearing lunch on a tray.

"I haven't had breakfast," I said, taking it. "Do you have any coffee? And a toothbrush?"

"Sorry, we don't usually keep prisoners here overnight," he said. "I'll see what I can do."

The meal consisted of a limp ham sandwich, vegetable soup, and a can of my favorite variety of ginger beer. Given the range of possibilities, I counted this as good luck, and dipped the bread into the soup. The officer returned a few minutes later with a mug of coffee and an apology for the missing toothbrush.

"Looks like your lawyer will get you out on bail," he said, as he was leaving. "But it might take another few hours for the paperwork to go through."

This news combined with the food to make me practically cheery. I sipped the coffee and wondered how I could prove that Madison had written the letters, as he was the most likely candidate. A warrant to go through his things ought to turn up plenty of evidence, but that would require convincing the police and a judge of probable cause. And yet I wondered. It would be convenient for Madison to be the author of my misery, but how would he have learned so much about my childhood? I hadn't kept my daddy's profession a secret, but not many people knew that I'd been raised to be a demon hunter. This implied someone I knew well, but everything in me recoiled from the idea. No one I trusted would be capable of something like this. I refused to believe it.

It was well into the evening before I finally heard voices again in the hallway. I recognized them both, to my surprise. Amir was chatting with McConnell, something about a hearing. For a moment, I could have sworn he was glowing like a knight in a fairy tale. I blinked.

"What are you doing here?" I asked.

"Your lawyer," McConnell said. "He said you hired him."

"Pro bono," Amir said smoothly and I stared.

"You're a lawyer?"

His lips quirked up. "A way to pass the time. I have a degree, but you'll want to find a trial lawyer if this mess goes any further."

"You've been granted bail, Miss Hollis," McConnell said, brushing past Amir to unlock the door. "Someone thought you were worth a hundred thousand dollars, so don't go running back to Montana."

This sum seemed so improbably large that I skipped over it entirely. "Did you call my family?"

For the first time since his arrival, I noticed that McConnell seemed genuinely angry, not merely gruff. "They were out," he said. "At least, after I identified myself as a police officer. Several calls went unanswered."

I closed my eyes. "Bloody stakes," I said. I should have known that Mama would go to ground after the scare with Daddy and the golem on the roof. But good luck explaining that to McConnell.

"Worried, Miss Hollis? I would be. You had me out chasing rainbows all afternoon. But at least now I've learned something useful."

"You have?"

"You were obviously worried that we would arrest you. So you warned your family not to speak to the police. But why do that if you're innocent, Miss Hollis?"

"You've been hounding me all week! And my family—"

McConnell leaned against the bars. "Knows we're investigating you. Knows we'd want to talk to them, though they shouldn't. Not if you're innocent. Not unless you knew the contents of those letters before I showed them to you. And how would you have managed that, Miss Hollis? Only if you'd written them."

Amir took a step forward. "Officer, we have paid bail. If necessary, I'll wake the judge."

McConnell shrugged and unlocked the door to my cell. "Enjoy freedom, Miss Hollis, if you can in this weather. I'll see you in court."

∞

"There's a car waiting just outside," Amir told me from the vestibule. "Keep your head down. Don't look at the cameras, don't answer questions."

I didn't ask him if he was overreacting. The buzz of eager reporters and protestors outside made me feel as though I were drowning in quicksand.

"Why did you get me out?" I asked. I adjusted my dress and wished that I didn't look quite so rumpled.

He gave me a sharp look, more despairing than I expected. "Do you know anyone else who could part with a hundred grand?"

His every look and gesture offered me something, but I didn't know how to accept it. I retreated behind insults.

"At least your profligacy is good for something."

"For something," Amir echoed, again in that strange tone. Was I treating him too harshly? Probably, but I didn't want to think about what would happen if I stopped.

"Would you like me to shield you?" he asked.

An abyss seemed to have opened up at my feet, the same shade as his dark hair. "Shield?"

"From the reporters," he said, softly. "I could put my arm around you. Act as a barrier."

I gave a hollow laugh. "No. That's quite all right. I've already cost you a hundred grand, let me not be responsible for ruining a suit with rotten eggs."

Amir smiled. "Ever brave, Zephyr."

I pushed open the door, into the yawning pit of unwanted fame.

The questions were relentless as Amir had warned. I ignored the voices and the flashbulbs alike, pushing blindly ahead to the black car waiting at the curb. Amir cleared the way ahead, but I had to fend off grasping hands all the same. Calls of "Why did you do it, Zephyr?" blended with chants of "Vampires are people!" and "We support *human* rights!" until they seemed to form a leviathan, a creature of misery and ill-intent. I elbowed aside a particularly insistent reporter and ran for the door, which Amir held open. I'd plunged inside before I realized that I shared the backseat with someone else.

"Nicholas?" I said, recognizing his silhouette. Amir climbed into the passenger side front seat and shut the door.

"We made it," Amir said, at the same moment that Nicholas turned to me—his face a mask of naked, animal fury—and slammed my body against the door and window. If I hadn't been so tired or frazzled, I might have managed to overpower him. As it was, he had a knife by my ribs and his fangs near my neck before I could catch my breath.

"Drive, Charlie," Nicholas rasped, and the car lurched forward.

My skin tingled; Amir had blasted enough heat to scorch the seats. "What in blazes are you—"

"Quiet, smoky," Nicholas said, the quiet of his voice in stark contrast with the wild fury in his eyes. "I'll stick her up the ribs if you more than breathe."

I shivered. The knife edge vibrated against my skin. "What is this, Nicholas?"

"You killed him," he said. His quiet voice broke on the last syllable. He sounded like a real thirteen-year-old boy, and that scared me more than anything. "You killed Kevin, and all this time you pretended to help."

"I didn't," I said. Even speaking was difficult, with my face squashed against the window glass.

"There's letters," Nicholas said. He pushed the knife until it nicked my skin. I hardly felt it.

"It's a frame-up. Someone else wrote those letters to implicate me."

"Who'd do that, Charity?"

"I don't know."

"Guess."

I hesitated, then realized plausibility ought to be my last concern. "Anyone with an axe to grind against vampires. Madison, maybe."

He moved his mouth a little from my neck. "Madison?" he said. "He's the one who said you did it."

"That would be clever of him," I said, and very carefully detached my cheek from the glass. Charlie was driving us southeast, toward the river. At this hour, the docks were deserted. No one would heed a call for help. It appalled me that I had forgotten how dangerous Nicholas could be. He had attacked me once before. I had seen his face when we visited the morgue. His grief then was his grief now, only now it had a target.

"It makes sense," said Charlie, timidly.

"I told you to stay out of this," Nicholas said. I had been watching his reflected image in the glass, but suddenly he leaned back in his seat and allowed me to turn around.

"Still got the knife," he said, looking between me and Amir. "Still faster than both of you. Don't try anything."

Amir studied my midsection, but the red of the dress would have masked any blood. "I'm all right," I said, before he could ask.

Nicholas gave a slow smile, showing off unretracted fangs. "*Two* boys sweet on you, Charity?" he said, tossing the knife from one hand to another. "That's some trick you got there. I told Charlie he liked you too much to see straight. He didn't think much of the idea that you'd killed Kevin and the others. But I'll tell you, Zephyr Hollis, I think you coulda done it. Maybe you didn't. You've always seemed on the up and up about this do-gooder business. You're a nice enough girl, but I ain't sweet on you. I remember how you gutted my papa on the floor of that heathen room of his. Right through the ribs, thatta girl, and there ain't a sucker in this city made it past five who can't tell who to watch out for. You're a Defender, Charity. I knew it the moment you pulled out that sword."

"I'm not a Defender," I said.

"Used to be."

"I gave it up. For charity, as you say."

He gave his knife a considering nod. "Maybe you just pretended?"

"I saved your life," I tried.

"You're still talking," he said.

I swallowed and fell silent.

He didn't seem inclined to speak, and Charlie and Amir didn't dare. We drove over the Brooklyn Bridge, the lights of the city suspended in a summer fog. The moon was lost behind clouds, but it still glowed brightly. I wondered if he would try to kill me; if I could move fast enough to stop it. I didn't think so. Just over the bridge, he slammed the knife in its sheath.

"Pull over, Charlie," he said.

Charlie turned the wheel with a screech of tires. "I knew you'd believe her, Nick!"

"I don't believe her. I'm just not sure. So here's how it goes, Charity. You've got a day to prove you didn't kill Kevin. No one kills one of my boys without answering for it. Not even you."

I doubted I could learn much in a day, but I nodded. What was one more impossible deadline to add to the list?

Nicholas left without another word. Charlie hesitated, looked back at me, and doffed his cap. "I'll make him see sense, Miss Zephyr," he said, and then stumbled out of the car.

Amir looked after them from the front seat. "I could kill him," he said, by way of an offer.

"No."

"You're that fond of him?" I didn't understand the flatness in Amir's voice. He wouldn't look at me.

"I'm . . . in a way. He sings like an angel."

"What if he kills like one, *habibti?*"

My breath caught. "If it comes to that, I'll do it. I owe him that much." Maybe he'd been right to call me a Defender. I'd never forgotten my training.

Amir sighed and turned around. The puddling streetlight made him look gaunt. I wondered how much effort it had taken to get me out of jail. Or perhaps he had been busy teleporting?

"What happens now, Amir?" I hadn't meant to say that. It was too open, too vulnerable. Amir was a paradox, a man whose mere presence invited me to let down my guard, and whose conduct least deserved it.

He reached out and cupped my cheek in his warm hand. "You go to trial, if necessary. You didn't do it, Zephyr. We'll find enough evidence to exonerate you."

He removed his hand a moment later, as though surprised to have found it there.

"You're so sure?" I asked.

He frowned. "Of your innocence? Don't be daft, Zeph."

"Everyone else believed Madison."

"It only seemed so to you. The circumstances of your arrest were colorful, but the letters can only damage you so much without other evidence. I was just speaking with your friend Elspeth and she doesn't believe a word of it."

"Elspeth! What did you want her for?"

He smiled. "About your plans to toss me into the rubbish heap tonight."

I sat up very straight. "You were trying to sabotage the ceremony, weren't you?"

"Even if that were possible, I'd hardly admit it."

"You'd say anything if you thought it would make me do what you want!" This anger, which had begun as a wan flame, grew larger and more comforting. Whereas the ordeal of jail and Nicholas's attack had left me feeling weak and frightened, my familiar anger at Amir's behavior served as a panacea. I could do anything as long as I hated him. "You've been manipulating me since we met."

"That word again. Do you know, Zephyr, I'm beginning to wonder if you aren't so obsessed with manipulation because you do so much of it yourself."

This hit a good deal harder than I was willing to admit. "The truth doesn't stop existing just because you twist it enough. It will always come back to you."

Amir leaned back against the dashboard, still facing me. I had a momentary pang of regret that we were still separated by the bulky car seats, but I didn't explore why. The anger was more appealing.

"Will it?" he said quietly. "That's fascinating, because running from the truth has worked for most of your life, as far as I can tell."

This was such an appalling, terrifying thing to say that my mouth fell open. "What are you talking about?" I asked.

"Your father," he said, "did something to you to make you immune. And yet every one of your siblings knows more about it than you do. Your father—"

"Did not do anything—*anything*—like the vile slander you've accused him of. I don't know what my immunity has to do with this, but however he did it—"

"How did he do it?"

It was a simple question, posed in a reasonable tone, but it absorbed my words like dry sand. I stared at him, desperate and afraid.

"You don't know," he said after a minute, when I couldn't speak.

No, I didn't. Did Harry? Did Vera? I thought of the little boy lying in our backyard, whose name I'd never known.

But no, Daddy would never have done anything like that.

"I'm leaving," I said abruptly, and pulled at the door handle. Amir opened his own door so that we stood, finally, with nothing between us but our own pride and fear.

"Where?" he asked. He seemed hopeful. I didn't understand why.

"Sofia's," I said. "I have an appointment."

"*She* isn't who you need to see," he said sharply. "You won't listen to me, I can see that, but you truly haven't figured it out by now?"

"Not who I *need* to see? You really have some gall. You have no right to tell me what to do."

He clasped his hands together. "Zephyr . . . don't."

I looked up at him. Would I ever see him again? The anger made every other emotion recede, but regret passed me like the smell of roses in Shadukiam.

"Why not?" I asked.

"It won't solve anything."

I laughed. "It will solve you."

CHAPTER FOURTEEN

I sat on a chair in the middle of a chalk circle, while Sofia drew holy words in Arabic in a careful pattern around another one. We were in her kitchen. I had asked if the spell would hurt her baking, but she laughed and said, "Holy ones like honey bees—give mystery." I wasn't entirely sure what this meant, but I supposed that was the point. While I waited, I nervously reviewed what Elspeth and Sofia had told me about the nature of the bargaining. I had to have things to offer whatever demon she summoned. I knew from my Montana days that demons weren't particularly interested in human tangible goods. I wouldn't get away with offering a priceless Ming vase, even if I had one to give. Demons were like bad witches in fairy tales; they wanted your firstborn child, your voice, your youth. In my present mood, even such an exorbitant price seemed worth it to get rid of Amir forever. But first I would try lesser goods: the red in my hair, my skill with a blade, perhaps even my singing voice. I hoped this would be enough.

I thought of Amir only as dust to be brushed away. I buried any recollections of our final conversation, of his face as he watched me turn from him. If his voice seemed to bubble up from the murky depths as I watched Sofia prepare the summoning, I firmly ignored it. She *isn't the one you need to see. You haven't figured it out by now?* I heard him say, and I smothered the voice with images of the endless boxes of Faust that Lily had photographed in his possession. He had no moral standing from which to lecture me. He had no further claim on my indulgence and certainly not on my affections. I would bargain with this demon, and Amir would go away, and that would be the end of it.

Sofia stood up. "Is all right?" she said. She looked younger tonight—perhaps from the soft glow of the candles placed around the room. She had changed from a matronly skirt and blouse to a simple black robe. Instead of a tight chignon, she'd bound her thick salt-and-pepper hair in two rope-like braids.

"It will be," I said, and this seemed to satisfy her. I felt absurd, still in the red dress I was afraid I would have to burn after all this was through. But I had only taken enough time to stop at home and take my remaining cash from the bottom of my trunk, along with ten dollars Aileen had given me without question. If I had dared to clean up and change, I had been afraid my anger would give way. Amir didn't deserve another moment's consideration. Sofia hadn't batted an eye at either my appearance or the dress, though she must have known of my circumstances before arrival. Imperturbability must be a good quality in a *sahir*.

Our language barrier hadn't mattered very much, at this late stage. Sofia had drawn herself a third circle opposite the main one. She stepped inside it and placed the chalk beside her foot.

"I start," she said. I braced myself, but she kept her hands at her side. "You sure?" she asked, after a moment. "The djinni . . ." she trailed off, struggling for words. "He not bad," she said, finally. "For djinni."

I felt as though she had slapped me. After all I had gone through just to get to this point? "I am sure," I snapped. This seemed sufficient; Sofia nodded, though I wasn't sure how to interpret the look in her eyes.

She began with a chant, low-throated and insistent. The air had already been stifling, but now it felt as though a charged storm cloud had blown through the windows. My hair began to lift around my head, and the layered skirt of the much-abused dress rustled in an invisible breeze. Sofia continued chanting. In the center of the main circle, smoke began to gather. Faintly, at first, like a guttered candle, and then burgeoning into a roiling, billowing mass. It glowed red and black and smelled like a forest fire. I'd only seen Daddy summon a demon once, and this didn't look anything like that last time. In fact, all that smoke reminded me of a—

Oh no.

Sofia's chant grew louder as the apparition in the circle expanded. It still hadn't resolved itself into anything I could recognize as a figure, but it appeared alive all the same. As though something inside that glowing mass were watching and evaluating me. A djinni. One I'd never met before—I'd been around Amir and Kardal enough to recognize them by the smell of their smoke. I watched it grow to fill the entire space inside the circle. I wondered if it would break through the ceiling, but the smoke seemed content to settle there, towering above the two of us. The smoke now blocked my view of Sofia, but her voice had not ceased chanting once during the astonishing display of her summoning. After another minute, the smoke began to coalesce, collapsing into something resembling a face and torso. I had thought Kardal made little effort to appear human, but this djinni made him look like Rudolph Valentino. His face shifted into shapes like a series of child's masks, though his eyes maintained their singular bright focus on me. His head was at least as large as his torso and anything below vanished into billowing smoke.

Sofia paused her chant, reached down to pick up the last bit of chalk and tossed it high in the air. As it sailed above her she spoke again: her rolling, decisive cadences somehow stilling the creature in the circle. It turned to her, but made no other move. The chalk had nearly finished its plunge when she said what must be the final words and it exploded into a shimmering, delicate powder that floated around her like snow. The djinni's face settled into a single countenance—glowing eyes, a wide forehead and hair that waved behind him. He half smiled in that same way Amir would in a mood of amused condescension. My hands gripped the side of the chair, but Sofia had instructed me to stay where I was.

"You've tied one of my sons to you, and now you want to cut him loose," the djinni said. His voice was deeper than even Kardal's, and painfully resonant. I realized who Sofia must have called.

"Are you Kashkash?" I said.

The impossibly large smile widened. "None other."

"Will you help me?" I tried without success to keep my voice from shaking.

His laugh made the ovens groan and my chair wobble. I flinched and forced myself to look back. "You know nothing," he said, "of what I am. Or what you ask me to do."

My anger at Amir had receded in a wave of terror and self-doubt. But I clung to its tattered remains because it was all my pride had left. "I know I wish to be free of your son's binding," I said.

Kashkash blinked his monstrous eyes and leaned forward. He could not cross the line of my circle, but he lowered his face until it was even with my chair and just a few feet away. His eyes were as big as my head; each tooth as large as my hand. I couldn't look at that, but I didn't dare look away. I stared at his nose, so grotesquely like Amir's, and trembled.

"He did not bind you, little human," Kashkash said. His voice blasted my ears. "You bound *him*."

"I saved his life!" I said. "The binding was just a side effect."

He lifted his head to the ceiling again and seemed to consider this. "And yet you hold on to it so fiercely."

"What do you mean?"

He manifested a finger and wagged it in the air. "Someone tested the bond. A foolish trap for my son to have fallen into, but still, a test. Someone else claiming Amir as his vessel should have damaged your bond—maybe even killed you, little human—and yet, here you are, asking me to break something you might have accomplished yourself."

That's what Jimmy Walker had meant to do with his scroll? "I had been hoping to manage it without dying!"

"Do you know how a bond is tested, little human?" he said, and I felt something like a bell go off inside me, a resonance with a conviction I couldn't put words to. *You haven't figured it out by now?* Amir had said. "The test is power"—he raised one hand—"against desire." He raised the other. "When they meet, which wins?" His hands smacked together, shaking the floor with its force. Dishes crashed to the floor and I had to stand to keep my chair from tipping.

"I don't understand," I said, when the echoes faded to silence.

That smile again. "You've willed yourself not to," he said. "You *wanted* that bond, little human. Enough to stand up against someone who wanted it very badly himself. You fought that battle without even knowing it, and that's the only reason you're alive right now."

"I . . ." The bell inside me tolled louder now, making me tremble with its force. I tried to push back.

"I hate Amir," I said. "He's abused my trust, manipulated and deceived me from the moment we met." But Kashkash's eyes were too much like Amir's. The bells thundered like I was in the tower of St. Michael's. I gasped, closed my eyes, and tried one last time:

"And he lied," I said. "About Daddy. He said . . . he said . . ."

How did you get immune?

I realized I was crying.

Sophia wasn't the one I needed to see, Amir had told me. So who? And then I knew.

"You summoned me," Kashkash said, "for a purpose. I am not used to being summoned. This great *sahir* of Washington Street is the only one to have dared it for a very long time. So this is my price, little human." He paused. "I will grant your wish."

I felt as though he had stabbed me in the throat. I stumbled forward. I wondered what would happen if I broke the circle, but I had that much sense remaining.

"No," I whispered. "Please."

Kashkash's face turned hard and inhuman. "You have treated my son very badly, Zephyr Hollis. I do this for his honor as much as my own."

"But, what will happen to him?"

"To him? Nothing, provided you keep this one condition."

I looked up and wiped my eyes. "What?"

"Do not bind him again. In word, thought, or deed. If you do, he will go away and may never return. This is the word of Kashkash and it is law."

His voice was so loud my ears rang in the ensuing silence.

"I understand," I said.

He nodded. "It is done," he said, and vanished.

⊷

I borrowed clothes from Sofia, who seemed to understand on some level that transcended language what had happened to me in her kitchen. I walked directly to the East Village where the last of the Yiddish theaters were getting out for the night, raucous theatergoers pouring onto the sidewalks to wait for their favorite stars. No one spared me a glance.

Ysabel lived on the top floor of one of the updated former tenements on Fourth Street, between Second and Third Avenues. *Know thyself*, the edict of the Oracle at Delphi, had always seemed to me like the vague aphorisms promoted in books of self-uplift. Now I knew it to be a warning, a statement of fear as profound as anything Dante carved above the first gate of hell. I was free, but I felt submerged, drowned by the mistakes of my father and my own willful refusal to see them. I should have come to Ysabel the moment I heard of the murders. Instead, I had ignored every hint of the truth.

Sofia's skirt was slightly too large for me; I hitched it up as I climbed the stairs to Ysabel's apartment. A carved prayer scroll had been nailed into the doorframe. I knocked on the door and fingered it as I waited. I couldn't read Hebrew. When she had marked a certain bag of blood with the word "forbidden," I wouldn't have known what it meant. I didn't know who would.

Ysabel's husband, Saul, opened the door. He was a gaunt man, stooped at the shoulders though still tall. He wore an embroidered yarmulke and was carrying a small, leather-bound book with Hebrew lettering embossed on the front.

"She's inside," he said, wearily. "She's been expecting you."

You haven't figured it out by now?

But now I had. At least this much of the puzzle.

I thanked Saul and let him lead me through the apartment I'd only visited once before. Then the occasion had been a dinner with other Blood Bank volunteers that my daddy would have disapproved of mightily had he known. Now, I wondered at the dishes piled in the sink, the broken crates in the corner of the living room, the dust on the mantelpiece. Ysabel was sitting in a chair in her bedroom.

"Sit down, *bubbala*," she said, gesturing toward the bed. *She looks deflated*, I thought. Dark bruises beneath her eyes, sallow cheeks, sagging, ghostly skin. I could only imagine how awful this week must have been.

"It's my blood, isn't it?" I said.

"Yes, dear," she said, with mingled misery and relief.

"How . . ." I didn't know where to start. I looked around the room instead: the handmade quilt on the bed, the photos on the dresser of Ysabel and Saul, far younger, sitting awkwardly for the picture with a fat-cheeked baby between them. A girl, I guessed, from the ribbon in her hair.

"How did you find out?" I asked.

Saul's voice came distantly from the other room. Ysabel looked up, realized he had picked up the phone, and sunk back into her chair.

"When you donated that first time. I never once worried—no marks on your arms, no red eyes, nothing to think you weren't perfectly healthy. And you are! Perfectly healthy. I didn't know. I gave it to, to a friend." She covered her eyes. I wanted to hold her hand, but I didn't know if she would want me to. I didn't know if she hated me.

The first time, she had said. Two years ago.

"Oh, Ysabel, why didn't you tell me?"

She wiped her eyes and took my own hand. "He died," she said, softly. "I couldn't bear to burden you with that. It was clear you didn't know. Always after I would take your bag and mark it so it wouldn't get lost with the others. Then I'd throw it away."

Forbidden, she had written, in careful Hebrew. But never in my sight.

"You never gave out another bag?" I said. "No one else died?"

She shook her head. "Never! Except . . ."

"Except now," I finished. "Do you know who stole it? How could they have gotten to it before you threw it out?"

"I . . . I grew careless. It's always so busy at the Bank, you know. Sometimes I would wait a whole day. What did it matter, I thought, no one else knew. But she did." A sob escaped her lips and she covered her mouth with her hands. "She knew and she took it, right after you gave last."

I'd last donated at Ysabel's around two weeks ago. Just when the letter-writer had sent Bradley Keck the poison blood.

My throat felt swollen and painful; it hurt to swallow. I shook with tension and exhaustion and the horror of the truth. McConnell had been right to arrest me. Whatever Keck's guilt and that of his anonymous enabler, it was ultimately my blood that had done the killing. My immunity had turned them halfway back to human again. I should have guessed in the morgue. Amir certainly had.

Saul walked into the room with a teapot and a cup. "You look like you could use it."

Just the sight of the teapot filled me with longing. I hadn't eaten since that meager meal back in my prison cell, and I hadn't had a drink in nearly that long. I thanked him so profusely that he laughed, a little bleakly. "Drink as much as you want."

I sipped the bitter tea (too impolite to ask for milk and sugar) while Saul said something to Ysabel in soft Yiddish. She frowned but he shook his head and patted her on the shoulder before leaving the room again. I could only imagine how he was taking this situation. Had he known the poor vampire that I'd killed? Did he know—"

I set down my cup and looked at her. "*She?*" I said, only now understanding the implications. "You know who took the bag?"

That meant that Ysabel knew the letter-writer. I could tell the police and Nicholas and clear my name!

But Ysabel started to cry. "You have to understand, *bubbala*, I wanted to tell you. Oh, this whole horrible week, how Saul and I argued. But I couldn't! She is wrong, I understand that, but she's been hurt so much and I couldn't, I just couldn't turn in my own child . . ."

Resonances shook me again, and by now I'd learned to pay attention. I felt hazy with disbelief, shock, and a sad understanding. I found myself kneeling on the floor in front of her chair.

"Ysabel," I whispered, taking her hand to steady myself. "Who did I kill? The first time, with my blood?"

"My son-in-law," Ysabel said, just as quietly. "Michael Brandon."

In the other room, Saul unlocked the door with a click. "Tateh," I heard Judith Brandon say as she walked inside her parent's home. "Thank you."

I looked up at Ysabel, though she slid in and out of focus. I'd been poisoned. Saul had seen to that, and maybe Ysabel had known.

"Her husband . . . was a vampire?"

"He became a *bruxa* when he worked for old Mayor Herod. They made him leave his job. Terrible business. And then . . ."

"I'm sorry," I said, slipping on one elbow to the floor.

"No, Zephyr," she said, crying again. "If someone goes to *Gehinnam* for this, it is me."

The last thing I saw was Judith Brandon's shoes, wet from the rain.

∽

I awoke alone, with my hands and feet bound and a gag in my mouth. This was a common predicament of heroines in the Mary Roberts Rinehart novels my sister Vera loved to read, but I had never imagined it to be quite this uncomfortable. Perhaps I could still count on an intrepid hero to find me before I suffered permanent damage to my shoulders?

Then I recalled how I had last left the only possible candidate for intrepid hero and allowed myself a sob. No, I could hardly count on Amir's help now.

I still felt groggy from the poison, but I forced my eyes open. So, she'd taken me to her office. It surprised me a little, but on the other hand, I could see why she would have deemed her isolated basement lair safe enough. Especially if she had expected me to remain insensate for longer. I propped myself up against a wall so as to get a better view of my latest prison. It was gloomier than I remembered, the only light coming from around the door and its opaque window.

I was a little surprised to be alive at all, and wondered if this unexpected gift could not be a sign that I was meant to have a chance to repent.

And to find my goddamned daddy.

I slid along the slightly dusty floor until I reached the door. I pushed the handle down awkwardly with my chin; locked, of course. I hadn't expected anything else, but I had to be sure. The sort of person who could plot a serial murder and frame someone else for the crime would tie knots securely and lock a door. I sat back down, the last of the effects of the poison waning. I was hungry, but my thirst felt even more painful than the ropes. A few more hours in here and I'd emulate Coleridge's ancient mariner.

I leaned back against the wall. The gag in my mouth effectively prevented screaming—indeed, it almost prevented breathing—and I tried to remember the way to her office from the main hall. Perhaps I could throw myself at the door in case someone happened to pass by? But my legs had been bound in such a way that when I tried to stand, I tipped over immediately. She had probably researched proper knot-tying of prisoners in the public library.

I fell over a second time and stayed on the floor, struggling to catch my breath. As I did so, I realized that I was staring at Judith Brandon's desk. And if I couldn't get out, perhaps I could get *in*. I wormed my way closer. The stacks of paper on top of the desk might be interesting, but were beyond me at the moment. However, to my delight she had not locked her drawers. I used my chin to pull out the topmost one and then knelt to peer inside. Unfortunately, I didn't have enough light to read well. I could only make out the large font of newspaper headlines, carefully clipped and stacked inside. "VAMPIRE KILLER STRIKES AGAIN!" read one from the *New York World*. I nosed the topmost ones aside: yes, every one was recently clipped, carefully documenting her murder spree of the past week. She'd also kept any mention of me. I had wondered how the letter-writer knew so much about me. Between what Ysabel must have told her and the newspapers, Mrs. Brandon had learned enough to be convincing. I turned around and used what little dexterity my bound hands possessed to dig deeper into the pile. At the very bottom, my fingers encountered a sheet of much heavier stock than newsprint. I bent awkwardly and pulled it out. I dropped it to the floor and turned around. An old photograph. I could hardly see it in the shadows behind the desk, and so I nosed it closer to the door.

I recognized my daddy first, though I'd never seen him so young. He was balancing a massive shotgun on his knee, which was perched on a stone. Four other men—two older, two about his age—had posed for the portrait. They stood tall and stern, each one carrying a gun or a stake. A hunting party sometime in the nineties, judging by their clothes and my daddy's youth. Daddy loved telling stories of his old hunting days, but this didn't look like anything I'd heard before. The rocks and trees behind them looked like Montana, for one, and I'd thought Daddy did most of his early hunting down south, in Georgia and Tennessee. I recognized one of the older men: Charles Simpson, a strange fixture of my early childhood who would come to town with the intention of drinking with Daddy, fighting, and then storming off for another year. I remember one year he and Daddy had a fistfight over the fact that I couldn't shoot straight. He died a few years after that, something wrong with his liver.

But there were three other men in this picture. A young man Daddy's age, to his left, with thunderous black eyebrows and a stake in one hand. Another older fellow, looking off to the side like he couldn't wait to get away. And, on the far right, a negro man, shorter than the others, with a sheathed sword on his back. Together, they looked like a seasoned hunting band, not some group tossed together for the sake of a photo.

I leaned down and saw that someone had inscribed the photograph in faint ink at the very bottom.

Gould hunt, 1897, it read. *Eric Simoley, Charles Simpson, Daniel Nussbaum, John Hollis, Benjamin Taylor.*

My heart clenched. I recognized another name, but not from my childhood. Zuckerman had told Aileen to investigate "the Nussbaum case," that it had something to do with the murders. Lily had said it was a dead end: a man who had killed his infant child and then taken his own life.

Footsteps echoed in the hallway. I picked the photograph up with my teeth and dropped it in the drawer just before Mrs. Brandon turned her key in the lock.

"I hadn't expected you to wake up yet," she said, closing the door behind her. "I would have come sooner."

As I couldn't speak, I contented myself with a grunt.

"I'll take off the gag, Zephyr, and give you water if you promise not to scream. No one will hear you in any case, but I'd rather not have the trouble."

I wondered if I shouldn't ignore her and try anyway, but she would just gag me again. I nodded and she untied and removed the cloth.

"There," she said. "Now, drink this. And then I believe it's time that you and I had a discussion."

She held the glass of water to my lips. I stared at it, and then decided she was unlikely to poison me again. "A discussion?" I said, after I had gulped it down, with just a little spilled down my shirt. I felt considerably revived, enough so that I started wondering if I could perhaps overpower her and escape.

"Yes," she said, seating herself at her desk. "Of options and exigencies. I imagine that you have worked this all out so I won't bore you with a confession, which I don't owe you in any case. What I want to make to you is an offer."

"And what would that consist of?"

"That you agree to place yourself in my power, for the mayor and I to use as we see fit. Your blood is very valuable, Zephyr. I'm sure you can see why."

"It *kills* vampires," I said.

"It turns vampires human. The killing is more of an unfortunate side effect. And something that can turn vampires human would be an extremely effective bargaining chip in the political sphere."

I stared at her. Could she really have reduced the monstrous pile of bodies in that morgue down to this petty political calculus? All this time I had pitied her, locked away in this basement room, marginalized and belittled for her sex when she clearly had capabilities equal to any of the men in the mayor's employ. But now any sympathy was washed away in a flood of contempt.

"And if I refuse?" I asked.

"You will be tried for murder. The evidence against you is solid, I have made sure of that."

"What if I tell the police the truth?"

"They won't believe you," she said. "And besides, I have the mayor's protection. Commissioner Warren is his close friend, and he'll make sure to steer things in the proper direction."

But her eyebrows lifted unsteadily as she said this, and I knew well the manner of someone attempting to convince herself of the truth of a dubious proposition.

"Even after your debacle with Madison at the supporters' banquet? Are you so sure?"

She drew herself up. "Madison *should* have agreed. But no matter, at this very moment, Faust is getting the required votes in the Board of Aldermen. I have pulled things from the brink, and Jimmy has seen that. In fact," she said, "I should thank you. Your falling out with that djinni was just the impetus he needed to bring us samples of the original brew. As we suspected, the current formulation is far less potent."

"He . . . he gave it to the mayor?"

Her smile was predatory. "Yes. Just yesterday. We got the results back less than an hour before the vote, but I believe we made it in time."

I felt the familiar wash of betrayal and anger, but a wiser feeling made me pause. Mrs. Brandon was probably telling the truth in her limited fashion, but I had no idea of the larger context. Amir might have told me had I been in any mood to listen. I wouldn't repeat the same mistake in less than twenty-four hours.

"Mrs. Brandon, I believe I can safely refuse your proposal."

She gave a breathy laugh. "Refuse? You'd rather go to jail? Have your hypocrisy exposed before the world?"

"My *hypocrisy*?"

"The vampire suffragette is a vampire killer! I didn't intend for Madison to accuse you in front of all those people, of course, but I've decided it only helps my case. Have you enjoyed the past day, Zephyr? The truth I've always known has been revealed to the world. You have never been who you pretend to be."

"But *I* didn't kill those vampires!"

She leaned forward and rapped me on the head. "Yes. You did. You've known all your life you have this power. Your blood did the killing. If you refuse, I will make sure that officer who hates you so much will learn it."

"How?"

"My mother will just have to confess."

"Ysabel wouldn't . . ." But I couldn't even finish the denial. I was here, wasn't I? If Ysabel felt any fondness for me, it hadn't trumped parental devotion.

"You are quite alone, Zephyr. Your lover has rejected you, your brother and friends have abandoned you, and your father has run away from his crimes. If you refuse me, all of this will be exposed. If you agree, I'll see to it that you are publicly exonerated."

I didn't give two figs about her offer, but she had mentioned one thing that sounded important. "Did you do something to my daddy? How do you . . ." I gasped. "The rabbi. The golem. You sent them?"

She leaned back in her chair, with an air of great satisfaction. "Rabbi Nussbaum has spent the last two decades wondering about his brother's suicide. I'd heard of his tragedy years ago—he's a friend of our local rabbi. When I learned Daniel had been a partner of your father's, I spoke to him. He agreed to visit your father in Montana and learn what he could. And what he learned, Zephyr, is that there is a very dark grimoire in your father's possession, one with a very dark ritual. A parent can give their first child immunity to vampires, but only through the blood of a brother. But then, you knew that."

But I hadn't. I had tried to stop myself from wondering this entire week, when the subject of my immunity had taken on such grotesque importance. Had my mother known? Had she even colluded with my daddy to produce his one perfect heir?

But I couldn't believe it. I'd seen his grief the one time I'd asked him about my dead brother. He hadn't done it callously or lightly. But why had he done it at all?

"And Daniel Nussbaum?" I said. "Why did he do it?"

Mrs. Brandon shrugged, apparently put out that I hadn't risen to her bait. "I don't know," she snapped. "I expect for the same reason. But the ritual didn't work for him. He killed his son and then the other child died as well."

And then he took his own life. I remembered Lily's hurried recitation of the facts: 1899, a murder in the Bronx. Two years after the Gould hunt, whatever that was. Four years before my own birth. My silence must have been especially irritating, because Mrs. Brandon stood up and nudged my legs.

"Well? The vote should be done by now, so we can just go up to Jimmy together. He's expecting me; I told him I have some big news. You'll let me do the talking."

I frowned. "I already told you no," I said.

"Don't be irrational! What other option do you have?"

"Sitting here?"

"You can't really—"

"No, Judith," I said, enjoying her momentary flash of indignation when I used her given name. "I really can. Tell anyone whatever you wish. I'll deal with the consequences, but I won't subject myself to the whims of a monster like you."

Her self-control—up to this point as rigid as her posture—snapped like a dry twig.

"You killed my *beshert*!" she screamed, as though she truly had no care for who might happen down the hallway. "You gave the blood that killed him, and I watched, I *watched*, you little bitch, as he choked on it, as the light left his eyes and his heart started to beat. It pumped the blood all over the floor. I was covered in it. He couldn't speak. He could only hold my hand. And that's how he died. Blind and dumb, with your blood on his face."

She leaned very close to me, so I could smell the musk of clove cigarettes on her jacket collar. Her face twisted like she was crying, but her eyes were dry.

"I'm sorry," I said. "It's my fault he died. I wish—"

I shouldn't have spoken. She screamed again with frightening, inarticulate rage and struck me hard against my cheek. My head snapped to the side, and before I could recover she hit me again, in my rib cage.

"Mrs. Brandon!" I gasped. "Judith, stop!"

But she didn't seem to hear me at all. I tried to move away, but there wasn't much I could do, bound as I was. A berserker fury had gripped Mrs. Brandon, and I was its object. "My Michael," she said. "My *beshert*, and you won't even pay me what you owe!" She punched me in the ribs again, nearly the same place. I groaned and struggled to throw myself against her. She shoved me back against the wall. "Jimmy will listen to me. He will, now that I have you. You'll just have to agree. You owe it to me!"

She stood suddenly and kicked me in the stomach. I grunted and fell over. I vomited bile and water, and nearly choked on it before I could catch my breath. Mrs. Brandon stopped suddenly, her head tilted as though she heard something. She looked at me as though she hardly knew who I was. I didn't bother to remind her. I wormed my way to the door, shoving all other considerations aside.

"Jimmy trusts me," she said, almost to herself. I turned around. She hadn't moved. She was staring at the door. I didn't understand what had happened—perhaps she had simply lost the last threads of her sanity. At the moment, I didn't much care. I made it to the door and used my chin to turn the unlocked knob. I collapsed into the hallway. The sudden brightness of the electric lights made me squint. Was someone else down here? I felt as hazy as I had after drinking the poisoned tea. I turned my head and saw Mrs. Brandon silhouetted in the doorway. She was looking down the hall.

"Judith? What is this?"

The mayor approached us. She must have heard him coming down the stairs. There was a man behind him. He called my name and ran toward me.

"Zeph!" Harry said. "Christ, Zeph, you look terrible."

He helped me sit up and started untying the knots. "So you didn't abandon me!" I found myself grinning. Why had I believed Mrs. Brandon for even one minute?

"Judith, tell me the truth," the mayor was saying. "You wrote those letters."

"There are significant political advantages to keeping the girl for our own purposes," Judith said mechanically, as though she didn't know what else to say now that her plans had been ruined.

The mayor shook his head. "A police officer, Judith," he said. "I can't overlook that. Commissioner Warren certainly can't. You'll have to turn yourself in."

Harry finished untying my legs. I moved gingerly, attempting to avoid jarring my bruises while letting the blood flow back into my sleeping limbs.

"We should get you out of here," he said.

"We?" I said.

"Your djinni is guarding the stairs."

My pulse surged. I looked down the hallway as though I could see him through the wall. "He's not mine anymore," I said.

Harry rubbed my shoulders. "He said something about that."

"You can't do this," Mrs. Brandon was saying. Jimmy Walker looked physically pained, his eyes shifting as though he longed to be anywhere else in the world. "Think of the political advantage," she said. "It's not too late."

"Judith, I appreciate all you've done for me, but this . . . this . . ."

He seemed at a loss for words. *For the first time,* I thought.

Harry helped me up, and then kept his arm around my waist. "Lady," he said, "it's too late. Your mother is at the police station right now, talking to Officer McConnell."

"She would never." She leaned against the doorjamb. "Oh God. You know who my mother is." She looked between Harry and Mayor Walker. "You both do."

Jimmy Walker put a pitying hand on her shoulder. "I'll make sure they treat you properly," he said. "I blame myself as much as anyone, Judith. I should have known how much stress you were under. I wanted to help you after that horrible business with Michael, of course. I thought I was doing the right thing to bring you here. But I see now . . . how could you have coped?"

Judith Brandon stared at him, wide-eyed and betrayed. Then she wrenched herself away and walked a few steps back into her office.

"Just give me an hour, Jimmy," she said. "Give me that much time. Then I'll do what I have to."

"Thank you, Judith," he said, relieved. "Come, let's leave her."

I waved off Harry's concerned arm and followed the mayor up the stairs. "A Jew," he muttered to himself. "Michael never mentioned that!"

Amir was waiting on the landing. He peered at me anxiously.

"This is getting to be a habit," I said.

"I believe we've reached the part where you tell me you're all right."

"I love you."

He snorted. "Or that."

The mayor shook his head. "You make me feel old, Miss Hollis."

"How so?"

He smiled. "I haven't the energy to love my dog at the moment. But I expect the feeling will pass with a highball or two. It always does."

CHAPTER FIFTEEN

"Judith Brandon is dead."

Lily sat down dramatically in our booth at Horace's speakeasy and tossed a paper on the table. It was the Tuesday edition of the *New Star-Ledger*. "Fire in City Hall kills aide, destroys evidence," she said, reading the headline aloud. I stared at her.

"How?" I asked. Aileen patted my hand awkwardly.

"In the fire, according to LeRoy. He mentions the investigation in the last graf. Fine reporter."

"How did she really die?" Aileen asked.

"Set fire to her files, then slit her wrists. Efficient."

I felt hollow. I had admired Mrs. Brandon, and even when I learned the truth, I hadn't wanted her to die.

Lily continued. "It looks like she destroyed any evidence about you, Zephyr. If she can't use you, no one can, I suppose."

The photograph! *Gould hunt, 1897.* I could picture it perfectly in my imagination, but I knew the image would degrade over time. And

I still had no idea what it meant. Despite our best attempts, no one had been able to find Daddy. I had been relying on getting Mrs. Brandon's files when the furor settled down. Now I never would.

"Damn," I said, shifting a little to ease my bruised ribs. I took another sip of Horace's firewater.

Harry, seated across from Lily, stared at the paper again. "*New-Star Ledger?* Didn't Zeph tell me you worked here? Why not write the story, if you knew more about the fire?"

Aileen and I shared a quick, worried glance. Trust Harry to blunder into the minefield with such male obliviousness.

Lily laughed and took a long gulp of her drink. I didn't know what it was, but I could smell the spirits from across the table. "Why *didn't* I write the story?" she said. "Very good question, young Mr. Hollis. And do you know, being a reporter, I went to my editor and I asked him. 'Breslin,' said I, 'why give that story to a two-bit hack like LeRoy when you have someone on staff who's been reporting on it from the beginning? He didn't even find out how the lady killed herself!'"

"Oh Lily!" Aileen said. "What happened then?"

Lily picked up her drink again. "He told me that he gave LeRoy the piece because the mayor's office called and said they wanted Mrs. Brandon's name kept out of the papers as much as possible, in the interest of the ongoing investigation. And he said he knew LeRoy was a safe pair of hands. Can you believe that?" Lily finished her drink and slammed the teacup on the table. "A safe pair of hands! I said, 'Breslin, what are we, journalists or public relations managers?' And Breslin said, 'That's the trouble with you, Lily, because you can't get it through your head that sometimes we're both. You think vampires are people, but sometimes they're just little bastards out to get your blood.'"

I gasped. "He didn't!"

Lily smiled. "He did."

"So what did you do?" Aileen asked.

"As of, ah, forty-five minutes ago, I am no longer an employee of the *New-Star Ledger*. No need to apologize. I'm intent on feeling very good about it for at least the next five hours. Now, who's with me?"

"I quit the Spiritualist Society," Aileen offered.

"Elspeth suggested that perhaps someone who regularly attends speakeasies shouldn't be a member of Friends Against Faust."

"And I had a very interesting conversation with Troy," Harry said. "I think I have to find a new apartment."

I shook my head, but smiled when I raised my glass with the others.

"To making your own way," Lily said.

Each of us had something entirely different on our minds when we echoed her, and each of us meant it equally.

᠀

Four hours later, Harry and I were doing a laughing, drunken foxtrot, while Lily and Aileen changed partners like cigarettes. Horace's band played like the Devil made them do it, and Horace himself made sure the drinks came strong. It had been so long since I had just let go like this. I felt like I had forgotten to have fun. Even my singing hobby had fallen by the wayside as the stress of the last few months piled upon me. In a way, I was grateful to Judith. Her actions had forced so many things out into the open. Perhaps now I could just be happy. Harry had promised to help me investigate Nussbaum and the Gould hunt. He'd been as shocked as I was to learn what Daddy had done to my twin brother, but he didn't try to deny it. He agreed that there had to have been some greater reason than just giving me immunity.

I'd learned the story yesterday of how Amir and Harry had come to rescue me in the bowels of City Hall. Amir had long suspected my blood was responsible for the deaths around the city, but he didn't have any reason to connect it to Judith Brandon. But when I was in jail, Mrs. Brandon had gone back to Aileen for one last séance with her dead husband. Aileen, desperate and tired of looking in vain for one lost spirit, thought to try going back to that same strange place where she'd successfully contacted Zuckerman. And she found him— Michael Brandon's shade had been roused by his wife's desire. Aileen wasn't entirely sure what they'd spoken of, but Judith Brandon had seemed confused and upset when she left. Aileen mentioned it to Lily, and they wondered if her husband had been a vampire killed in the same strange way as the others. When I disappeared, Amir contacted them both to ask if they'd seen me. Together, they began to wonder if there was something connecting Mrs. Brandon to the St. Marks Blood Bank where the killer must have gotten my blood. Lily searched through old newspapers. Michael Brandon's death notice mentioned nothing, but then she found a marriage notice: Judith Cohen, daughter of Saul and Ysabel Cohen, married to Michael Brandon. The rest had unraveled as I'd witnessed.

The band finished "East St. Louis Toodle-Oo" and paused for a brief water break. Harry and I took the opportunity to refresh our drinks.

"I've been meaning to tell you," I said, after ordering a sidecar. "I got the strangest telegram from McConnell today. He said he wouldn't be investigating me anymore. That he'd seen my family's 'young charge' and had been convinced. Was he talking about Judah? What on earth did he mean?"

"Oh!" Harry blushed a little. "I, well, so I . . . James was still hot under the collar about you saving Judah—"

"James?"

"McConnell," he said hurriedly. "Anyway—"

"When did you have the opportunity to get on a first-name basis with . . . Harry! Did you sleep with my investigating officer?"

"Shh!" Harry said, looking around. "Not everyone is as tolerant of buggery as you, Zeph. And it happened on Sunday. He'd found me to corroborate some information about Daddy and our family in the letters and well, one thing led to another, and then he told me about how you insisted that underage vampires could be something less than little killing machines—"

I shook my head with a small smile. "Pillow talk!"

Harry grinned. "The stories I could tell you . . ."

"Don't, Harry. You're still my little brother. There's only so much my heart can take."

"So after a rousing game of backgammon," he said, and I elbowed him, "I decided, why the hell not, and arranged for him to visit the compound. He must have gotten there this morning if he cabled you."

"Wonders upon wonders," I said. The bartender poured my sidecar with a flourish and pushed it closer to me. "I'm very grateful to you, however you effected it," I said.

"The least I can do, Zeph." He looked up. "Would you mind terribly if I left you alone for a few minutes? There's a gentleman who just walked in . . ."

I laughed. "Off with you! Don't stay with your old maid of a sister."

Harry gave me a strange smile and sauntered off. I sipped my sidecar and watched Lily and Aileen laughing together in the corner. I felt very content. A man sat down beside me.

"I'd buy you a drink, but you already seem to have one."

My breath hitched a little, but I covered it with a sip. Strong, like everything at Horace's. "Then I suppose you'll just have to get me something else."

Amir turned to me. "Would a ride to my apartment suffice?"

"Goodness," I said. I looked at him, bereft of pretense. I had said I loved him and he had disappeared with hardly another word. And now he found me again with nothing less than a proposition? I might love him, but I doubted I would ever know what to make of him. How do a djinni and a human love? What could he really feel for me?

But still, he seemed both pensive and hopeful. It seemed like my answer mattered, and that was a great comfort.

"What's the rush?" I asked.

He shrugged. "I have a trip to take in the morning. And some things I'd like to say to you."

This was more than enough to take me out the door and into the waiting taxi. We were silent on the ride over, me glancing nervously at his pensive profile and then out the open windows. The air was heavy and wet; we drove through Central Park, and it seemed to me like we were in a jungle. I could smell the flowers and the leaves, just as much a part of the air of this city as exhaust or manure.

I realized that we were headed to the east side, away from the Ritz.

"Where are we going?" I asked him.

"I thought it prudent to rent new rooms," he said, "when I was afraid you might go to trial. And then it seemed like a good idea anyway, circumstances being what they are."

This sounded ominous. "What sort of trip are you taking?"

"In due time, Zephyr," he said. I wished, suddenly, that I had drunk more back at Horace's. I was too tipsy to feel in control, and not splifficated enough to feel brave. I longed for him in that desperate, headlong, unthinking way that had always terrified me. I loved him, but I didn't understand him.

The taxi pulled over in front of a building fronting Central Park on Sixty-first Street. A doorman helped me out while Amir paid the driver.

"Eric," Amir said, when the taxi had driven off, "this is Zephyr Hollis."

The doorman nodded as though this meant something to him, and held out his hand. "A pleasure to meet you, miss. Just let me know if you need anything. The lift is this way."

He directed us to the elevator, and we took it to the seventh floor.

"Not the penthouse?" I said, when we stepped into the carpeted hallway. "Such restraint!"

Amir laughed in that way he had, like he hadn't meant to and couldn't quite regret it. "It had already been let," he said. "They assured me these rooms were equally spacious. But I have it on good authority the building is owned by communists."

"In that case, I forgive you for being an instrument of capitalist hegemony."

Amir unlocked a door at the far end of the hallway. "My relief," he said, "is boundless."

The furnishing was surprisingly spartan, given my familiarity with Amir's opulent taste. Oak table and chairs in the kitchen, two seats and a coffee table in the parlor, and absolutely nothing in the foyer.

"When were you planning to move in?" I said, frowning.

"I'm not," he said.

"I thought you said you just let the apartment?"

"Yes. Zephyr . . . do you think we could sit?"

I felt frightened, for no reason I could articulate. I didn't like his expression. It reminded me of before, when he was dying of vampire poison and he wouldn't tell me. Only he wasn't dying, and I wasn't going to jail, and perhaps I didn't know what had happened to my daddy, but overall, really, things had turned out remarkably well and why did I insist on thinking otherwise?

"Where, Amir?" I said, far too acidly. "The floor?"

"There's a couch in the parlor," he said mildly. I blushed and followed him to it.

"So what's all this about?" I asked. He sat as far away from me as possible. We had not touched once this evening. I looked at his hands and wondered what it might cost for me to try. "Where are you going?"

"I have to leave tomorrow at dawn," he said, which I noted did not answer my question. "I'm not sure when I'll be back. Or if."

"If?" I let out a baffled laugh. "You sound like you're going off to war."

"Something like that," he said. He looked almost serene. But all I felt was this horrific certainty that I had been right; that everything would not work out in the end. That the man I had finally admitted I loved now seemed to be leaving me forever.

"What is *something like* a war? If you don't want me just say so, no need to make up such melodrama."

He had been looking away, but now he whirled on me. His expression was a revelation: a longing as deep and passionate as my own, as rife with self-doubt and blame and as convinced of its own futility. I gasped. Had he always felt this way about me? Had I just ignored what I didn't want to see?

"Zeph." His voice broke. He wanted me but dared not touch me. The heat of him, that smell I had never been able to forget, reached out across the river separating us. Two feet, a million miles, it was all the same when my eyes met his across an unbridgeable distance. I thought, *Can I trust you? Will you always want me?* But these questions had no answers. So I asked one that did.

"Why did you give the mayor the old Faust?" I asked. The bill had passed just as Judith claimed; the last two hold-out aldermen relented after receiving proof. I couldn't say that the result upset me very much, in the end. Elspeth would find other means to fight. I would back out gracefully. Elspeth had been remarkably kind during our last, awkward conversation. She said it was clear that we could no longer work with each other on this issue, and I didn't deny it. But she had said something else, something that had resonated deeply with my newfound understanding of myself.

"Do not blame him too much for his nature," she had said. "Or you for yours."

I knew she was speaking of Amir. And I knew she was right.

But now Amir laughed incredulously. "You tally every mark against me, don't you? And I know I'm swimming against the tide, but I try to earn a few points in that other column, just to offset the matter, just in the general spirit of persuasion, but who am I fooling? Certainly not you, *habibti*. Nothing I do now can come close to equaling the single black mark of Faust. So why did I do it?" He shrugged. "Because you were rotting in a jail cell and no one could get to you and there was a judge with a fair mind to bow to the howling mob outside and ship you to the Ludlow Street jail for the foreseeable future. So I took myself to the mayor's office and encouraged him to send a message to the bench that bail would be acceptable, so long as it was suitably high, and I gave him the bottle and that was that."

I slipped off my shoes and pulled my knees to my chest. There was too much going on inside; I had to hold it close, or else it might burst.

"A business transaction," I said.

"Yes," he said, his eyes black, "or a coward's ploy, though you're too polite to say so. I hadn't the guts to keep you in prison for your own principles, so I violated them to get you out."

"Amir—"

"But it will be all right," he said, a cruel parody of my earlier thoughts. "I'll be gone in the morning. I just need to tell you some things before then."

"But I don't—"

"First," he said, as though he hadn't heard me. "This apartment is yours. I've leased it in your name, with the whole matter paid up for the next three years. I've arranged for my bank to send you an allowance—"

All of this was entirely astonishing to me, but I couldn't bear to hear his falsely bright, brittle voice any longer. "Amir!"

I stood up in my stockinged feet. Amir put down his hand and looked up at me. I couldn't make out his expression at all, except he smelled like frankincense and that had never been a bad thing before.

"Maybe I haven't entirely forgiven you, or maybe I'm not sure, but for heaven's sake stop arrogating to yourself all the blame for everything that Faust has done. Has it ever occurred to you that perhaps Faust would have found its way here no matter what? The man had invented it, after all. What did you think he planned to do, store it in his basement? You saw an opportunity, and you seized on it. Perhaps your opportunity was a thoughtless social experiment, a little joke, a game, but someone else would have heard of this wonder drug. Someone else would have brought it to the city for all the money it could make. You've been hoarding the blame like it's pirate's treasure. Haven't you any humility?"

Amir stared at me. He opened his mouth and closed it. The frankincense smell grew stronger, and an ember seemed to light in his eyes. He started to tremble and I had a moment of fear before I understood that he was laughing.

"Humility," Amir said. "*Humility!*" He slid from the couch to the floor, so that, to my utter astonishment, he knelt before me. "Zephyr, darling, Zephyr, *habibti, wild spirit which art moving everywhere; destroyer and preserver*—"

"What?" I took his hands.

"Shelley," Amir said, still laughing.

"First you're off to war and now you're quoting dead Romantics?"

"'Ode to the West Wind,'" he said, and I felt very warm and very full.

"Why are you laughing?"

"You love me."

"Didn't I say so!"

Amir took a deep breath, quieted. "Princes are not generally given to humility," he said, "but I shall endeavor to be an exception."

His hands felt so warm in mine, so happy and perfect that I knelt down myself. I put one hand against my cheek and felt, through his fingers, how wide I was smiling. "I believe this is the point at which you indicate reciprocal emotion," I said.

"Pardon?"

"Say you love me, you dolt."

Very carefully, like I was a Fabergé egg he was stealing from a jeweler, Amir took my face between his hands.

"It needs saying?"

"Always, everywhere. Otherwise I'll find means of convincing myself it isn't true."

"That would be a shame," he agreed.

"Because it's true?"

He smiled. I kissed him. It took quite a long time, that kiss, and never once did I consider where our noses should go or whether his hands had strayed too low or any of the hundred innumerable things that had run through my mind during other, inadequate kisses. His hands in my hair, mine around his waist. I climbed into his lap, just to get closer.

"Yes," he said, after we had finished.

I felt groggy with joy, too stupid to remember what I had been saying just five minutes before. "Yes, what?"

"Yes I love you, you dolt."

∞

It hurt, at first. I hadn't expected it to, given the number of erotic novels Aileen had passed my way over the years. In my naiveté, I'd expected that such advice would overcome the hundred ignorances and confusions involved in conjoining two bodies, however temporarily.

But Amir was a patient and tender lover. He even offered me the use of a condom, though he admitted that there was no chance of a djinn and a human producing a baby. I bravely said I trusted him and he laughed and put it on anyway.

"I don't blame you for doubting me," he said. "I hope I can earn your trust, if I return," he said, and I ignored that *if I return* as thoroughly as I had once ignored my love for him. *I will make him stay* was my only thought.

Afterward, we lay together, my head against his shoulder, his arm around my back. I hardly moved and my only thoughts were a lazy, disbelieving joy, a languor that suffused my entire body. Amir stroked my hair with his other hand. I wanted to keep the moment forever, I wanted to tell him I loved him and beg him to never leave, I wanted to plan a hundred things we could do together just tomorrow, but instead I fell asleep.

When I awoke, Amir wasn't in the bed. I sprung upright, in blind panic, but he was seated just a few feet away in a chair facing the window. It was the room's only other piece of furniture.

He turned to me. "I was just going to wake you," he said. "I have to leave soon."

"Still? I don't understand. Where could you possibly have to go?"

Amir walked over to the bed. His clothes were strange: white silk pants and a loose top of the same pristine shade. The sort of outfit that Kardal favored.

"I'll make it simple," he said. "No time for anything else. When Kashkash agreed to release the binding, he told you that you must never bind me again."

"Yes," I said. "And I didn't!"

He sighed and sat on the edge of the bed. I reached for his hand unthinkingly. "You did. Kashkash is very clever, *habibti*, and not particularly nice. He said you couldn't bind me in thought, word, or deed. Well, that includes bindings other than becoming a vessel. He understood quite well that you couldn't help binding me."

He paused and waited for me to grasp his meaning. And when I did I started to laugh. It was all I could do. "I told you I loved you," I said. "The first words out of my mouth and Kashkash wins. But why do you have to leave?"

"He's taken Kardal," Amir said quietly. "Taken him deep into the netherworlds and left him in Kashkash knows what dimension. I'm the only one who can find him. And if I don't leave at dawn, then Kardal will be there forever."

I sat up. He wouldn't look at me, but he seemed so sad that I embraced him anyway. I wanted to cry but I forced the tears back. If this were the last time I saw him—

"You'll come back, right?" I said.

"If I can. Kashkash doesn't set these tests lightly. He may love us all, but his weak sons receive no mercy. Four hundred years ago, Umar went into the netherworlds after his older brother Aban. Neither of them have ever returned."

So Kardal had been telling the truth, in a fashion. Exiled forever. And if I asked Amir to stay, to abandon his brother and live with me until I died?

But I could never ask it, any more than he could stay.

"I should give you a token," I said. "If you're going to be a knight off to battle."

"Zephyr—"

"Oh, I have just the thing. Not a ribbon or a handkerchief, but hopefully it will prove more useful. It's all I can think of, anyway, and I wouldn't want you to forget me while you're off battling demons . . ."

I babbled furiously as I tumbled off the bed, heedless of my nakedness, and searched the floor for my discarded possessions. There— right beside the garter. I picked up my knife, the blessed silver blade that had been my constant companion since moving to New York, and handed it to my lover.

He took it solemnly. "Are you sure?"

I lifted his chin until he met my eyes. "Come back," I said. "I love you. When you find your brother, tell him I'm sorry for being such a fool."

He pulled me close, so abruptly that I let out a startled yelp. "There's more . . . about your father."

I pulled away slightly. "Daddy?"

"Just listen, it's nearly dawn. There's different kinds of vampires. Normal ones, like Nicholas and Charlie, don't have a choice. Others are like Rinaldo, but he had only a fraction of the powers of a fully Chosen vampire."

"Yes, I remember. Kardal told me."

"The ritual to deliberately turn yourself into a vampire is almost impossible. One in a thousand people who try will succeed, and not many try. So Chosen vampires are rare. But when they come into this world . . . Zephyr, the destruction is unimaginable. The ritual is so monstrous that only a monster would try. But it changes them anyway, into a harder, stronger, deadlier version of their worst selves. Your Defenders worry about piddling vampires like Nicholas, but Defenders *exist* for the Chosen ones. Your father performed a ritual on you and your brother—he used the blood of a sibling to summon a demon. And that demon gave you immunity. But Zephyr, that immunity *isn't the point.* It's a side effect. That demon can only be summoned when a Chosen vampire is alive. And the demon gives the child the power to kill it."

"Kill it? How? With my blood?"

"It's stranger than that. You've probably seen revenants before? Shambling corpses crawling from their graves? Well, Chosen vampires create armies of them. They can't help it—wherever they go, graveyards rise up in their wake. Allow a Chosen to roam long enough, and the whole world would drown in corpses. Nothing human can kill Chosen vampires. Not even you. Only revenants can. But revenants are dumb and slow. No Chosen would ever be in danger from them, normally. But your blood can control revenants, Zeph. That's why the demon's curse exists. A little of your blood will make any revenant obey your will."

"My will? You mean . . ."

"Your blood will let you command a horde of them. You can *make* them deadly."

"And kill a Chosen," I whispered into his neck. Had I just teased Harry about grisly pillow talk? I thought I would weep. "So there's a Chosen alive right now? Who? I haven't heard of packs of revenants roaming the streets. Is that why Daddy . . ."

But all I could see was that picture that Judith Brandon had destroyed. *Gould hunt, 1897.* Two years later, one man tried to summon the demon and failed. Six years later, another one tried and succeeded.

"I don't know. I only put this together yesterday, when you told me about Nussbaum. Your mother didn't know anything about what your father had done, though she suspected. He never told her, she never asked."

"And now he's gone," I said. Vampire hunting?

The window in this room looked out over the park. A beautiful view, but to the west. I wouldn't be bothered by the sunrise in here. The brightening of my day would be subtle and mysterious, until eventually I couldn't deny the light that lit the trees and the wide boulevard of Central Park East.

I embraced him once, fiercely, and let him go.

"Come back," I said, as though I could possibly demand such a thing; as though he could possibly promise it.

He smiled, though it seemed wrenched out of him. "Do you remember when I fought that vampire in the snow and how you harangued me for coming to your rescue?"

I laughed, surprised that I could manage it. "Of course. God, how you annoyed me!"

"That was when I first loved you."

I would not cry. That would not be his last sight of me. The light grew brighter. I blinked. Amir noticed it too, he gave a sharp nod and stood up.

"If I'm not back in two years, forget about me," he said.

"I won't forget about you."

He took my hands. *"Ma'a as-Salaama, habibti."*

He was gone before his last echo. My hands felt a moment of dislocated warmth, my nostrils a vanished scent.

I stared out the window until the sun shone on the park. I realized I was still naked and went searching for my blouse. He would be back, of course. Two years, he said. I hoped it wouldn't take that long, but no one would describe me as flighty. Indeed, I fell in love with great difficulty. I would not lose him.

But for now, I found myself unexpectedly in possession of a palatial apartment on the Upper East Side and a monthly allowance of an undisclosed amount. I had two dear friends who seemed to have found themselves at loose ends. What couldn't we do with a decent space and a little money? Had Amir asked me, I would have refused him out of hand. But in the current circumstances, I felt like that money could do anything I wanted. Any mad, foolish, extravagant dream of social change I could dream up.

I ran back to the living room, where I had seen a telephone. Amir had left his cuff links and vest on the couch. I folded the vest and put the cuff links on top very carefully. I didn't think. I refused to think.

Just as I was about to pick up the phone, it rang. I stared at it for several seconds.

But my fate had already been decided long ago, on a hunt before I'd been born.

"Yes? Who is this?"

"Zeph, is that you?"

"Daddy? Where are—"

"I ain't got time, sweetie. Just listen: whatever you do don't go anywhere near that Ludlow jail."

"What?" The Ludlow jail was down the street from Mrs. Brodsky's. I passed it all the time. "Whyever not?"

"Because I think that's where he's locked up."

"Where who's locked up, Daddy?" I said.

"I got a lot to tell you, Zeph, and you aren't going to like any of it.

But there's a nasty kind of vampire down there who's been locked behind some good wards the last twenty-odd years, and he's mad as hell about it. I think he's about to break out, but I can't tell from here. And Zeph, if you go in that jail, I think it'll outright break the wards that are holding him."

"What happens then?" I asked because I had to. I had to hear it again, so I might begin to believe it.

"Then? Well, sweetie. Then the dead rise up."

"Oh, Daddy."

Amir was gone, and New York had hundreds of graveyards.

What would I do?

I would wait for him. And in the meantime, my blood would lead an army of revenants.

ML   4-12